# RUSSIAN RESURGENCE

# RUSSIAN RESURGENCE

*A Craig Page Thriller*

## ALLAN TOPOL

SelectBooks, Inc.
*New York*

This edition published by SelectBooks, Inc.
For information address SelectBooks, Inc., New York, New York.
First Edition

ISBN 978-1-59079-449-4


Library of Congress Cataloging-in-Publication Data

Names: Topol, Allan, author.
Title: Russian resurgence : a Craig Page thriller / by Allan Topol.
Description: First edition. | New York : Selectbooks, [2018]
Identifiers: LCCN 2017043720 | ISBN 9781590794494 (softcover : acid-free paper)
Subjects: LCSH: United States. Central Intelligence Agency–Officials and employees–Fiction. | Murder–Investigation–Fiction. | Women journalists–Fiction. | Conspiracies–Fiction. | Political fiction. | GSAFD: Suspense fiction. | Mystery fiction.
Classification: LCC PS3570.O64 R88 2018 | DDC 813/.54–dc23 LC record available at https://lccn.loc.gov/2017043720


Manufactured in the United States of America
10 9 8 7 6 5 4 3 2 1

*Dedicated to my wife, Barbara*

# Acknowledgments

This is my sixth novel with Kenzi Sugihara, the founder of SelectBooks. I am indeed fortunate to be working with such an outstanding publisher. From our first discussion, Kenzi understood the significance of *Russian Resurgence* and its relevance to critical issues facing the US and the world today.

Nancy Sugihara and Molly Stern did an outstanding job of editing. They smoothed the sentences and caught grammatical errors. More important, they found inconsistencies and unlikely plot points in the draft, which compelled me to revise the manuscript.

Kenichi Sugihara, the marketing director, has come up with still another fabulous and creative cover. He has formulated the marketing program with energy and enthusiasm.

My agent, Pam Ahearn, provided enormous help in shaping this story. With Pam's assistance, I was able to weave together present events involving Russia and Hungary with their past relationship, as well as Peter's present with his past. I am very grateful to have her as my agent.

Finally, I want to acknowledge the assistance of my wife, Barbara. From our first trip to Hungary, she continually encouraged me to make that country a critical part of the novel. She then tirelessly read drafts and offered valuable editorial suggestions.

"If you want to talk about a nation that could pose an existential threat to the United States, I would have to point to Russia. And if you look at their behavior, it's nothing short of alarming."

*—From testimony of General Joseph F. Dunford Jr.,*
*Chairman of the Joint Chiefs of Staff, at his*
*Senate confirmation hearing in July 2015*

# RUSSIAN RESURGENCE

# Potomac, Maryland, and Dulles Airport

## The Present

**N**ick Toth loved baseball. The twelve-year-old played second base and had been voted MVP on his youth team. He had meticulously compiled his batting average during the season, which had ended the previous week—a league best at .408. With the games now over until spring, Nick turned his baseball obsession to the Washington Nationals, who were locked in a tight first place battle with the Mets.

That evening the Nats were playing in Los Angeles. That meant a 10:15 p.m. start, Washington time. When Nick asked if he could watch, his grandpa said, "Positively not."

Always resourceful and never willing to take no for an answer, Nick lay awake quietly in his second-floor bedroom at his grandparents' house. Nick lived with his grandparents at the luxurious estate, which was built on six acres along River Road in Potomac, Maryland.

At ten minutes before midnight he tiptoed down the hall to his grandparents' bedroom and looked in the open door.

*They're both asleep*, he thought with joy. Swiftly returning to his own room, he grabbed his iPad. Then, dressed in Washington Nats pajamas, he sneaked softly down two carpeted flights to the rec room on the lower level, where a billiard table sat on one side and a bridge table on the other. Using a flashlight he had hidden in a drawer at the beginning of the season for evenings like this, Nick settled down in a chair next to the bridge table and turned on his iPad to the game.

It was the top of the seventh and the Nats were leading three to two. He watched without sound, not only because he didn't want his grandparents to hear him if one of them should wake up, but also because he found the babbling of sports announcers distracting.

"Watching on mute is much more like being at the game," his father had told him. Thinking about his father caused tears to well up in Nick's eyes. It was hard to believe it had already been a year. Those words "Viktor and Ellina Toth" and "boating accident" cut through Nick like a knife. The first time he had heard them—from a grim-faced Maryland state trooper—Nick had been at his grandparents' house swimming in their pool. It had been a fateful, hot, and muggy Sunday afternoon, July 15, just the year before.

An only child, Nick had loved his mother, but his incredibly close bond was with his father. It was Dad who taught Nick about baseball—spending hours helping him perfect his swing. Dad had also pushed him hard at school, telling Nick, "You have enormous talent and intellect. You can do anything you want in life." Then in a single moment he had lost both of them.

Nick had spent hours on the bay in the catamaran with his dad, who was an excellent sailor, so he couldn't understand how something like this could have happened on a sunny, mild afternoon. "The bay can be tricky," the state trooper had said. "Freak winds sometimes arise from nowhere."

In the end, the why and how didn't matter. The reality was that his parents were both gone. He had moved in with his grandfather, Peter—his father's father—and his grandmother, Reka. They couldn't be better to him, and yet he missed his parents every single day. After the accident, regardless of how hot it was, he refused to swim in his grandparents' pool because it reminded him of that horrific day. Last September his grandfather, knowing how Nick felt, had the pool filled in.

While watching the baseball game, Nick stayed alert. If he heard his grandparents calling him, he planned to hide the iPad in a closet, claim he couldn't sleep, and offer to go back to bed and try again. He wouldn't like lying to his grandparents, but this was an important game. The Mets had lost a day game to the Pirates, and if the Nats won that evening, they would be in first place by two full games.

Half an hour later, Nick heard voices from upstairs—but it wasn't his grandparents. Straining his ears, he heard two men speaking in a foreign language. He couldn't understand what they were saying, but he was sure it was Russian. Nick was paralyzed at the thought of what these men were doing in his house. Were they here to hurt him and his grandparents? The house had a security system, but maybe the intruders had disarmed it.

Nick's knees shook, and perspiration started to dot his forehead as he recalled his grandfather warning him always to be alert to his surroundings and to beware of anyone speaking Russian. After his parents had died, he had told Nick that someone might try to break into the house to harm them. When Nick had asked why, his grandfather had responded, "Ever since I was eight years old the Russians have been my enemy." Then he had rolled up the sleeve of his shirt, and on the upper right arm, Nick saw a hammer and sickle symbol of the Communist empire branded into grandfather's arm.

"Who did that to you?" Nick had asked.

"A horrible man. A Russian colonel by the name of Suslov."

"It must have hurt when he did it."

"Then, and for a long time after."

"What happened to Colonel Suslov?" Nick asked.

"Someone killed him. But enough about that. Come with me, I want to show you something."

Grandpa had then taken Nick to the rec room, walked over to the brick wall, and removed several bricks. They concealed a hiding place. In it, Nick saw a small black case.

"If we're ever attacked in the house," Grandpa said, "I want you to come down here, grab the case, and escape through that window." He pointed to a window that was above ground and opened to the back of the house. "Then you run like hell. When you get to a safe place, open the case; it will have instructions for you to get in touch Emma Miller. Remember her? She's the woman you met when I took you to Paris.

She'll take care of you. Don't worry about me and your grandmother. Just do what I told you."

Grandpa had said it in a forceful way, and Nick realized there was no point asking for an explanation.

Grandpa had repeated the same instructions just the previous day. "I want to make sure you really understand," he had explained. At the end of this session Grandpa said, "Good. You'll be able to do this. You're wise and clever well beyond your years. You must be strong."

Now Nick realized the time had come to comply with his grandfather's directive. Though he was terrified, with his grandfather's words "be strong" reverberating in his mind, Nick raced across the room, slipped into a pair of sneakers, and quietly removed the bricks. He pulled out the black case, grabbed a nearby flashlight, and then moved a chair under the window next to the bridge table. Standing on the chair, he was able to slide the window up. He tossed the black case outside onto the grass. After shoving the flashlight into his pajama pocket, he grabbed the window ledge, boosted himself up, and twisted out of the open window. He grabbed the case from the moist grass and then ran as fast as he could from the house.

When he was a hundred yards away, breathing heavily but refusing to stop, he turned right, in a southeasterly direction, toward Washington and made a large loop around the house. Once he reached River Road, Nick cut off onto a small county back road, deciding it would be safer. As he did, he heard a loud explosion from behind. Nick stopped and turned around. To his horror, he saw a huge fire. Flames were shooting up from his grandparents' house. He wanted to turn around to go back, but his promise to his grandpa was pounding in his brain.

Not watching his footing, Nick stumbled in a pothole. He fell to the ground and scraped his knee on the rough, unevenly paved road. With the dark woods around him, exhausted and terrified, he considered remaining there. Then he recalled his grandfather's words: "Be strong."

Shrugging off the pain, he rose to his feet and resumed running. Fortunately, the night air was cool, and he soon reached a main road called Seven Locks. An occasional car passed him as he ran. He kept going until he reached a small shopping mall—the Cabin John Center. It was deserted except for several parked cars.

Nick headed for a dimly lit corner and collapsed on a concrete step. The temptation to go back to the road, flag down a car, and have the driver get him to a police station was great. But Nick couldn't do that. He couldn't defy his grandfather's directive. Thinking about his grandparents and recalling the fire, Nick clenched his fists. He had always been close to them, but even more so after he lost his parents. And now they must both be . . . he choked as the word "dead" came to his lips, and tears began to roll down his cheeks. No one could have lived through that explosion. Nick felt a pang of anger deep in his chest toward the two unknown Russian men.

After allowing himself to cry for a few more minutes, he again recalled his grandfather's words and pulled himself together. *I will be strong.*

He wiped away the tears with the sleeve of his shirt and opened the black case. Inside he found a passport with his picture, but the name next to it wasn't Nicholas Toth—it was Jonathan Hart. He saw a cell phone and a sealed envelope with the name "Emma Miller" on the front. He fingered the envelope but didn't open it. There was also a stack of hundred-dollar bills and another of fifty-euro notes, each held together by a rubber band. Next, he saw a small pad and a pencil. Finally there was a piece of paper that had the name Emma Miller, a Paris phone number, and the address 98 Place des Vosges, which Nick recalled from a trip to Paris with his grandfather was where Emma lived. Also, he saw a note in his grandfather's handwriting that said, "Call Emma. Use this Paris phone number. She will tell you what to do. AND BE STRONG."

Nick picked up the cell phone and dialed Emma. He heard her say, "Allo," in a sleepy voice.

"This is Nicholas Toth," he said, forcing his voice to sound firm. "Grandpa's dead."

"What happened?" she asked in a quavering voice.

"I—I'm not sure. I heard intruders and ran. I saw the house on fire and heard a huge explosion. Grandpa and grandma were both inside." He choked back the tears.

"Are you all right?" she asked, now sounding fully awake.

"Yes. I did just what grandpa told me to do."

"Where are you?"

"In a shopping area a couple miles from the house. Grandpa told me to call you. That you would tell me what to do."

"Come to Paris. Do you have your Jonathan Hart passport?"

"Yes, and I have a lot of money."

"Stay on the phone. I'll make an airplane reservation for you." After a couple of minutes, Emma was back, "Nick, listen. I made a reservation for you in the name of Jonathan Hart on Air France this evening at 6:15 from Dulles Airport to Paris. The ticket has been paid for. Can you get to Dulles Airport?"

"Yes. I know where to get a cab."

"Good. You're on flight 55. I will meet you at the airport after you come through baggage claim. I'll see you in Paris tomorrow. And be careful, Nick."

Though he was horrified and devastated by what had happened to his grandparents, through the haze of numbness that threatened to engulf him, Nick began to feel a prickle of relief that he was no longer alone in the world. He knew that Emma had worked with his grandfather because Nick had gone on two business trips to Paris with him—one when he was six and the other a month after his parents had died. Both times Nick had spent some time alone with Emma while Grandpa had been busy in meetings. She had been really nice. After the second trip Grandpa had said, "If anything happens to me, I've arranged for Emma to take care of you."

Emma must have been close to Grandpa. She even knew that he would be traveling as Jonathan Hart. Knowing how much his grandparents loved him and how smart his grandfather was to arrange this escape plan for him fortified the boy's resolve.

Nick put the contents back into the black case. No longer feeling the need to run, he left the mall, crossed the road, and set off on foot toward downtown Bethesda. Though his knee hurt, he ignored it. Good ballplayers never let pain stop them.

Almost three hours later, he reached the Hyatt Hotel in downtown Bethesda. After using the bathroom and washing his face as well as his knee, he went through the revolving door and outside again. Several cabs were parked in front of the hotel. He could take a cab to Dulles, then spend the day waiting for his plane.

As he started toward the first cab, he stopped in his tracks. That could be risky because cab drivers kept records of their fares, so it would be easy to track him. And even though no one was following him, it was possible that the Russians could have set a trap for him, planting cab drivers in places he might go. The Metro would be better, he decided. The trains ran close to Dulles, and he could get a bus from there. Nick remembered reading a spy book of his father's in which the spy changed subway trains to avoid detection. That's what he would do.

As Nick waited anxiously in the dim light for Metro to open, he looked around for anyone who might be pursuing him, and kept his ears open for anyone speaking in Russian, but he didn't see or hear anything suspicious.

As soon as the Metro opened, Nick took a train to Reagan National Airport. There he transferred to a train that ran out into Virginia close to Dulles Airport. At the end of the line, he took a bus to Dulles. He looked around nervously, but it didn't seem like anyone was following him.

As he rode in the bus, Nick thought about the other times he had gone to Dulles Airport—at least twice a year with his parents since he was five. His dad had been a lawyer with a large Washington law firm and the three of them would go to Southern California in the summer to vacation for a week or two and to Aspen in the winter to ski. That was another sport Nick loved, although not as much as baseball. They had spent enough time waiting for planes that Nick knew his way around the airport.

It was only a little after eight in the morning when he arrived at Dulles. He walked over to the Air France counter where he saw a sign: "Closed. Will open at 1 p.m." He'd come back then to get his boarding pass.

Though it felt like his whole life had fallen apart, Nick drew on inner resources of strength he didn't know he had. He had to somehow survive this ordeal and get to Emma. Though the anxiety and fear of the previous night had left him with no appetite, he realized he had to maintain his strength. He took the escalator to the lower level where he remembered seeing a small café. Once he got off the escalator, he looked back apprehensively, but no one was following him.

In the café, he bought a turkey sandwich, a banana, and a bottle of water, paying with one of the hundred-dollar bills from the black case. The heavyset woman at the cash register raised her eyebrows, but didn't say anything.

The café was otherwise deserted. Nick took the food over to a table across from a television tuned to CNN. He saw a blazing fire on the screen followed by smoldering ashes.

The announcer said, "This devastating fire occurred in a mansion on River Road in a tony area of Potomac, Maryland. According to neighbors, the house had three occupants: Peter Toth, his wife, Reka, and their twelve-year-old grandson, Nicholas. A Montgomery County police spokesman has stated the fire was so intense that the house was totally destroyed. The remains found were unidentifiable. All are presumed to be dead—burnt beyond recognition."

As he listened, Nick began shaking. His teeth were chattering, and tears welled up in his eyes. "No," he whispered to himself. "No." It was so bizarre. He felt as if he were a character in a horror movie who was finding out about his own death on the news.

The announcer continued, "The cause of the fire is believed to be accidental, most likely started by the rupture of a gas line."

As a picture of his grandfather flashed on the screen, Nick leaned forward to make sure he heard every word. The announcer continued, "Peter Toth, aged seventy, was born in Hungary. He became a prominent industrialist after Hungary achieved independence from Russia in 1989. Tragedy also struck this family a year ago when Peter Toth's only child, Viktor, and Viktor's wife, Ellina, were killed in a mysterious boating accident on the Chesapeake Bay. . . . Now let's turn to financial news."

Nick struggled against the blanket of grief and fear that threatened to overwhelm him. He was on the cusp of surrendering to it and the accompanying paralysis, but one factor pulled him back from the precipice—his grandfather's words: "Be strong."

## Moscow

Fyodor Kuznov, the Russian president, sat in his palatial Kremlin office behind the ornate, gold-embroidered, red leather-topped desk—rumored to have been used by one of the czars—and looked at the television tuned to CNN. As he heard the announcer reporting on the fire in Maryland, a cruel smile crossed his face. He walked over to the map of Europe taped on the wall.

The map had been prepared in 1980, and it depicted the world as it was then: Russia in control of the USSR, and Russia dominating Central Europe (often described erroneously in the Western media as Eastern Europe) all the way west to Berlin and beyond. For Kuznov, the events of the late 1980s and early 90s when the Soviet Union collapsed were a self-inflicted tragedy. The Berlin wall came down, and Moscow lost its control of Central Europe.

At the time Kuznov had been a mid-level official with the KGB working with the Russian army to put down the violent revolution launched by Chechnya to join the exodus from Russian rule. Kuznov believed the best way to kill a snake was to cut off its head. Thanks in large part to Kuznov's ruthlessness in destroying the Chechen leaders, Russia smashed the revolution, laying waste to much of the capital of Grozny in the process.

Following the war, Kuznov returned to Moscow expecting a hero's welcome, but the country's leadership didn't care. They were concerned with the dismantling of the Soviet Union and the creation of democracy in Russia. Kuznov had thought it was a farce—democracy could no more take root in Russia than roses could grow in an oil field.

For Kuznov, the dismemberment of the Soviet Union was a travesty, neither inevitable nor compelled by the force of events. Rather, in Kuznov's view, this horrendous outcome could be attributed to a lack of effective leadership in the Kremlin. Even the spineless Gorbachev, who became along with his wife, Raisa, the darling of the Western press, conceded that the Soviet Union could and should have been preserved. Yeltsin, who followed him, was a drunk and plunged the country into economic chaos. He couldn't lead a class of school children to the bathroom, even on one of those rare days when he was sober. Had Stalin, Khrushchev, or Kuznov been in power, the map of Europe would now look exactly as it had in 1980.

Some leaders would whine and bemoan what had happened to their nations. Not Kuznov. The Russian leader didn't believe in wasting time crying over spilled milk. Instead, he wanted to find a way to refill the bottle.

To achieve that ambitious goal, Kuznov decided to utilize the democracy he despised in order to catapult himself from KGB apparatchik to national leader. He grabbed on to the coattails of Ivan Samoren, the then mayor of Moscow, rising from Ivan's director of security to deputy mayor. With Kuznov's KGB training, it was easy to arrange Ivan's death by poisoning without leaving any evidence that might point back to him. As Ivan's deputy, Kuznov was a natural choice to succeed his hapless benefactor, whose wife, Catherine, was in Kuznov's bed the night her husband died. When he tired of Catherine a year later, he dispatched her on a one-way trip to the gulag.

One of the things Kuznov had learned from Ivan was that it was possible to fix elections in Russia. By the time Kuznov ran for president, after being Moscow's mayor for five years, he had assembled a coterie of oligarchs whose wealth had been acquired by stealing assets from the state during the shift from Communism to a market economy. Those oligarchs financed his election campaign, and former KGB colleagues supplied the muscle to destroy opponents. With that combination, Kuznov sailed into the presidency.

Once he had secured his position, he focused on his burning desire to rebuild the Soviet Empire and develop enough power to pose a threat to Germany, France, and even the United States. In the first stage of his program, he rebuilt and strengthened the Russian military, aided by an alliance with Beijing, which supplied military technology to Russia in return for Moscow constructing a pipeline to transport badly needed oil and gas to China.

Now Kuznov was ready for the second stage. He raised his hand and placed a finger on Hungary. Hungary was the key. The secret agreement he had reached with Hungarian Prime Minister Szabo, referred to as the Friendship Pact, was to be announced in a little over two weeks at a public ceremony in Budapest. This pact would go a long way toward enabling Russia to regain control over Central Europe, since it would permit Russia to station its troops and military equipment in Hungary.

In Szabo, Kuznov found an unlikely but willing ally. Franz Szabo had been a left-leaning socialist when he became prime minister of Hungary fifteen years ago. Like Kuznov, Szabo was a totally amoral leader. While he might have started out with political convictions, wanting to improve the lives of the Hungarian people, the longer he remained in office, the more he was driven by a desire to solidify and to tighten his hold on power while expanding his personal prerogatives.

Recognizing that his primary opposition was coming from the right, Szabo moved in that direction to commandeer the support of his right-wing opponents. He became indifferent to the left. They had nowhere to go. And there was something else driving Szabo that Kuznov could exploit: The Hungarian leader despised the German chancellor. Szabo was convinced she was trying to establish German hegemony over the entire continent. He was unwilling to let Hungary become a vassal state in the new Teutonic empire.

Once Kuznov realized what was motivating Szabo, the Russian leader reached out to his Hungarian counterpart with an invitation to that year's Defender of the Fatherland Day celebration. Watching in a position of honor close to Kuznov in the reviewing stand, Szabo was dazzled by the Russian show of military force. Kuznov invited him to a celebratory dinner that night and arranged for two voluptuous women to visit Szabo in his hotel room. At breakfast the next morning, Kuznov opened discussions with Szabo about the Friendship Pact. The Hungarian had dragged his feet, appearing reluctant to enter into the agreement during the endless rounds of negotiation with Dimitri, Kuznov's trusted aide.

Finally, three weeks earlier, Szabo flew to Moscow and they shook hands on the deal, which was to be publicly announced on August 16 at a signing ceremony in Budapest. Its most critical provisions were that Russia would expand the nuclear power plant it had built for Hungary during the Communist period and construct a second nuclear plant. The two combined would supply virtually all the electricity Hungary needed, freeing them from dependence on oil and gas imports. In return, Russia would be allowed to station its troops and military equipment in Hungary.

Looking at the map, Kuznov moved his finger east and then north from Budapest. With Hungary as a jumping off point, Russia could take over the Czech Republic and Poland. In the meantime, other troops would roll west from Russia, conquering Ukraine and Romania, later joining up with the troops advancing from Hungary.

Kuznov was not concerned that he would meet resistance from France, Germany, or England. He viewed their leaders as weak and spineless. If you pushed against them, they gave way. In the case of Germany, as long as Kuznov signaled that he would not cross their border, they would look the other way. All they cared about was expanding their economy—they wouldn't want to get involved in anything this messy. Moreover, making his move with Hungary right now in August was a stroke of genius. The Western Europeans never liked to do anything that interfered with their prized August vacations.

As for US President Worth, Kuznov was strongly of the view that the people in Congress, exhausted from wars in the Middle East, would never countenance involvement in a European war until it was too late—until Kuznov had a tight grip over Central Europe. It would be déjà vu, the 1930s all over again in terms of Washington overlooking unpleasant realities in Europe and hoping it would all blow over. His plan had been brilliantly developed. Once his agreement with Hungary was announced, Kuznov could begin implementation.

Everything had been proceeding smoothly until ten days ago when an upset Szabo had called Kuznov to say they had a problem. Peter Toth, who had been a powerful Hungarian industrialist and was now living in the United States, had somehow learned about the secret agreement between Kuznov and Szabo. Now Toth, aided by Emma Miller, his former CFO, was threatening to torpedo the agreement. In that phone call Kuznov had assured Szabo not to worry. "Nobody, and I mean nobody will stop this agreement from going into effect," he had said.

Kuznov turned back to the map. He looked at the Russian border with Ukraine. He would airlift Russian troops and supplies over Ukraine and into Hungary. Ukraine wouldn't dare to try and stop them.

Kuznov heard his intercom buzz. Then the sound of his secretary's voice came, informing him that his aide, Dimitri, had arrived.

"Send him in," Kuznov said.

The Russian president moved from the map to his desk.

Dimitri, a tall, thin man in his thirties with hollow cheeks and sunken eyes, was the son of one of the generals Kuznov had worked with in Chechnya. He had a brilliant mind and had studied political science at the University of Moscow. What Kuznov most appreciated was Dimitri's loyalty and his desire to complete every assignment Kuznov gave him successfully.

As soon as he saw Dimitri, Kuznov was struck by the worried expression on his face. Before Dimitri had a chance to speak, Kuznov said, "I heard on CNN about the fire at Peter Toth's house. Were our men able to learn anything before killing Peter and the others?"

Dimitri shook his head. "If they had, they were instructed to go immediately to our embassy and to communicate with me. I haven't heard anything so the answer must be no. Judging from all the reports in the American media and the statements by the local police, it is clear that Peter Toth, his wife, Reka, and grandson, Nicholas, are all dead."

"Dammit," said Kuznov, frustrated they hadn't learned anything about what plans Toth may have set in motion. But there was still hope, he remembered. "What about the woman in Paris?"

"Everything is proceeding on schedule."

Kuznov narrowed his eyes at Dimitri. "What else? Why do you look worried?"

"I just returned from Budapest where I was making arrangements for the Friendship Pact signing ceremony. During a private meeting with Prime Minister Szabo I was suggesting that we should have it in front of their parliament building when suddenly, without any warning, Szabo said, 'The agreement is off. I won't sign it.'"

Kuznov was flabbergasted. "What?"

The Friendship Pact was the linchpin of his entire European initiative. Enraged, he pounded his fist on the desk and shot to his feet. "Fucking Hungarian! I want you to have him killed. Make it look like an accident."

Dimitri shook his head.

"You're daring to disagree with me?" Kuznov hissed.

Dimitri cowered in the chair. "Not disagreeing, Mr. President. With all due respect, I merely want to raise a point for your consideration."

"Okay. I'm listening."

"Szabo's deputy and likely successor if anything happens to him has developed a very close relationship with the German chancellor and the French president. He wants better relations with the West and will never even for one moment consider the Friendship Pact."

"How do you know this?" Kuznov asked.

"He explained it to me in a private conversation. He wanted me to know that he disagreed with what Szabo was doing. He also said that the justice minister, Janos Rajk, disagrees as well."

"Suppose you were to tell Szabo's deputy why Szabo was murdered."

"He would leak it to the press," said Dimitri.

"So you're telling me we're finished in Hungary. That means my entire plan to rebuild the Russian empire collapses."

"No, sir. Not at all."

Kuznov was mystified. "What, then?"

"In my opinion, Szabo is behaving like a rug merchant. He wants a better deal."

"We've agreed to construct enough nuclear energy facilities to supply virtually all of Hungary's electricity. I won't do any more."

"I think he's looking for a personal payoff."

"What do you base that on?"

"He said that he won't be gaining enough from the agreement, and that with the opposition Toth has stirred up, he'll be facing too many risks. I reminded him that in addition to the nuclear energy facilities, he will be striking a blow against the Western Europeans, who he hates."

"And?"

"He repeated, 'I gain nothing from the agreement.'"

Kuznov pondered Dimitri's words.

"What do you want me to do?" Dimitri asked.

Before responding, Kuznov thought about the systemic corruption in Russia. He was convinced that practically every top official in his government had stolen money from the State and stashed it in foreign banks. Kuznov himself had numbered accounts in three banks—one in Switzerland, one in Andorra, and one in Panama. He could hardly be upset at Szabo for trying to line his own pockets. In this respect, why should Hungarians be any different from Russians? Or leaders in just about every country in the world?

Besides, the Russian had three favorite ways of dealing with his opponents: arrest them, kill them, or bribe them.

"Return to Budapest," Kuznov said. "Offer Szabo 100 million euros to be deposited in the bank of his choice if he will agree to sign the Friendship Pact."

"That might work," Dimitri conceded.

"Not might. It has to work. This is critical for me, so that means it's critical for you."

The unstated threat hung in the air.

# Paris

The sun was struggling to break through thick gray clouds in the eastern sky on what was predicted to be a cool but dry day, more like fall than summer. For Craig Page, this was perfect weather for a morning run.

Craig had a regular routine. He normally left the still sleeping Elizabeth Crowder in bed at their apartment, which was on the left bank close to Boulevard Saint-Germain, not far from Saint-Sulpice. He then crossed the Pont Royal, continued past the Louvre around the Jardin du Carrousel, and turned around and ran to Place de la Concorde, where he crossed the river. Then down to the Quai Anatole-France along the Seine.

That morning the first part of his routine was shattered. While he was looking for his running shoes, Elizabeth's cell phone began to ring. He looked at her anxiously as she sat up in bed, reached over to the nightstand, and grabbed the phone.

"Yes," she said. "Yes. Give me that address again. . . . Okay. . . . Got it. I'll be right there."

She put down the phone and jumped out of bed.

"What happened?" Craig asked.

"It was Henri. A woman was murdered in a house on Place des Vosges. He wants me to go there and cover the story."

"Why you? You're the foreign news editor, not some damn police reporter."

"Henri says it has an international component. The woman was a Hungarian national and a big deal with a Swiss investment bank."

"Oh bullshit, all of his police reporters are probably off on August holiday."

She came over, kissed him, and said, "Now, now. No grumbling. Henri rotates the August assignments and this is my year. Besides, you have next month's car race to prepare for. And after that, we're going deep sea diving off Australia. It's not a tough life."

He wrapped his arms around her. "It would be easy to placate me and it wouldn't take long," he murmured.

"Down boy," she laughed, slipping away and heading into the bathroom where she turned on the shower.

Craig went into the kitchen, returning moments later with two cups of double espresso. While Elizabeth dried her hair, he placed one on the sink nearby.

"Thanks," she said.

"As long as one of us has to work, I'm glad it's you," Craig quipped.

She put down the hair dryer and picked up the espresso. "Very funny. If I had received a five-million-euro bequest from my benefactor I wouldn't be working either."

He laughed. "I doubt that. You'll always be working."

"And you'll always be trying to get yourself killed."

Her words stopped Craig. She had been after him lately to give up car racing but he had refused. He loved what Fittipaldi, the famous Brazilian driver had called, "the zensation of speed." And he was convinced the crash in Sardinia that landed him in the hospital had been a freak event—once in a lifetime. He was a better driver now. He was confident it wouldn't reoccur.

Still, he regretted that his racing was their one bone of contention since they had been living together in Paris. She repeatedly told him, "I can't believe I'm more worried about you now than when you were doing counterterrorism. Why don't you go back to private security work the way you did when you left the CIA the first time? At least then you had a gun for protection."

"Too boring," he had replied. "I want the zensation of speed."

After finishing his espresso, Craig finally found his running shoes and made to leave for his delayed run.

"When will I see you," Elizabeth asked as he headed toward the stairs.

"Hard to say. I'm going out to the track later in the morning. Bruno wants to make some adjustments to the Jag."

"Don't be late. I made a nine o'clock reservation at a new little place in Le Marais. It's very trendy right now."

He loved that she was always coming up with new restaurants for dinner. He tended to stick with the tried and true. "You're dull when it comes to restaurants," she once told him. "This is Paris. An incredible number of chefs here can really cook. My goal is to try as many of them as possible."

He had to admit she had a point.

Craig kissed her goodbye, then raced down the one flight of stairs to the ground floor and outside. He took a couple of minutes to stretch. Then he set off.

As Craig ran, he reflected on his current situation. His personal life with Elizabeth was ideal. They had fun together. The sex was great. And she wasn't talking about marriage any longer. Craig was relieved. Having lost both his wife, Carolyn, and his daughter, Francesca, Craig had no desire to get married again.

Career wise, he was becoming restless. For the last year, following the wrap up to the murder of Federico Castiglione, who Elizabeth had referred to as his benefactor, Craig hadn't been involved in any espionage or counterterrorism work. It was the longest stretch in his life. Car racing was exciting and a challenge, but he missed the action of the world of espionage—his world.

As the sun broke through the clouds, Paris was coming to life. It was a gorgeous morning. Energized, Craig picked up his pace as he passed the Musée de l'Orangerie and approached the Place de la Concorde.

Elizabeth was convinced he missed "the game" and was itching to get back into counterterrorism. Though he denied it, she was right, of course. Still, he was thoroughly immersed in rally racing. After his victory in Stresa the previous year racing as Enrico Marino, he had gained prominence in the world of rally racing. His next big race would be in a month in the Swiss Alps, starting and ending in Geneva. According to one of the racing rags, Enrico Marino was the favorite.

An hour later, Craig wasn't the least bit winded as he ran down the stairs to the Quai Anatole-France. At the bottom, he dashed straight ahead along the Seine. The path was concrete, unlike the dirt and grassy area on the right bank. He disliked the hard surface, which was brutal on his knees and hips—a reminder that he was no longer in his twenties.

Normally cars were barred from the Quai, but up ahead he saw four vehicles parked along the embankment. One was a police car, another an ambulance. Coming closer, he saw eight people milling around and peering into the river. Three were in police uniforms.

At a distance of ten yards from the scene, Craig stopped and looked at what was happening. None of them paid any attention to him. As he watched, he noticed two men in the river in wetsuits. It had rained heavily the previous day, and the Seine was brown with runoff. They had placed the still body of a man into a harness-like contraption, and those on the embankment were in the process of raising it. Craig heard the word "mort" as someone stated the obvious: of course, the man was dead.

Instinctively from his years in espionage and counterterrorism, Craig moved closer to get a look at the man. He must have died a short while ago because his facial features were still intact. Dark skin, maybe Arabic. A mustache but no beard. A full head of black curly hair.

Suddenly, Craig stopped in his tracks, a horrified look on his face. He recognized the dead man: Amos Neir, an Israeli from a family of Moroccan Jews. Amos had been a Mossad agent when Craig worked with him in the Middle East in his former life as a CIA agent. But more than that, they had become friends over the years.

Craig inched a bit closer and looked at the body. Amos was fully dressed in a dark suit with a blue shirt open at the collar. Craig saw discoloration around the neck. He might have been strangled before being dumped into the river, Craig thought.

Not wanting to be interrogated by the French police since his relationship with Amos involved classified CIA work, Craig turned around and ran back in the direction he had come.

He recrossed the river and reached the Tuileries, safely out of the crime area, then he sat down on a park bench and put his head in his hands. He wept for his friend Amos. But he had to do more than cry. Craig called his friend Giuseppe, who had succeeded him as the director of the EU Counterterrorism Agency.

"Where are you?" Craig asked when he had Giuseppe on the line.

"My office in Paris"

"I need to see you."

"When?"

"How about thirty minutes?"

"Come to the office. I'll move things around."

That was all Craig needed to hear—he quickly ran over to flag a passing cab.

Giuseppe split his time between his offices in Rome and Paris, unlike Craig, who only had a Paris office when he was the head of EU Counterterrorism. In Paris, Giuseppe had retained Craig's office in the La Defense complex as well as his secretary, Maxine.

In the cab, Craig recalled the first time he had met Amos. Craig had been a young CIA agent assigned to the Middle East at the time. He had been operating undercover in Jordan when he received a summons to Langley to meet with Ralph Bogart, the director of Special Ops. He was surprised and thrilled to be invited to attend a meeting with some of the top CIA leadership as well as Deputy National Security Advisor Veronica "Ronni" Moss, and a US Army and Air Force general.

He had no idea what the subject was until Ronni Moss began speaking. "We've become increasingly worried about Iran's effort to build nuclear weapons," she had said. "The regime in place since the mullahs deposed the Shah is a horror. We can't allow them to attain nuclear weapons—not at any cost."

As he listened to an hour-long discussion about the Iran nuclear program and the risks it posed to the United States and her allies, Craig was puzzled as to why he had been invited.

Then Bogart said, "The Israelis have developed a very detailed plan to damage a critical component of the Iranian program by blowing up the computer control center for Iran's uranium enrichment facility in Natanz, which is south of Tehran, about eighty kilometers southeast of Kashan. They have a Mossad agent, Amos Neir, who has been undercover in Iran and knows the area. It's a two-man job. They're prepared to supply a second man and do it alone, but they've given us an offer to join them. We would like to accept that offer. Craig, are you willing to take on this assignment? In view of the risks involved, the decision is up to you."

Craig was both pleased and flattered. An assignment like this could be a wonderful opportunity to advance his career at the CIA. He eagerly accepted.

The next day Craig flew to Israel for intensive planning sessions with Amos. The two of them hit it off immediately and enjoyed being together.

While both were married with young daughters, ethnically and culturally they were very different. Amos was descended from Jews who had lived in Morocco for six hundred years after the Jews had been expelled from Spain when Ferdinand and Isabella conquered the country. His grandparents had moved to Paris while his parents immigrated to Israel.

Craig's father, the only survivor in his family from the Nazis, was rescued as a small child in Northern Italy by a US Army officer and raised in Monessen, Pennsylvania, where Craig was born and grew up. Craig and Amos shared a desire to make their countries and the world a safer place. Both were fearless. Amos, who studied and read history extensively, saw the world in terms of a broader historical perspective.

The Mossad had planned the operation down to the last detail. Craig and Amos had papers identifying them as employees of a French consulting firm that had a contract to work in Iran.

Everything was proceeding according to plan. They succeeded in blowing up the computer control center and were slipping back to their escape vehicle when they were spotted by two Revolutionary Guards.

Their instructions were that if either were captured, the other should try and escape to provide an eyewitness account of what they had seen in the facility. When the guards moved up on Craig and Amos, Craig went on the offense, shouting for Amos to run. Though Craig fought hard, they managed to knock him to the ground and began beating him.

Disregarding their instructions, Amos refused to leave Craig behind. Instead, he whipped out a knife and stabbed both Iranian guards, likely saving Craig's life. Then they hightailed it out of the facility to a safe house. From there they were transported in the back of a vegetable truck to a Caspian port.

Both the United States and Israel had been extremely pleased with the result of the operation, and Craig's CIA career took a major leap forward

Craig was jarred from his reverie as the Paris cab pulled up in front of the La Defense complex. He hurriedly paid the driver before finding his way to the building's elevator.

When he entered Giuseppe's suite, Craig's former secretary, Maxine, smartly dressed in a powder blue suit with a white silk blouse, looked up from her computer. She peered over the top of brown-framed glasses resting halfway down her nose and said, "Nice outfit, Craig."

"I was jogging."

"Gee, I would never have figured that out. Giuseppe's waiting for you," she added.

Craig opened the door and entered the office, which looked exactly as Craig had left it. "Monastic," a French official had once described the interior. The only furniture was a desk and a couple of chairs. A small oriental carpet covered part of the wooden floor. Craig had neither the time nor the interest in decorating. By the time Craig and Giuseppe greeted each other, Maxine was walking through the door with two double espressos.

Giuseppe said, "Not for me. I have to do something about my blood pressure."

After Maxine had left, Craig collapsed into a chair and closed his eyes, thinking with anguish about Amos, Daphna, and their children—such an incredibly close family.

"You look like hell," Giuseppe said. "What happened?"

Craig described what he had just seen.

"I remember you telling me about your relationship with Amos Neir. I'm so very sorry to hear that. . . . Do you know whether he was still with the Mossad?"

"I know he was nine months ago when we last got together in Milan. He was talking about retirement sometime late this year. So I assume the answer to your question is yes, but I have no idea whether he was in Paris on Mossad business."

"Let me check something," said Giuseppe, turning to his computer. After a pause he turned back to Craig. "I checked a list of Mossad agents operating in Europe that we got from Tel Aviv. He's not on it."

"Those lists are never complete. Moshe tells you what he feels like."

"For sure. Regardless, if a Mossad agent is killed in Paris, whether he's on an operation or not, and dumped into the Seine, we have to assume it's the work of terrorists."

"Absolutely. That's why I called you immediately."

"I better let Moshe know that one of his people was killed," sighed Giuseppe, reaching for an encrypted phone.

Craig listened while Giuseppe told Moshe about how the Paris police had pulled Amos Neir's body out of the Seine.

Craig wondered what the venerable Mossad director's reaction was as he watched Giuseppe listening intently, finally stating only, "Yes, I understand," before hanging up. With a thoughtful expression, Giuseppe returned the phone to his desk drawer.

"Well?" Craig asked impatiently.

"Moshe said he'll talk to his prime minister and have him call the French president. The goal is to get Amos's body out of France and back to Israel immediately—before his death is picked up by the press and becomes a major incident."

"You think he'll be able to pull it off? Once the head of French intelligence finds out, he may insist on an investigation before Amos's body is sent back to Israel."

"The good news is that Jean-Claude is in Turkey for a couple of days."

"I notice you didn't ask him what Amos was doing in France. Whether it was Mossad work or something else."

"No," Giuseppe said. "I'd like you to do that for me. I assume you're going to Israel for the funeral."

Craig nodded.

"I think you'll have a better chance of getting reliable information in person."

"Agreed."

"Good. I'll call Moshe back and tell him to talk to you as my representative."

"You're forgetting one small problem," Craig reminded him.

"What's that?"

"After my plastic surgery, I don't look like Craig Page did when I worked with Mossad people, and my passport and all of my IDs are in the name of Enrico Marino."

"I'll explain that to Moshe."

"It still won't be easy."

"You'll find a way to get around the obstacles," Giuseppe assured him.

"I appreciate your confidence."

Giuseppe reached into the credenza behind his desk, pulled out a cell phone, and handed it to Craig. "It's encrypted. French state of the art. Almost as good as Israeli. You can use it to call me."

"I better head home to pack," said Craig.

"Elizabeth will be pleased that you're getting back into the game. The last time the three of us had dinner, while you were in the men's room she told me how much she hates your car racing. 'Craig's putting his life on the line for nothing,' she said. And now it will be for something."

"All I want to do is find out who killed Amos Neir. I'm not putting my life on the line."

"Regardless of what happens, this will be for a good cause. My car and driver are out front. He'll run you back to your apartment."

As they made their way slowly across town in heavy Paris traffic, Craig thought about the call Elizabeth had received that morning concerning the murder of a Hungarian national working for a Swiss bank. The woman had been killed at about the same time as Amos. Both in Paris. To be sure, this was a huge city and it was easy to conclude two deaths on the same day was a coincidence. But maybe not, Craig wondered. Amos was likely tracking a terrorist in Paris. Was that terrorist the one who killed the Hungarian woman and eliminated Amos when he realized Amos was in pursuit?

Craig realized his mind was off on a flight of fancy with no hard evidence. All he had to go on was a gut feeling based on his experience, but those had often been correct in the past. He'd be interested in Elizabeth's reaction.

*        *        *

Despite being exhausted from a sleepless night after the fire, Nick was barely able to close his eyes as the Air France plane made its way to Paris. He kept seeing flames shooting up from his grandparents' house and engulfing them—he couldn't get the image out of his head. The CNN announcer's words, "burnt beyond recognition" reverberated over and over again in his brain and sent chills through his body.

Nick wrapped a blanket around himself and tried to keep his arms from shaking and his teeth from chattering. At least he had Emma

Miller to take care of him. Thank God for that. Though he tried not to think about the fire, he couldn't help it. He wondered what had happened. Did the Russians shoot his grandparents first and then set the house on fire? Or did they set the fire while they were still alive and sleeping? Either way, it was too horrible to contemplate.

For a diversion he turned on an airplane movie. Explosions went off in the violent action film—no relief there. Midway across the Atlantic, he started to think about the reason he was flying to Paris. Emma would take care of him. And the black case he was clutching contained a sealed envelope with a message for her. Grandpa had entrusted him with this important assignment, and he had to concentrate on completing it.

At long last he heard the pilot say they would be beginning their descent into Charles de Gaulle Airport.

Nick tried to calm his apprehension as he followed the throng of passengers moving from the plane through the space-age glass and steel Air France terminal. He followed the signs for "ARRIVING PASSENGERS," and "BAGGAGE CLAIM."

Approaching passport control, Nick felt a wave of anxiety. He was traveling under a false passport. What if the agent asked him questions about Jonathan Hart? How could he answer? With moist fingers, he slipped his passport under the window to the bored and tired-looking man behind the glass and held his breath. The agent yawned, never even glancing at Nick, and stamped the passport.

Nick took his passport and followed the signs for baggage claim. Not having checked any bags, he went right to the exit. Emma had told him that she would meet him when he had exited.

Once he walked through the sliding glass doors, he saw lots of people milling around and a score of men in suits and ties holding signs. He looked everywhere but didn't see Emma. He wandered around the area, but there was still no sign of her. Perhaps she was stuck in traffic and would be there soon.

An hour later, when Emma still hadn't come, Nick called her phone number, but no one answered. He struggled to stave off panic.

He decided that he had only one option: He'd take a cab to her house. So Nick made his way to the end of the taxi line, and fifteen minutes later he was getting into a cab driven by a tall, dark-skinned man. The radio was playing some kind of African music, Nick thought.

He showed the driver Emma's address. The driver nodded and pulled away from the curb.

Once they had left the airport and merged onto the highway, they were mired in heavy morning rush-hour traffic. Nick couldn't keep his eyes open. After the hours of fear and uncertainty, he fell asleep.

He didn't know how long he slept until he was awakened by the driver calling to him, "You want 98 Place des Vosges?"

The cab was stopped. Nick sat up with a start. "Yes. That's right."

"Something has happened in this area. The police have the street blocked off. This is as far as I can go. There's the place you want."

The driver was pointing to a four-story pink brick town house just ahead on the left. It housed a restaurant on the ground floor. In front Nick saw three police cars and an ambulance, all with flashing red lights on the roof.

*Oh my God. I hope nothing happened to Emma,* he thought.

Nick steeled his courage. "I'll get out here," he told the driver.

He paid the cabbie and, with his knees wobbling, got out of the cab, looking around. He had never visited Emma's home or been in the Place des Vosges before. It had a green parklike garden in the center that was bisected by gravel paths and edged with trees. Two larger buildings were on either side of the square and a number of elegant brick town houses surrounded it.

Nick walked toward number ninety-eight. After he had taken several steps, he decided this was a mistake. He didn't want to answer questions from the French police. It'd be better to lay low for a little while and try to find out what was happening.

Nick ducked behind a parked car, out of sight of the dozen or so police and officers. Looking out from behind it he saw a number of people with steno pads—probably reporters—milling around the entrance to number ninety-eight. A few onlookers had stopped and were gawking, and he saw a man talking into a microphone in front of a television camera.

They were all speaking French, which Nick didn't understand, except for one woman, who was speaking in English. She looked like his history teacher, around forty with short brown hair. He heard her say to a man, "I just spoke to the police captain. The victim's name was Emma Miller. She was a Hungarian national, and she was dead when the police arrived. He refused to tell me the cause of death."

The woman's words cut through Nick like a machete. Emma Miller had been his lifeline. In horror, tightly clutching the black case, he collapsed to the ground. As he sat there he saw a gurney being carried out of number ninety-eight with dark green canvas covering what must have been Emma's body.

He thought about the last time he had seen Emma in Paris, about a year ago. Grandpa had to go off to a meeting, and Nick had spent a fun day with Emma. He remembered her taking him up to the restaurant in the Eiffel Tower, and what an incredible view of the city it offered. And she had ordered a flaming dessert with cherries, something he had never seen before.

What he had liked even more than the dessert was being with Emma. She was so interested in him and everything he was doing—in school and in sports. At the end of the day, he asked his grandfather if they could come to Paris again and spend more time with Emma. He promised they would.

Nick felt nauseous as he watched the police wheel the gurney toward the ambulance and load it in the back. The door slammed with finality. It was the end of Emma's life. The end of Nick's connection with his grandfather. He truly was all alone in a strange city, in a foreign country, with people speaking a language he didn't understand. He didn't know a single person. He was only twelve years old!

On the verge of panic, he stood up and watched the crowd breaking up. Onlookers were moving away while the police climbed back into their cars. The reporters were doing the same. As he looked around, he saw something terrifying. Twenty yards away, a blonde man with a large round face was staring at Nick through the open window of a black Citroën.

*What in the world am I going to do?* The onrushing fear threatened to paralyze him. He forced himself to think. There had to be something he could do.

*Run to one of the police cars before they pull away?* That was an option, but his grandfather had never trusted the police. Besides, they might not speak English. Then what?

As he thought about his next step, the police cars drove away. That option had vanished. The man in the Citroën was still watching him. His whole body felt cold, and he was shaking.

Nick saw the female reporter with short brown hair, the one who had been speaking English, heading toward a dark blue Audi parked close to him.

Without a second thought, Nick staggered after her. He clutched the black case as he approached the woman. Maybe she would help him. She was his only chance.

By the time Nick was close enough to speak, she had her hand on the car door. Feeling terrified, he opened his mouth to say, "Please help me." But nothing came out.

*He couldn't speak!*

This had never happened to him before.

He formed the words again and opened his mouth.

*Nothing!*

*Silence!*

*What?*

*He couldn't speak!*

After all the other terrible things that had happened, now he had lost his voice, too. It was all too much for Nick. The courage he had felt was dissipating. He couldn't bear the pain and grief any longer. Tears formed in his eyes and ran down his cheeks, and he let out a sob.

The startled woman turned around and saw Nick standing behind her with tears streaming down his face. She reached into her jacket pocket, took out a handkerchief, and handed it to him.

"Who are you?" she asked kindly.

The words still wouldn't come. Nick shook his head, distraught.

The woman opened up her bag, removed a pad and pen, and handed them to him.

She understood.

He wrote on the pad: "I lost my voice. Will you help me?"

She nodded her head. "Tell me where you want to go."

He wrote: "I came from Washington to see Emma Miller. Now she is dead. I don't know anyone else in Paris."

After he passed the pad back this time, she placed a comforting hand on his shoulder while she read his words.

Then she looked at him with compassion. "I'm Elizabeth Crowder. I'm an American living in Paris. Would you like to come with me? I will help you."

When he nodded, she opened the back door of the car for him. He looked in the direction where the black Citroën had been. He wanted to tell her about the man who had been watching him, but the Citroën was gone. So he climbed inside her car and fastened his seatbelt.

She got into the front and started the car. As she did, he was clasping the black case tightly with both hands, as if his life depended on it.

\*        \*        \*

Elizabeth thought how bizarre her unexpected encounter was while she drove the young boy back to her apartment, glancing from time to time into the rearview mirror to check on him. An American kid doesn't just appear out of thin air on a Paris street—and at a murder scene, no less.

Also, something was radically wrong with this child. His note had said he'd lost his voice. Maybe he had suffered some trauma that had rendered him mute. He had come from the States to meet Emma Miller and arrived at the scene of her murder. He looked terrified. Was he related to Emma Miller? Or a witness to her murder? Was he in shock because of what had happened to her? Elizabeth mulled over the possibilities.

Whatever it was, he needed sympathy and care. She was unwilling to turn him over to the police, who might not be understanding—at least not until she found out who he was.

She parked in front of her apartment, helped him out of the car, and led him up the stairs to the second floor. Once they were inside, it occurred to her that he might be hungry. She took him to the kitchen and pointed to the butcher block table. The boy sat down, still clutching his case.

"Would you like something to eat?" Elizabeth asked.

He nodded.

She toasted a baguette from the day before and fixed a plate with three different types of cheese and some melon. She placed the food on the table, and he ate eagerly, nodding to her to say thank you.

She poured a glass of water for him and fixed a coffee for herself. Then, without saying a word, she sat down across from him.

When he had finished all the food, she asked, "Would you like more?"

He shook his head.

To help him, she had to find out who he was.

"Can I see your passport?" she asked.

He reached into the case and pulled out a US passport, which he then handed to her.

After looking at it and his picture, she said, "I will try to help you, Jonathan."

As soon as the words were out of her mouth, he started shaking his head vigorously.

She was puzzled. "You don't want my help?"

He shook his head again, reached into his pocket, and pulled out a crumpled piece of paper. He unfolded it and placed it on the table. As she watched, he slid it across to her. It was white with a gold border.

Elizabeth read: "Potomac, MD, Bears Baseball Team—Most Valuable Player Award Presented to Nicholas Toth."

He reached across the table and pointed to the name Nicholas Toth, then he pointed to himself.

"Oh my God!" Elizabeth put her hand to her mouth in surprise.

While passing the time at the murder scene earlier that morning waiting for the police to provide information, she had been watching CNN. She had seen the report about the fire in Potomac, Maryland, and remembered the announcer stating that twelve-year-old Nicholas Toth had died in the home along with his grandparents. But Nicholas Toth was here in her apartment. He had either not been in the house or had escaped after the fire started. And after these horrific events, this boy had then flown to Paris to see Emma Miller. He had arrived in time to witness Emma's dead body being removed from her apartment. It wasn't surprising that he couldn't speak.

Just then she heard the front door open. From the living room, Craig called out. "Elizabeth, are you home?"

Terrified, Nicholas sprang to his feet. He dashed toward the open walk-in pantry, climbed inside, and pulled the door shut.

Walking into the kitchen in his running clothes carrying a baguette, Craig asked, "What are you doing home?"

"It's a long story," she replied, walking to the pantry. "I'll tell you in a moment." Standing in front of the pantry door she said, "It's okay, Nicholas, you can come out."

The door slowly crept open, and with small steps and a frightened expression, the boy reappeared.

A startled Craig dropped the baguette on the floor. Nicholas moved behind Elizabeth, watching him warily.

"This is Craig," said Elizabeth comfortingly. "He's a good man. He lives here with me. He'll help you, too. Won't you, Craig?"

"Who is he?" Craig asked.

"Patience. Tell him you'll help."

"Of course. I'd be glad to help."

She turned back to Nicholas. "Would you like to take a shower and get some sleep?"

He nodded.

"Good. I'll get you some of Craig's clean clothes. They'll be large, but they'll do for now."

After Nicholas had showered, Elizabeth provided him with a pair of Craig's pajamas and led him into the second bedroom, where she motioned for him to climb into bed. Seconds later he was sound asleep.

She found Craig in the kitchen munching on bread and sipping coffee.

"Now do you want to tell me what the hell's going on?" he asked.

"Sh, keep your voice down. Nicholas is sleeping."

"Okay. But tell me."

She explained how Nicholas had approached her on the street outside of the murder scene. Then she told Craig what she knew based on the CNN report and what she had learned from the boy. "He had come to Paris to see Emma Miller."

"The woman who was murdered?"

"Exactly. So with the terrible shock of everything that happened he lost his voice."

Craig thought about it for a minute. "Makes sense. There has to be a relationship between the fire and Emma Miller's murder, doesn't there?"

"For sure. According to CNN the boy's grandfather, Peter Toth, had extensive Hungarian connections. From the Paris police I learned that Emma Miller was a Hungarian national."

"What will you do with the boy?"

"He has to be at serious risk," said Elizabeth. "Whoever killed Peter and Emma must have a great deal at stake. Once they found out that

Nicholas is still alive—and they probably will at some point—they'll come after him to find out what he might have learned from his grandfather. Or if he saw the people who set the fire."

"Definitely," Craig agreed. "So we have to protect him until we find out what's happening. Any ideas?"

"I have a friend, Jules Cardin, a psychiatrist, who runs a clinic outside of Paris for children suffering from trauma. It's a good place and safe. Lots of security to keep troubled kids from leaving the facility. Also, Nick has a passport with a phony name so they won't be able to locate him there."

"That sounds perfect."

"My thought is that Nick should stay here tonight in the hope that being with us in a home environment might bring his voice back. And you and I can protect him. Then if he still can't talk in the morning and he agrees, I'll take him to the clinic and check him in for treatment. While he's staying in the clinic, I'll try to find out what the connection is between Emma Miller and the Potomac fire."

Craig pushed back some hair that had fallen over his eyes. "There's only one problem with that plan."

"What's that?"

"I'll be in Tel Aviv tonight."

"Tel Aviv? What for?" asked Elizabeth in surprise.

"Amos Neir was murdered. They pulled his body out of the Seine."

"Oh, Craig, I know how much he meant to you."

Craig narrowed his eyes. "I sure as hell am going to find out who killed Amos."

"You're going to Israel for the funeral?"

"That and to get some information that will help me find his killer."

"Don't worry about me tonight. I've got my gun. I can protect the boy."

"It would be better to take him to the clinic today."

She shook her head emphatically. "He's been through so much, and a night in a home environment might help him talk."

Craig sighed. "I can see that I won't change your mind. I'll arrange for a couple of security men who used to be with EU Counterterrorism to get over here as soon as possible. They'll provide protection for you and Nick."

"But tell them to remain outside and be unobtrusive."

"Of course. They'll do that. I'll call you when I'm on the way to the airport and give you a contact name and number. It'll probably be Pierre, who was with the French special ops. You met him once. At any rate, keep the security men here as long as you need them. Nick should be okay at the clinic, provided they don't follow you there."

"Agreed. I'll make sure they don't."

"Now come into the bedroom while I pack. I have a suggestion for you."

As Craig tossed clothes and toiletries into a suitcase, he said, "I think you should call Betty Richards and tell her about Nick. With the Hungarian connection, there's an international component."

"Good idea. I'll call Betty. Also, as the CIA director, she'll be able to get the cooperation of the FBI on investigating the Potomac fire."

Craig kissed Elizabeth at the door. "I'll call you from Israel," he said. "And be really careful. A lot's going on here."

"Is it conceivable that Amos Neir's murder is somehow related to Emma's?"

"I've been wondering that. As you know, I've never been big on coincidence in a situation like this."

Once Craig had left, Elizabeth reached for her phone to call Betty. Then she reconsidered. She had to learn more before she could involve the CIA director.

In view of the Emma Miller murder, she was convinced that the fire at Nick's grandparents' house had been intentional, but she didn't have any factual basis for her conclusion. The CNN announcer had said the cause of the fire was believed to be accidental, most likely caused by the rupture of a gas line. To Elizabeth, that seemed wrong given the intensity of the fire and that the bodies were burnt beyond recognition. But she was no expert on fires.

She did know one, however. Her dad had been a member of the NYPD, and one of his drinking buddies was Kevin Collins, former head of the New York City Fire Department. She had sought his opinion once before when she had been working in New York, and he had told her to call him anytime.

She checked her watch. It was almost seven in the morning in New York. She gave it a try.

Kevin answered in a sleepy voice. "Who's calling?"

"It's Elizabeth Crowder, Mr. Collins." She always called her dad's friends mister. When Elizabeth was growing up, her mother insisted on it, and she never got out of the habit.

"Sean's girl. Good to hear from you. I liked that book you wrote a couple years ago about Muslims in Europe."

"Glad to hear that, Mr. Collins."

"With all that's happened since, you should write a sequel."

Elizabeth had considered doing that but didn't know where she'd find the time. "I'm thinking about it. Meantime, I need help."

"I'll do what I can."

She described the situation for Collins. When she was finished, he asked, "The house was totally destroyed, and the bodies were burnt to the point of being unidentifiable?"

"That's what they said on CNN, quoting a police spokesperson."

"Had to be arson. For a huge house like that they must have used a highly flammable liquid as an accelerant and lots of it."

"You don't think it could have been the rupture of a gas line?" she persisted.

"No way."

Elizabeth thanked Kevin and hung up. After refilling her empty coffee cup she thought about where to go next. Focus on the victims, her reporter's instinct told her. They had to be the key to what had happened.

She went online and found the obit in the *Washington Post* for Peter Toth. Two paragraphs made a powerful impression on Elizabeth:

Peter Toth was born in Budapest, Hungary, in 1948. In 1977 when he was twenty-nine years old, he came to the US as a member of a Hungarian hockey team. He defected at that time and remained in the United States. In 1991, shortly after Russia relinquished control of Hungary, he returned to his home country and became a wealthy industrialist. For many years Peter Toth was very close with Franz Szabo, the current prime minister, who began as a young liberal politician in 1989. Toth and Szabo had a falling out two years ago, as Szabo's politics became increasingly right-wing. At that time, Peter Toth liquidated most of his interests and moved back to the United States.

Peter Toth's father, Zoltan Toth, now ninety-five, is still alive and living in the Washington area. Zoltan Toth was an important leader among the pro-independence Hungarians who directed the unsuccessful 1956 uprising against Russia. At the time, Zoltan Toth came to New York to plead the rebels' case to the UN. He was barred from returning to Hungary by the Russians. He settled in the United States, while his wife and eight-year-old child, Peter, were prohibited from leaving Hungary.

Elizabeth picked up a pencil and a pad. On a blank page she wrote the name Peter Toth. Under it she drew a timeline.

| Date of Birth | Hungarian Uprising | Defection to US | Return to Hungary | Move to US |
|---|---|---|---|---|
| 1948 | 1956 | 1977 | 1991 | 2016 |

At this point Elizabeth believed she had enough information to talk to Betty Richards, who had succeeded Craig as CIA director. As a result of Craig bringing them together, the two women had developed a close relationship. Betty had been a help to Elizabeth not just professionally, but in dealing with Craig, who Elizabeth loved, but who could be a pain in the ass. When they joined forces against him, Craig called it "the sisterhood at work."

Not knowing where Betty was, Elizabeth decided to email and schedule a call.

"I have to talk to you on a secure phone. What do you suggest?" she wrote.

A minute later the response came. "I'm currently in Berlin for a NATO security conference. I could stop in Paris tomorrow on my way home. How about 6 p.m. at the embassy?"

Elizabeth immediately replied, "I'll be there."

Next, Elizabeth had to call Henri, her boss at the paper. As the foreign editor, she had a lot of freedom to pursue her own stories, but with one as complex and time-consuming as the murder of Peter Toth was likely to be, it was best to get Henri on board early in the process. If not, he could become an impediment. This time she had the perfect opening.

"Henri," she said, "I have a little more information on the woman who was murdered this morning."

"Do the police have any leads?"

"Nothing so far, but as I was working on my article, I came across a peculiar fact."

"What's that?"

"Hours before Emma Miller was killed, there was a mysterious fire in Potomac, Maryland, a suburb of Washington and Peter Toth—"

"I heard about the fire. Peter Toth was an enemy of the Hungarian prime minister, Szabo." Henri sounded excited. "I've met Szabo a couple of times. The man's a horror, a right-wing demagogue, and vicious. He told me how much he admires Kuznov, and one of Kuznov's most charming characteristics is how he murders his political opponents. Emma Miller could have been involved with Peter Toth. Suppose Szabo took a page from Kuznov's playbook? And if he did that, he might have arranged Emma Miller's death as well. This could be big."

She was thrilled Henri saw where she was going with this, but had no intention of telling him about Nick. "That's what I was thinking," she replied.

"I want you to get on this right away. Full steam ahead with your connections. Being an American, you should have a leg up on any other journalist in Europe. Go to Washington if you think that would be helpful. I'll set up a special expense account for the story. You can always edit other pieces from the road or dump them off on Dominique."

Elizabeth was ecstatic. "Will do."

"Just keep me informed."

"Don't I always?"

"No is the answer to that question," came Henri's exasperated reply.

"I will this time. I promise."

"I've heard that before. Do you know the value of that particular promise?"

She was smiling. "I'll play your silly game. Several thousand euros?"

"Wrong. Three US pennies. And by the way, if you involve Craig and this turns dangerous, as most of your escapades with him do, then don't worry about my loss from your demise."

"Why's that?"

"I've taken out a life insurance policy on you and made the newspaper the beneficiary."

Elizabeth wanted to say, "That's not funny," but she didn't think Henri was joking.

After hanging up the phone, she walked over to the window and looked out. As she did, two black BMW SUVs pulled up in front of her apartment building. It had to be Craig's friends.

A man wearing sunglasses got out of one of the vehicles. He was short and squat and looked hard as nails. This was Pierre. She remembered meeting him once at a function with Craig. He was retired from the French military—special ops. Elizabeth opened the window and waved to him. He waved back.

Then she walked into the bedroom and moved her gun from the closet to the drawer of the bedside table. She was ready in case they came for Nick.

# Northern Israel

Craig arrived in Israel late that evening. After checking into the Dan Hotel on the beachfront in Tel Aviv, he arranged for a rental car to be delivered early the next morning. He wanted to drive himself to northern Israel for the funeral.

Amos had been a member of a kibbutz north of Haifa, close to the Mediterranean. When the kibbutz had been founded in 1948, the same year as the establishment of the state of Israel, it had been an agricultural kibbutz. Its revenue came primarily from oranges, peaches, and lychees. That changed about twenty years ago. Keeping pace with the new Israel, the kibbutz abandoned agriculture and moved aggressively into tech. It now served as an incubator for high-tech start-ups. Already six companies had been launched from the kibbutz that were on the NASDAQ.

Though it was 11:30 p.m. when Craig had finished making his rental car arrangements, he had no intention of going to sleep. Tel Aviv had a frenetic pace, particularly in the summer, which went well into the morning hours. He set off on foot for Dizengoff Street, which was lined with bustling outdoor cafes and restaurants. After walking for half an hour, he found an empty table at a Yemenite restaurant where he ate salad and grilled lamb accompanied by a good red blend of cabernet, merlot, and cabernet franc from the Golan.

After Craig had finished his meal, he made his way back to the hotel, taking in his surroundings and enjoying the warm night air. Looking around at the people in the restaurants, on the street, and even on busses, he had the same thought that he always had in Rome: How do these people get up for work in the morning?

Craig was up early the next morning and driving his rental car out of the hotel parking lot by six o'clock. The sun was already up. Welcome to Israel in the summer. It was a picture-perfect day with not a cloud in the robin's egg blue sky. Nobody should have to be buried on such a beautiful day, Craig thought somberly.

On the highway, Craig kept pace with the flow of heavy traffic, which fortunately lightened as he got further from the city. He had no need for GPS. Over the years when he had been stationed in the Middle East, he had made this drive many other times. He and his wife, Carolyn, and their daughter, Francesca, had often gone to visit Amos and his wife, Daphna. They had a daughter, Gila, who had been Francesca's age, which would make her twenty-eight now, and a son two years younger. The two families had been close, taking vacations together in Turkey and Morocco.

Craig's last visit to the kibbutz had been six months before Carolyn died of bacterial meningitis in Dubai. When he had called to let them know that Carolyn was in the hospital and seriously ill, Amos had arranged for her to fly to Israel, which had the best medical facilities in the Middle East. But by the time she got there, it was too late.

Craig reached the kibbutz an hour before the funeral was scheduled to begin. As he pulled up to the metal gate at the entrance, he immediately became aware of the high level of security. Two soldiers armed with semiautomatic weapons stood on each side of the gate. Another was checking IDs.

Craig rolled down the window and held out his Italian passport.

"Pull over and park," the soldier said curtly, pointing to a dirt area off to the side.

Craig did as he was told. Two soldiers descended on him. "Out of the car," one of them ordered.

Craig climbed out and raised his hands. One of the soldiers roughly patted him down while two other soldiers examined his car.

"Why are you here?" the soldier asked.

"Amos and I worked together. We were friends. I know his wife, Daphna. I've been here many times to visit him."

The soldier didn't seem convinced. "Who can confirm your identity?"

"Talk to Moshe."

Craig had learned long ago that no one ever used the last name or the title of the venerable Mossad director. They simply referred to him as Moshe.

The soldier took out his cell phone and said something in Hebrew. Minutes later he directed Craig to a jeep parked inside the gate. Craig climbed into the vehicle. With a soldier driving, they rode up the hill and parked next to the kibbutz administration building.

Moshe was waiting in front. His gray hair, once thick, was thinning. With heavy bags under his bloodshot eyes, he looked weary and much older than Craig remembered. He had once told Craig, "Every time I bury one of my people it takes years off my life." And Craig knew that Amos had been a favorite of Moshe's.

When Craig got out of the car, Moshe's head snapped back in surprise. "Giuseppe told me that you had some plastic surgery," he said. "Still, I wasn't expecting such a difference. Your doctor did a good job."

"I like living. So I made a change to stay alive. After that, I managed to kill the devil who was after me."

"This was your battle with the Zhou brothers."

Craig was startled. Israel hadn't been involved.

"It's my business to know what's happening everywhere in this small world," Moshe remarked. "With globalization, we're now all interconnected. I'm familiar with what you did in Argentina as well."

"Unfortunately, I can't go back to looking like Craig Page."

"I don't know, Craig. Plastic surgeons can do miraculous things."

"Now I have a new career as a race car driver. My fans wouldn't like it."

"Giuseppe said you and I should talk about Amos and his death."

Craig nodded.

"My office, this evening at seven o'clock."

"I'll be there. Do you know where Daphna is now?"

"Their house." He pointed to a path that went up a slight hill between two rows of trees.

With the hot sun beating down, Craig walked along a cracked cement path, passing a school and a soccer field, until he arrived at a modest stone structure that was identical to others around it. Craig recalled it was one floor with two bedrooms, a living room, a small kitchen, and a bath. Meals were taken in the communal dining room. Despite the wealth of the kibbutz, members refused to alter their lifestyle. Those who wanted more left to live in Haifa or Tel Aviv.

People were milling around outside of the house. Craig saw a couple of familiar faces from the Mossad, but decided it would be too complicated to explain who he was so he moved past them. With the crowd of people inside the house and the absence of air conditioning, it was hot. Craig felt perspiration soaking the white button-down under his suit jacket.

He saw Daphna sitting on a sofa, her son, Danny, on one side and her daughter, Gila, on the other. Daphna's eyes were puffy and red from crying. She had one of the saddest expressions Craig had ever seen.

Going over to her, he said, "Daphna. I'm so very sorry."

Confusion was on her face as she stood up. "Do I know you?"

"Amos was a wonderful man," he added, hoping she would recognize his voice.

"Craig?"

"Yeah. I had a little work done on my face."

She hugged him. Then she broke down and cried. He took the handkerchief from his pocket and handed it to her.

"I can't believe you came. Thank you. Thank you. Amos loved you like a brother."

Craig had no intention of telling her he had seen the police pulling Amos's body out of the Seine so he simply responded, "I had to be here."

She wiped the tears from her eyes. "We heard about your loss with Francesca. She was a very special person—brilliant and a joy to be with. I was so sorry to hear."

"Thank you," Craig said looking down at the ground and choking back his own tears and the sadness he felt when he thought about Francesca.

"I had been pressing Amos to retire for several years. I told him it was a young man's business. Finally, last June he agreed to retire in September—next month, right before Rosh Hashanah." She began crying again. "He . . . he almost made it."

Other people were waiting to talk to Daphna, and as they drew her attention Craig pulled away. He left the house and climbed the rocky path leading up a hill to the kibbutz cemetery. He looked at the markers—so many young people from the kibbutz had lost their lives in Israel's wars: 1948, 1956, 1967, 1973, and the more recent ones in Lebanon and Gaza. Craig was convinced that peace would never come to this part of the Middle East, and it didn't matter what actions the Israeli government took. All it could do was remain strong in confronting its implacable enemies.

*          *          *

Craig didn't feel like talking to anyone, so when the funeral began he hung back. It seemed to pass in a blur, a kaleidoscope of memories. In his mind he replayed times he had spent with Amos. The Israeli could be intense and hard-driving when the situation required it, but he was also fun to be with. He had often made jokes and poked fun at politicians, and he was an incredible soccer player—daring and fast as the wind. More than anything he had loved his family.

As the ceremony was ending, people started chanting the mourner's kaddish. Craig joined in. Afterwards, he stopped briefly at the house to say goodbye to Daphna. In the crowded room, she pulled him to one side. "Craig," she said. "I know you retired from the CIA, but you still have contacts. Please, please find out who did this and make them pay for it." Her voice cracked with emotion.

"Daphna, I loved Amos. I promise you that I'll do it for you and for me."

## Paris

Elizabeth slept fitfully. Every hour or so she woke up and reached into the drawer, making certain the gun was still there. She also walked over to the window and looked out to check that Pierre and his colleague were in place. Everything outside looked normal.

She wanted to believe that Emma and Peter's killers wouldn't have had enough time to figure out Nick was with her. She hoped that was right.

Finally, at about five in the morning, she fell into a deep sleep. What felt like moments later she awoke again to the sound of a ball smacking against a wall: whack . . . whack . . . whack.

Pulling on a robe, she went out to the living room. Nick had on her baseball glove and was tossing a rubber ball against the red brick wall, catching it, and tossing it again.

Looking startled and embarrassed when he saw her, he took off the glove and returned it to the top of the bookcase where she kept it. The ball rolled across the floor.

"That's okay," she said.

Hoping he could talk, she added, "It's my glove. I'm a pitcher. What position do you play?" She held her breath.

He opened his mouth as if to speak, but nothing came out. He raised two fingers.

"Second base," she said.

He nodded.

"Why don't you get dressed? I'll fix breakfast."

Once he had disappeared into the bathroom, Elizabeth called Pierre on the number Craig had given her. "Hi Pierre, this is Elizabeth. Anything happen during the night?"

"All quiet."

"Can I bring you down some food and hot coffee?"

"That's very nice of you, but we loaded up at the patisserie on the corner. I'll probably gain ten pounds on this job."

"The chocolate croissants are particularly good."

"Already had two of them."

After hanging up, Elizabeth cut up a melon and made Nick a tomato and cheese omelet along with a side of smoked salmon. There was nothing wrong with his appetite—he devoured everything.

As Elizabeth was finishing her second double espresso, she said, "I've been thinking about your situation. I want to help you, and I have an idea."

He listened wide-eyed, anxious to hear what was coming next.

"I assume you could speak before all this happened."

He nodded.

"I would like to help you speak again, but I'm no doctor. I don't know how to do that. However I have a good friend, Dr. Cardin, who runs a clinic outside of Paris for children who have suffered trauma. I would like to take you there and have you stay at the clinic so Dr. Cardin can help you."

From Nick's face, she saw anxiety give way to fear.

"You will be completely safe at Dr. Cardin's clinic. You can use your identity as Jonathan Hart. Neither Dr. Cardin nor anyone else at the clinic will know that you are Nicholas Toth."

Nick took a deep breath and blew it out, then rubbed his hand through his hair.

She cautioned herself to go slowly. He was only a twelve-year-old, and he had been through a lot.

"I won't take you if you don't want to go," she added. "But if you do I will visit you often. Tell me what you think."

She passed a pad and pencil across the table to him. Nick made no effort to pick it up. A minute, then two passed. He didn't move. She couldn't even imagine what was running through his mind.

Finally, he picked up the pencil. She watched him write on the pad, then slide it across the table.

She read: "If I don't like the clinic, can I leave?"

She looked at him. "Absolutely. You just tell me on one of my visits."

When Nick didn't respond, she continued, "I prefer the clinic because Dr. Cardin and his people are very good." She started to say, "I think they will be able to restore your speech," but caught herself. She didn't want to promise what she wasn't certain she could deliver. So instead, she added, "I'm hopeful they'll be able to help you speak again."

Nick looked a little less anxious.

"So is the clinic okay?" she asked.

He nodded.

"Good. On the way to the clinic, we'll stop and buy you some clothes. While I'm getting dressed, you can look in the bookcase in the living room. I have lots of English novels. Pick out the ones you'd like to read and you can take them with you."

Nick raised his right hand and stood up. She guessed he was asking her to wait. He raced into the bedroom he had been using and returned with the black case. After sitting down at the table, he opened it, removed a sealed envelope with Emma Miller's name on the front, and handed it to her.

"Emma Miller is dead," she said.

He nodded. Then he wrote on the pad, "Open the envelope."

She did, hoping it might unlock the mystery of the fire and Emma's murder. Inside she found a typed note.

Emma:

Continue the operation without me, and take good care of Nick.

Peter

Elizabeth wondered what operation Peter and Emma had been planning. Regardless of what it was, she was convinced it had led to both of their murders.

She showed the note to Nick. "Do you know what operation your grandpa was talking about?"

Nick shook his head.

"Can I keep this note?"

He nodded.

"Okay. I'm going to get dressed. Why don't you pick out some books in the living room that you'd like?"

Alone in her bedroom, she closed the door and called Dr. Cardin. In explaining the situation, she told him that Jonathan Hart was a cousin from the United States who had been entrusted to her care. She also briefly explained how he had lost his grandparents in a fire and might still be in danger, but kept the details intentionally vague. As she expected, he was incredibly sympathetic and didn't press her for details about the fire.

"Of course you can bring Jonathan. We'll do everything we can to restore his speech."

Her next call was to Pierre. "In a few minutes I'll be leaving the apartment with a boy. We'll be getting into the blue Audi parked in front and driving away. I'd like you to follow me."

"Will do."

"If we have company, could you find a way to disable them?"

"That should be easy. Meantime, I'll ask Simon in the other car to remain here at the apartment in case anyone tries to break in."

As she left the apartment, Elizabeth was relieved Craig had arranged for security. Pierre, in his black BMW SUV, had no trouble following her while maintaining a comfortable distance.

She parked in front of a men's clothing store on Boulevard Saint-Germain close to Saint-Germain-des-Prés. While she and Nick went into the shop, Pierre remained outside. Nobody seemed to be following them.

Watching the clerk help Nick select several shirts, slacks, shoes, and underwear, Elizabeth felt a pang of sadness. She was forty and had never had a child and never would because of the severe endometriosis she had suffered at the age of twenty-two.

From the clothing store, with Pierre following, she drove north to the clinic on the outskirts of the city, breathing a sigh of relief when they arrived without incident. Again Pierre remained outside.

From the moment they entered Dr. Cardin's office, Nick seemed to like the doctor. He was impressed with the photographs on the walls showing Dr. Cardin climbing various mountains.

Dr. Cardin led them along an immaculate corridor with white walls that looked as though they had been recently painted. Nick's room at the end of the corridor was bright and airy with a bed, a desk, and a couple of chairs. Sunlight was streaming through pine trees outside and into the sparkling windows. The clinic was clearly well maintained.

After Dr. Cardin had introduced Nick to some of the staff he withdrew, leaving Elizabeth alone with Nick.

"You'll be okay here?" Elizabeth asked.

Nick nodded.

She hugged him before turning to leave, tears beginning to well in her eyes. He was such a nice kid. It wasn't fair that this had happened to him.

In front of the clinic, she approached Pierre. "Thanks for everything you've done," she said. "The boy is safely stowed away, so your mission is complete."

"No, Mademoiselle Crowder, my instructions came from Craig," he replied, his suntanned face almost apologetic.

"What did he tell you?"

"We're supposed to remain with you until he returns to Paris."

"Oh, for God's sake. That's ridiculous."

"Those are my orders, Mademoiselle Crowder. So you go anywhere you have to, and I'll follow without drawing any attention."

She was convinced it was unnecessary, but Craig wasn't here to argue with. "Okay. I understand."

She got into the Audi and drove away. Ten minutes later, Craig called. "How's it going?" he asked.

"No issues. I just dropped Nick at the clinic."

"Happy to hear that."

"You can let Pierre and his people go. I don't need them anymore."

"Wrong," Craig said emphatically. "They stay until I get back tomorrow."

"Do you really think that's necessary?"

"Listen, Elizabeth." He sounded emotional. "I just came from the funeral of a good friend. It wasn't so long ago that I buried my daughter, as you'll recall. I don't intend to bury you as well."

"Okay, okay. I get it. Have you learned anything about what Amos was doing in Paris?"

"Only that he was still with the Mossad. I'll find out more this evening. We'll talk tomorrow when I get back."

As she drove, Elizabeth thought about Nick. Hopefully Dr. Cardin would be able to help him get better, but in any event what would happen to him? From the CNN story she had learned that he was an only child and that his parents had died the year before. He had been living with his grandparents, but they were now dead. His great-grandfather Zoltan had to be too old to take care of a child. She had no idea whether Nick had any relatives who would want to raise him. No other family members had been mentioned in the media. When all this was over, she couldn't just abandon him.

For now, she had done what she could to help Nick. She had to stop worrying about him and concentrate on Peter and Emma to learn about the operation the two of them had been planning, which had undoubtedly gotten them killed. The police captain at the scene of Emma's murder had refused to provide any details about her death, which was unusual. Elizabeth had to get some information. It was time to collect on a large IOU.

Last year a terrorist had killed a French diplomat in India. The French had tracked the man to the United States, where he was hiding outside of Los Angeles. When they had sought extradition from the US to try him for the murder, the State Department had inexplicably dragged its feet. During her time in Paris, Elizabeth had developed a good relationship with Alain Rousseau, the director of the French Foreign Ministry's security branch. Alain knew that Elizabeth was close with Betty, the CIA director, and asked her to intervene. Elizabeth never knew how Betty did it, but two days after Elizabeth's call, the terrorist was on a plane to Paris where he was tried, convicted, and sent to jail. Alain had told her he would owe her big time.

So when she called Alain from her car and asked if he was free for lunch he said, "I'd love to. I imagine it's time for me to pay you back."

"That's right."

"Any background you can give me so I can do some prep work before we meet?"

"A Hungarian national was murdered yesterday in her apartment in Place des Vosges."

"Emma Miller."

"How do you know about it already?"

"The combination of Emma being a Hungarian national and working for a foreign bank was enough to get me copied on the emails. I'll see what I can find out. How about Chiberta at one o'clock?"

"With pleasure. See you then."

One of the things Elizabeth liked about Alain was that he still enjoyed a two-hour lunch. Parisians, even top professionals like Elizabeth, had increasingly started copying their American counterparts by opting for a quick lunch at a fast-food restaurant or a sandwich at their desk. But not Alain.

When Elizabeth reached the dimly lit Chiberta, with its sleek modern interior and well-spaced tables, Alain was already seated. Dressed in a double-breasted, pin-striped suit, white shirt, and red Hermes tie, Alain had a full head of gray hair and an almost aristocratic appearance. As he rose to kiss her on the each cheek, he said, "Good to see you again, Elizabeth. I'm glad you called."

The waiter came over and they ordered—salad and sea bass for Elizabeth and pâté and duck breast for Alain. Alain also selected a Vosne-Romanée from Domaine Daniel Rion for them to share.

When the waiter departed, Alain said, "A lot about this case is sensitive." He looked troubled. "So can we do it off the record, strictly for background? And you won't incorporate anything I tell you in your article?"

"I can agree to that," Elizabeth responded. "I'm not looking for a story about Emma Miller." She paused. "Well actually I am, in the long run, but it's more complicated than that."

"Go ahead. I'm listening."

Elizabeth briefly pondered how to explain the situation to Alain without involving Nick. After careful consideration, she said, "My primary focus is on a story about a suspicious fire outside of Washington in which a Hungarian industrialist named Peter Toth died. Shortly after that fire, Emma Miller was murdered. Perhaps there's no connection, but more likely, what happened to Emma may shed light on what happened to Peter. Regardless, I won't incorporate anything you tell me in my story about Peter. And it will be off the record."

"Fair enough."

After the waiter brought the wine their first courses arrived. As Elizabeth picked up her fork, Alain said, "It was awful what happened to Emma Miller."

She put the fork back down. "What do you mean?"

"The woman was tortured horribly. She had bruises over almost her entire face. Four fingers had been broken. The autopsy showed she had been raped and sodomized. Then she was stabbed multiple times in the chest, causing her death."

Elizabeth was rapidly coming to the conclusion that the people responsible for this were trying to obtain information about the operation that Emma and Peter had been planning. Fortunately, Elizabeth had been able to safeguard Nick or God only knows what these people would have done to him.

"Who called the police?" Elizabeth asked.

"A neighbor in the next building, which has a common wall with Emma's house. He said he heard screams. He also heard men shouting in a foreign language. He thought it was a Slavic language, perhaps Russian."

Elizabeth sat up in alarm. Peter's obit was full of how Russian involvement had marked his life.

Noticing her reaction, Alain said, "Something I said struck a chord?"

"The Russians under Kuznov are making plenty of trouble," she remarked.

"Don't rely too heavily on what I said. The neighbor wasn't sure. The police are pulling out all the stops, but so far they don't have any leads."

"What about Emma's job?"

"She worked for Credit Suisse evaluating business investments in Asia, nothing related to Eastern Europe or Russia, and that's all I could learn."

For the rest of lunch they discussed foreign policy matters. Then Alain returned the topic to Russia, expressing how worried he was about Kuznov.

Elizabeth could hardly eat. Alain's description of what had happened to Emma squelched her appetite. She merely pushed her food around on the plate while she drank a couple of glasses of wine.

Once they separated after lunch, Elizabeth was determined to find out more about Emma Miller. She still had time to do some research before her meeting with Betty, so she went to a brasserie close to the US Embassy and settled in a corner with a cappuccino and her computer. It was clear to Elizabeth that Emma was a critical part of this puzzle. She had to see what she could find out about the Hungarian woman.

From the internet, Elizabeth discovered that Emma was nineteen years younger than Peter. Her father had been a leader in the 1956 uprising against Russia, just like Peter's father. She had never married. Elizabeth saw a picture of Emma taken twenty years ago and another from last year. The woman was positively beautiful with blonde hair, blue eyes, and a model's figure.

Born in Budapest, Emma had gotten a degree in finance at the London School of Economics. Following that, she returned to Budapest to work for a London-based international bank. Shortly after Peter had set up his business in Hungary, she joined him as the company's chief finance officer. Two years ago, when Peter liquidated most of the company and moved to the States, Emma relocated to Paris where she took a job as vice president of finance with the huge Swiss bank Credit Suisse.

Next, Elizabeth Googled Peter Toth Industries. It was a privately owned firm with Peter Toth as the only stockholder. Ten years ago it had huge holdings in Hungary in telecommunications and energy. Two years ago almost all of the assets were sold off, and Peter Toth moved to the United States.

Currently, the resident agent in Budapest for Peter Toth Industries was Gyorgy Kovacs, who had been with the company since its inception. She saw an address, phone number, and email address for the company. With Peter and Emma both dead, Gyorgy was likely to be her best source for information. He might have some idea of what was happening.

As Elizabeth reached for her phone, she decided against identifying herself as a reporter. Gyorgy might not be willing to meet with her. Two people he must have been close with had been murdered within twenty-four hours of each other. Gyorgy would have to be worried himself.

So when he answered the phone she identified herself as "Jane Wilson, a friend of Peter's in Washington."

"Why are you calling?" he asked with wariness in his voice.

"I am currently in Paris and would like to fly to Budapest to meet with you tomorrow afternoon."

"For what purpose?"

"It would be better if we spoke in person." When he didn't respond, she added, "Please, if you cared about Peter then we have to talk."

After a few minutes, he said, "Come to my office at 3:00 p.m. tomorrow. Number 6, Szalay U, along the square in front of the parliament building."

Elizabeth felt as if she were starting to make progress.

*       *       *

Betty was waiting for Elizabeth in a palatial VIP visitor's office at the US Embassy. Four months ago, Elizabeth had been in this very room interviewing US Secretary of State Harrison Barton about President Kuznov's unveiling of powerful new weapons during a parade in Moscow. The secretary of state refused to express alarm, telling her the show of weaponry was "only to lift the spirits of the Russian people suffering economic hardship." Elizabeth had retorted, "Don't boys always use their new toys?"

Barton had dismissed her concern and promptly terminated the interview. The next day Elizabeth wrote up the interview and characterized Barton as being "nonchalant about the threat posed by Kuznov."

Today, Elizabeth picked a different bergère than the one she had sat in during her interview with the secretary of state. She didn't want to jinx this meeting. When she explained to Betty why she was sitting in that particular chair, the CIA director burst out laughing.

"Barton has a noodle for a spine," she said, grinning. "President Worth should have sacked him long ago."

"I assume you told your leader that?"

"Of course. Craig taught me that to be a good CIA director, you have to speak your mind with the president. Of course, following that approach got Craig fired."

They both laughed.

"How was the NATO security conference?" Elizabeth asked.

"A tough session. For two days we did nothing but talk about Russia. As far as I'm concerned, the sixty-four-thousand-dollar question is how to contain Kuznov. I strongly believe, and the French agree, that he is no longer content with controlling Crimea and battling Ukraine. His ultimate dream, in our view, is to gobble up other countries in Central Europe and reassemble the Russian Empire."

"The Germans don't agree?"

"They have their heads in the sand. They want to avoid any confrontation that would be bad for business—their business."

"And the British?"

"No opinion as usual, 'on the one hand and on the other hand.' It's a shame the British don't have three hands."

Elizabeth smiled. "Your people did a good job of concealing those differences. I sent a reporter to Berlin to cover the conference. He didn't pick up these nuances."

"Glad to hear that. We tried to sweep it all under the carpet—a friendly disagreement within the family. Okay Elizabeth, what's on your mind?"

"First, let me say I really appreciate you making a pit stop in Paris to see me."

"If you want to talk to me, I know it has to be important," Betty replied with a shrug.

Elizabeth had no hesitation telling Betty about Nick. She described what happened from the moment she reached Emma Miller's apartment, to dropping Nick off at Dr. Cardin's facility and her lunch with Alain.

At the end, Betty removed her coke-bottle glasses and twirled them slowly between her fingers, her face pensive. "That's quite a story," she eventually remarked. "Whatever operation Peter and Emma were planning must have been significant enough to get them both murdered."

"Exactly my conclusion. Do you think that Peter, with Emma's help, was planning to overthrow Szabo and launch a revolution in Hungary?"

Betty thought about it for a minute. "The Potomac fire was too sophisticated to be the work of Hungarian intelligence agents. Also, I doubt if they would go into Paris and torture Emma Miller that way. Perhaps I spent too much time in the last two days talking about Kuznov and Russia, but to me this has Kuznov's fingerprints all over it."

Elizabeth nodded. "You're right on the mark. A source in the French Foreign Ministry told me that Emma's killers may have been Russian. But what I can't figure out is why Kuznov would even be involved."

Betty shrugged. "I don't know. All we have to go on is the note Peter gave Nick for Emma. The two of them were planning some type of operation. Would it have adversely affected Kuznov? Did the Russian leader find out about it? I'm grasping at straws because we have nothing else. Perhaps if we had a clear understanding of Peter and his life we might be able to come up with answers."

"I'm flying to Budapest tomorrow to meet with Gyorgy Kovacs, Peter's business associate who is based in Hungary. He may be able to supply critical background information about Peter."

Betty's face lit up. "That could be an enormous help. My instinct tells me that understanding Peter Toth is the key to unlocking who perpetrated the Potomac fire and Emma's murder. When I get back to Washington I'll talk to Chris Murphy, the FBI director, and have him put the FBI on the Potomac fire investigation."

Elizabeth was concerned. "Please don't tell Chris about Nick. The kid's life is in danger, and I'm so worried about him."

"If you don't want me to, I won't."

"Thank you."

"That's all right, but Elizabeth, I'm surprised you're so emotionally involved with this kid."

"I don't know what it is. I have eleven nieces and nephews, but I've never seen a kid like Nick. He's so stoic and resourceful. After all he's been through . . . he really is amazing."

"What's Craig say about Nick?" Betty asked.

"He only saw him briefly before he flew off to Tel Aviv."

"To race?"

Elizabeth explained about the murder of Amos Neir.

"Do the French know Amos was Mossad?" Betty asked.

"I don't think so. I have a feeling Craig and Giuseppe will let them know when Craig comes back."

"Jean-Claude will go through the roof."

Elizabeth was alarmed. "You won't tell him, will you?"

"Of course not. I'm a lot of things, but not a masochist. Craig and Giuseppe can step in front of that chainsaw."

As Elizabeth stood and thanked Betty again for stopping in Paris Betty said, "One other thing. I just recalled something from our Berlin meeting that could be useful to you."

"What's that?"

"How much do you know about Franz Szabo, the current Hungarian prime minister?"

"Henri, the publisher of my paper, described him as a horror, a right-wing demagogue, and vicious."

"Henri's spot on. Szabo is constantly moving to the right and quashing civil liberties. He's been doing his darndest to convert Hungary into a dictatorship. Add to that one other fact I just learned in Berlin: We've received reliable information that Szabo is making a strong pivot toward Russia. He's negotiating a trade deal with Kuznov for the supply of nuclear energy. That's upsetting England, France, and Germany, who are sure there must be a quid pro quo."

"I'm glad to hear the three of them agree on something."

"Kuznov doesn't care. He's playing by Moscow rules. Do you know what those are?"

Elizabeth shook her head.

"The rules that Kuznov makes up as he goes along. And they generally involve the use of force. So Kuznov and Szabo getting together, if it were to happen, is a nightmare scenario, not merely for Europe, but for the United States as well."

Elizabeth mulled over Betty's words as she left the embassy and made her way back to the car. As she opened the car door, her phone rang. It was Pierre.

"I left one of my colleagues at your apartment," he reported. "He said that somebody in a black Citroën pulled up, parked in front of your building, and was waiting. He looked suspicious, so my colleague walked over and flashed a Paris police ID. When he saw it, the man drove away."

Elizabeth was startled. They must know she had had contact with Nick. Hopefully they didn't know where she had taken him.

"Listen, Pierre," she said, "can you have one of your men go up to the clinic where we took the boy this morning and stand guard there?"

"Will do, but what about you? Do you still want to stay in your apartment tonight?"

"Damn right. Let 'em come. We'll be waiting for them. You okay with that?"

"For sure. That's what I get paid to do."

# Moscow

Kuznov had constructed a private gym next to his Kremlin office. Aides knew that when he was working out he didn't like to be disturbed. It had to be for something extremely important. So as he pedaled furiously on the stationary bike, the Russian president was surprised to see Dimitri walk into the room and approach him.

Perspiring heavily, Kuznov reduced his pace. "What happened with Szabo? Did he agree to my terms?"

"I haven't gone yet. I'm flying to Budapest this evening."

Kuznov stopped pedaling and grabbed his water bottle, chugging greedily. His face was red from the workout and from anger. He told Dimitri, "You disappoint me that you haven't already fixed this with Szabo. It was your top priority. What could have been more important?"

Dimitri looked chagrined. "Believe me, I was ready to go immediately after our last meeting, but Szabo claimed to be too busy to see me until tomorrow morning."

"It's all an act. Fucking Hungarian. He's playing you like a violin. Once this agreement is implemented and I don't need him anymore, he's a dead man."

Dimitri took a deep breath. "I have some more news you won't like."

Kuznov gripped the bike to steady himself. "Tell me."

"Boris, who was responsible for the Emma Miller assignment in Paris, just got back to Moscow and gave me a report."

"I saw the news stories about her death."

"She wouldn't tell them anything about Peter Toth's plans to wreck the Friendship Pact—even after extreme interrogation."

"Then they didn't do a good job," Kuznov spat. "I never failed."

"But there's another problem Boris told me about. At the time the two men went into Emma Miller's apartment, they left a third man, Anatol, in a car parked close to the building. Anatol remained in place even when the other two left the area. After Emma's body was taken away, Anatol saw a frightened boy, age about ten to twelve, get out of a cab and hide behind a car. When the police had gone, the boy approached the reporter Elizabeth Crowder."

"From the *International Herald*?"

"Exactly. She took the boy away."

"How did Anatol know it was Elizabeth Crowder?"

"He lives in Paris," Dimitri explained. "Sometimes she's on the television. He recognized her."

Kuznov pounded his fist on the side of the bike. "What a moron. Why didn't Anatol snatch the boy before Elizabeth could take him away?"

"That's what I said. Boris told me that Anatol wouldn't do anything like that unless he had specific orders."

"Is he a man or a fucking robot?"

"Boris also told me that Anatol was able to take a covert picture of the boy before he got into Elizabeth's car. I immediately sent it to our people. On a hunch, I ordered them to locate photos of Peter Toth's grandson, Nicholas Toth, to see if it matched up."

Kuznov jumped off the bike, fuming. "How could those idiots in Washington have let the boy escape?"

"Maybe he wasn't even at home at the time," Dimitri suggested. "At any rate, let's wait until we get confirmation that it's Nicholas Toth."

Kuznov looked irate. "I'm not waiting for anything. Of course the kid's Toth. He has to be. This could be a good opportunity. He lived with his grandfather. We should seize him. He may have overheard what his grandfather was planning—the information we couldn't get from Emma Miller. After that, they can kill him. We can't leave a kid out there who could endanger our plans for the Friendship Pact. I want you to tell Boris to get his ass on the first plane to Paris and find that kid. I assume that Anatol and the rest of his team are still in Paris?"

"Correct."

"Good. Then Boris can order them to move on Elizabeth Crowder's apartment first. Nicholas Toth might be there. I want that kid."

## Tel Aviv

When Craig arrived at the unmarked, heavily fortified building in northern Tel Aviv that served as Mossad headquarters, an attractive young woman in a fitted khaki skirt led him to a private dining room on the top floor with a view of the Mediterranean. A gorgeous red fireball sun was setting across the shimmering water. He noticed the table was set for three.

A few minutes later, Moshe entered the room accompanied by a man Craig didn't know.

"Craig, meet Gideon Baruch, my head of operations," he said.

Baruch was a tall, tough-looking man in his forties. He had short brown hair, and a layer of coarse stubble blanketed his face.

Craig stuck out his hand. "Pleased to meet you."

Baruch squeezed Craig's hand so firmly it sent shock waves all the way up to his shoulder. *I'm glad we're on the same side*, Craig thought.

"Let me tell you, Gideon," Moshe said, "Craig Page is a unique intelligence asset. After God made him, he threw away the mold. Now he's a race car driver. Do you know why?"

Gideon shook his head.

"I'll tell you why. Because he refused to take crap from anybody in authority. He's the only man to be fired as both director of the CIA and head of EU Counterterrorism. Are there any other jobs you've been sacked from Craig?" Moshe asked.

"Head of Mideast operations for the CIA," Craig replied promptly. "That was before I became director. Let's just say I don't suffer fools very well."

"I thought there were only wise men in Washington," Moshe retorted.

"Yeah. Right."

"I'm honored to meet you," Gideon said.

"Don't say stuff like that," Moshe responded. "Page's head is already large enough."

Craig laughed. As they sat down, two waiters entered carrying trays. One held salads; the other grilled fish. The wine on the table was a cabernet from the Golan. After taking a bite, Craig commented on how excellent the fish was.

"It was caught this morning," Moshe replied. "Gourmet experts always criticize our food. They say we can't cook like the French or Italians. Of course we can't. We're not French or Italian. We have to forget about outside criticism and do what we have to do. I don't just mean in food. We have to do what's right for us in foreign affairs as well. This is a circuitous way of getting to Amos Neir."

Moshe's words were too nebulous for Craig to understand, but he didn't ask for clarification. He expected to find out before long.

"It was good of you to come today," Moshe added.

"Giuseppe asked me to do it."

"No, I mean to the kibbutz this morning. It meant a lot to Daphna. You didn't have to do that."

"When my wife was still alive we spent a lot of time there with Daphna and Amos. Our daughters became good friends. Francesca loved the kibbutz." Even now Craig found it difficult to talk about his daughter.

"I was truly sorry to hear about Francesca's death," Moshe said. "I'm devastated every time I bury one of my agents—but a child. I can't imagine." Moshe gave a deep sigh.

"Well," he continued after a moment, shifting the topic with his usual brusque, businesslike tone, "let's talk about Amos Neir. What does Giuseppe want to know?"

"One of your Mossad agents was killed in Paris and pulled from the Seine. As the head of EU Counterterrorism, Giuseppe assumes it was the work of terrorists. Not surprisingly, he wants to know who they are and what they're up to. You can't argue with that."

"Of course not."

"His first question is whether Amos was still with the Mossad. This morning I learned the answer is yes. So the next one is: What was he doing in Paris?"

When neither Moshe nor Gideon replied, Craig added, "Obviously he wasn't on vacation with Daphna."

They still didn't respond. Craig pressed ahead. "Listen, Moshe, I know you like to play your cards close to your vest. I understand that. You have enemies the French don't, and you want to pursue them. However, in a couple of days Jean-Claude, who fortunately happened to be in Turkey when this occurred, will return to Paris. He'll connect the dots, learn that the deceased was a Mossad agent, and come pounding on your door. You'd be better off letting me and Giuseppe take the heat for you, or at least some of it. I also need to find out who killed Amos. I told Daphna I would do that."

Moshe sighed deeply again. *He does that well,* Craig thought. Must have had lots of practice. Moshe pointed to Gideon. "Okay, tell him."

Gideon took a sip of water, then said, "The commentators in the media love to go on at great length about the political rift between France and Israel. In the intelligence area, nothing could be further from the truth. Over the years we have developed and maintained a close and cooperative relationship with the French intelligence agencies. We consider them a valuable ally, and we have a great deal of respect for their organization and abilities. I believe they feel the same way about us."

"However?" Craig prompted impatiently.

"The French police and intelligence agencies have their hands full worrying about attacks on their general population—in theaters, at soccer games and other sports events, and in restaurants, for example. We decided they need some help in stopping attacks aimed specifically against Jews and Israelis in France, particularly in Paris, where a myriad of those attacks occur every year.

"We figured that the French intelligence agencies could use help in infiltrating the Muslim communities in Paris. As you know, Amos's parents moved to Paris after spending their entire lives in Morocco. He was born in Paris and lived there until he was fourteen, when his parents moved to Israel. With his dark skin and French language skills, Amos was able to move into Clichy-sous-Bois, a primarily Muslim suburb of Paris that is home to a significant number of jihadists. Blending into that community, for the last six months he was operating as an undercover agent, posing as a Moroccan businessman named Ahmed Hussein. His assignment was to end next month."

"Daphna told me it was his last assignment before retirement."

"Correct," Moshe confirmed with sadness.

"Do you have any other agents in Paris doing this same work?"

"No, he was the only one we sent," Gideon responded. "It was a trial assignment. If it worked out, we planned to send others later in the year. Before his death, Amos discovered three planned terrorist attacks, not aimed particularly at Jews, but at Paris targets—the opera, the French Open tennis tournament, and the Louvre during a Bastille Day celebration. Each time he alerted the authorities anonymously, and all were stopped. No announcement was ever made in the media. But the bottom line is this: Amos Neir saved scores if not hundreds of French lives."

Craig was digesting what he had just heard. "So it's likely the jihadists found out what Amos was doing and killed him."

"That's what we figure," Gideon said. "Amos was strangled, then dumped into the river. According to Paris police, they received an anonymous call from someone who saw a body being tossed from a car into the Seine."

"So Amos's assassin could be any of the jihadists in Paris, and there are quite a few of them."

"We think we can narrow the field to one leading suspect."

"That would be helpful."

Gideon pulled a laptop from his briefcase. He showed the screen to Craig, where he had brought up a photo depicting a bearded man.

Craig didn't recognize him. "Who is he?"

"Omar Basayev, known as Omar the Chechen. A week ago Amos informed us that a man revered by the Chechens had arrived in Clichy and seemed to be engaged in suspicious activity. Amos sent his photo, and we made the ID. We were surprised Omar was in Paris because all of his activities to date have been aimed at Russia. We asked Amos to do surveillance on Omar. If we found out what he was doing in Paris and passed it on to Jean-Claude, it would earn us a lot of points with French intelligence."

"What did Amos learn about Omar's activities in Paris?" Craig asked.

"That he was recruiting young men for some type of terrorist attack," said Gideon. "Unfortunately Amos wasn't able to find out the target or the date. How much do you know about Omar?"

"I never had an assignment in Chechnya or one involving Chechens so my knowledge is limited," Craig replied. "I heard Omar's name mentioned a couple of times in intelligence briefings at Langley. That's all."

"Omar is both a fascinating and terrifying character," Gideon said. "In order to understand him, I have first to give you some background about Chechnya. This rugged land in the Caucasus Mountains in Southern Russia is home to many Muslims who, for centuries, have been determined to resist Russian domination and control. This goes all the way back at least to Peter the Great, who sent troops in 1722 to subjugate them and failed. In the time since, the Russians moved in with cruel troops, aiming to suppress this unyielding region or else destroy every last Chechen, and they often suffered heavy losses as a result.

"In 1944 Stalin, claiming that the Chechens were collaborating with the Germans, ordered the deportation of the entire population of Chechnya—half a million people—to Kazakhstan. They remained there until Khrushchev let them return home."

"Even for the Russians that was pretty extreme," Craig remarked.

"It shows what the Russians think of the Chechens," Gideon explained. "The Russians named the capital of Chechnya "Grozny," which means 'terrible' in Russian, more confirmation of how the Russians regarded the region. This brings us to Omar. He was a young professor of European history in Grozny in 1994, when the first of the two modern Chechen wars with Russia began. When the Soviet Union disintegrated in 1991 and entities in the former USSR like Georgia, Uzbekistan, and Ukraine were declaring independence and freedom from Russian dominion, the Chechens said, 'We want our freedom, too.' This was too much for Moscow. The Russians said 'nyet' and sent troops to enforce their will.

"Omar became the leader of one of the nationalist groups pressing for independence. His group wasn't militant—in fact, it eschewed violence and wanted to negotiate with Moscow. That didn't matter to Kuznov, who was the highest ranking intelligence officer accompanying the Russian troops that rolled into Grozny. Kuznov's theory was that if he lowered the boom on the peaceful secessionists, it would break the back of the independence movement. So he sent troops to Omar's house one night. Omar was chained to a pillar and forced to watch while they gang-raped and murdered his wife, then tortured and killed his two young daughters. Kuznov decided to leave Omar alive to tell the grim tale, expecting it would have a chilling effect on the independence movement. But that was a big mistake."

Gideon paused, choosing his words carefully. "Omar was well liked by the Chechens," he continued. "This barbaric act intensified their opposition to Russia. It also drove the history professor into the arms of the militants and jihadists who gave him training and turned him loose to conduct hit-and-run operations against the Russians, including an attempt on Kuznov's life in Grozny. This attempt would have succeeded had Kuznov not changed cars at the last minute in the motorcade. A powerful bomb, arranged by Omar, completely destroyed the car Kuznov was supposed to have been riding in.

"Kuznov responded by ordering a ruthless and relentless campaign in Grozny. It lasted two years and killed tens of thousands of civilians, leaving the city in ruins. The independence movement and opposition to Russia disintegrated in the city—or what was left of it. Grozny had been suppressed. The war was over."

"What happened to Omar after that?" Craig asked.

"He went underground. In 1999 the Russians launched the Second Chechen War in an effort to squelch the embers of the independence movement and the growing threat of radical Islam. Omar carried out hit-and-run operations against Russian troops in the mountains of the Caucasus.

"When that war ended, he returned to Grozny. The city had been rebuilt into a modern city with glass skyscrapers. Kuznov had installed Daud Mollah to be the despotic ruler of Chechnya and its capital Grozny, with complete subservience to Moscow.

"Omar was well hidden by supporters. According to a Russian defector who immigrated to Israel, Kuznov and Omar reached an understanding: Omar would not carry out any attacks in Russia, including Chechnya, and Kuznov would not try to kill him. It was a strange deal that both sides recognized might not hold, but it was the only agreement they could reach to stop the mutual bloodshed, at least for a while. Periodically, Omar ventured out of Chechnya and conducted attacks against Russian troops in foreign countries including Crimea and Syria."

"But there aren't any Russian troops in Paris," Craig pointed out.

"That's what worried us. Our assumption is that another jihadist group with assets in France has recruited Omar to conduct an operation for them in Paris, hoping to capitalize on the fact that he's not on French intelligence's radar."

"What would Omar gain from it?"

"Money to finance attacks against Russians. Some of those jihadist organizations are loaded with cash."

"So your assessment is that Amos stumbled across a terrorist operation being planned by a Chechen terrorist in France, and that he paid for it with his life."

"All of the facts point to that conclusion."

"You should know, Craig," Moshe interjected, "that as soon as I learned that Omar was the terrorist Amos had uncovered in Paris, I asked Amos to come home because I knew how vicious the man could be. I told Amos we would pass the information along to Jean-Claude, and they could deal with it. Amos strongly resisted, telling me that he wanted to find out what Omar was planning and that he thought he was close. He wanted me to wait until he had that information."

*That certainly sounds like Amos,* Craig thought.

"I could have ordered him home," Moshe added with remorse in his voice. "And I should have. It's a decision I regret every hour since I learned of Amos's death, and I'm sure I will for the rest of my life."

Stiff from sitting, Craig stood up and walked around the room to stretch his legs. As he did, he thought about what he had just learned.

"How much of this am I allowed to tell Jean-Claude?" he asked.

Gideon looked at Moshe, who said, "All of it. He'll bluster for a while because we didn't inform him, but he'll soon realize he should be grateful to us, that we're giving him a gold mine of information."

"Do you have anything else for me?"

Gideon reached into his bag and pulled out two photographs. "One of Amos and one of Omar. These may be useful."

"Where did the photo of Omar come from?"

"Taken by Amos and sent to us electronically. That's how we made the ID."

Gideon slid the photos across to Craig. Then he took out a piece of paper and handed that to Craig as well. "It's the address of the apartment Amos used in Clichy. We had one of our people search it, but they didn't find anything. However, somebody in the neighborhood may have information. Are you familiar with that suburb of Paris?"

"Very much, from my time as head of EU Counterterrorism. Jihadists control part of it. The French police try and stay out, for their own safety."

"Then you know the risks you're facing if you decide to go in."

"That's right," Craig mused thoughtfully. "Amos looked like he belonged."

Moshe finished Craig's thought. "You won't. You'll arouse suspicion and become a target."

*       *       *

After the meeting Craig went back to his hotel. He called Giuseppe and said, "I'm in Israel. We have to meet tomorrow. Will you be in Rome or Paris?"

"Rome."

"I'll take a morning flight and come right to your office."

"Mission accomplished?"

"Sadly, yes."

He booked a plane ticket to Rome, then called Elizabeth. "I'm flying back to Rome in the morning to meet Giuseppe."

"Oh, Craig, you sound terrible. I'm so sorry."

"How are you doing?" he asked.

"I've made some progress. I don't want to tell you on the phone. We'll talk when we're together, but it can't be tomorrow. I'm going to Budapest."

"Okay, but be careful. How's your new friend?"

"Safe, as we planned. Pierre was an incredible help. Once I get on my plane tomorrow morning at ten, you can cancel the security on me and at the apartment."

"All right, will do. Hey, I love you, and safe travels."

## Paris

Nick was asleep in his bed in the clinic. Suddenly, he felt a tapping on his shoulder. He shot to an upright position. Standing next to him was his grandpa. It couldn't be.

"Grandpa, what are you doing here?" Nick gasped. "I thought you were dead."

Grandpa put a finger over his lips. "Sh . . . be quiet Nick. Get dressed. You're coming with me."

Nick sprang out of bed and dressed quickly. Together the two of them raced silently down the halls and out the front door of the clinic.

Nick didn't see a car parked in front.

"Where's your car?"

"We have to run through the woods." He pointed. "That's where I parked. Follow me."

Grandpa began running. He was fast and far ahead of Nick, who was struggling to keep up.

The boy stumbled on a tree branch and fell to the ground. When he scrambled up, he couldn't tell which direction his grandfather had gone. He began running into the woods. He had no idea which way to go.

He stopped running and screamed, "Grandpa! Grandpa! Grandpa!"

But it was hopeless. Grandpa didn't answer.

Nick awoke with a start. Not realizing he had been dreaming, he jumped out of bed and ran down the corridor in the clinic. One of the nurses stopped him, holding him tight. He began flailing his arms wildly. The nurse called for two of her colleagues. They gave Nick a shot to calm him down. Then they took him back to his room.

Nick lay in bed the rest of the night crying.

*       *       *

At eight in the morning, Omar was at the apartment in Clichy that he and his aide Shamil were sharing. While they were eating breakfast, he watched an envelope slide under the front door. Omar grabbed the gun on the table, ran to the door, and opened it. He saw a boy scampering down the stairs. Omar recognized him as an errand runner for the Imam in the local mosque.

Omar didn't chase the boy. Instead, he returned to the apartment and opened the envelope. Inside was a note from the Imam: "Come as soon as you can."

It was only six blocks to the largest mosque in the area. Omar and Shamil left the apartment and walked over. With Shamil standing guard in front of the mosque, Omar went into the white-bearded Imam's office.

"I suggest that you complete your work in Clichy and leave as quickly as possible," the Imam said.

"What happened?" Omar asked.

"I heard from a source in the police department that the body of Ahmed Hussein was pulled from the Seine and immediately shipped to Israel. He was likely a Mossad agent."

Omar wasn't surprised to learn that Ahmed had been an undercover agent, although he would have guessed that the man was working for French intelligence and not the Mossad. The only reason Omar had come to Paris was to recruit three young men to help with a twenty-million-euro job. When he had been conducting interviews one evening to find three who were right for the assignment, he had noticed a man with black curly hair at a nearby table in Brasserie Rabat pretending to read a newspaper while he sipped a coffee. Omar wasn't fooled. He had a very sensitive antenna for intelligence agents. That's how he had managed to stay alive. Omar was convinced that the man was straining his ears to overhear what Omar was saying.

After Omar had finished the last interview at ten in the evening, he took out his phone and called Shamil, who was standing guard outside of the brasserie. He told his aide, loud enough for the curly-haired man to hear, "I'm coming right now to give you all of the details. Meet me at number 15 Rue Bonaparte."

Watching Omar's discreet body language through the brasserie window, Shamil immediately understood what Omar needed from him.

As soon as they concluded their call, Omar watched Shamil move away and head in the direction of Rue Bonaparte. Before leaving the brasserie, Omar waited long enough for Shamil to get in place, hiding in the doorway of the deserted building at the end of a narrow street—really nothing more than an alley—which reached a dead end at number 15.

The trap had been set.

Omar left the brasserie and walked to Rue Bonaparte. If the black-haired man followed, that would confirm to Omar that he was an undercover agent. He seemed anxious to know what Omar was planning, and this would be his best way of finding out.

As Omar walked under the full moon, he didn't notice anyone following him. Either the man was very good at his craft or Omar was wrong about him. Entering the building, Omar looked back. No sign of the curly-haired man. He climbed the stairs to the first landing, leaving Shamil concealed behind the door in place on the ground floor.

Five minutes later, the curly-haired man walked slowly into the building. In the dim light filtering in from outside, Omar saw the man pull a gun, look around, and then start up the stairs. Once he was on the second stair, Shamil jumped him from behind. With the element of surprise and Shamil's incredible strength, the gun dropped from the man's hand and Shamil drove him to the floor.

Shamil was on top of the man, who was face down, and his hands were tight around the man's throat. The man thrashed, but to no avail.

Omar ran down the stairs.

"Kill him," he ordered in a voice devoid of emotion.

After Shamil had strangled the man, he raced four blocks away to get their white van. In the meantime Omar checked the dead man's ID. It said he was Ahmed Hussein and listed a Clichy address. He had to be an intelligence agent, probably sent by the French government to infiltrate jihadists in Clichy. Omar returned the ID to the dead man's pocket.

When Shamil returned with the van they loaded the body in the back. Then they waited until 5:00 a.m. to drop it in the Seine at a location far from Clichy. Unfortunately someone must have seen them toss the body in the river and called the police.

That was two days ago. Now Omar studied the Imam's heavily creased face. "What will happen?" Omar asked.

"My source told me that Jean-Claude, the head of French military intelligence, will be returning to Paris from a trip to Turkey today. We can expect police and military units to come into Clichy very soon in a show of force to find the killer. That's why you should leave."

Omar didn't ask the Imam how he had deduced that Omar had killed Amos. The cleric had incredible sources of information in Clichy and elsewhere in Paris. Besides, it didn't matter. If the Imam knew it, others would as well.

"I understand. Thank you for the warning."

Once he had exited the mosque, Omar called the three men he had selected for the job. He told them to meet him at Brasserie Rabat. The three men—Mohammad, Yassir, and Rachid—were from Algerian and Moroccan families. As he had planned the operation, Omar had seen the need for additional support for him and Shamil. He was unwilling to use Chechens because he didn't want it to seem like a Chechen operation, which could result in reprisals against his people, so he had come to Paris to recruit men who would be right for the job.

The three were unemployed, like so many other Muslim men in their twenties living in Paris. All seemed healthy and strong. Each had been arrested at least once for petty crimes like theft. Yesterday Omar had given each of them an offer: ten thousand euros for ten days of work. They would receive five thousand before they left with Omar for a location outside of France, which Omar had not disclosed, and the other five thousand when they returned to Paris in two weeks' time. In an hour, Omar would begin meeting separately with each of the three men to hear their decisions.

He and Shamil returned to their apartment, loaded all of their things into the van, and drove to Brasserie Rabat.

It was still twenty minutes before the three would begin arriving. Shamil waited outside and stood guard while Omar, carrying a briefcase, walked into the brasserie. He nodded to Habib, the owner, picked up a coffee at the bar, and took a table in the corner. It was too early for lunch, and the brasserie was deserted.

Waiting for Muhammed, the first man to come, Omar recalled the stranger from Washington who had hired him for this job. Peter Toth had come to Omar's fortress in the mountains outside of Grozny. Though Omar had never met Peter Toth before, he was willing to talk with anyone Yuri Brodervich sent to him.

Though the assignment meant operating in unfamiliar places in Europe, for twenty million euros, Omar decided to do it. The first ten were already in his bank account in Andorra; the rest would be transferred when he completed the job.

As Omar contemplated the details of his plan, Muhammad entered the brasserie and walked toward Omar's table. When he was seated, Omar gave him a speech he would give the others as well. "We're leaving in an hour for this mission. I have to know whether you are coming with me or not. If yes, I'll give you five thousand euros now. The other five when we return to Clichy after the job. You can take the money home and hide it or give it to your family. Pack some clothes and toiletries. Then get back here in one hour." Omar looked at Mohammad. "In or out?"

"In," he said quickly.

Omar reached into his bag and handed him an envelope. "Five thousand euros are inside."

After Mohammad had departed, Yassir came. "In or out?" Omar asked.

Yassir looked around nervously. "In," he replied softly, and Omar gave him an envelope.

Rachid was last.

"Are you in?" Omar asked.

Rachid hesitated. "Where are we going?"

Omar was annoyed. "I told you that you'd find out when we get there. Now, is it yes or no?"

With Rachid still hesitating, Omar considered canceling his offer. However, as he had planned the operation, he preferred three of them, and after what the Imam had just told him, he didn't have time to select a substitute.

"Well?" Omar asked.

"In," Rachid replied in a voice filled with anxiety.

Omar gave him an envelope. "Now let me remind you of what I've already told you. Bring only one bag. And no cell phones. Not in your pocket or in your bag. Is that clear?"

"Yes," Rachid said.

An hour later, the white van pulled away with Shamil driving and Omar in the front seat. Mohammad, Yassir, and Rachid were seated in the back.

Omar was still feeling uncomfortable about having Rachid along. If he made one wrong move, Omar would kill him. He'd then change his plan and carry out the operation with the remaining two and Shamil.

## Paris and Budapest

Before flying to Budapest, Elizabeth decided to stop at the clinic and see Nick. Parked in the driveway, she recognized one of Pierre's men in the car watching the clinic. She nodded to him as she walked into the building.

When she identified herself to the receptionist inside the front door and said she wanted to see Jonathan, the woman replied, "I'll call Dr. Cardin." That made Elizabeth apprehensive. A minute later Cardin appeared.

"Is Jonathan okay?" Elizabeth asked.

"He's fine now. In the middle of the night, around 2:00 a.m., he woke up frightened and ran out in the corridor. Our nurses gave him a mild sedative and he went back to sleep. This morning as soon as I got in, I asked him about it and gave him a pad and pencil to reply. He wrote that he had a bad dream. He dreamt that his grandfather was still alive and came to take him away from the clinic. They were running in the woods outside the clinic when he became separated from his grandfather. That prompted him to wake up and begin running down the corridor.

"This morning he seemed all right. It's good you're here because he asked me when he would see you again. I was planning to call you later this morning after I had a chance to observe him a little more."

"What about his speech?"

"Yesterday I had Dr. Morey, our chief therapist, analyze and work with Nick. She's very optimistic, but she said we'll have to be patient. Cases like this induced by trauma often take time."

"Can I talk to Jonathan?"

"Of course, and I think it'd be best if you do that alone. Do you remember where his room is?"

"Sure."

Walking along the corridor, she hoped that Nick wouldn't want her to take him out of the clinic. He really needed the expert care to regain his speech.

When she entered Nick's room, she saw him sitting at the desk engrossed in reading. As soon as he saw her, he put down the book. Elizabeth noticed it was *Eye of the Needle*, one of her books. It might not be the best choice, with that terrifying climax on the island, she thought, but she wasn't about to tell him that.

Nick rushed over and hugged her.

She felt so sorry for the kid that she wanted to cry. It tore at her heart. His parents had only died a year ago. Now his grandparents were gone, too. The trauma from the fire and then Emma Miller. Losing his speech. It was a wonder he could even get out of bed in the morning.

She said, "I heard from Dr. Cardin you had a bad dream last night."

Looking chagrined, he went over to his desk, picked up a pad and wrote something, which he handed to her. She read, "I'm okay now. Dr. Cardin is very nice. And Dr. Morey thinks she will be able to help me speak."

Elizabeth felt relieved. At least he wasn't completely miserable at the clinic.

"Listen, Nick," she said. "I have to leave Paris for a few days for work."

He looked sad.

"It's only for one or two days," she added. She had to do something to cheer him up. Suddenly, she had an idea. "Listen Nick, today is Friday. For sure I'll be back by Saturday evening. Then Sunday morning I have a baseball game in the Bois de Boulogne, a big Paris park, with some of my American friends."

He looked at her wide-eyed with anticipation.

She continued, "Our regular second baseman had to fly home to the States, and I was hoping you could play." That wasn't true, but what the hell. Carl was a friend; he'd be willing to pass up the game this time.

Excited, Nick pounded his right hand into his left palm as if it were a glove. Now he was smiling broadly.

"Wait here for a minute," she said. "I have to go out to my car and get something."

Once in the parking lot, she scrounged around in the messy trunk until she found what she was looking for: a baseball glove and a ball. She carried them back into the clinic and placed them on Nick's desk. "You can use the glove Sunday."

He slipped it onto his hand. It fit perfectly. While she watched, he pounded the ball into the glove several times. With the glove still on, he walked across the room and gave her a hug. She held him tightly.

"I won't let any more bad things happen to you," she vowed.

Feeling much better, Elizabeth left the clinic and drove to Charles de Gaulle Airport. Once she was on the plane she called Pierre. "I'm safely on board. Craig said you and your colleagues don't have to worry about me or the apartment, but it would be good if you could keep surveillance at the clinic."

"Absolutely," he replied.

*     *     *

When she arrived in Budapest, Elizabeth took a cab to Gyorgy's office in the building that housed what was left of Peter Toth Industries. It was a drab and dingy looking six-story structure that occupied half a block abutting the square in front of the magnificent Hungarian Parliament Building, the largest structure in Hungary. It was located along the Danube, which separated flat, commercial Pest from the more residential and hilly Buda. Before going inside to meet Gyorgy, Elizabeth paused to admire the parliament building, its neo-Gothic, Romanesque Revival architecture inspired by London's rebuilt palace of Westminster. It was surfaced with limestone and had numerous spires shooting into the air.

Turning back to Peter's building, she noticed that some of the windows on the top floor had been broken. Looking from the outside, she had the impression that very few of the offices were occupied. The three concrete steps in front were cracked.

Above the front entrance was a sign that read, "Peter Toth Industries." It had been defaced with splattered black paint.

Entering the building, she saw a heavyset, middle-aged receptionist behind a wooden desk. "Can I help you?" the woman asked.

"I'm here to see Gyorgy Kovacs. I'm Jane Wilson from Washington. He's expecting me."

The woman pointed Elizabeth to a bank of elevators on the right side of the lobby. "Take the elevator to six. He'll be waiting for you."

Once Elizabeth exited the elevator, a dapper looking man in a suit and tie with thick gray hair greeted her.

"Jane, I'm Gyorgy Kovacs." He looked at her with a peculiar expression as he reached out to shake her hand.

"Thanks for taking the time to meet with me."

"My pleasure. I thought we'd go to a café a couple blocks away to talk."

"Whatever you'd like."

As soon as they were out on the street and walking, he said, "I recognize you from TV. You're Elizabeth Crowder, the newspaper reporter." He looked frightened. "What's this all about? And why did you lie to me?"

She took a deep breath, hoping Gyorgy wouldn't terminate their discussion. The time had come to level with him. "You're right, I am Elizabeth Crowder. I don't believe the Potomac fire was an accident. I'm convinced Peter was murdered, and I want to find out who did it."

He didn't look surprised. "For your newspaper?" he asked.

"That's right. I lied to you because I know that Prime Minister Szabo and Peter were enemies. I didn't want to create problems for you if Szabo was listening in on your phone calls."

"Thank you. I appreciate that. For the same reason, I didn't want to talk to you in my office. I'm afraid it may be bugged."

"I hope you'll talk to me now."

Without hesitating, he said, "I was devastated by Peter's death, and I'm convinced Szabo is responsible. I want you to establish that and broadcast it to the entire world."

"If the facts support that conclusion, I certainly will."

"That Szabo . . . he hates—excuse me—hated Peter. He would do anything to strike at Peter. Look at the condition of our office building. It was once the finest in Budapest when Peter Toth Industries was thriving. We occupied the top five floors, and the first was retail. We had a large neon sign on the roof with 'Peter Toth Industries' in bright red letters."

"And then Peter sold off his companies?"

"It was more than that," Gyorgy replied with a sigh. "Peter Toth Industries still owns the building, but Szabo directed the police to take down the neon sign on the roof. I learned from a police source that Szabo gave the order to deface the sign in front of the building. From time to time windows are broken at night, but the government has refused to permit any repairs. They tried to buy the building for a pittance of its worth, but Peter turned down their offer. Szabo is now threatening to take it over and not pay anything. As you may be aware, our prime minister doesn't have any respect for the rule of law. Now with Peter's death, I'm afraid Szabo is directing his venom toward me."

After two left turns, they arrived at the Picard Cafe, which was half full. Gyorgy led them to a table in the back. They both ordered cappuccinos, and Gyorgy asked for a couple of pastries.

When the waiter was gone, Gyorgy said, "I can't tell you how sad I was to hear of Peter's death. He was more than a business partner and a good friend. He was a great human being, a man of enormous political principle. When he sold most of the business, I remained in Budapest to handle the disposition and to manage what was left."

"How long did you work with him?" Elizabeth asked.

"I first met him in 1991 shortly after the Soviet Empire had collapsed and Hungary achieved its independence from Russia. He told me about his business plans in Hungary, and I agreed to work for him. We started out slowly for the first few years. Once privatization came in 1995, we hit the ground running."

Gyorgy paused as the waiter returned with their peach and blueberry cakes. Elizabeth sipped her cappuccino.

When they were alone again, Gyorgy resumed talking. "Peter was born in Hungary and then lived in the US from 1977 to 1991, but he wasn't happy there."

"Why do you say that?"

"It may be hard for you Americans to understand, but many Hungarians have an incredible nationalism in their blood. We're not content living anywhere else, even if that place has material advantages. And Peter certainly lived comfortably in the United States. In 1980, he married Reka, a woman from Cleveland whose father was also a Hungarian refugee. They had one child, a son named Viktor."

"Who died a year ago?"

"Exactly." Gyorgy paused to sip his cappuccino, then continued. "The reason I thought Peter wasn't happy in the United States was because as soon as Hungary became independent, he arrived in Budapest to start a business."

"Did Reka and Viktor come with him?"

Gyorgy shook his head. "She didn't want to leave her family in the States, and she hated Hungary. He spent almost all of his time here, only visiting Reka in Cleveland a few times a year. With the free market economy taking off in Hungary, it was a great time for Peter to build a business empire. Fortunately, he had some money from his father-in-law to invest and the state was privatizing, which is a fancy word for selling off state assets for a fraction of their worth.

"Peter also had another advantage. He was well connected with Franz Szabo and Janos Rajk, who were rising political stars and with whom he became close friends. With their help he got control of a major portion of Hungary's telecommunications and energy sectors. For about twenty years Peter was making a fortune in these businesses. Our company was flying high."

"Then what happened?" Elizabeth asked, picking at her pastry and watching him intently.

"His good friend Szabo became prime minister and Szabo's politics changed."

"What do you mean?"

"When Peter first came to Budapest," Gyorgy explained, "he, Szabo, and Janos were all liberals. But over the years as Szabo sought to become prime minister and then to hold on to power, he moved more to the right."

"Did Szabo's views change?"

"It may have been that, or it may have been his effort to deal with the increasing right-wing movement in the country by broadening his base and seizing his political opponent's support from the center right."

"I've seen it happen elsewhere," Elizabeth commented.

"But regardless," Gyorgy continued, "Peter and Szabo would increasingly argue, and their disputes became more and more bitter. Janos, who is now justice minister, frequently tried to serve as a mediator or referee, but that eventually became too difficult. Finally, about two years ago when Szabo signaled a tilt toward Kuznov and Russia and away from NATO and the West, it was too much for Peter. He had suffered so much at the hands of the Russians when they ruled Hungary that his hatred for Moscow knew no bounds. After learning that Szabo was sucking up to Kuznov, as Peter put it, he and Szabo had a bitter argument and a total break in their relationship. This time Janos couldn't repair the damage. Peter went berserk, attacking Szabo in the media. He even told me that he wanted to kill Szabo."

"He actually said that?"

"Yes, but I don't think he ever attempted to act on it. At any rate, after Peter's diatribe in the press, Szabo gave him six months to liquidate his business interests and leave the country. Otherwise Szabo said he would confiscate everything and find a reason to arrest Peter. As I said, our prime minister doesn't respect the rule of law. Peter complied."

"How did Emma Miller enter into all this?"

"Emma Miller," Gyorgy whispered, dropping his head into his hands. "I can't believe she's dead too." He took a deep breath, and then blew it out. "I need some air. Let's go outside to talk about Emma."

Gyorgy led the way to a small park two blocks away. It was deserted. They sat on a bench.

"Beautiful, brilliant Emma," Gyorgy sighed. "I feel so terrible."

"How long did she know Peter?"

"She and I both started with him at the beginning in 1991. She had been born in Budapest, educated at the London School of Economics, and was working in Budapest for a London-based international bank at the time Peter met her. She was amazing with finances—the smartest person I've ever met. Increasingly, Peter relied on her to build his business. She was the CFO. I was the COO. When Peter liquidated, Emma moved to Paris and took a job with Credit Suisse."

"Did Emma and Peter have a personal relationship as well?"

Gyorgy fiddled with his tie. "Why do you ask?"

"As you said, she was beautiful. Peter was here without his wife. Emma wasn't married. It wouldn't be surprising."

Gyorgy smiled. "I understand why you're so successful as a reporter. You're very good at interrogation."

"I promise you that I will never write anything about their personal relationship," Elizabeth reassured him.

"I guess it doesn't matter if I talk about it. Everyone involved is dead. The answer is that Peter and Emma fell in love and were lovers for about fifteen years. Even after she moved to Paris, he traveled there about once a month to see her. And there's something else."

Gyorgy paused for a minute. Then he continued, "Twelve years ago, Emma, who was nineteen years younger than Peter, became pregnant with Peter's child. She wanted to have an abortion because a child would interfere with her career. Emma didn't have great maternal instincts. At the time, Peter knew that his son and daughter-in-law couldn't have a child and were trying to adopt. So Peter convinced Emma to have the child as a remembrance of their love. He told his son and daughter-in-law that he had learned through a connection in Budapest of a woman who wanted to put a newborn up for adoption. Peter worked out all the legal details and flew to Washington with a nurse and the baby. It was a boy who they named Nicholas."

Elizabeth nearly fell off the bench. *Holy shit*, she thought. Peter was Nick's father, and the kid had no idea.

"To my knowledge," Gyorgy added, "Peter never told Viktor or Ellina that he was Nicholas's biological father."

"What do you know about the death of Peter's son, Viktor, and Ellina?"

"Nothing at all. Peter believed Kuznov had them killed, but he never gave me any basis for that. He . . ." Gyorgy stopped talking and looked at Elizabeth. "You're American?"

"Correct."

"Do you work with the CIA as well as the *International Herald*? I know they use reporters from time to time."

She believed she could trust Gyorgy. "Let's just say that the CIA director and I are good friends."

"Well tell your friend the director that Peter and Emma dying within hours of each other could not have been a coincidence."

"Who do you think was responsible?"

Gyorgy looked around nervously, then said, "As I told you a few moments ago, our prime minister doesn't respect the rule of law."

Elizabeth pondered Gyorgy's words for a moment. "But what would Szabo gain from killing Peter and Emma?" she eventually asked.

"He would be eliminating vocal opponents. Remember, I told you that Szabo was pivoting toward Moscow, and that's straight from the Russian playbook."

Elizabeth wasn't convinced. "Perhaps, but I need your help. I would like to meet with the justice minister, Janos Rajk, the other member of the triumvirate with Peter and Szabo. Do you know Janos?"

"Reasonably well. Peter included me in a number of meetings with Janos."

"Could you call him and arrange a meeting for me?"

"What should I tell him?"

"That Elizabeth Crowder, the reporter from the *International Herald*, is doing a piece on Peter's life and would like to get his perspective on a longtime friend."

"Okay. I'll try."

Gyorgy took out his phone. Listening to him conduct the conversation in Hungarian, all Elizabeth understood were the words, "Elizabeth Crowder." When he put down the phone he said, "Janos is tied up today, but he can meet you tomorrow at 10:00 a.m. in his office."

"Thanks. I'll be there."

"What will you do this evening?"

"I don't know. I hadn't planned to stay overnight. Get a room at the Four Seasons I guess."

"I have a proposal for you. How much do you know about the 1956 Hungarian revolt against Russia?"

"Only what I remember from a modern European history course at Harvard."

"Well if you want to understand Peter, who he was, and what motivated him, you have to focus on 1956. Those events shaped his entire life."

"I do know that Peter was eight at the time, and that his father, Zoltan, was a leader in the rebel movement."

"Correct. My father, Lajos, was seventeen then. Although he didn't know Zoltan or Peter, he was very much involved in our fight for freedom. It would help you to hear from him what really happened."

For Elizabeth, this was a great offer. "I would love that."

"Good. Let's do it over dinner. We'll pick you up at the Four Seasons at eight."

"Don't you have to see if your father's available?"

Gyorgy smiled. "Since my mother died last year, my dad doesn't go out much. His mind is sharp, and he loves talking about his 'contribution to history,' as he describes it."

*        *        *

The restaurant, Café Kor, was five blocks from the Four Seasons and close to the magnificent St. Stephen's Basilica. Walking through the door behind Gyorgy and his father, Lajos, Elizabeth's eyes adjusted to the dimly lit interior. Gyorgy must have been a regular patron because the maître d', a young man with black curly hair dressed in jeans and a plaid shirt, gave him a warm greeting.

The restaurant was crowded. As they walked to their table, Elizabeth was struck by the resemblance of Gyorgy to his father. Both were tall at six foot two with thick gray hair and an old world look enhanced by their white shirts and dark blue blazers. Father and son stood ramrod straight as they moved through the restaurant.

Once they were seated and had perused the menus, a waiter came over to take their order.

"What would you recommend?" Elizabeth asked Gyorgy.

"I'm having the goose liver pâté and the grilled duck breast."

"That sounds great, I'll have the same."

When the waiter had departed Lajos said, "I'm a beer man myself, but my son's a bit of a wine snob so when I'm with him, I'm forced to go over to the other side."

Gyorgy smiled. "You always say that, Dad, but you have to admit Hungarian wines have gotten a lot better in the last ten or so years."

"Everything's gotten better since the Russians left."

The waiter rushed back with the wine Gyorgy had ordered. It really was quite good, with a gorgeous deep red color and enticing aroma. Speaking of wine snobs, Elizabeth thought, this one might even suit Craig. "What's the grape?" Elizabeth asked.

"The wine's called Sauska Cuvee 7. It's a blend of several grapes including merlot and cabernet and is produced in the south of Hungary."

Lajos turned to Elizabeth. "Gyorgy said you wanted to hear about our '56 revolt against the Russians and my contribution to history."

"I would like that very much, if you don't mind talking about it."

"He loves talking about it," Gyorgy interjected. "It was his day in the sun."

Ignoring Gyorgy, Lajos shook his head, his face somber. "I don't get many chances to describe what happened," he began. "Some Hungarians still recall those events vividly, and we have days of remembrance on October 23, since the fall of Communism, but much of our population has a collective amnesia about what happened in 1956. Young people only know the post-Soviet world that began in 1989 when the Russians left. And to be fair to them, during the period from

1956 to 1989, the events of '56 weren't taught in schools. The Russians pretended our revolt never happened or treated it as a Western imperialist-inspired putsch. For many people of my generation, guilt makes them bury the events of that time in the backs of their minds."

"Guilt?" Elizabeth asked.

"For sure, if they hadn't been intimidated by the Russians and had the courage to act instead of hiding in their houses, we might have prevailed."

"How did you happen to get involved?"

Their first courses came and Lajos paused to eat before responding. The pâté was quite good, Elizabeth thought.

Lajos put down his fork and replied, "I was a first-year student at the Technical University in Buda on October 23. It was a beautiful fall day, lots of sunshine, crisp air, blue skies. My two best friends, Ferenc and Gabor, and I joined thousands of other students in a peaceful march. We were heading toward Bem Square. At the beginning of the march we didn't have a clear objective. Young people in Poland had recently demonstrated against Communist rule and we were calling for solidarity with Poland." He shrugged. "Maybe we were just students rebelling against authority, the way students always do. Or letting off steam on a nice fall day.

"But then a strange thing occurred. As we marched first to Bem Square in Buda and then across the Danube to the parliament in Pest through the business and commercial heart of the city, huge numbers of people joined us. You have to realize none of this was planned. Workers left their offices and factory jobs and marched with us. Gradually, we became more than two hundred thousand strong. Nothing like this had ever happened. It was a spontaneous mass of people lacking organization and leaders. But now we now had an objective. The marchers were crying out, 'Russians go home.'

"At first the Communist regime in Budapest, comprised of puppets who took their orders from Moscow, was uncertain how to respond to the protestors. I suspect at that point uncertainty reigned among Khrushchev and the other Russian officials in Moscow as well. They had never seen anything like this."

"What happened when you got to the parliament?" Elizabeth asked.

"It was already evening. Gerő, the Communist Party boss, used a radio broadcast to tell everyone to go home. That only inflamed the crowd. Some of the protestors tried to seize the radio station. At this point Ferenc, Gabor, and I ran over to Heroes' Square. We joined others who were struggling to pull down a giant bronze statue of Stalin. We viewed this as a symbol of Russian enslavement. The Hungarian army couldn't stop us, or perhaps they didn't want to. Though we heard that AVH, those cruel and sadistic bastards in the Hungarian secret police, were shooting protestors in front of the parliament. In Heroes' Square we struggled for hours until some protestors brought large construction equipment to help. We cheered wildly when Stalin fell to the ground and only his boots remained."

Elizabeth was mesmerized by Lajos's words. "What happened then?"

"At around 2:00 a.m. the Russians decided to send in their own troops and tanks, which had been stationed outside of town, to break up the protests. We weren't organized, but many of us came to the same conclusion: We had to fight the Russian army to achieve our freedom. We managed to get rifles from sympathetic Hungarian soldiers, and we made Molotov cocktails. We may have been the most ragtag group ever to fight the Russian army, but fight we did. Once we spotted their troops, we opened fire on them, then raced into alleyways to escape. We tossed Molotov cocktails at tanks and ran. We began calling ourselves freedom fighters and declared this was a revolution.

"Ferenc, Gabor, and I joined other fighters in the Corvin Cinema in central Pest. This was one of the largest cinemas in the city. Strategically located, we could hit the Russian troops as they made their way into the city. When the troops arrived, we fired at them and then raced into the cinema to hide. We also threw grenades in the turrets of their tanks. Gabor was killed in the fighting, hit by a Russian tank. Ferenc and I had to pull his body out of the street while the battle continued to rage." Tears welled up in Lajos's eyes as he spoke.

"Even though our average age was about eighteen," he continued, "we refused to quit. Then we got lucky. Some of the Hungarian troops came over to our side along with their tanks and antitank guns. Once we had that support, we were able to hold the Corvin Cinema. The Russians pulled back. We took turns sleeping, waiting for their next attack.

"It came on October 25 when the Russian troops mounted a new attack aided by AVH troops. In front of parliament, they massacred three hundred protestors. At the Corvin Cinema we managed to drive their forces off, and we even captured some of their equipment. Ferenc and I took charge of one of their antitank guns and turned it on their T-54s."

Gyorgy interjected, "I never knew you did those things."

Lajos laughed. "Well you never asked." He looked at Elizabeth. "What does your father do?"

"He's a retired New York City policeman."

"I'll bet you don't know much about some of the operations he conducted."

"That's true," she admitted.

As Lajos excused himself to go to the bathroom, the waiter came to clear their first courses.

Elizabeth turned to Gyorgy. "Your dad has amazing recall," she remarked. "That must have happened more than sixty years ago."

"I guess if you live with your memories the way he does, you don't forget."

"Did your dad work in business or finance as you do?"

Gyorgy shook his head. "He was a chemical engineer, working in a plastics plant."

Lajos returned to the table, and a few minutes later their main courses arrived. For several moments, they ate in silence, enjoying the perfectly cooked food. Then Lajos turned to Elizabeth, "What happened next in our battle with the Russians was very particular," he said.

"What do you mean?" she asked.

"While we were fighting their troops to a standoff during these three days, we heard rumors that they were increasing their military strength in the country. We were anticipating a vicious attack, but it didn't come. Instead they drew back their troops, tanks, and planes. Incredibly, they negotiated a cease-fire on October 28 with the Hungarian government. It appeared as if they wanted a political solution. During the next two days the cease-fire held, and Russia started pulling its troops and tanks out of Budapest. Those of us in the Corvin Cinema were afraid to believe the fighting was over. We held our breaths and remained vigilant, guns in hand.

"Finally on the thirty-first, all the Russian troops had left the city. At long last, we put down our guns. That evening, exhausted, we left the Corvin Cinema and made our way to Kossuth Square, where the

Hungarian Parliament Building is located, the scene of a wild celebration. A gypsy band was playing national songs. People were danc-
ing. They were cracking open bottles of champagne and passing them
around."

Lajos paused for a moment and closed his eyes. Elizabeth guessed he
was recalling the scene.

He opened them again and continued, "We exchanged stories about
the battles. We laughed and we cried for our dead comrades like Gabor.
It was a miracle. We had defeated the Russian army. Ferenc and I got
drunk that night. Close to dawn we staggered back to the Corvin
Cinema, which had become our home in Budapest, and fell asleep on
the floor.

"And then?" Elizabeth said.

"Those bastards . . ." Lajos cursed. "They do it every time. We were
stupid not to realize it. That's the one constant in Moscow's military
playbook."

Elizabeth realized what was coming next. She listened while Lajos
explained.

"Russia never enters into a cease-fire to arrive at a political solution.
It's always to rearm and reinforce their military, and to plan for the next
round of fighting."

Elizabeth nodded. "The events in Syria in 2016 certainly support
what you're saying. Two days after Secretary of State John Kerry entered
into a cease-fire with Russia, they and their Syrian allies unleashed a
horrendous bombardment on the unarmed civilians in Aleppo, even
targeting hospitals."

But Lajos looked like he was seeing something from the past. She
sensed that he hadn't even heard what she had said, that his mind was
back in 1956.

He took a deep breath and exhaled. "When I woke up around
noon, I heard one of my comrades cry out. He had just heard reports
that Russian troops and tanks were crossing the Soviet border from
Ukraine. They had entered Hungary close to the Czechoslovak border
and had occupied the towns in the east, which control the rail lines into
Budapest. Many of the residents in these towns had no involvement
in the revolution. They regarded it as an uprising of the intelligentsia
in Budapest. Once we heard about the Russian troop movements, we

knew the cease-fire was a ploy. As soon as they choked off Budapest, they would act against us with such a massive show of force that we would have no chance to resist."

Lajos paused to take a breath. "In response to this dire news, someone else said that Chairman of the Council of Ministers Imre Nagy, who had replaced the Communist András Hegedüs on October 24, had sent a representative named Zoltan Toth to the United States. Gyorgy worked for Zoltan's son, Peter, for many years. Did you know that?" Elizabeth nodded and Lajos continued, "Well anyhow, Zoltan was supposed to get help either from the US or the UN."

"Did you believe he would succeed?" Elizabeth asked.

"Some of my colleagues were convinced the US would help us. After all, their Radio Free Europe and the CIA had been encouraging us to revolt and throw off the yoke of Soviet oppression for years. Even Ferenc thought the US would help, but I didn't believe it. Not for a second.

"Growing up in Budapest I had a Jewish friend who told me how Catholic farmers in a small town in rural Hungary had hid his parents on their farm when the Nazis were rounding up Jews and sending them to the death camps. He said this was late in the war. The allies had control of the skies and could have bombed the railroad tracks leading to the death camps, but President Roosevelt refused to do that. As I recalled his story, I was certain that President Eisenhower wouldn't lift a finger to help the Hungarian people, despite all of their urging for us to revolt, and despite the arguments of Zoltan Toth."

"And you were right," Elizabeth said sadly. "Unfortunately, in the last seventy-five years, the United States has often disappointed those who it promised to help."

"Yes. Well, the Russians weren't taking any chances," Lajos continued. "They brought 150,000 troops, 2,500 modern tanks, and lots of bombers to provide air support. Early in the morning on Sunday, November 4, they began indiscriminately bombing and shelling practically every building in Budapest. They wreaked destruction even if they didn't see freedom fighters and even if the buildings didn't have military significance. It was cruel and barbaric, leveling block after block."

"Were you in the Corvin Cinema at the time of the bombardment?"

He nodded. "From November 4 to November 6. Fortunately we were able to access a series of underground tunnels in which we could hide. My friend Ferenc began to become unglued mentally from the constant shelling. I tried to calm him down, but he snapped. He eluded me and ran out into the street, shooting wildly at Russian soldiers. He killed two before they mowed him down."

"How did you survive?"

"When it was only six of us left, the commander told us it was hope-less and that we should try to escape individually. He said that way we'd have a better chance of surviving and being able to tell the story of what happened. I used the tunnels as far as I could. When I surfaced, I was next to the deserted barracks of a Hungarian army installation. I found a uniform in a closet, which I put on. Then I hotwired a mili-tary transport and headed toward the Austrian border. Driving through what was left of Budapest, I saw nothing but dead bodies and rubble. It was a horrific scene, with the stench of human flesh and death in the air. Limbs were severed from bodies, children, even babies. It was the ultimate example of man's inhumanity to his own race.

"When I reached the Austrian border, I found a point at which the guards were letting refugees slip across in return for money. There were so many that in the confusion I managed to join in with a large group of several families. One of them was going from Austria to Italy. When I told one of the men, Tibor Esterhazy, I had fought at the Corvin Cinema, he regarded me as a hero and offered to take me to Italy with them. Tibor had owned a chemical company in Budapest, and he had a relationship with a company based in Torino. Once I told him I had been a student at the Technical University studying chemical engineer-ing, he offered to pay for my education. I would treat it as a loan and work with him after I graduated. He was a wonderful man."

Elizabeth took a sip of her wine before asking, "How long did you stay in Italy?"

"Until the Russians left Hungary in 1989. The following year, I per-suaded my wife, Lucia, who was Italian, and son, Gyorgy, to move to Budapest. So we returned here and began a new life."

Gyorgy interjected, "I had gotten a degree in business from the University in Bologna and was working in Torino at the time. I wasn't married, so I decided to move with my parents. I figured there would be opportunities when Hungary shifted from Communism to the free market. That proved to be true. I met Peter Toth a year after we arrived in Budapest, and he hired me. You know the rest."

When Gyorgy went up front to pay the bill, Elizabeth thanked Lajos for providing such valuable information.

"We all suffered so much at the hands of the Russians," he said. "Not only in 1956, but afterwards too. In Budapest on Andrássy Avenue is a museum called the House of Terror. You should go there if you have time. It will help you appreciate what happened at the time and what the secret police did to us. But the irony is that the Hungarian people fought so hard for our freedom in 1956, and now we have elected Szabo, this neofascist megalomaniac who's on his way to converting our democracy into a dictatorship. He needs to be stopped."

## Rome and Paris

Giuseppe was waiting for Craig in his office when he arrived. Once Craig had walked through the door, Giuseppe called to his secretary for two double espressos.

"What happened to your blood pressure?" Craig asked.

"Ah, the hell with it," Giuseppe grumbled. "If I can't drink coffee and red wine, what's the point of living?"

Craig laughed. "That's how I feel."

"Besides, dealing with you always elevates my blood pressure, regardless of what I drink."

As they sat down at a conference table, Giuseppe said, "Tell me what happened with Moshe."

Craig reported in detail on his dinner meeting with Moshe and Gideon. As Craig spoke, Giuseppe looked increasingly worried and heavy creases appeared on his forehead.

"We already have scores of terrorist groups operating in Europe," he growled when Craig had finished. "We definitely do not need Chechen radicals as well."

"Agreed," said Craig. "It seems as if Paris is attracting jihadists like a magnet."

"We'll have to fly to Paris and tell Jean-Claude."

"That 'we' better mean both of us. I'm not going alone to tell him about Moshe's little operation in France."

"I wouldn't do that to you. Fortunately for both of us Jean-Claude may be preoccupied. He had to rush back to Paris because of the brutal murder of a Hungarian national named Emma Miller."

Craig sat up with a start. "I'm familiar with Emma Miller's murder. Elizabeth was covering the story before I left for Tel Aviv. She told me about it. But Emma Miller's death has another component."

"What's that?" Giuseppe inquired.

"I'll only tell you if you promise not to mention it to Jean-Claude or anyone else."

"If that's what you want, of course I'll honor it."

Craig and Giuseppe had developed such a close relationship over the years that Craig could rely with confidence on his promises. So Craig explained about Elizabeth finding Nicholas Toth in the Place des Vosges and what she had learned about the fire in Potomac, Maryland. "The key point is that Peter Toth had a strong Hungarian involvement," he concluded.

"So there's definitely a connection between the Potomac fire and Emma Miller's murder."

"Exactly. In fact, Elizabeth is now in Budapest trying to find out who might have been responsible."

"What did she do with Nicholas?"

"She has a friend who operates a clinic for children suffering from trauma. She took him there."

"Can I do anything to help Elizabeth—perhaps provide security for her or for Nicholas?"

"Thanks, Giuseppe, but I already have it covered."

"Listen Craig, I won't say anything if you don't want me to, but don't you think you should tell Jean-Claude about Nicholas?"

"Absolutely not. You know what he's like. Once he hears about Nicholas, he'll head right to that clinic and try to compel the boy to talk. He'll traumatize the kid so badly that he'll never recover his speech."

"Okay, I'll do it your way. I'll pretend you never told me. What I don't know I can't repeat."

"Thanks, Giuseppe. Remember, a kid's life is at stake."

In his mind, Craig saw terrified Nicholas coming out of the closet in his kitchen. Speaking deliberately, he added, "If the Russians who killed Peter Toth and Emma Miller learn that Nicholas is alive, they'll do everything they can to find him and kill him."

Giuseppe didn't argue. Instead, he buzzed his secretary. "Craig and I are flying to Paris. Please get us on the first available flight."

In the car on the way to the airport, Craig said to Giuseppe, "One fact keeps bothering me. Amos and Emma Miller were killed in Paris on the same day."

"You think the two homicides are related?"

"Right now, I don't have evidence to link them, but my instinct tells me yes."

Giuseppe thought about it for a minute. "You may have a point. If we exclude terror bombings, there were only seventy-three homicides in Paris in all of last year. Here we have two on the same day and both have an international component. You may be on to something."

"Which means if we solve one of these murders, the other will fall into place."

*       *       *

Four hours later Craig and Giuseppe filed into Jean-Claude's office. The head of the French intelligence agency didn't even wait for them to sit down before he barked out, "I'm furious at the two of you," his face red with anger.

*Uh-oh*, Craig thought.

"What happened?" Giuseppe asked, as if he had no idea what was on Jean-Claude's mind.

"I can't believe you knew the Israelis were flying Amos Neir's body home and didn't inform me. That violates every rule of cooperation we have."

"You were in Turkey," Giuseppe said. "The Israeli prime minister arranged it with your president. I assumed he would let you know. Didn't he?"

"No, he didn't," Jean-Claude snapped. "Moshe called a little while ago to tell me that the two of you would be coming to talk to me about Amos Neir and what he was doing in Paris. When I heard that, I gave it to Moshe with both barrels. He has no right running an intelligence operation in France without my knowledge and approval."

"Can we sit down and talk about this?" Giuseppe asked.

Jean-Claude pointed to a conference table in the corner. "Sit if you want, but you two better not try to justify what Moshe did. Those damn Israelis are always operating on their own. Now I find out you two are in bed with them."

Craig decided to intervene. He couldn't let Giuseppe take all the heat. "First of all," he said, "neither Giuseppe nor I had any idea that Amos Neir was even in France until I saw his body being pulled from the Seine. And second, every nation has a right to defend its own security."

"If Moshe had clued me in, Amos Neir might still be alive."

"That's doubtful," Giuseppe said. "In any event, wait until you hear what Craig has to tell you. I think you'll be grateful to Moshe and Amos Neir."

Jean-Claude shook his head emphatically without responding. Craig almost thought he would refuse to listen. Finally, he said. "Tell me."

Craig decided to omit the reason Moshe had given Amos this assignment. He cut right to the results. "Amos Neir was a dark-skinned Moroccan Jew—the perfect candidate for infiltrating Clichy. In the last several months he provided the French police with three anonymous tips on major terror attacks being planned by jihadists in Paris. As a result of his tips, you were able to thwart all three."

Jean-Claude didn't disagree. Instead, he said, "So you expect me to award this Israeli a medal?"

"No, but I'd at least like you to acknowledge that he saved French lives."

"I don't care how many lives he saved. It's still outrageous that Moshe didn't let me know Amos was operating undercover in my country."

"Maybe he should have, but he didn't."

Giuseppe intervened. "All of that's irrelevant. Amos is now dead. He may have been uncovering something big, and he paid for it with his life."

Jean-Claude responded, "Maybe he was killed because of the attacks he thwarted. Maybe he didn't discover anything new."

Jean-Claude was really stubborn, Craig thought, not willing to yield an inch.

"Moshe thinks Amos was onto a new suspect," Craig said.

"Who?"

"Have you heard of Omar Basayev?"

Jean-Claude sat up with a start. "Omar the Chechen."

Craig nodded.

"The man's a horror," Jean-Claude said. "Brutal and cruel, but also cunning. He's given Moscow fits with his attacks on Russian targets there, in the Ukraine, and in Syria. You're not going to tell me Omar's in France."

"Amos spotted him in Clichy. He was trying to find out what Omar was doing when he was killed."

"Are we certain it's Omar?"

Craig took the picture Gideon had given him in Israel and passed it to Jean-Claude. "Amos photographed this man in Clichy and forwarded it electronically to Tel Aviv. The Mossad people made the ID."

Jean-Claude looked alarmed. "We have a small Chechen population in Clichy," he conceded. "Omar could have blended in with them. He may be planning to hit a Russian target in Paris. Their embassy, perhaps."

"Or," Giuseppe interjected, "Omar may be joining up with other non-Chechen jihadists for an attack in France that doesn't involve a Russian target."

Jean-Claude shook his head. "Unlikely. That doesn't fit his MO."

"He may have been offered enough money to do a job here. He could then use those funds to finance other operations against Russia. These terrorists sometimes freelance."

"That's possible," Jean-Claude admitted.

"During my time as director of the EU Counterterrorism Agency, I established relationships with informants in Clichy," Craig said. "I could go up there and talk to them."

Jean-Claude dismissed Craig's offer with a wave of his hand. "This is a matter for the French intelligence and military. I'll send in some of my people this evening. We'll find out what Omar is planning. We'll also take him into custody."

"There's a lot of hostility to the French government in that area," Craig pointed out.

"Are you telling me how to run an operation in my own country?" Jean-Claude snarled.

"I spent time in Clichy. I'm just trying to be helpful," Craig replied with a shrug.

Jean-Claude pounded his fist on the table. "With a show of force, we'll get what we want. I'll accompany intelligence agents with troops fully armed."

*Sounds like a prescription for a riot*, Craig thought. And it was doomed to fail. But he didn't argue any more.

Jean-Claude stood up, signaling the meeting was over. Before leaving, Craig considered asking Jean-Claude where he was in his investigation of Emma Miller's death, but decided that would be a mistake as long as he wasn't willing to talk about Nicholas.

On the way out of the office, Craig thought about Jean-Claude's plan for going into Clichy. He had no intention of leaving the search for Omar up to Jean Claude and his people. Amos had been Craig's friend. To hell with Jean-Claude. If the Frenchman didn't get results that evening, Craig intended to go into Clichy himself the next day. He'd find Omar and make him talk. He wanted to know exactly what he was planning, and what had happened to Amos.

From Jean-Claude's office, Giuseppe drove to the airport to fly back to Rome. Craig checked his phone on his way back to the apartment. It was seven in the evening. He had a text from Elizabeth telling him she'd be staying that night in Budapest. He hoped she was learning something.

When he turned the key and opened the door, he saw a lamp turned on in the living room. Craig immediately grabbed the gun in his bag. Elizabeth was compulsive about turning off lights. As he moved through the apartment silently, Craig checked and rechecked, but nobody was there and he couldn't find anything missing. Even the forty euros he had left on the bureau were still there. But he was certain some of his papers had been moved. Elizabeth's computer was turned on. She would never have left it that way. There was no question about it: Somebody had been in the apartment.

The only explanation was that whoever had killed Emma Miller knew that Nick had gone off with Elizabeth, and they were searching for the boy. Satisfied no one was hiding in the apartment, he put down the gun and called Elizabeth on the encrypted phones they used.

"Where are you?" he asked.

"Four Seasons Gresham Palace in Budapest."

"Can you talk?"

"Absolutely."

He told her about the apartment break-in.

"Did you have anything in the apartment that identifies where you took the boy?"

"Nothing."

"Anything on your computer?"

"Not a thing," she asserted, "but they could never get in anyhow. I'm paranoid about hackers so I change the password daily."

"Okay. These guys play rough. I heard from Giuseppe what they did to Emma Miller. I'm going to move into the Bristol. You can come right there when you return to Paris. After that, we'll go over to the apartment together to get the things you need. Meantime, I'll call Pierre and have him position someone to watch the apartment and someone outside my suite at the Bristol."

"You think all that's necessary?" Elizabeth asked.

"For sure. When are you coming home?"

"Tomorrow afternoon. I had a good meeting with a business associate of Peter's today, and I'm meeting with the justice minister tomorrow. He was a friend of Peter's. I'll give you a report when I get back."

"Okay. Take care of yourself."

*       *       *

Craig had dinner alone at Au 41 Penthièvre, a small restaurant close to the Bristol. As he walked back to the hotel at ten o'clock, his phone rang. It was Giuseppe.

"Have you heard the news?" Giuseppe asked.

"No. What happened?"

"The police backed by military troops went into Clichy with a show of force. That was Jean-Claude's effort to grab Omar. The locals fire-bombed a couple of police cars and a military vehicle. It was a real mess."

"Gee, what a surprise. Have you spoken to Jean-Claude?"

"A couple of minutes ago. They couldn't locate Omar. If he was still there, he was hiding, and no one was talking."

"I'm going up to Clichy tomorrow, early afternoon, when things have settled down a little," said Craig.

"You telling Jean-Claude ahead of time?"

"No."

"Well, I can't tell him either because I don't know about it. Good luck."

## Russia, near the Black Sea

President Kuznov had a large summer house along the Black Sea. He liked traveling there for several days at a time in August. Typically, he brought along his wife, Svetlana, and his much younger mistress, Natasha. At six in the evening Kuznov and Natasha were nude, frolicking in the hot tub behind the house. Looking up, he saw Svetlana watching them disapprovingly from a second-floor window, but he ignored her gaze. He reached for a glass of champagne resting on the edge of the tub and took a sip.

Suddenly, from behind, he heard Dimitri's unmistakable voice say, "Mr. President, we have to talk."

Kuznov turned around and said, "Dimitri, your timing is horrible."

"Mr. President, I think you'll want to hear this immediately."

Kuznov looked at Natasha, who was frowning. "Wait for me in the bedroom," he said.

In a pout, she climbed out of the tub, tossed a towel over her shoulder, and brushed past Dimitri.

"Get in," Kuznov said. "We can talk in the hot tub. It'll do you good to relax. You work too hard."

Dimitri stripped off his clothes before gingerly lowering himself into the hot water. When he was in the tub, Kuznov said, "Now tell me what's so important that it couldn't wait an hour."

"I just returned from Budapest. Szabo and I had a tough negotiation session. Eventually we got down to 100 million euros, your number, which was where I drew the line."

"And?"

"Szabo wants to think about it. He'll get back to me."

"So you're nowhere."

"I think he'll take it."

"How confident are you?"

Dimitri thought about it for a moment, then said, "Very confident."

"Good. In the morning I'll give the order to begin assembling troops and tanks at airfields near Ukraine. Once the Friendship Pact is signed we'll airlift those troops and tanks over Ukraine to Hungary."

"Won't Ukraine object?"

"They wouldn't dare. They know I'll destroy their entire military in twelve hours. Now tell me about Nicholas Toth."

"Our technical people analyzed the photo Anatol took of the boy."

"And?" Kuznov asked impatiently.

"We found yearbook photos of Nicholas Toth from the last few years. The boy who went off with Elizabeth Crowder is unquestionably Peter Toth's grandson."

"But I told you that without any additional analysis. What I want to know is whether Boris has been able to locate the kid."

"Not yet. Anatol broke into Elizabeth Crowder's apartment, but nobody was there at the time."

"What did he find?"

"Nothing related to the boy. From what he saw, she lives with a race car driver named Enrico Marino."

Kuznov was becoming increasingly annoyed. "So far you haven't told me a damn thing."

"I'm getting to it. Anatol found baseball equipment in Elizabeth's closet: bats, gloves, and balls. He remembered reading in one of the French newspapers that she plays baseball Sunday mornings in the summer in the Bois de Boulogne with other American expats."

"So if she plays this Sunday," Kuznov said, completing the thought, "Boris could send people to grab her and they could force her to tell them where the boy is."

"Definitely. And perhaps even better, she might bring Nicholas to the game."

"Then we could seize Nicholas and find out what he knows."

"Precisely."

"Talk to Boris and have him set this up. I don't want the boy to get away this time."

# Budapest

Janos Rajk was tall and thin with a receding hairline above a wrinkled brow. When Elizabeth entered his spacious office in the Justice Ministry, she thought he looked worried. Still, he greeted her graciously.

A secretary brought in coffee in china cups and Janos pointed to the living area, motioning Elizabeth to the sofa. He sat on a straight chair facing her.

"I appreciate your meeting with me," she said.

"I'm happy to do so. You're a well-respected journalist and Peter Toth was my good friend for many years. I was saddened and distraught to learn of his sudden death, and I'd like the world to remember his many good qualities."

Elizabeth removed a pad and pen from her bag. "Could you tell me about those good qualities?"

"Peter had an incredible love for Hungary. He would do anything to help his native country. That patriotism may have something to do with his background."

"What do you mean?"

"His mother was descended from Hungarian aristocrats related to the monarchy and instilled in him from birth a love for Hungary. His father was one of the leaders of the 1956 uprising against Russia. Peter returned to Hungary right after the wall fell because he wanted to help rebuild our economy and turn Hungary into an economic powerhouse."

"And while doing that, he made an enormous amount of money."

Janos smiled and sipped his coffee. "That's true, his investments did pay off. At the same time, he supplied us with badly needed knowledge of the American economy and how free markets operate. As you are no doubt aware, we were emerging from the dark ages of Communism. Peter played a major role in shaping our economy under these radically different circumstances. You Americans have an expression: doing well by doing good. That applies to Peter Toth."

"He also had a close relationship with Franz Szabo, who was a rising power in politics and is now prime minister," Elizabeth pointed out. "That must have helped Peter tremendously in building his business."

Rajk frowned. "If you're implying there were payoffs, then you're entirely wrong. The three of us were close friends over many years. I can tell you that Peter never paid anything to Franz or me for influence."

"So what happened to end this great friendship Peter had with Szabo?"

"In a word, politics," Rajk replied with a sigh. "We were all initially liberals, but after becoming prime minister, Szabo started moving the country to the right. So to remain true to his beliefs, Peter supported political candidates who were Szabo's competitors. He believed Szabo had grown too strong and that he was becoming like Erdogan in Turkey, minus the religious bent."

"Did you join Peter in supporting candidates on the left?"

Janos shook his head. "I believed it was better to achieve change from the inside. When I became justice minister five years ago, Peter came to me with claims that Szabo was corrupt and had taken bribes from other businessmen. I asked Peter to provide me with evidence and I would prosecute him."

"What happened?"

"He never did. When Szabo pivoted toward Russia two years ago, Peter went ballistic. He funded a PR campaign against the pro-Russian move. In response, Szabo threatened to confiscate his companies."

"Could he have done that? You're the justice minister."

Janos shifted in his chair, looking uncomfortable. "I don't know how that would have played out," he replied. "I advised Peter to liquidate his business and leave the country. I'm glad he took my advice, mooting the issue."

"Have you maintained your own close relationship with Szabo?"

Janos was silent for a few moments. Finally, he said, "I would prefer not to answer that question. This interview is about Peter."

Elizabeth nodded. "Fair enough, let me ask you this: Why was Peter so adamant about Szabo's pivot toward Russia?"

"He had suffered under the Russians after the 1956 uprising."

"Suffered how?"

"Peter's father, Zoltan Toth, left the country in the midst of the revolution in 1956 to plead our case before the United States and the UN. He had been sent by Chairman Imre Nagy. Were you aware of that?"

Elizabeth nodded. "And I'm aware that Peter, who was eight at the time, remained in Budapest with his mother."

"That's right. Zoltan had planned to take Peter and Anna with him, but something happened at the last minute and he ended up going alone. Afterwards, Peter and his mother, Anna, were barred from leaving Hungary, and Zoltan wasn't permitted to return. Once the fighting ended, Peter and Anna suffered horribly. A Russian colonel named Suslov moved into Zoltan's house and forced Anna to become his mistress. He changed Peter's name from Peter Toth to Lazlo Suslov, and he beat the child mercilessly. He even branded a hammer and sickle on Peter's arm. As Peter got older he turned to hockey as a means of escaping the colonel. As a star player, he was able to move into the athletic dorm, where he lived until he defected to the States in 1977 while on a tour with his hockey team."

"What happened to Anna, Peter's mother?"

"Peter told me that when he came back to Hungary in 1991, after the Russians left, he spoke to the woman who lived next to his parents' house in Budapest. She informed him that in 1978 an ambulance had come suddenly to take his mother away. She never returned. The neighbor later learned that she had wound up in a mental institution and died a month later. According to the neighbor, Suslov kept the house until the Russians left in 1989. While he was there, he moved in one young girl after another."

Janos took a deep breath, hesitating for a few seconds as though reluctant to tell her any more. Then he said, "There's one more piece to story."

Elizabeth took a sip of her coffee, waiting for him to continue.

"In 2005 Suslov returned from Moscow to Budapest for a visit. He was on a honeymoon with his new wife. When the maid at their hotel went into the room one morning, she found the wife drugged and tied up in the living room. Suslov was in the bed in a pool of his own blood. He had been strangled and castrated, his penis stuffed into his mouth. The incident was never reported in the media. The police investigated, but no suspects were ever identified."

She thought about what Gyorgy had told her yesterday. Peter had told him that he wanted to kill Szabo. "Do you think Peter killed Suslov or hired people to do it?"

Janos shrugged. "There were rumors of Peter's involvement, but I never saw any evidence of that. You should be aware, however, that there were a lot of people in Budapest that hated Suslov. He was one of the most despised Russians from the occupation." He paused, then added, "Rumors can be false. I trust that you wouldn't write something based on rumors."

"Of course not. I would never write about something like this without reliable confirmation."

"I'm happy to hear that. As I said, Peter was my friend. Even when he liquidated his business and moved back to the US, we saw each other from time to time, either when I visited or when he came to Paris."

"What brought him to Paris?"

"Some business, I think, and some friends."

Elizabeth had no intention of questioning Janos about Peter's relationship with Emma Miller. She had already gotten the facts from Gyorgy, and she was certain Janos wouldn't talk about it.

As she glanced over her notes to see if she had any follow-up questions, Janos said, "Since you're researching Peter, you will be interested to know that next Tuesday in Bethesda, Maryland, I'll be speaking at a memorial service for Peter and his wife, Reka, and their grandson, Nicholas, at the Church of the Little Flower."

"I appreciate your telling me. Can I ask who invited you to speak?"

"Our ambassador in Washington. He liked Peter as well and considered him to be a true Hungarian patriot, a man to whom this nation owed a tremendous debt of gratitude for its economic rebuilding."

As Elizabeth left the Justice Ministry, she decided to walk back to the Four Seasons where she would pack and take a cab to the airport. Though it was August it was surprisingly cool, with low humidity.

While she walked, she thought about what Janos had told her. She wondered whether the Russians had killed Peter and his family as payback for Suslov's murder. It was too early to jump to a conclusion like that, but one thing was clear: Peter Toth had been an exceedingly complex man who had lived a bizarre life.

## Paris

Craig expected trouble in Clichy. At noon on Saturday he had rented a small black Renault, then driven north toward Clichy.

Driving with the hot August sun beating down, Craig thought about the divided city Paris had become. Since the 2015 terrorist attacks, Muslim-inhabited suburbs like Clichy, or banlieues as they were called, had become even more separate and cut off from the white Christian majority that ruled Paris. The influx of refugees from Syria, Iraq, Afghanistan, and other Middle Eastern countries had only exacerbated the situation. After last night's riot he realized it would be risky to venture into the area alone. However, he was determined to find Omar.

After arriving in Clichy, Craig parked near a soccer field and got out of his car. He glanced around, but didn't see anything suspicious, so he walked to a nearby auto repair shop. Abdullah, the owner, had his shaved head ducked under the hood of a truck.

When Craig had been the director of EU Counterterrorism, he had made Paris his base and developed relationships with people in Clichy like Abdullah, warning them when trouble was coming so they could lock up and shutter their businesses. Grateful, they were willing to repay the favor with information. What made today's visit awkward was that after his plastic surgery, Craig no longer looked like Craig

Page—and he didn't want to disclose his new identity any more than was absolutely essential to find out more about Amos and Omar.

"Hey Abdullah," Craig said.

The mechanic pulled his head out from under the hood of the truck and stared at his visitor.

"Who are you?" he asked.

"I'm a friend of Craig Page. He sent me to speak with you."

A mechanic in the next bay was eyeing Craig warily, and Craig was glad he had a gun holstered under his jacket.

"Why don't you come into the office?" Abdullah suggested.

Craig followed Abdullah across the grease-stained floor to an office with papers piled on a dingy desk. Old engine parts were scattered around, and several unopened cardboard boxes were piled in a corner.

Abdullah kicked the door shut with a thud. Craig had no idea what Abdullah was thinking, and he didn't try to figure it out. All he wanted to do was get some information and then get the hell out of there before that mechanic called some of his buddies.

Abdullah sat behind the desk and pointed to a chair in front of it. Craig removed a box of spark plugs and sat down.

"I gather you had some plastic surgery," Abdullah said.

"That's right. How did you recognize me?"

"I'm good with voices. Yours is distinctive. Now tell me what's going on, Craig."

"What do you mean?" Craig asked.

"French intelligence agents and police came into Clichy last night accompanied by soldiers dressed for war. They started breaking the bones of Muslim men, trying to find out where a Chechen terrorist by the name of Omar was hiding."

"Believe me, I had nothing to do with that. You know that's not how I operate."

"It was stupid," Abdullah said, shaking his head. "First of all, we hate the Chechens. They're trouble. And second, tell your friends Jean-Claude and Giuseppe this is no way to obtain cooperation."

"You're right." Craig nodded ruefully. He took the pictures of Amos and Omar out of his pocket and put them down on the desk. "Have you seen either of these men?"

Abdullah picked up the photo of Amos and looked at it intently.

"He's a Moroccan Jew living in Clichy. Polite. Works in some kind of international business."

Craig was startled. "What makes you think he's a Jew?"

"He came in here a couple of times to get his car fixed. I was born in Morocco. I knew lots of Jews there. We got along. I can tell. Anyhow, what'd he do?"

"Somebody killed him and dumped his body into the Seine."

"Can I count on you not to identify me as the source of information?"

"Of course. Haven't we always operated that way?"

Abdullah pointed to the picture of Omar. "That guy killed the Jew."

"How do you know?" Craig asked.

"This is a small community. People talk." Abdullah shook his head and pointed to the picture of Omar again. "He's no good, that one. A thug from Chechnya."

"He's the one the French police are looking for."

"I hope they catch him. We're just recovering from the last round of riots. Now this Chechen bastard is bringing more trouble to the area."

"Who could help me locate him?" Craig asked.

Abdullah thought about it for a minute. "Do you know the Brasserie Rabat on Rue Balzac?"

"Yeah. I was in there once. I don't know the owner, though."

"Guy by the name of Habib runs it. I haven't talked to him about this situation, but he has many Chechen customers, and he hears a lot. He could be helpful. It's worth a try."

"Will he talk to me?"

"I'll call and ask him to," said Abdullah. "I can't guarantee that he will, but it's your best shot."

"I appreciate it," Craig replied, feeling like he was finally starting to get somewhere.

"I'd like you to catch this Chechen thug. I don't like the cops busting the heads of our people on his account."

Walking from Abdullah's garage to the Brasserie Rabat, Craig passed the largest mosque in Clichy. Heavy clouds had formed in the sky, and a thunderstorm seemed likely.

He decided to take a detour, heading toward the office in the back of the mosque. There, he found the Imam alone reading a book. Craig knew him from his former job as head of EU Counterterrorism. Unlike Abdullah, Craig and the Iman had never liked each other. Though Craig had looked to the Iman for support, he always suspected the gray-bearded man of fomenting trouble.

Before Craig had a chance to open his mouth, the Imam said, "If Jean-Claude Dumas sent you, then get out of here."

"Nobody sent me."

"Then what do you want?" he asked, drawing his eyebrows together.

Craig showed him the picture of Amos. "This man was my friend. Somebody killed him and dumped him into the Seine Wednesday morning."

"So that's why Jean-Claude launched a reign of terror on Clichy."

"My friend was killed by a Chechen—Omar Basayev." Craig handed the Imam Omar's picture. "Have you seen him?"

The Imam studied it and handed it back. "He was here for a few days last week and left before your friend was killed. He went back to Chechnya. Go look for him there."

"What was he doing in Paris?" Craig persisted.

"You'll have to ask him. So fly to Grozny and stop bothering me."

"I thought that's what you'd say. I was hoping your desire to avoid further violence might induce you to cooperate."

"Get out of here," the Imam snapped.

As Craig left the mosque, he mulled over what the Imam had said. He wasn't sure he believed him, though it was possible that Omar had returned to Chechnya after Amos's body was discovered.

Leaving the mosque, Craig saw three young men on the corner, watching him with hostility. He ignored them and kept walking.

Ten minutes later he entered Brassiere Rabat. He took in his surroundings through the lens of the heavy, cigarette smoke-filled air. In Clichy, the government didn't enforce regulations like those that banned smoking in bars and restaurants. The place was about half full. Craig went up to the zinc bar, and a woman in a black uniform, her head covered by a brown hijab, came forward to take his order. After requesting an espresso, he dropped two euros on the bar and asked, "Where's Habib?"

She turned and pointed to a heavyset man leaning over a griddle behind her. He was scraping it down with a spatula. At the sound of his name, Habib wheeled around. He was a middle-aged man wearing a stained white apron and black-framed glasses, and his black hair was interspersed with gray. Habib must have realized Craig was the man Abdullah had called about because he pointed toward the swinging door that led to the back of the brassiere and headed that way. Espresso in hand, Craig followed him.

They went into a cramped office where a small desk was piled high with various papers, most of which looked like bills.

Habib remained standing. "You just spoke to Abdullah," he said.

"That's right." Craig nodded. "He thought you could help me find someone." He handed Habib Omar's picture. "His name is Omar Basayev, a Chechen."

Habib gave the photo a quick glance and handed it back. "I've never seen the man."

From the cursory way Habib had glanced at the photo, Craig was confident he was lying. "Are you sure?" he asked. "This is important. Perhaps you want to take a closer look."

"I told you, I've never seen the man," Habib repeated, sounding irritated now.

"Abdullah said you have a lot of Chechen customers. Perhaps you could introduce me to one who might help me."

"That's impossible," Habib replied curtly. "Now you had better leave. I have to get back to work."

Observing Habib's demeanor, Craig was positive he knew something and wasn't talking, either from fear or to protect someone. But he had no way to force him to divulge what he knew.

Craig picked up a blank piece of paper and a pen from the desk, wrote down his phone number, and handed it to Habib.

"If you remember seeing this man or can help me in any way to find him, please call."

Habib tossed the paper on his desk among the many others, grunting in reply as Craig walked back out through the kitchen.

As he left the brassiere and walked toward his car, Craig was certain the three young men he had spotted earlier were following him. The sky had turned very dark now, and the air was heavy with moisture.

Craig pretended not to notice the men as he crossed the street to his car. One of the three had gotten there first. He was standing between

Craig and the car door. The others held back on each end of the car near the edge of the soccer field.

"You want something?" Craig asked coldly.

"Yeah. You don't belong here," said the young man, his face contorting in anger.

"You don't have to worry. I'm leaving. Now get out of my way."

The young man pulled out a switchblade and snapped it open, holding it toward Craig hostilely. He looked as though he were preparing to lunge when suddenly the skies opened up and released a torrential downpour.

It was the diversion Craig needed. Ignoring the rain soaking him to the bone, Craig swung his right arm sideways in a single swift motion, grabbed the man's right forearm, and smashed it against the car, knocking the knife from his hand. Craig then raised his leg and slammed the pointed toe of his shoe into the man's groin in a powerful blow. The man screamed in agony as he dropped to the ground.

One of his friends charged Craig from the right, but Craig took him down with a powerful fist to the head. As he did, the third man jumped on Craig and knocked him to the ground into a puddle. Craig was on his back, his assailant on top raising a fist high in the air, ready to shatter Craig's skull. Nearly blinded by the rain, Craig quickly rolled to the side, pushing him off, then spun around, smashing him in the face and breaking his nose. Blood mixed on the ground with the rainwater.

Craig pinned the battered man to the pavement by his throat, shouting, "Where's Omar?"

When the man didn't reply, Craig squeezed tighter. "Tell me, you bastard, or I'll kill you."

"Fuck you."

Craig squeezed harder, but as the man's face started to turn purple, Craig suddenly heard a gunshot coming from the soccer field. He sprang to his feet and yanked open the car door. As he did, he saw three more men racing across the soccer field toward him. One was holding a metal pipe in his hand, and another had a gun, which he was firing in Craig's direction. A bullet flew over Craig's head.

Craig reached under his jacket for his gun, swiftly pointing it at the oncoming men. He forced himself to focus his sights through the blinding rain, aimed for the pipe, and then pulled the trigger, hitting the pipe squarely and knocking it to the ground.

Stunned, the three stopped in their tracks. Craig took advantage of their surprise to throw himself into the car and start the engine. He floored the accelerator, but as he peeled away he could still hear gunshots coming from the soccer field. A bullet smashed the back window, and Craig ducked to avoid the flying shards of glass. He continued to drive, watching the men in the rearview mirror chasing after him on foot. He reached the corner and darted out into a stream of cars. Ignoring the honking horns, he made a sharp turn in a direction that had a reasonably open road. Traffic was his enemy. If he had to stop, they might catch up.

It wasn't until he reached the highway heading south that he felt relief. Once he arrived at the Arc de Triomphe, he pulled off onto Avenue de Friedland and parked the car. The rain had stopped. His clothes were soaked and muddy. As he got out of the car, he brushed the glass off the back of his jacket and pulled a few pieces from his hair. Fortunately he wasn't bleeding. And he was glad he had taken insurance for the rental.

Walking back to the Bristol, he checked his phone and saw a text message from Elizabeth. "Should be at the Bristol 6 p.m. Made dinner reservations 8 p.m. at L'Arome. Love, Elizabeth."

In the hotel suite, Craig sent his wet clothes off to housekeeping and took a long shower, washing his cuts and scrapes with warm, soapy water. He felt exhausted from the last few days, which surprised him. Normally he was never tired—maybe age was starting to creep up on him. He dismissed the thought impatiently, running through everything he'd done since he had gone for a run Wednesday morning. Now it was Saturday afternoon and he'd been going nonstop. No wonder he was tired.

He left a message at the front desk for them to give Elizabeth a key to the suite, climbed into bed, and immediately fell sound asleep.

The next thing Craig felt was a woman's warm mouth enveloping his cock. While she sucked, she ran her fingernails over his balls and his upper thigh. Craig felt himself getting rock hard. He was convinced he was dreaming until he heard Elizabeth voice telling him she wanted him inside of her.

They moved their bodies together, gradually increasing the tempo, faster and faster, until they came together in a mighty climax.

Craig slid off and held her in his arms. "That was a helluva way to wake me."

"I hope you don't mind. I've never come home to find you sleeping before."

"I'll have to nap more often."

"Now you have to feed me," she said. "This woman has appetites."

"So I've noticed."

*       *       *

L'Arome, on Rue Saint-Philippe-du-Roule, was a gem of restaurant with an incredible chef, making it one of their favorites in Paris. Their usual table was just in front of the kitchen and relatively isolated, so they could talk discreetly if they kept their voices down.

They ate crab in a tomato gelée followed by a sublime lobster in butter sauce, then grilled filet of beef, all the while sipping on an excellent Saint-Joseph the sommelier had recommended. Craig listened entranced as Elizabeth told him about Nick and what she had learned in Budapest. He was especially blown away when she told him that Nick's real parents were Peter and Emma; and the kid had no idea.

When she had finished telling him everything, Craig told her about Israel and Clichy, playing down the attack, but explaining how frustrated he was in his search for Omar.

When dessert, an excellent chocolate mousse, came Elizabeth said, "After dinner can we stop at the apartment to pick up some of my things?"

"Sure. Pierre has a man in front watching the building. I'll let him know."

"You really think we have to stay at the Bristol?"

"Definitely. The people who killed Peter and Emma must have realized that Nicholas escaped the fire. They want to find him and kill him."

"Why would they want to kill the kid?" she asked.

"They're worried Peter may have told him something or that he could recognize the men who set the fire," Craig explained.

"But how would they have made the connection between Nicholas and me?"

"I've been thinking about that. My guess is that they had a man on the street watching Emma Miller's house. They probably saw Nick leaving with you."

Elizabeth paused, dipping her spoon into the mousse. "They could have recognized me, I guess."

"Of course. You appear on TV quite a bit. Goons like this may not be able to read, but they certainly watch TV. I think you had better cancel the baseball game tomorrow."

She shook her head emphatically. "I couldn't do that to Nick. On the way back from the airport to the Bristol I stopped at the clinic. They've made no progress on his speech, and he looked so sad. Dr. Cardin told me that's how he always looks, and one of the nurse's told me that he cried through the night. You can't blame the kid—he's lost every person he had in the world. It tore at my heart. The only time he smiled is when I reminded him about the baseball game tomorrow. This game means so much to Nick. I can't disappoint him. Besides if he were to play, that might trigger his speech returning."

"Dr. Cardin said that?" Craig asked.

She shook her head. "No, but it seems reasonable."

"Please don't get angry at me, Elizabeth, if I tell you something."

She straightened up. "What's that?"

"Normally, you're levelheaded and clear-thinking, which makes you an incredible reporter. But you've become so emotional about this kid that it's clouding your judgment."

"I don't think it is," she said stubbornly.

"It really is. You're totally ignoring the danger you'll be exposing Nick to, as well as yourself, if you bring him to that baseball game."

"These people will never find out about it."

He shook his head. "You're kidding yourself. Last month *Figaro* ran a feature about the Sunday morning baseball game American teams play in the Bois de Boulogne. You were mentioned in the article. 'The star pitcher is a woman, Elizabeth Crowder, the *International Herald* foreign news editor,' they wrote. If someone Googles you, the article will come up."

"But this means so much to Nick. I can't disappoint him."

Craig took a deep breath and exhaled. He realized he would never change her mind. There was only one solution.

"Listen, Elizabeth," Craig said. "I was planning to work on my car with the mechanic tomorrow morning. I'll cancel that and go to the game with you and Nick. I'll be armed and ready for them."

She reached over, grabbed his hand, and squeezed it. "I love you, Craig Paige."

*       *       *

Sunday morning over breakfast in the suite Craig asked Elizabeth whether she had informed her teammates that Nick would be playing that day.

"I emailed them when I was in Budapest. Told them my twelve-year-old nephew Jonathan was visiting from the US, and that he can't speak as a result of trauma, but he's a terrific second baseman. Carl, who's our regular second baseman, said he'd sit this one out, and the others agreed."

"Are you pitching?"

"Yeah."

Recalling the break-in at their apartment, Craig still believed the baseball game was a foolish and potentially risky move, but he had no intention of rehashing that decision. He had learned long ago that once Elizabeth had made up her mind on something, it was hopeless to try to change it. Besides, he now saw a potential upside. He wanted to get some more information about who broke into their apartment and what they wanted. This might flush them out, though it meant placing Nick in the line of fire.

Before they left, Elizabeth put on a navy T-shirt with white letters on the front that said "Paris Yanks" and had the number 3 on the back. She looked nervous as she tucked a second T-shirt into her bag.

"Did I ever tell you that you look sexy in that shirt?" Craig asked, trying to get her to relax.

"I believe you've mentioned that several times," she replied, trying to smile. But her voice betrayed her anxiety.

With Elizabeth behind the wheel of the Audi, they drove to the clinic. Craig rode shotgun with a Glock pistol in his hand, his eyes constantly roving around the surrounding. He breathed a sigh of relief when he determined that nobody was following them.

When they arrived, Elizabeth went into the clinic alone while Craig explained their plan to Pierre, who was parked at the end of the driveway.

"Do you want me to come with you?" Pierre asked.

Craig thought about it for a minute. Pierre would be a help, but there was a possibility there could be an attack on the clinic if they didn't realize the boy was gone. Pierre could help prevent harm being done to Dr. Cardin and the clinic if he stayed, and he might be able to capture the assailants, too. Craig was sure he could protect Nick and Elizabeth himself.

"No, I think it's better if you stay here," he replied.

A few minutes later, Elizabeth came out of the clinic. Right behind her was Nick, also wearing a Paris Yanks shirt, bat in one hand, glove in the other, and a huge smile on his face. Though guarding him would be difficult, seeing his smile made Craig believe it was worth the risk.

When Nick approached Craig, he gave Craig a high five. Craig opened the back door of the Audi for Nick while Elizabeth got behind the wheel again. The sun was shining brightly, and they made it to the ball field in the Bois de Boulogne without incident. It was a gorgeous summer day in Paris.

The other members of Elizabeth's team, seven men and one woman, were already on the field warming up. The opposing team hadn't arrived yet. Nick raced out to second base while Elizabeth threw warm-up pitches with the catcher. Meanwhile Craig found a good observation position on a slightly elevated grassy area in front of a storage shed behind the Yanks bench on the third base side. That gave him good visibility of the area. Though the temperature was rising and it would soon be hot, Craig wore a light jacket, allowing him to conceal his holstered gun.

He glanced at the field. Nick was tossing a ball around with the other infielders. The kid was graceful and self-confident, and he had a strong arm. Nick could definitely play ball. And surprisingly, he didn't seem nervous playing with adults.

A few minutes later two gray minivans arrived. Craig watched anxiously as the side doors opened. Eight men and four women climbed out, all wearing red shirts with yellow lettering that said "Nationals." The irony struck Craig. Even in Paris it was New York versus Washington. Craig looked around again. Nothing suspicious.

They played a six inning game, with the Nationals up first. Elizabeth, really smoking the ball, struck out the side. Nick was batting sixth and didn't get up in the first inning.

In the top of the second, a Nationals batter hit a sharp grounder between first and second. Nick got a good jump on the ball, fielded it smoothly, and tossed it to the first baseman for the out.

"Way to go, Jonathan," the shortstop shouted.

Nick was up at bat in the bottom of the second with the bases empty. After taking a ball and two called strikes, he whacked the fourth pitch, a line drive, between the shortstop and third baseman for a solid single.

The next hitter doubled to right field and Nick raced home with the first run. Nick was beaming as the other players gave him high fives. Craig was thrilled for the kid, but his joy rapidly dissipated when he saw two men standing in a cluster of trees just off the right field line, halfway between the first baseman and the right fielder. Both were blonde and beefy and could easily be members of a Russian hit squad. They seemed to be watching the game.

The next couple of innings passed without incident, with the two men remaining in the same position. Nick singled again in the fifth but didn't score. In the field, he caught a line drive for an out and scooped up two more ground balls, which he tossed to the first baseman for outs.

With the Yanks coming to bat in the bottom of the sixth, the score was tied at one apiece. Elizabeth was the second batter up. Craig wondered whether she had noticed the two men who were still standing off the first base line. If she had, it certainly hadn't distracted her excellent pitching. Now he was anxious to see how she'd hit.

The count went to two balls and two strikes. The Nationals pitcher leaned back and let fly with a fastball. Elizabeth was waiting for it. She pulled back her bat and swung hard, smashing the ball over the head of the left fielder. The ball was still rolling when it landed in a creek.

Craig saw Nick jump to his feet. When Elizabeth had run the bases and was back at home plate, Nick shouted, "Great hit, Elizabeth!"

Elizabeth stopped in her tracks, then raced over to Nick. "What did you say?"

"Great hit, Elizabeth."

"You can talk!" she cried, hugging him.

When Craig glanced at the right field line, he saw that the two blond men were gone. He wanted to believe they had just come to watch the game, but it was too unlikely.

Remaining vigilant, Craig moved down the hill close to Elizabeth and Nick. The other Yanks were congratulating Elizabeth and telling Nick what a great game he had played.

As the others drifted away, Elizabeth said to Nick, "We have to get ice cream to celebrate you getting your voice back!"

"Yes!" said Nick. "I love ice cream. And we have to celebrate your home run, too."

Craig cringed. If Elizabeth had asked him, he would have said they should get to a safe place as soon as possible, but he wasn't about to ruin the party.

Elizabeth drove them to a nearby Häagen-Dazs, and once inside, Craig picked out a table in the back that had a clear view of the front door while Elizabeth and Nick got the ice cream. Elizabeth didn't ask Craig what he wanted—she knew he always ordered java chip with hot fudge. Elizabeth had pralines and cream with hot fudge, and Nick had a banana split. Once they reached the table, ice cream in hand, Craig offered Nick the seat between him and Elizabeth.

After Nick had eaten about half of his banana split, Elizabeth said to him, "You're a very brave boy coming to Paris all by yourself."

Nick put his spoon down. "My grandfather told me what to do if anything like this ever happened," he said, his voice wavering slightly. "I didn't want to run away when he and Grandma were in trouble, but he ordered me to follow his instructions and get to Paris as quickly as I could, where Emma Miller would take care of me. He drilled me on it so many times my reaction felt almost automatic."

Through the open door, Craig caught sudden movement out of the corner of his eye. Whipping around, he saw the two blond men running toward the ice cream parlor. Each had a gun in his hand. Craig didn't know whether they wanted to seize Nick or kill him, but it didn't matter. With other patrons in the shop, he couldn't let them get inside or there'd be a bloodbath.

Reacting instantly, Craig reached for his gun. At the same moment, Elizabeth yelled, "Under the table," pushing Nick down and shielding him with her body.

When the men were just a few steps away from the open door of the shop, Craig raised his gun and opened fire. He hit both of them squarely before either of them could get off a shot. People in the shop were screaming hysterically, and the two ice cream servers hit the ground behind the counter.

Gun in hand, Craig ran toward the door. Both men were on the ground. One was writhing and cursing, but the other was mostly still aside from the ragged breaths that struggled from his lungs. The bullet had hit him in the chest, and he was close to death. Craig turned to the other man, who was bleeding from his shoulder. As he got close to him, Craig saw him slip something into his mouth.

Damn it. Cyanide.

He wanted to force the man to talk, to find out who sent them, but it was probably too late for that. He reached into the man's mouth, but the pill was already gone. Saliva was forming, and the smell of cyanide was in the air.

"Who sent you?" Craig shouted, grabbing him around the neck. The man gave Craig a crazed smile before his eyes flickered shut for the last time. It was hopeless. He checked for IDs, but neither man was carrying one.

Craig looked at the man's muscular right arm. He had a tattoo of a vampire bat that Craig recognized—he was a member of a gang in Moscow that Kuznov used for jobs, which included executing pesky journalists. The Russian president had to be behind this attack, Craig decided. Maybe these were the thugs that had broken into Craig and Elizabeth's apartment as well.

Behind him, Craig heard one of the ice cream shop employees calling the police. Though Jean-Claude could help him get out of dealing with the police, he didn't want to use that chit. They had to get out of there before the police came.

Elizabeth and Nick had gotten up from the floor and were standing next to the table.

"Let's go," he called to Elizabeth.

She grabbed Nick's hand, and the three of them ran to the Audi. Craig got behind the wheel and floored the accelerator at the sound of approaching sirens. As they drove, they passed police cars coming the other way.

Craig quickly realized they were being followed by a black Citroën, although it looked like the only person in the car was the driver. Craig drove fast, weaving in and out of lanes, but the Citroën kept pace. Craig wasn't concerned—once they reached the highway, he was confident he'd lose him.

Once they reached the ramp, Craig immediately cut across three lanes to the left. The Citroën followed suit. As an exit approached on the right, Craig waited for the last possible second, then cut across the two right lanes, ignoring the honking horns.

The Citroën tried to follow. Craig heard the sound of a crash, and through the rearview mirror he saw that a Mercedes had collided with the Citroën and sent it spinning back toward the median barrier. *Too bad*, Craig thought.

Staying well above the speed limit, Craig drove to the automobile race track where he practiced. He had an office where they could talk.

Without a race that Sunday, the track was deserted. When they were seated in Craig's office with the door open to afford Craig an unobstructed view outside, he asked Nick, "How are you doing? Are you scared or upset?"

The boy looked a little shaken, but he was still smiling. "Nice shooting, Craig. I . . . I think I'm okay. I saw that man who was driving the black Citroën at Emma Miller's apartment when I first got to Paris. He was watching me."

"That's very useful," Craig said. "It explains how they knew from the get-go that you were with Elizabeth."

"Were those men who tried to attack us at the ice cream shop Russian?" Nick asked.

"They were," Craig affirmed. "How did you know?"

"That evening of the fire I snuck down to the basement to watch a Nats game. It was around midnight, because the game was in Los Angeles, and my grandparents were asleep on the second floor. Suddenly, I heard two men on the first floor. They were intruders who had gotten through the security system—they were talking in Russian."

"How did you know it was Russian?" Elizabeth asked.

"Grandpa hated the Russians. They made him suffer when he was a boy in Budapest. And he was sure they had killed my parents and made it look like a boating accident."

"Did he have any proof?" asked Craig.

"No, and the police couldn't find anything," said Nick, shaking his head. "But my dad was a good sailor and it was a calm day. My grandpa thought there must have been foul play. At that point, Grandpa made me learn Russian from a tutor. He said I had to know my enemy."

"Nick," Elizabeth interjected, "your grandpa told you to go to Emma Miller in Paris if anything happened . . ."

"That's right."

"But what about your grandpa's father, your great-grandfather Zoltan? He lives in the Washington area. Why didn't your grandpa ask you to go there?"

"Great-grandpa Zoltan lives in Deerwood, a facility for old people. He's not sick, but he's ninety-one. He has trouble walking, so he couldn't take care of me. And also . . ." Nick hesitated.

"You can tell us, Nick," Elizabeth encouraged him.

"Great-grandpa Zoltan always seemed angry at my grandpa. They did not have a good relationship. I asked Grandpa about it a couple of times and he said that some things had happened between them a long time ago. When I asked what they were, he said he would tell me one day. But . . ." Nick choked up. "Now he never can . . ."

"I know how difficult all this is for you," Elizabeth said, putting her hand on his shoulder. "You're such a brave boy, Nick. Craig and I want to protect you."

Nick nodded slowly, looking at her.

"To do that," she continued, "we want to find out who killed your grandparents and Emma Miller and make sure they're punished. While we're doing that, we need a safe place for you to stay. I think the clinic would be best. Even though you can speak, Dr. Cardin will let you stay there. Everyone, including Dr. Cardin, thinks you're Jonathan Hart, so that's some protection. Also, they have good security at the clinic."

"And I already have a man stationed there," Craig interjected. "I'll add a couple more armed men—former French special ops—to watch the facility from the outside."

"With all of that, are you okay with going back to Dr. Cardin's clinic?" Elizabeth asked.

"How long do you think it will be for?" Nick asked.

"I don't know for sure. My guess is a week at most."

Nick nodded. "That's okay."

Elizabeth looked at Nick. "You had a cell phone in the black case when you arrived in Paris. Do you still have it?"

"Yes."

Elizabeth wrote down her phone number and gave it to Nick.

"Call us anytime, day or night, if you see anything suspicious."

"Wait," he said. "I just remembered something else."

They both looked at him alertly.

"About a week ago on a Friday Grandpa and I were watching a Nats game on TV when he received a call from Emma. He seemed upset. I was pretending to watch the game, but I was really listening to him." Nick looked chagrined. "I know I shouldn't have, but I couldn't help it."

"What happened?" Elizabeth asked.

"Grandpa was angry. He wanted Emma to do something, and she was refusing. Grandpa shouted something about how he wouldn't let Szabo and Kuznov get away it—that it would take them back to 1956 with Russian troops in Hungary again."

"He said Szabo and Kuznov?" Elizabeth asked.

"Uh-huh. I don't know what Grandpa wanted Emma to do, but finally she agreed to it. When he hung up I wanted to ask him what they were arguing about, but I didn't want him to know I'd been listening, so I didn't say anything."

Craig checked the date on his phone. "That Friday was July 28. The Nats played the Mets at home, an evening game. Is that right?"

"For sure. The Nats won three to two with a homer in the ninth."

"Glad you remembered that," Elizabeth said. "It could be important. Now let's get you back to the clinic."

As they stood up to leave, Nick examined the photos in the office of Craig in a racing uniform next to his rebuilt blue Jag XK8.

"Hey, Craig," Nick said. "When this is all over, will you take me for a ride in your car on the track?"

"Absolutely. And we'll get that sucker up to 125 miles per hour."

"That'd be awesome!" said Nick.

"No, you won't," cried Elizabeth.

"We just won't tell her," Craig added in a mock whisper.

\*       \*       \*

After dropping off Nick, Craig and Elizabeth returned to their Bristol suite.

"We have to decide on our next move," said Craig.

"That can wait until morning." Elizabeth picked up the phone and reserved a table downstairs at Le Epicure, the Bristol's gourmet restaurant. "We're going to celebrate," she told Craig.

"What are we celebrating?"

"Life. We dodged bullets today. That calls for a party. So let's clean up and get going."

Two hours later, while eating some of the most incredible food they'd had in a long time, including duck and line-caught seabass from St. Gilles, accompanied by a 2005 Chambertin by Latour, Elizabeth and Craig talked about trips they hoped to take and places they wanted to go. They didn't say a word about Peter Toth or Amos. Then for dessert they shared an ethereal orb of dark chocolate with a gold leaf on top. They finished off dinner with glasses of Armagnac.

On the elevator ride back up to their suite, Craig put his arms around Elizabeth and held her tight, leaning in to kiss her deeply. Their bodies fused together until the elevator stopped.

Back in their suite, on fire with passion, Elizabeth tossed her bag on the floor and Craig pulled her close to resume kissing her. Tugging at his shirt and fumbling with the buttons, they began to undress each other.

"I love you so much," she said.

"And I love you."

Suddenly, he heard a cell phone ringing in the bag Elizabeth had dropped on the floor.

"Ignore it," Craig said.

She pulled away. "I can't. From the ring I can tell it's Betty on the encrypted phone she gave me. It might be about Nick."

"Thanks, Betty," he grumbled.

Elizabeth picked up the phone. Craig heard her say, "Hi Betty . . . . I can talk. . . . I'm here with Craig. Just the two of us. I'll put it on speaker."

Elizabeth placed the phone on the desk. His erection withering, Craig pulled up a chair and sat down near the desk. Elizabeth grabbed a robe and tossed him one.

"Can you hear me?" Betty asked.

"Yes," Elizabeth replied.

"Hi Craig."

"Always happy to hear from you," Craig replied, suppressing his annoyance.

"I just received information from the FBI director."

"Go ahead."

"They were examining Peter Toth's finances."

"What'd they find?" Craig asked curiously.

"On July 28 Peter transferred ten million euros to Emma Miller's bank account at Credit Suisse in Paris. A day later that same sum was transferred from her bank to an Andorra bank, to an account in the name of Omar Basayev, a Russian citizen from Chechnya."

Craig was astounded. He didn't think Peter was perfect, but he wouldn't have guessed that he'd hire a terrorist. He also wondered how Peter knew Omar.

Pushing that aside, Craig noted, "Our two strands are converging— Omar's killing of Amos and the murders of Peter and Emma."

"What's your next move?" Betty asked.

"I want to call a time-out," Craig said. "Let me and Elizabeth think about this for a little bit, and we'll get back to you."

With his mind fuzzy from the glass of champagne, three glasses of red wine, and Armagnac he had drunk at dinner, Craig went into the bathroom and splashed cold water on his face. When he returned to the living room of the suite, Elizabeth was sitting at the desk writing.

"What are you doing?" Craig asked.

"Making a timeline," she explained. "I think better when I can see it. According to Betty, Peter transferred the ten million euros to Emma on July 28. That evening in Washington Nick said Emma called Peter and they argued."

"She must have been resisting whatever his arrangement was with Omar."

"Exactly," Emma agreed. "What Nick overheard Peter telling Emma is critical. Peter must have learned that Szabo had made a deal with Kuznov that would enable Russia to bring troops into Hungary. Betty told me Szabo was negotiating a trade deal with Kuznov for the supply of nuclear energy, so this must be what Russia is getting in return. Once

Peter found out, he could have hired Omar to kill Szabo." Elizabeth put down her pencil. "That would make sense. Gyorgy told me that at one point Peter mentioned wanting to kill Szabo, but he didn't think he had ever attempted to act on it."

"That's valuable information," Craig said. "This time Peter was prepared to act on it and Emma was balking—for whatever reason. I'm sure she didn't have the same level of hatred toward Russia that Peter had, since she didn't suffer in the same way. Peter was asking for a helluva lot to make her an accomplice in a political assassination of the Hungarian prime minister."

"But she caved," Elizabeth noted. "And wired the money to Omar the next day."

"Once Omar got his money, he must have gone to Paris to arrange the hit on Szabo," Craig added, excitedly pacing around the suite as he talked.

"Why Paris?"

"Possibly he was recruiting helpers there. Or perhaps Szabo is planning to come to Paris and that's where the hit will be. Regardless, Amos was trying to find out what Omar was doing in Paris, so Omar killed him. Meantime, Kuznov found out that Peter wanted to wreck his alliance with Szabo and arranged to have Peter killed."

Elizabeth looked down at the paper on the desk. "I think we're right," she said, "but our analysis raises one big question: Once Peter was dead, why didn't Omar close up shop and head home to Grozny? No doubt Peter's ten million was only a down payment. Peter's estate would hardly have sued Omar for breach of contract."

Craig laughed. "You hang out with a lot of lawyers."

"But I'm serious."

Craig thought about it for a minute, and then threw up his hands. "I can't answer that. What I do know is that this situation is now too large for the two of us. We have to go to Washington and brief Betty. This is so important I'm sure she'll want to involve President Worth. We can work with Betty and the president on a strategy going forward. Worth and I parted on good terms after that Ascona business. Fortunately, I kept my mouth shut for a change."

"Even though he used and manipulated you."

"You don't have to put it that way."

"Those were your words," Elizabeth reminded him.

"Fair enough. But the bottom line is that President Worth was grateful to me and I have an entrée to go back to him. Let's call Betty back and ask her to set it up. We can fly to Washington tomorrow."

"We?"

"Yes, I'd like you to come because you have firsthand knowledge and have been closer to the Hungarian angle. Is there any reason you can't go?"

"One twelve-year-old boy," she said. "I can't leave Nick here alone while you and I are half a world away. I would never forgive myself is something happened to him."

"We have security at the clinic."

"I don't care."

She was looking hard at Craig, and he could tell it was hopeless to argue. But then it occurred to him that Nick could be an asset in Washington.

"We could bring Nick," Craig proposed. "Having him with us could be an advantage. If President Worth hears from Nick what Peter said about Russian troops moving back into Hungary, it will underscore what's on the line for the US. Knowing President Worth, I doubt that he will want to be another Eisenhower."

Elizabeth seemed relieved. "Good point. We can pick Nick up at the clinic in the morning on the way to the airport."

They called Betty on speaker. The CIA director was a quick study. She interrupted Craig after his opening few sentences and said, "Hold tight. I'll check with Karen and see when I can get you on the calendar."

A minute later, she came back. "Tuesday, 3:00 p.m. is your slot. She blocked out an hour but hopes you won't need it all."

"Excellent," Craig said. "One other thing."

"With you there's always something else."

"Can you arrange for two armed FBI agents to meet us at the airport and stick with us 24–7 while we're in Washington? We'll be staying at my Georgetown house, but we need two units in case Elizabeth and I decide to split up."

"Will do."

"And restrict the purpose of our meeting with Worth on a need to know basis."

"What are you concerned about?" Betty asked.

"The Potomac fire shows that Kuznov has a powerful Washington presence."

"You can say that again," she grumbled. "I heard last month from the FBI director that Kuznov now has scores of agents in Washington. He wants to bring back the Cold War. There is definitely a Russian resurgence."

As soon as they hung up the phone with Betty, Craig called Giuseppe. "Can you come by the Bristol for breakfast at seven tomorrow?"

"I'll be there."

*       *       *

When Giuseppe entered the suite, Craig and Elizabeth's suitcases were packed and standing next to the door.

"You two going somewhere?" Giuseppe asked.

"Your perception of the obvious is acute," Craig said.

Elizabeth came forward to greet Giuseppe, and he kissed her on each cheek. "I'm glad one of you has good manners," he said.

"I have a piece to edit," she said. "I'll be in the other room, so you boys can talk."

Over coffee and croissants, Craig told Giuseppe about everything that had happened the day before and their decision to go to Washington.

"I heard about the ice cream parlor incident," he said. "The surveillance camera in the shop was broken. The French police are going berserk trying to figure out what happened."

"The world's a better place without those two thugs."

"Agreed. What do you need from me at this point?"

"Not a thing. I just wanted to brief you."

Giuseppe tapped his fingers on the table. "I have a thought for you. On September 1, EU member heads of state are meeting in Brussels and Szabo is scheduled to attend."

"With the proximity of Paris to Brussels and the ease of hiring thugs here to help, that could explain why Omar came to Paris to plan his operation," Craig interjected. "Chances are the hit will take place in Brussels. Assuming Omar left Clichy, which is likely, he and his entourage may already be in Brussels, hidden by one of the numerous jihadists cells in that city."

Giuseppe linked the fingers of his hands together. "Brussels is a terrorist's dream: a nightmare to defend and almost impossible to locate a terrorist in. The police don't have anything like the organization in France or Germany. And there are so many damn jihadists, I think they outnumber the police."

"That's a sobering thought," said Craig.

"Well, regardless," Giuseppe replied, "I'll head up there this morning. Get them to launch a manhunt for Omar and beef up security for the September 1 summit. I'll let you know if I learn anything."

## MOSCOW

Monday morning, Russian President Kuznov was becoming increasingly angry as he listened to his finance minister and the chief economist report. He had never known such negative people in his life. Every slide they put on the screen had numbers in red and only red. According to them, GDP, investment, wages, and consumption per person were all sharply down.

To be sure, he realized the Russian economy was encountering stiff headwinds because of low oil prices and declining manufacturing. At the same time, consumer prices were rising sharply. Even with all of that, these Cassandras of gloom and doom were unbelievable. He was seriously considering having them both arrested for crimes against the state and finding replacements that were more optimistic. At that moment, Kuznov's secretary opened the door and said, "Dimitri is here. He says it's urgent."

Kuznov turned to the two officials, "We're finished today. Come back next week with a more realistic assessment."

"But—" the economist began.

The finance minister cut him off. "Yes, sir. We will."

Kuznov hoped Dimitri brought good news, but he was already grateful to his aide for giving him a reason to conclude the economic meeting.

Dimitri's face was flushed with excitement as he entered the room. "Everything has been finalized," he said. "Szabo has agreed to sign the Friendship Pact at a ceremony a week from Wednesday, ten days from now, in Budapest's Parliament Square. In return, I transferred fifty million euros to his bank account at the Republic Bank in Lucerne. He will get the other fifty on Friday, two days after the signing."

"Excellent. That is very good news."

Though it was only noon, Kuznov walked over to a credenza along one wall and pulled out a special vodka made only for him. He poured out a glass for each of them, then he raised his glass. "To the Russian–Hungarian Friendship Pact."

For Kuznov, this agreement was the key to Russia's resurgence and the re-creation of its empire. Under the pact, Russia would be able to station troops in Hungary and operate freely from that country as a base. That meant Russia could control Central Europe again. Then Russian troops could travel west from Russia through Ukraine and north and east from Hungary to conquer Poland, the Czech Republic, and Romania.

Thinking about his just concluded finance and economic meeting, Kuznov saw another advantage. By focusing on foreign conquest and Russia's expansion, Kuznov would increase his popular support. He could divert attention from the economic misery rampant throughout Russia. The people's bellies might not be full but their national pride would be bursting.

"What are the logistics for the execution of the Friendship Pact?" Kuznov asked Dimitri.

"You will fly to Budapest on that Wednesday, arriving at ten o'clock in the morning. The ceremony will be at noon in front of the parliament building. There will not be any advanced public announcement on the subject of the gathering or even that you will be in Budapest. The media will be told Prime Minster Szabo has an important statement to make. That should produce a crowd. You and Szabo will appear on the platform in front of parliament. With so many of the Western leaders away on August vacations, this is the perfect time to do it."

Kuznov broke out in a broad smile, something he rarely did. "Excellent. I will give the order to the generals to begin moving our troops into Hungary on Thursday, the day after the ceremony. Now tell me what happened with Nicholas Toth."

"Boris flew to Moscow last evening and provided me with a report. I thought it would be better if you heard it directly from him. He's waiting outside."

Kuznov frowned. This had to be bad news. Dimitri didn't want to be the one to deliver it. If it had been good, Kuznov knew Dimitri would have provided the report himself, taking credit for the result.

"Bring Boris in," Kuznov snarled.

When the three of them were seated around the conference table, Kuznov stared at Boris who looked away. "Were you able to seize the boy?" he asked.

"No sir, Mr. President," Boris stammered.

"Well, what happened?"

"Elizabeth Crowder brought him to the baseball game in the park. I used two of my best men for the job. I watched everything from a distance and remained in constant contact with them. My men could have easily killed him during the game, but I understood that our primary objective was to capture him and force him to talk."

"Correct," Kuznov said.

"So, I told my men to follow Elizabeth and the boy after the game, when they would have a better chance to seize him. After the game they went to an ice cream shop."

"Who is *they*?" Kuznov asked sharply.

"The boy, Elizabeth, and a man with her. I recognized him from pictures in Elizabeth's apartment to be the Italian race car driver Enrico Marino, who is her boyfriend. I told my men to go into the ice cream shop armed and to seize the boy. I was waiting outside a little distance away."

Kuznov was at the edge of his chair. "What happened then?"

"Before they could get to the kid, Enrico Marino opened fire and killed both of them. He grabbed Elizabeth and the kid and escaped by car before the police got there."

"Didn't you try to stop them?"

"Absolutely, Anatol was in a car a block away. I gave him the order to crash their car and grab the kid. Anatol chased them, but Enrico is a race car driver," Boris added sounding defensive. "He couldn't keep up."

Kuznov sighed deeply. What a bunch of fucking incompetents. He recalled that Elizabeth had been involved with Craig Page when Kuznov had last dealt with him, but that had been a couple of years ago. Still, this shootout sounded like something Page would do.

He turned to Dimitri. "Go outside to Irina and ask her to find out how long Enrico Marino has been racing cars. Also, have her print me a picture of Marino."

Kuznov thought possibly the answer would be about two years, confirming his suspicion that Enrico Marino was really Craig Page.

Two years was the answer Dimitri returned with a few minutes later. The picture Dimitri handed Kuznov didn't look like Craig Page. He must have had plastic surgery, Kuznov decided.

"You know him?" Dimitri asked.

"As Craig Page before plastic surgery."

"The former head of EU Counterterrorism?"

"Precisely. Craig and I have a history. We did some business together before he reinvented himself as Enrico Marino. He's tough and ruthless, but also smart."

"Sounds as if you like him."

"Respect would be more accurate."

"So you think Craig Page killed the two men I sent to grab the boy?"

"Exactly. And he must have figured out they were Russians."

"Suppose he did. What can he do with that information?"

Kuznov leaned back in his chair and closed his eyes, trying to think like Craig Page.

It took Kuznov two minutes to come up with the answer. "Craig Page will fly to Moscow and confront me. He'll demand to know why I wanted to kill or kidnap Nicholas Toth."

"That would be insane," Dimitri said, the disbelief evident on his face. "You're in control here."

"Of course I am, but Page is gutsy. He takes chances no one else would. I learned never to underestimate him."

"Suppose you're right, and—"

Kuznov was irritated. He didn't like his judgments being questioned. "I am right," he said, cutting Dimitri off curtly.

Dimitri's face turned red. "Of course you're right. What should I do to deal with him?"

"Alert all the airports in the country to be on the lookout for Enrico Marino. When he enters the country, tell them to hold him in a detention room and immediately let you know. Then you tell me."

"What will you do with him?"

Kuznov thought about killing Craig, but the former CIA director might have friends in high places in Washington, and as long as he could get Craig out of circulation, he wouldn't pose a threat to Kuznov.

"Transfer him to a prison and lock him up until after the ceremony in Budapest. I don't want Craig Page or anyone to stop that ceremony from taking place. I'm afraid if he were on the loose, he'd find a way to do that."

"What do we do about the kid, Nicholas?" Dimitri asked.

Now that Page was in the act, Kuznov had no doubt that Craig had learned everything Nick knew and that he had stashed the boy somewhere so hidden or well-fortified that they would never be able to get to him. Recognizing a hopeless situation when he saw one, Kuznov decided not to waste any more resources in a futile effort to find the kid. Instead, they had to shift their attention to Craig Page.

Kuznov ordered, "Forget about the kid. We have Craig Page in our sights. As long as we control Craig, we control the situation."

## Washington and Maryland

When Elizabeth told Nick early Monday morning at the clinic that he would be flying to Washington with her and Craig and that he might even be going to the White House to meet the president, the boy was thrilled. As Elizabeth helped him pack, Craig was outside conferring with their security for the ride to the airport and in the terminal.

An eventless two hours later they were in an Air France business cabin winging their way to Washington. Elizabeth was on the window, Nick next to her, and Craig across the aisle. When people saw them, Elizabeth thought, they looked like a happy family.

On the flight, Craig and Nick watched action movies and Elizabeth read a history of the 1956 revolution. She wanted to learn more about Zoltan Toth, who she was planning to meet with as soon as they arrived in Washington. Her hope was that Zoltan, notwithstanding what Nick had said about his relationship with Peter, might be able to shed some light on what Peter was planning.

Elizabeth read through events leading up to the revolt and its early days, much of which she had heard from Gyorgy's father. Finally, she came to material about Zoltan Toth.

> While the cease-fire held in Budapest, Zoltan Toth, the special emissary of the Free Hungarian Government, arrived at the UN. "We cannot believe that we are alone," Toth said. "We cannot believe that the world will sit by passively and let our freedom be crushed, the flowering of our manhood annihilated." To the American government, Zoltan Toth pleaded, "You told us to revolt. We believed in you. Now, help us."

Elizabeth saw a picture of Zoltan Toth taken at the UN. Glancing at Nick in the seat next to her, she was struck by their resemblance.

The author went on to describe Zoltan Toth as "a freedom fighter turned diplomat," who was earning high marks with diplomats at the UN. Elizabeth read:

> Zoltan Toth was born in Budapest in 1920, the oldest son of a judge and well-respected legal scholar. It was always expected that Zoltan Toth would become a lawyer himself, and he did not disappoint his father, who saw that dream realized when Toth completed his education at Eötvös József College, the elite training school for lawyers, only months before the Germans began their invasion of Hungary. During the war both of Toth's parents were killed by Germans.

> After the war, Zoltan Toth joined the Communist Party. He became a practicing lawyer in Budapest and an articulate spokesman for the government in international forums. Later he, like many other members of the party, became disillusioned with the severity of the regime and joined the freedom fighters. During the early days of the struggle, Zoltan Toth manned a rifle that he seized from an AVH guard. Then words became his weapons.

Toth was married, with an eight-year-old son at the time. His wife, Anna, and son, Peter, did not come to New York with Zoltan Toth, but rather remained in Hungary.

Zoltan Toth failed to gain any support from either the UN or the United States. In Washington, his words fell on deaf ears. All of the attention of John Foster Dulles's State Department was riveted on Egypt. The seizure of the Suez Canal by Britain and France had so infuriated Dulles and President Eisenhower that they had little time for other concerns. The dignity of Nasser, the Egyptian dictator, had to be preserved at all costs. America's oldest and best allies had to be punished. In any case, Dulles and Eisenhower had no desire to confront Russia at this critical time.

Zoltan Toth then received an urgent message from his colleagues in Budapest reporting that the Russians had begun a military attack on the city. He returned from Washington to New York, driven nearly to the point of despair, and again pleaded Hungary's cause before the UN Security Council. "It is now a matter of life and death," he said. "It will be death for thousands of our people if you do not act immediately."

The Soviet ambassador calmly responded that Mr. Toth's hysterics were totally uncalled for. "Just now," he said, "our negotiations in Budapest are making great progress. Give us a three-day recess, and it will all be ended peacefully."

The Western nations agreed. The three-day recess was voted for, prompting the *New York Times* to conclude that "the big Western powers appear to have decided to keep the Hungarian question to one side for the moment, until such time as it becomes clear that the anti-Soviet rebellion has either attained its objectives or has been checked."

Without any help from the US or the UN, the result was inevitable. The Red Army smashed into Budapest destroying everything and everyone in its path.

The author included a dozen photographs showing the devastation in Budapest. Rubble was everywhere, and dead bodies littered the streets.

Looking at them made a powerful impression on Elizabeth. It was outrageous that the US government, after urging an uprising, had permitted this slaughter to take place.

She turned back to two sentences which had stuck with her. "Zoltan's wife, Anna, and son, Peter, did not come to New York with Zoltan Toth, but rather remained in Hungary."

She hoped that Zoltan could tell her what happened to Peter then and afterwards. Her reporter's instinct told her that the trail to understanding the fire at Peter's house in Potomac began when Peter was eight years old in Budapest in 1956.

*       *       *

When Elizabeth, Craig, and Nick exited baggage claim at Dulles Airport, two teams of FBI agents were waiting for them. One drove Craig and Nick to Craig's house in Georgetown, while the other took Elizabeth to Deerwood Senior Facility in Potomac. It was a hot and muggy day—par for the course for Washington in August. Elizabeth did not miss the summer weather of the nation's capital, which had been built on a swamp.

Deerwood was a high-end operation with three stages as residents moved from apartments to full-time assisted living and then nursing care. Elizabeth imagined the fees were astronomical, but Peter had been wealthy, and according to Nick, Peter had been paying the bills.

After stepping out of the FBI car on the Deerwood premises, Elizabeth went right to the director's office. Mary Jane Gorman, the director of Deerwood, was a kindly gray-haired woman.

Elizabeth identified herself as a friend of Peter Toth's and said she'd like to talk to Zoltan.

"Terrible accident that fire," Mary Jane said. "Zoltan was very upset when he first learned about it, although he's starting to do a little better now."

"I understand that his mind is very sharp."

"Incredible for someone that age."

"Where can I find him?" Elizabeth asked.

"Zoltan spends a lot of time sitting outside in the garden in the back, often reading. Let me take a look."

She stood up, turned to the window behind her desk, and looked out. "He's there now. I'll take you out."

Mary Jane led Elizabeth along an immaculate, blue-carpeted corridor and through a door behind the building. They were in a well-kept garden filled with flowers. Elizabeth saw a solitary figure seated on a wooden bench dressed in gray slacks and a white shirt. He was clean-shaven, with a thick head of bushy white hair and black-framed glasses. Next to the bench was a walker. He was dozing, and his book had fallen to the ground at his feet.

"Mr. Toth," Mary Jane said as they approached, waking him up, "you have a visitor. This is Elizabeth Crowder. She's a friend of Peter's."

Zoltan looked intently at Elizabeth, trying to decide if he recognized her.

"Well, I'll leave you two alone," Mary Jane said and withdrew.

Zoltan was alone in the garden. Elizabeth picked up his book and handed it to him before pulling over a chair.

"Have I met you before?" Zoltan asked.

Deciding what to divulge was tricky, Elizabeth thought. She hated lying to Zoltan, but she couldn't tell him his great-grandson was still alive.

"We haven't met, Mr. Toth. I live in Paris, which was where I became acquainted with Peter." Well that was sort of true. "He was an amazing individual. I was so sorry to learn of his death, and I flew here for the memorial service tomorrow."

"It's an awful experience," Zoltan said, his eyes filled with pain, "to have a child die, even if a parent is as old as I am." He shook his head and, seeming to recover himself, asked, "What do you do in Paris, Miss Crowder?"

"I'm a newspaper reporter with the *International Herald*. Actually the foreign news editor."

He looked at Elizabeth for a moment without saying a word. She guessed he was trying to decide whether he should talk to her or not. Elizabeth frequently evoked that reaction when people first learned she was a reporter. Some decided they had to be careful lest something troublesome appear in one of her articles; others decided they could use the press to achieve some objective. She hoped that Zoltan fell into the latter category, that way she might learn something useful.

Finally, he said, "I think the Russians set the fire and killed Peter, Reka, and Nick."

"Why do you say that, Mr. Toth?"

"About a week ago or so, I'm not sure how long, I lose track of time, Peter came to me. He said he wanted to forgive me, and that he had a plan to repay the Russians for everything they did to us. Not just in Hungary but in murdering Viktor and Ellina, too.'"

"Did he have any evidence that the Russians killed Viktor?"

"If he did, he didn't tell me, but losing his son, his only child, was unbearable." He paused, and then added, "I, too, lost mine, more or less, when he was just a child."

"Did he tell you what he planned to do?"

"I asked him, but he wouldn't say. Only that I would read about it in the newspaper. I told him to be careful." Zoltan took a deep breath. "So that's why I think the Russians killed him. They found out what he was planning to do and murdered him before he could act."

Elizabeth thought about what Mary Jane had said. Zoltan's mind was incredibly sharp. He had put together what had happened.

Zoltan said, "You're probably wondering why I've told you all this. After all, you're a stranger."

"That thought has occurred to me."

"If you're a reporter who covers international stories, I figure you might start digging and make out a case against the Russians for the fire, or at least tell someone in the FBI or the police. Will you do that?"

"I will investigate the fire. I promise you that."

He nodded with satisfaction.

"Let me ask you," Elizabeth said, proceeding gingerly into what had to be a sensitive family matter, "you told me a few minutes ago that Peter told you that he finally forgave you."

"That's right," he replied softly, perhaps sorry that he had told her that.

"Can I ask you to explain what for?"

When he didn't immediately respond, she added, "It might be relevant to your son's death."

He took a deep breath. "How much do you know about my life in 1956?"

"That you were a hero of the revolution. That Imre Nagy sent you to the US to plead Hungary's case at the UN and in Washington."

"At which I failed miserably."

"You can't blame yourself," said Elizabeth. "You were playing with a stacked deck."

"I wanted my wife, Anna, and son, Peter, to come with me in case I wasn't able to return to Hungary. I had arranged for them to come."

"So what happened?"

"The plan was for Peter and me to ride in the back of an army truck to the Austrian border. I was in a Hungarian soldier's uniform. We covered Peter with a tarp on the floor. That way we made it through Russian checkpoints."

Elizabeth was at the edge of her chair. "And Anna?"

"I set it up for a Hungarian farmer to pick her up at our house. She had papers showing that she was his wife. She was supposed to meet us at the border crossing. I had bribed the guards who were there until midnight. The next shift would never have let me cross. Peter and I arrived at a little after ten. Anna should have been there by eleven, but she never came."

"Why not?"

"I learned later that Anna had changed her mind at the last minute. Perhaps she was afraid that she wouldn't be able to return to her beloved Hungary. So she sent the farmer away."

"Why didn't you take Peter with you?"

"I planned to, but he became frightened when his mother didn't come. I waited until the last possible minute for Anna to come. At five minutes to midnight, Peter ran into the woods to find his mother. The guards told me that I had to cross the border immediately, or I would have no chance of getting to Austria, and from there to the US. It was impossible to catch Peter in time to cross. So I ran toward the Austrian border." Zoltan had tears of shame in his eyes. "As I ran, I felt horrible. I was leaving behind my son, my only child, who I loved dearly, because his mother was such a fool. I learned later that Russian soldiers captured Peter in the woods and turned him over to Colonel Suslov, who had been searching for me. The colonel moved into my house, made Anna his sex slave, and treated Peter cruelly."

"But then in 1977 Peter defected here. Did he find you then?"

"He came to Cleveland, a center for Hungarian refugees, where I was living. For a long time, Peter would barely even talk to me. He blamed me for deserting him and his mother and causing them so much pain. I tried to make him understand that I didn't have a choice, that I had to go to the US to try and save the country to prevent thousands more from dying. He told me, 'You certainly did a good job of that.'

"In the last couple of years, we had a bit of a thaw in our relation-ship. I had moved to Washington and was living in the area when Peter moved here as well after selling his business in Hungary to be with his son. Actually Viktor, my grandson, leaned on Peter to reconcile with me. Reluctantly, he tried. But he never really forgave me until that last time we were together."

Elizabeth stayed silent as she listened, moved by the story.

"I loved my son," Zoltan added, a tear rolling down his crinkled cheek. "I loved Peter. Even during all those years when he wouldn't have anything to do with me. I never meant to desert him. If I could do it again, I would have done it differently."

"You mean you wouldn't have come to the US?"

"No. At the border I would have kept a tight grip on Peter. When it was clear Anna wasn't coming, I would have picked the boy up and run with him, whether he wanted to go or not. Believe me, I never thought he'd run away. But life doesn't give us another chance."

Elizabeth looked at Zoltan, wracked with sorrow and remorse, and thought about the handsome young man she had seen in a photograph in the book she had read on the plane, the freedom fighter who had come to the United States to plead Hungary's case, leaving behind his wife and eight-year-old son.

The phrase "vicissitudes of old age" entered her mind. She thought about her own life. What would she be like when she was Zoltan's age, if she lived that long? And if she was in a facility like this, who would come to visit her? Not Craig. He was ten years older and unlikely to be alive, and she didn't have any children who would come to see her.

She thanked Zoltan for talking with her.

"And you promise to investigate my son's murder?" he asked.

"I will do everything I possibly can," she assured him.

In the car on the way to meet Craig and Nick at the house in Georgetown, Elizabeth thought about her relationship with Craig. Where were they going? Craig didn't want to get married again. And she had never even told Craig that she couldn't have children.

On the plane she had felt as if the three of them were a family. It had been a great feeling. She thought about Nick. When this was all over who would take care of him? Certainly, Zoltan couldn't do it. Reka probably had relatives in Cleveland—that was a possibility. But

Elizabeth thought of a better one for Nick. She and Craig could adopt him. But she wasn't ready to discuss it with Craig yet.

She picked up her cell and called Craig. "I just left Deerwood," she said. "I'm on my way to Georgetown, planning to stop en route to pick up some food unless you already did."

"Nope. We've been in the house," said Craig. He sounded distracted, and Elizabeth wondered what he was up to.

An hour and a half later, carrying two heavy bags of groceries, she walked into the house. Peering into the study, she spotted Craig and Nick hunched over a computer. Cars were racing across the screen in some type of racing game.

She stood in the doorway watching them. They had no idea she was even there, which explained why Craig had seemed so distracted on the phone.

"Gotcha," Nick cried out. "My game."

"Dammit. That's three in a row," Craig moaned.

"Hi boys," Elizabeth said. "I'm home."

Craig got up and kissed her. "Good timing. Now I have a reason to quit. This kid's killing me."

Elizabeth took charge. "Nick, you go upstairs and get cleaned up. Craig, I'm putting you to work in the kitchen helping me with dinner."

She figured that was a good way to peel Craig off from Nick so she could tell him what she had learned from Zoltan.

An hour later, the three of them sat down at the dining room table. Elizabeth had kept it simple: steaks that Craig cooked on the grill in the back, a corn and tomato salad, and sautéed and diced eggplant, pepper, and zucchini.

Their bodies were still on Paris time, and after eating watermelon for dessert, Nick was practically falling asleep at the table. Elizabeth sent him up to bed while she and Craig finished a bottle of Vajra Barolo and cleaned up.

Before they went to bed, Elizabeth looked out of the windows. Two FBI cars were in place. In the back of the house an FBI agent was sitting in the yard, watching the back fence. If anybody came, they would be ready for them.

*    *    *

Craig slept soundly and woke up at 6:30 a.m. He left Elizabeth asleep in the bed and hurried down to the gym in the basement where he ran on the treadmill, pushing himself hard. Fifteen minutes later, he had company. Nick climbed on the exercise bike and started pedaling fast. *The kid's obviously in good shape*, Craig thought.

That was how Elizabeth found the two of them half an hour later.

"Isn't this a cute scene?" she said.

"Would you like the bike?" Nick asked her.

"You've got to be kidding," she laughed. "My idea of a morning workout is raising a cup of coffee while I read the paper."

After breakfast, Elizabeth took Craig aside and said, "I'm going to the memorial service for Peter and Reka. When do you want to leave for the White House?"

"Two o'clock. I'll call Betty and tell her to meet us there at 2:30. That'll give us a little prep time.

"Okay. I'll be back by two. What will you and Nick do until then?"

He shrugged. "Hang out I guess."

"I know you, Craig," she said. "You have something in mind. But I really think you and Nick should stay in the house. I don't want you taking any chances with him."

"I wouldn't dream of it."

"I don't believe you."

"We'll see you here at two."

Five minutes after Elizabeth left, Craig said to Nick, "You ever been to the Spy Museum?"

Nick shook his head. "I always wanted to go."

"Good, then get dressed. That's where we're going."

Craig figured that accompanied by two FBI agents they would be safe. And after the museum, he and Nick could get some pizza and still be back in time to leave by two o'clock.

\*        \*        \*

At thirty minutes before ten, Elizabeth entered the Church of the Little Flower on Massachusetts Avenue in Bethesda, Maryland. Not knowing what she hoped to learn, she sat down in the last pew to have a clear view of others in attendance.

At ten o'clock, the church was about a quarter full with two hundred attendees. Seated in the front row she saw Zoltan with Mary Jane from Deerwood at his side and Janos Rajk, the Hungarian justice minister.

The pastor spoke first. He talked about Peter's life, but the lack of personal details made Elizabeth think he didn't know Peter very well. As the pastor spoke about Peter, Elizabeth noticed a gray-haired woman in the second pew, her shoulders shaking as she sobbed softly. Elizabeth couldn't see her face.

The pastor then spoke about Peter's wife, Reka, describing her as a devoted member of the parish, "Outgoing and gregarious, she supplied strong support for Peter's work in Hungary." Then he added, "Both Reka and Peter provided loving care and nurturance to their twelve-year-old grandson, Nicholas, who was also a victim in the fire, following the untimely death of his parents last year. It is so unfortunate that Nicholas had his promising life ended at such an early age."

Speaking after the pastor was Jane Jordan, who had been a close friend of Reka's.

"Reka was a wonderful woman," Jane said. "We became good friends when she and Peter moved to this area from Cleveland two years ago to be with their son's family."

Jane recited the many community organizations to which Reka had belonged. Then she added, "Reka never had an easy life. Peter was gone much of the time in Hungary; and yet she managed to make a life for herself. Tragedy struck a year ago with the untimely death of their son and only child, Viktor, and his wife, Ellina, in a boating accident. Still, Reka continued her community involvement."

The woman in the second pew didn't seem to be as affected by the words about Reka, and Elizabeth wondered whether this woman had been another one of Peter's lovers.

When Jane sat down, Janos Rajk climbed up to the pulpit.

"I am Janos Rajk, the Hungarian justice minister. I have flown from Budapest because I want all of you in attendance and indeed the whole world . . ." he paused and looked around, "to understand and to appreciate what a patriotic Hungarian Peter Toth was. Russia slapped a virtual straitjacket over our country from the end of the Second World War until 1989 when the wall fell and the Soviet Union imploded.

"Hungary is a wonderful country with great natural resources and incredibly talented, creative people. However our nation faced the difficult task of building an economy out of the mess that Russia left. Perceiving this necessity, Peter Toth left the US in order to bring his business expertise to our reborn nation. To a great extent, we owe our current economic vitality to Peter Toth.

"On a personal level, I have had the pleasure of Peter's friendship for more than twenty years. I have found him to be a warm and caring individual who would do anything for a friend, while at the same time devoting himself to Hungary, the country he loved so much."

After Janos Rajk had finished speaking, the pastor recited a few prayers and the service ended.

While people filed out, Elizabeth kept her eyes on the gray-haired woman in the second pew. She hadn't risen when everyone else had left. Janos stopped when he saw Elizabeth and introduced her to the Hungarian ambassador.

"Excellent words, Mr. Rajk," she said.

"Thank you," he replied. "I look forward to reading your article about Peter."

Janos moved to the door with the ambassador, then Zoltan and Mary Jane filed by. Elizabeth nodded to them. At last the woman in the second pew stood up and turned around. Elizabeth thought she looked familiar, but at first she couldn't place her. As she walked down the aisle, coming closer to Elizabeth, recognition clicked into place. Her name was Tracy Thomas. Elizabeth had met her about ten years ago while she was still living in New York. It had been at the Press Club in Washington. The Foreign Press Association was honoring Tracy, who was retiring, for her years of distinguished foreign reporting for a Philadelphia daily.

Tracy stopped when she caught sight of Elizabeth. Her face was tear-stained, although she had stopped crying. "I know you, don't I?" she asked.

"Elizabeth Crowder. I met you at the Press Club when I was with the *New York Tribune*."

"Of course. Now you're with the *International Herald*. The foreign news editor in Paris. What brings you here today?"

"Can we go somewhere and talk?"

"I'm staying at the Hyatt in Bethesda. They have a coffee shop."

"I'll meet you there."

*         *         *

Elizabeth's curiosity was piqued as her FBI escort drove her to the Hyatt. She wondered what kind of relationship Tracy might have had with Peter.

When Elizabeth arrived, Tracy was already seated in an isolated corner. A waitress came over and they ordered two coffees.

"Were you a friend of Peter's?" Elizabeth asked.

Tracy smiled. "I wouldn't describe us as friends. We were lovers in the seventies. A long time ago," she added wistfully, "before he married Reka. I haven't seen him in many years. Now tell me what brings you here?"

Elizabeth chose her words carefully, not wanting to give too much away. "Peter was an international businessman, and he died under mysterious circumstances. My editor thinks there might be a story here. You know how that goes. I have family in the States, so I was happy to come."

"You think it was arson?" Tracy asked, instinct from her years as a reporter kicking in. "Not the rupture of a gas line as the police claim?"

Elizabeth shrugged. "I have a friend in the New York Fire Department who told me that the rupture of a gas line wouldn't produce a fire so devastating that the bodies were burnt beyond recognition. Let's assume he's right. Then I have to understand Peter. What he did and who his enemies were. Any help you could give me would be appreciated."

Tracy took a deep breath before responding. At last she said, "I helped Peter defect. It was December 1977. He was in Philadelphia with a Hungarian hockey team playing an evening exhibition match against the Flyers. Though my beat was international, my editor saw a good story here. It was the height of the Cold War and the right-wing fringe in Philadelphia had decided to use this match as a way of protesting against Communism."

"Did it occur to them that there was a difference between Hungary and Russia?"

"With a Moscow-controlled puppet government in Budapest, that difference was too subtle for our hockey fans. At any rate, Peter decided to defect that evening, and I reluctantly became his accomplice."

"Will you tell me about it?"

"Better than that, I'll send you a piece that I wrote for the memoir I never finished. What's your email address? You can read it on the plane back to Paris."

"Thank you," said Elizabeth, handing Tracy her card.

"Bear in mind as you read this story that I was pretty gutsy in those days. Though my father had been a general in the U.S. Air Force and Chairman of the Joint Chiefs in 1977, I had previously been active in the anti-war movement. I was even arrested in Chicago at the 1968 Democratic convention, which almost drove my father crazy. So I was willing to take chances to help Peter."

"And you became lovers?"

Tracy looked wistful. "I fell in love with Peter. Our relationship only lasted a couple of months. Then we split."

"Did you ever see him again?"

Tracy shook her head. "I followed his business career in the media and on the internet. I knew that he married Reka, a Hungarian American whose father was a wealthy lawyer and real estate developer in Cleveland. And of course that Peter became a successful businessman in Hungary after the Russians left."

"He hated the Russians, didn't he?"

Tracy looked grim. "That's an understatement. Peter suffered horribly under them. Colonel Suslov, who raped his mother and moved into their house, branded a hammer and sickle on his arm. Peter would have done anything humanly possible to get revenge."

*      *      *

When Elizabeth returned to the house at 1:30 p.m., Craig and Nick weren't there. Of course Craig hadn't stayed in the house as she had requested.

She called him on his cell.

"Where are you?"

"Eating pizza with Nick. We'll be back by two. We're fine. No need to worry."

Elizabeth was annoyed that Craig hadn't listened to her. It was vintage Craig. He always did as he wanted regardless of the risk. But there wasn't much she could do at this point, so she put aside her irritation with a sigh.

With a little time to kill, she couldn't resist taking out her iPad and at least starting the piece Tracy had sent her.

*The Hungarian Hockey Player and the Newspaper Reporter*

Philadelphia's Spectrum was sold out for the exhibition hockey game between the Philadelphia Flyers and the Hungarian national team. It was a loud, angry crowd determined to make the evening into a Cold War statement.

They were an army of fifteen thousand strong, on their feet loudly singing the "Star Spangled Banner." It was a hostile and belligerent crowd, displaying their animosity toward Russia.

The intensity and ferocity of the "boos" from the crowd had startled Peter Toth, the starting center for the Hungarian team, when he and his teammates emerged on the ice.

A great crescendo of emotion was building as the song came to its end, and the whole crowd was singing fervently. With the last note, a huge animallike roar went up from one end of the Spectrum.

"Kill the Commie bastards," they shouted.

The referee dropped the puck to start the match. Two minutes later, Peter Toth stole the puck from an American player. He was racing along the right, the puck on his stick heading toward the goal, when he saw a small, bright orange object flying toward him.

Peter raised his hand reflexively to block the object, but it was too late. The speeding orange projectile crashed into his groin with a terrible ferocity, smashing against his genitals. An excruciating look of pain consumed his face as he collapsed. He lay motionless on the ice.

The rock, painted orange, rested beside him where it had dropped. Its message was spelled out in dark blue letters: "Free Central Europe."

A horrified silence settled over the arena as he lay prostrate, and the team's physician rushed out to assess him. Peter's head began to move back and forth, and he strained to sit up, but the pain was too much.

A stretcher was called for, and there was a flurry of activity in the tunnel leading to the locker room. Finally a stretcher was brought out and Peter was carefully placed on the dark green canvas, and then carried off the ice.

"Good God!" Hal Cross, the sports reporter for the *Bulletin* called out to me. "He got it right in the nuts!"

Only moments before I had framed the opening lines of this article: "The Spectrum was a carnival of madness, a celebration of insanity." Those lines now seemed apt.

The injured hockey player disappeared into the tunnel on the way to the locker room. Another gladiator skated out to take his place on the ice. The crowd remained silent. The match would go forward.

"Did you catch the guy's name who was hurt?" Cross asked.

I had heard him announced as Lazlo Suslov, but didn't respond. I was already on my feet shoving my pad and pencil into a large brown canvas purse and bolting for the exit to the press box. Here was the best story in town. All I had to do was find out where they took the Hungarian hockey player. Then I'd get an exclusive.

Using my press credentials, I learned that the Hungarian team was staying at the Wings Hotel, ten minutes from the spectrum. I found Peter there in the hotel dining room.

"Mind if I join you for dinner?" I asked. "There seems to be a shortage of tables, and I don't want to wait."

Before he had a chance to respond, I introduced myself and told him I was sorry for the way the people at the hockey match had behaved.

Over dinner I asked him about his life in Hungary. He gave short factual answers—but no opinions.

I wanted to make him feel comfortable talking to me, so I told him about how I had been active in the anti-war movement during the Vietnam War. I told him about how we were constantly harassed by the same kind of people he might have dealt with in Hungary.

Deep furrows appeared on Peter's brow, and he glanced around nervously at these words. Abruptly, he lowered his head and leaned across the table. His eyes were very serious now, and his mouth tightened into a grim expression. His right hand was stretched out on the table—it trembled with excitement. "I need your help," he whispered tensely. "Will you help me?"

We agreed to discuss the situation in private, but we couldn't be seen going to his room together. Peter said the team's security was watching him.

He dropped a room key on the blue carpet near his feet, then kicked it over to my side of the table.

Back in his room, Peter turned the deadbolt and slipped the chain on the lock. Without saying a word he turned on the radio, skipping two rock stations until he found a Mozart concerto.

"Do you still want to help me?" he asked. "My name is Peter Toth. Not Lazlo Suslov. That was the name that Russian bastard gave me. Tonight, I'm planning to defect."

When I agreed to help him, he explained his plan to me.

"Listen carefully. Go to the lobby. First, make certain there is a tax-icab outside. Talk to the driver and have him stand by. Call me here on the house phone when you've done that."

"And then?" I replied quickly.

"I'll call Boris in the lobby and tell him to bring a pain killer to my room."

"Boris?"

"One of my two Russian guards. You saw those two big men in the lobby playing chess?"

I nodded.

"As soon as Boris starts toward the elevator, call me here. I'll go down the stairs as fast as I can. Once I get to the lobby, you have to distract Igor, the other guard, long enough for me to get out of the front door and into the cab."

"How do you want me to distract him?"

"That's up to you, but be careful. He's got a gun and they're taught to do what's necessary in every situation."

"I'll be able to handle him," I replied. "Don't worry. What happens to you then?"

"The Russians will think I'm just another Central European defector, escaping from their great prison. They'll file a complaint with your government, but not much else will happen."

I told him he was kidding himself, that it wouldn't be that easy. More than likely the US government would make an effort to find him. But he was prepared to take his chances.

"Are you ready to go downstairs?" he asked me.

"Ready. Just one question first. How will you get around? Did they give you money?"

He hadn't thought of money. The players hadn't been given American money to cut down on their chances of defecting. I reached into my wallet and gave him what I had, but he refused to take it until I gave him my number so he could repay me.

In front of the hotel, I found an empty cab waiting for a fare. "Can you take a passenger?" I asked the driver. "He'll be down in a couple of minutes. He's blond with a foreign accent."

The cabbie nodded and turned on his "in service" light.

Back inside the hotel I grabbed a scotch and soda from the bar, then called Peter to report on the waiting cab.

A few seconds later, the bellman called one of the Russian guards to the house phone. I heard him talking in Russian, but couldn't understand what he was saying. He took a small bottle of pills from his pocket, then walked over and conferred with his comrade. When he started toward the elevator, I called Peter again. "He's on his way up."

Then I walked into the lobby and approached the other Russian guard, who was sitting next to the chess table. I stood next to him and tried to engage him in conversation, acting drunk, slurring my words, and leaning on his shoulder.

Through the corner of my eye, I spotted Peter moving swiftly from the stairs to the front door. Immediately, I dropped my drink on the chess table, then collapsed on the Russian guard, embracing him and touching his cheek with my mouth. I whispered for him to come upstairs with me, but suddenly he caught sight of Peter. He pushed me roughly away and ran after him.

"Halt," he shouted. "Halt." He pulled a gun from a small holster belted to his chest.

On my knees where the man had shoved me I watched Peter. He was already through the front door when the guard reached it. The door was closing, but the Russian kept running, gun in hand, expecting the door to open again. His legs were driving his bulky frame like a powerful engine.

It was too late when he realized he was wrong, that the door wasn't going to open again in time. He struck it broadside at full speed. His head hit first, then he bounced backward to the floor, instantly unconscious.

As I headed to the lower level parking garage to retrieve my car, I thought about how I had the best damn story in Philadelphia, but couldn't write a word of it for fear of endangering the Hungarian hockey player.

I never expected to hear from Peter Toth again, but three days later . . .

Elizabeth heard the front door open.

"Hi Elizabeth, we're home," Craig called out.

She checked her watch. It was five minutes to two. She put her iPad down and met them in the entrance hall. "Did you two have a good time?" she asked.

"Great," Nick said. "He took me to the Spy Museum, and then we had lunch at a wonderful cafe."

Elizabeth smiled, enjoying his enthusiasm. "Okay," she said. "Time to go to the White House."

*       *       *

Craig, Elizabeth, Nick, and Betty met in a small room in the White House close to the Oval Office.

"Dealing with President Worth can be tricky," Betty said. "He has a lot on his mind, so it may be necessary to bring him along slowly to get him on board."

Recalling his past interactions with Worth, Craig didn't disagree. "So how do you want to handle this?"

"My suggestion is that you, Craig, and I begin with the president, providing him with background, while Elizabeth and Nick remain here. At the appropriate time, we'll call for Elizabeth and Nick to join us."

"Makes sense," Craig agreed. He also imagined that unspoken by Betty was a concern that the president wouldn't want to say too much in front of Nick, who after all was still a child, while he would want to hear what the boy had to say.

A few minutes later, the president's secretary led Craig and Betty into the Oval Office. It had only been fourteen months since Craig had last seen Worth in this same room, but as Worth got up from his desk and came forward to greet Craig and Betty, Craig was struck by how much Worth had aged in that time. His brown hair had markedly turned gray, and there were deep creases in his forehead that Craig had never noticed before. He looked tired. He had certainly paid a price for being the most powerful man in the world.

"It's good to see you again, Craig," Worth said, holding out a hand. "With the passage of time, I hope you've forgiven me for how I handled our last operation together."

"There is nothing to forgive, Mr. President. I would have acted the same in your position."

"I'm glad to hear you say that."

"I appreciate your agreeing to meet with us," Craig added.

"I know you, Craig. If you weren't involved in something important to the United States, you wouldn't be here. Would the two of you like something to drink?"

Worth was being gracious. Craig didn't want to take any more of his time than necessary. "No thank you, Mr. President."

Worth pointed to the living area and moved toward a straight chair. Craig took one facing him, while Betty sat on a sofa off to one side.

"Okay, what's this about?" the president asked.

While Craig and Nick had eaten their lunch, Craig had rehearsed in his mind how he would summarize this complex situation, beginning with the Potomac fire and the murder of Amos Neir. Craig had it down to about fifteen minutes, and Betty didn't interrupt.

At the end, he said, "I am convinced that Kuznov and Szabo have reached some type of agreement that will have adverse consequences for our European allies and for the US. I am also convinced that before his death, Peter Toth set in motion a plan to have Omar Basayev assassinate Szabo, most likely in Brussels on September 1, to block this agreement from going into effect. We wanted you to know about this situation so you could take appropriate action."

Worth leaned back in his chair and closed his eyes. As he did, he removed a small white rubber ball from his pocket and began squeezing it. After a minute, he opened his eyes and leaned forward, looking troubled.

Worth turned to Betty. "Do you accept Craig's two conclusions?"

"I do, Mr. President."

Craig saw that Worth had trouble accepting what Craig had said, but in fairness to the president, it was a lot to come out of the blue. Craig had one more card to play to convince the president. "I brought Nick and Elizabeth with me. They're in the office down the hall. I think it might help if you heard directly from Nick."

"That's a good idea." Worth put the white ball back into his pocket and buzzed for his secretary to bring them in.

Craig could tell that Nick was nervous about entering the Oval Office. The president must have sensed that as well because he said, "Craig told me what you did. You are a very brave boy, and I'm honored to meet you."

That made Nick smile. "Thank you, sir."

Worth reached out a hand to Elizabeth, which she grasped. "I'm one of your best readers," Worth said. "I gave my aides an order to include your articles in my morning briefing book."

"Thank you, Mr. President."

Craig pulled over two more chairs and they all sat down.

"I hear you're a Nats baseball fan, Nick."

"For sure."

"I am, too. Will we win the World Series this year, you think?"

"I think so."

"I do, too, but you can never count the Dodgers out," Worth said with a smile.

"I'm worried about the Red Sox, too," said Nick, his nervousness beginning to fade.

"Craig told me that you were watching a Nats game a couple of weeks ago when you heard your grandfather say something about Hungarian Prime Minister Szabo and Russian President Kuznov. Do you remember what it was?"

"Yes, sir. My grandpa told Emma that they couldn't let Szabo and Kuznov get away with something, that it would take them back to 1956 with Russian troops in Hungary again. My grandfather sounded upset. . . . He suffered a lot under the Russians in 1956."

Worth was now looking at Elizabeth. "Do you share Craig's conclusions about the agreement and about Omar?"

"Yes. I was just in Budapest where I obtained support for these conclusions from Peter Toth's closest business associate and from the justice minister."

"I have no doubt that you did probing interviews with them. I've never been on the receiving end, but I can imagine."

She laughed. "When this is over, I'd be honored to interview you."

Worth laughed as well. "I'm sure you would."

"Well, unless you have something else to ask Nick or me, Mr. President, we'll return to the office outside and wait for Craig."

*Thanks, Elizabeth*, Craig mouthed silently.

When they were gone, Craig said, "Nick is a great kid."

"He is," Worth responded. "And I like Elizabeth a lot. When are you going to marry her?"

Betty chimed in. "Yeah, when?"

Craig blushed. "Can we return to Russia and Hungary?"

"Fair enough," Worth said. "You have me convinced that Peter set up this assassination attempt on Szabo before his death. Do you think Omar has or will abort because of Peter's death? Generally these assassins receive a partial payment up front. He could keep the payment without needing to go through with the deal."

"I don't think Omar will abort," Craig said. He was determined to find and to kill Omar because of Amos, and he'd do anything to get the president's support. To retain credibility, he added, "At any rate, it's too risky to make that assumption."

Worth took out the white ball and began squeezing it again.

"Unfortunately," the president said, "we've received some independent evidence corroborating your conclusion that Kuznov and Szabo have entered into some type of agreement and that Peter Toth was right. It could be 1956 all over again."

"What evidence?" Craig asked.

"Tell him about the satellite photos," Worth told Betty.

"Yesterday from routine surveillance we obtained photos showing Russian troop movements on the Russian border with Ukraine. This could be a staging area to move them into Hungary once the agreement is signed by Kuznov and Szabo. President Worth and I have been worried about Kuznov's plans for further aggression and were wondering what the reason was for these troop movements. Your report provides the answer."

"Sorry to be the bearer of bad news," Craig said.

"Of course Kuznov will still have to move his troops and equipment through Ukraine," the president remarked.

Craig shook his head. "He'll fly over."

"And risk Ukraine shooting down a Russian plane in their airspace?"

"Absolutely. This Hungarian ploy means too much to Kuznov. He'll play chicken with the Ukrainians. He'll gamble that they'd never have the guts to do that and risk an all-out Russian attack, with Kuznov claiming the plane was in Russian airspace. And I think he'll win his gamble."

"Once those Russian troops are in Hungary," Betty said, "they'll be a threat to Germany. This isn't some obscure Middle Eastern country. It's Europe, and it's contrary to US interests."

"I won't be like President Eisenhower," Worth said. "I won't stand by and let Russia dominate Central Europe."

This was good news to Craig, but he wondered how far Worth would go to stop it.

As if reading his mind, Worth added, "I know Kuznov well enough to realize that calling and demanding that he not pursue this ploy in Hungary would be a waste of time. All he understands is brute force. I'll give the order to move US ships and other military resources into the Mediterranean. He'll notice that. My hope is he'll back off when he sees our show of force."

And if Kuznov didn't back off, Craig wondered whether Worth was prepared to go to war over this issue.

Betty spoke up. "We may have another alternative. Suppose we let Omar assassinate Szabo? Szabo's death would throw a monkey wrench into Kuznov's plan."

The president raised his hand to his face and stroked his chin. For a whole minute he thought about Betty's proposal. Finally he said, "I don't like it for two reasons. First of all, I can't knowingly let another world leader be assassinated for reasons of foreign policy. In the long run that could put every occupant of this office at risk of assassination by foreign leaders. And second, it's hard to predict the fallout from Szabo's assassination, especially if it comes out that we had advanced knowledge. Don't forget, the First World War was started because of an assassination. I think if we can prevent Omar from assassinating Szabo, we should."

"Okay, flip it then," Betty said. "Suppose we warn Szabo."

"He's barely talking to me, and we don't have hard enough evidence," said Worth. "He'll laugh it off."

"Well, I know what I have to do," Betty said. "I'll alert our people in Brussels and have them assist Giuseppe and the Belgium authorities to locate Omar and take him into custody."

"I like that. Meantime, Craig, you've been on the trail of Omar. I want you to continue on it. You're good at this sort of thing."

Craig was glad to have the president's vote of confidence. "I'll do that, Mr. President."

As soon as they returned to Europe and stashed Nick at the clinic with extra protection, Craig planned to go to Brussels and assist Giuseppe in the search for Omar.

Betty's phone rang in her bag. She pulled it out and looked at the caller ID. "The FBI director," she said, looking at the president.

"Take it," Worth told her.

The call lasted two minutes. It was a monologue by the FBI director. All Betty said was "yes" and "I understand."

When she put down the phone, she said, "The State Department has learned about Peter Toth's travels in the days before his death. On July 25 he traveled to Grozny by a circuitous route: Washington, Sardinia, and then Grozny via Rome and Moscow. He arrived in Grozny on the twenty-sixth. He was only there a few hours. After that he returned to Washington via Moscow and Paris."

"In Grozny he must have recruited Omar," Craig said.

"But why Sardinia?" Betty asked.

Craig shrugged. "No idea. I'll have to get Giuseppe on that. And once we get back to Europe, I'm flying to Grozny."

"What in the world for?" Betty asked.

"If we're right, the attack isn't until September 1. It's possible that once Omar finished his preparations in France and Belgium, he went back to Grozny to avoid detection."

Craig recalled what Gideon had told him when he had been in Israel for Amos's funeral. Omar and Kuznov were bitter enemies.

With that in mind, Craig added, "If I can find Omar, I may be able to convince him that by trying to kill Szabo he's walking into a trap set by Kuznov, and that he should abort."

"And if he doesn't agree to do that?" Worth asked.

"I'll kill him."

Betty looked skeptical. "The odds are long that he returned to Grozny. More likely he's holed up somewhere in Belgium or northern France."

"The Imam in Clichy told me that Omar went back to Grozny."

"That's a reliable source," Betty said sarcastically.

"Giuseppe already has enough people in Brussels trying to find Omar. I won't have anything to contribute there, but nobody's in Grozny. Even if Omar's not in Grozny, I may be able to hook up with one of his friends or confidantes. One way or another, I may be able to convince them to tell me where Omar is."

"It'll be risky for you," Worth said.

"I'm prepared to take that risk, Mr. President."

## Over the Atlantic

On the return flight to Paris, Craig and Nick sat beside each other with Elizabeth across the aisle.

Once the plane had leveled off, Elizabeth took out her iPad, opened it to Tracy's draft, and resumed reading on her iPad.

I never expected to hear from Peter Toth again, but three days later as I sat at my desk in the newspaper office, the phone rang.

When I answered, I heard a frantic voice: "It's the Hungarian hockey player. I'm hurt. I need help."

I went to the motel in Pittsburgh where he had been staying as fast as I could. Peter opened the door, sheets soaked with blood wrapped around his ribs.

"They shot me," he said weakly.

The Russian guards from Philadelphia had found him, it turned out, although he had managed to escape.

He looked light-headed. I helped him put on his blood-soaked jacket, grabbed his suitcase, and pulled him out of the door and along the corridor.

Fortunately in the lobby neither the room clerk nor the bellboy were visible. Nobody noticed as I led Peter to my car, helping him into the back seat so he could lie down.

He needed a doctor. I recalled that Barry Firestone, one of my close friends in the anti-war movement, had settled down in Pittsburgh, gone to medical school, and become a doctor in Mt. Lebanon.

I arranged to meet him at his home office. Barry Firestone had gotten fat and bald, but he was a very good doctor. Working without the aid of a nurse, it took him more than an hour to treat Peter. He cleaned the wound and used six stitches to close it up. After he bandaged Peter, he gave him some pills for infection and for pain. Then he took Peter into one of his upstairs bedrooms and put him to bed. He had lost a lot of blood but Barry said he would be okay. While Peter slept, I made up my mind to take him back to Philadelphia and hide him in my house.

The next morning we drove back to Philadelphia. On the way I asked him what he had been doing in Pittsburgh. The Hungarian Refugees Relief Agency had told him that most of the refugees had gone to Cleveland after 1956. He had been on his way there, but had to change buses in Pittsburgh, when the Russians caught up with him.

In the next two weeks while Peter recovered from his wound we became lovers. I enlisted the help of my father, U.S. Air Force General and Chairman of the Joint Chiefs Alvin Thomas, to use his government contacts to obtain asylum and citizenship for Peter in the United States.

After everything had been settled, Peter told me one morning over coffee that he had decided to move to Cleveland. He wanted to be with other Hungarian people. I was heartbroken but understood.

So on a cold but sunny January morning, I dropped Peter Toth at a bus station in Philadelphia.

And on that morning, my Hungarian hockey player disappeared from my life forever—just as abruptly as he had entered it.

Elizabeth closed her eyes. She recalled Tracy's final words at the Hyatt Hotel in Bethesda following the memorial service, about how Peter would have done anything in his power to get revenge on the Russians.

Tracy's story underscored those words. Everything that happened and was happening must have been set in motion by Peter's desire for revenge.

## Paris

Pierre and two of his men met Craig, Elizabeth, and Nick when they got off the plane at Charles de Gaulle Airport in Paris. From there, he drove them straight to the clinic.

Craig knew Elizabeth would go berserk when she heard about his going to Grozny, so he didn't want to tell her until they had taken Nick to the clinic and Craig's security for the boy was in place.

In Nick's room, the boy hugged both Elizabeth and Craig. "You understand," she said, "that you're only staying here until I can be sure that you'll be safe outside of the clinic, don't you?"

He nodded. "I'm okay with that. I know I'll be safe here."

Nick didn't ask and Elizabeth didn't say what would happen to Nick after that.

It was three in the afternoon. When they were back in the living room of their suite at the Bristol, Elizabeth asked Craig if he'd be going to Brussels to work with the authorities to locate Omar.

Craig took a deep breath and said, "Tomorrow morning I'm flying to Russia, to Grozny."

When she didn't respond, he added, "The capital of Chechnya, which is a part of Russia . . ."

"That's insulting," she replied in a surly voice. "I know where Grozny is. I didn't reply because that's the most asinine idea I've ever heard. Even from you."

"Don't hold back, tell me what you really think."

"What could you possibly hope to accomplish?"

"Omar may be holed up there until it's time to go to Brussels. And even if he's not, I may be able to convince his confidantes to tell me where he's hiding."

Elizabeth shook her head in exasperation. "That is so stupid. You won't learn a damn thing in Grozny. Even worse, you'll never make it out alive. Between Omar's terrorist friends and Kuznov's thugs, somebody will kill you. You might as well be going into Russia with a big bull's eye painted on your back."

"But I'll be Enrico Marino."

"You're being delusional. You already have a history with Kuznov, and he knows the two of us are together. By now he has no doubt learned that two of his thugs were killed in Paris by a man with Elizabeth Crowder. When they broke into our apartment, they must have learned that Enrico Marino was living with Elizabeth Crowder. It will take them about ten minutes to learn that Enrico Marino's life began two years ago, and that he is Craig Page. And for confirmation, Kuznov won't believe that any race car driver could bring down two of his people with a single shot each." She looked at Craig. "You know I'm right."

"I'm going anyhow."

"You'll never get out alive."

"I'll find a way to do this."

"You're just being stubborn and pigheaded."

To gain Elizabeth's support, Craig said, "It's our only way to find out about the cause of Peter's death. That means it's the only way to ensure Nick's safety."

"Oh bullshit. You're just saying that to manipulate me into dropping my opposition. The truth is you want to find Omar and kill him to avenge the death of your friend. That's what's driving you."

Elizabeth began to cry. He got up, walked over, and took her into his arms. She punched her fists against his chest. Then she stopped and let him hold her.

For a few moments, he held her tightly. Then she pulled away.

"A little while ago, when you and I and Nick were on the plane, I was so happy. Now this," she said.

Tears were streaming down her cheeks.

"I'll be back. I promise."

"Yeah, right. I don't plan to waste my time on the widow's walk. I have my job at the newspaper," she said, her voice cracking. Then she stormed into the bedroom and slammed the door behind her.

*That certainly went well*, Craig thought.

Craig called Giuseppe. "Where are you?" he asked.

"Paris."

"Can you meet me at the place where we had breakfast a couple of days ago?"

"Be there in an hour."

When Giuseppe arrived, Craig knocked on the bedroom door.

"Giuseppe's here," he called to Elizabeth through the closed door.

When she came out, she said to Giuseppe, "Has he told you the stupid thing he plans to do?"

Giuseppe looked puzzled. "Not yet. I just arrived."

"Why don't we start by telling Giuseppe what happened in Washington?" Craig suggested.

"Okay, you tell him," she said angrily.

Craig began speaking and Elizabeth jumped in to talk about Zoltan and the memorial service. "Bottom line," Craig said, "President Worth wants me to find Omar."

"And you're going to Grozny, which is why Elizabeth's upset."

"What are you, a mind reader?" asked Craig.

"I've known the two of you for quite a while."

"And don't you think this is stupid?" Elizabeth asked.

"Listen. I care for the two of you, and I hate to get into the middle of this."

"Just tell me what you think," she demanded.

"It's Craig—he's always taken chances that I and others wouldn't. Somehow he always survives."

"I really do think Omar may be there or I'll be able to find out where he is from one of his people," Craig insisted.

Elizabeth sighed and shook her head. Craig figured she knew a hopeless cause.

"Let's talk about Sardinia," Giuseppe said, changing the topic. "Why do you think Peter stopped there?"

"I have no idea," Craig replied, relieved that they were no longer discussing Grozny.

"While you're in Grozny, let me move up on Sardinia."

"That would be great. What's happening in Brussels?"

"I've distributed Omar's picture to all the Belgian security and police agencies and to the people in northern France. So far no leads. But I'm hopeful we'll find him before September 1."

# Moscow and Grozny

On Monday, Craig flew on Air France to Moscow's Sheremetyevo Airport. There, he planned to change planes to Aeroflot for the flight to Grozny.

In the busy new terminal at Sheremetyevo Craig carried his duffle toward passport control. In the slow-moving line, Craig thought about how vulnerable international travelers were, totally at the mercy of foreign governments and their law enforcement personnel.

When he reached the front of the line, Craig slid his Italian Enrico Marino passport under the glass. The agent studied it with a bored expression. He glanced up at his computer screen and suddenly, he looked alert.

Craig noticed him reaching down with one hand and pressing a red button on a panel next to his seat. *That spells trouble*, Craig thought to himself.

"What are you doing in Moscow?" the official asked.

"I'm in transit. Going to Grozny."

"Purpose of the trip?"

"Business."

"What type of business?"

"I'm looking for possible investments," Craig replied.

Two armed soldiers closed in on Craig as they spoke, one from each side. The soldiers were large, burly men toting automatic weapons.

"Come with us," one of the soldiers told Craig in English.

"Why? What did I do?"

The other soldier shoved Craig with the handle of his gun, effectively ending the discussion.

They led Craig to a small windowless room with a metal table and two chairs. Once Craig was inside, one of the soldiers grabbed Craig's duffel and tossed all the contents—clothes, toiletries, and books—on the floor. Then the soldiers left, slamming the door. Craig heard a deadbolt click into place.

He had to figure out what was going on—and fast. After about a minute's deliberation, he decided that Elizabeth must be correct: Kuznov had figured out that Craig had killed his two thugs in Paris, and that Craig was now Enrico Marino. It was unlikely that Kuznov had deduced why Craig had come to Russia. If they blocked Craig from going to Grozny, at least he might be able to get a meeting with Kuznov to try to obtain some useful information. After all, he and the Russian president had helped each other in the past.

Satisfied that he had a plan, Craig sat down in one of the chairs and waited for someone to come for him.

*       *       *

Dimitri burst into Kuznov's office. "You were right, Mr. President," he said.

"Don't sound so surprised," Kuznov replied. "I'm always right. What happened?'

"Enrico Marino has just landed at Sheremetyevo. He's been taken into custody. I could have him transferred to a jail until after the ceremony in Budapest."

"Where was he flying from?"

"Paris. He was connecting to Grozny."

Kuznov was startled. "Did you say Grozny?"

"Correct."

This changed everything. Kuznov's assumption had been that Craig was coming to Russia to confront him, but obviously that wasn't the case. But Grozny? Why Grozny?

Kuznov knew that Craig had access to Nicholas Toth, and it was possible the boy had trusted him enough to tell him what he knew about his grandfather's plans to put an end to the Russian–Hungarian Friendship Pact. And now Craig was going to Grozny.

Kuznov called the director of the Transportation Ministry and asked him to access travel records. "Tell me whether Peter Toth made any airplane trips to Grozny in the last month."

Kuznov held on the line. A few minutes later he heard the answer. "Peter Toth traveled to Grozny on July 26. He stayed a few hours before flying back to Paris."

Now Craig Page was going to Grozny, undoubtedly to find out what Peter had done there. Kuznov was aware that he had plenty of enemies in Chechnya. Perhaps Peter had enlisted one of them to keep the Friendship Pact from being finalized. In that case, Craig could be a valuable asset for Kuznov. By following Craig, Kuznov might find out what Peter had been planning.

Kuznov turned to Dimitri. "Order the airport guards to release Page. Have them tell him that his detention was a mistake, that we confused him with an Italian terrorist. I want him to fly to Grozny as he planned. Hold his plane if need be."

Kuznov saw a perplexed look on Dimitri's face, but he had no intention of explaining why he had changed his orders.

Once Dimitri was gone, Kuznov called Daud Mollah, who ruled the Russian republic of Chechnya as his own private empire but was loyal to Kuznov.

"Daud," Kuznov said, "you will have a visitor, an Italian race car driver by the name of Enrico Marino. He'll be arriving sometime today on a flight from Moscow. I want to find out what he's doing in Grozny, who he's talking to, and what they're saying. This is very important."

"Understood. We'll follow him from the moment he arrives."

"A loose tail. He will be on high alert, and I don't want him to know."

"Understood."

Kuznov was aware that Daud enjoyed using brute force wherever and whenever possible, so he added, "One other thing. I don't want you to take any action against Enrico Marino. I don't want him harmed when he's in Chechnya. Report to me personally in real time about all of Marino's activities."

After he put the phone down, Kuznov closed his eyes and thought about the situation. On Peter Toth's trip to Grozny, he must have set a plan in motion to disrupt the execution of the Friendship Pact. Perhaps even after his death that plan was still proceeding. He certainly couldn't risk assuming it wasn't. Kuznov would let Craig uncover that plan. Then he would pounce.

\*        \*        \*

When Craig heard the lock turn on the door, he stood up, ready to invoke Kuznov's name and his relationship with the Russian president, hoping that would get him better treatment and maybe even a meeting with Kuznov.

Instead of soldiers, a middle-aged man in a suit and tie, black-framed glasses, and thinning brown hair entered. Craig held his breath, wondering what was coming next.

"Unfortunately, there has been an error," the man said. "You were confused with a suspected terrorist traveling with an Italian passport. We regret the mistake. You're not only free to go, but we've held your flight to Grozny to give you a chance to board."

Craig was flabbergasted. He wondered what the hell was going on. The official sounded convincing, but Craig was reluctant to accept his story. It seemed highly unlikely they would have delayed the flight on his behalf, whether they had made a mistake in detaining him or not. On the other hand, with the incredible arbitrariness of justice in Russia, anything was possible.

Craig simply said, "Thank you," picked up his bag, and followed the official out of the room. The man led Craig to a doorway that opened onto the airfield. A minivan was waiting for Craig, its engine idling. It drove him across the field to his Aeroflot plane to Grozny.

After an uneventful flight, Craig checked into the Hotel Grozny City at six o'clock that evening. It was a thirty-two floor, sleek modern building with a series of gray steel columns running along the sides from the ground to the top. The hotel was in the new redeveloped center of the city and a stone's throw from the main mosque. This was the part of Grozny that the Russians had rebuilt after they pulverized the drab old city to rubble in the 1990s, proving once again that wars are good for contractors.

But the hope for an influx of tourists had never materialized. Walking through the thick red carpeted lobby, Craig saw very few people and little activity. Build it and they will come often turned out to be a phony promise.

Once Craig had dropped his bag off in his spacious suite on the thirtieth floor, he took the elevator back down to the lobby. The concierge, a tall, thin man with a shiny shaved head and neatly trimmed black beard and mustache, was standing behind a desk talking in French with an anxious sounding woman about restaurants in Grozny. She was peppering the concierge with an endless stream of queries. Craig held back, waiting for her to finish, while silently rolling his eyes. Grozny wasn't exactly a culinary mecca.

When the concierge was free Craig moved up to the desk and slid five one-hundred euro notes across the counter to the concierge, who swiftly pocketed the bills.

"I'm Enrico in room 3010," Craig said. "I'd like to talk to you in private. Do you have somewhere we can go?"

"My office. Follow me."

The mirror behind the desk was a door leading to an office. Craig followed the concierge inside. Once he closed the door, he asked Craig, "What can I do for you?"

"I want to meet Omar Basayev, sometimes known as Omar the Chechen."

All of the color drained from the concierge's face. He was pale and his hands were trembling. At least he knows who I'm talking about, Craig thought.

"I don't know that individual," he eventually replied. He held out Craig's money, anxious to return it.

Craig didn't take it back. Instead, he pressed ahead. "If you make an introduction for me, I'll give you another two thousand."

Craig sat down in a chair, making himself comfortable while the concierge agonized over how to respond.

"Yours is a difficult request," he finally said. "There are risks for me."

"Three thousand euros."

"Four thousand and I'll do what I can. I can't make any guarantees. I think you can understand."

"It's a deal," said Craig.

"Good. I'll call you if and when I've made arrangements."

"I'll be in the dining room up on the thirty-second floor. After that, in my room. I'll be expecting your call."

An hour later Craig was finishing a disappointing dinner of over-cooked, dry roast chicken washed down by a mediocre bottle of Bulgarian wine when the maître d' brought over a phone. "The concierge is calling," he said, handing the phone to Craig and departing quickly.

"I've made the introduction you wanted," came the concierge's voice over the phone. "In fifteen minutes, a man named Mikhail will call you on the phone in your room. He'll give you an address. Take a cab there.

Mikhail will be waiting for you there in a black car. He'll take you to meet the man you want to see."

Craig was apprehensive. It had been too fast and too easy. It just didn't seem right. On the other hand, if the concierge had a line to Omar and Omar knew that a Western European had come to see him while he was planning a job in Brussels, he might be curious to meet the man. And if he wasn't there, Craig might be able to persuade one of Omar's confidants to tell him where he was. Once he had his location, he could go there and kill him.

"I'm going back to my room to take the call."

"First, bring me my money."

"Two thousand when I leave the hotel to meet Mikhail. The other two thousand when I return to the hotel."

"I took risks for you," said the concierge, sounding furious.

"That's the way I'm doing it," Craig replied with finality.

In the elevator, Craig focused on the fact that he didn't have a weapon. Bringing one with him would have been too risky. Back in his suite, he looked around. The mini bar had a classic corkscrew with a knife that opened up. That would do the job.

Fifteen minutes later, the phone rang in Craig's room.

"This is Mikhail," said a voice on the other end. "Take a cab to the concert hall. I'll be waiting for you in front in a black car."

Craig paid the snarling concierge two thousand euros and got into the only cab waiting in front of the hotel. He realized there was a good chance the driver was with state security or reporting to them, but he didn't have a choice. Mikhail would have to deal with that.

"Concert hall," he told the driver.

It was dark when the cab came to a stop thirty minutes later and the driver told him they had arrived. Craig paid him in cash before getting out to look around. He saw a black car parked in front of the concert hall, its engine idling. The driver's window was rolled down.

"Mikhail," Craig said as he approached.

"Yes," said the man in the car. "Quickly, get in the back of the car."

As soon as Craig climbed in, a man who had been crouched down in the back of the car jumped at Craig, a club clutched in one fist. Off balance, Craig didn't react in time and the man smacked him on the side of the head. Though dizzy and barely conscious, Craig was still aware of his assailant taking a syringe from a bag and inserting it into his arm. Then he blacked out.

*        *        *

Irina, Kuznov's secretary, buzzed Kuznov on the intercom. "The Chechen president is calling," she said.

Kuznov picked up immediately, hoping Daud would have news about Craig Page.

"I had my best security people follow Enrico Marino from the minute he got off the plane in Grozny," Daud reported.

"And?" Kuznov asked.

"At six o'clock earlier this evening, he checked into the Hotel Grozny City. One of the men I had placed in the lobby saw him go into a private room with the concierge. He was there with the concierge for fifteen minutes. Two hours later, he left in a taxicab driven by one of my men. He asked to go to the concert hall. While my man drove him via a circuitous route, security people in the hotel forced the concierge to tell them what he had discussed with Marino. It took some persuasion, but the concierge finally admitted that Marino had asked to meet with Omar Basayev. The plan was for Marino to meet up with Mikhail, a member of Omar Basayev's gang, in front of the concert hall, and Mikhail would then take him to Omar from there."

"Why did the concierge agree to this?"

"Money. I'll have him executed immediately," said Daud obsequiously.

"No. Don't do that," Kuznov ordered. "Leave him in place. You'll own him now. You'll be able to use him whenever you want."

"Understood."

Kuznov wondered if Page was seeking Omar out because he had something to do with Toth's plan to prevent the Friendship Pact from being consummated. The Friendship Pact was too important—he was prepared to break his truce with Omar over it. He would have him murdered before he would risk having him interfere with that agreement.

"Have Marino and Mikhail met with Omar yet?" Kuznov asked.

"I don't know if Omar will be there or if he is even in Grozny, but Mikhail and another man just got out of Mikhail's car in front of a deserted warehouse. They carried Marino into the warehouse. It looked like he had been incapacitated in some way. My men can see inside with binoculars through a broken window, but they can't overhear conversations in the building. Tell me what you want me to do."

Kuznov paused for a second to process what Daud had told him. He had a number of objectives. First, he wanted to learn why Craig wanted to meet with Omar. It must have something to do with Peter Toth. Second, he wanted Omar dead.

He told Daud, "Wait a little while to see if Omar is there or if he comes. If your men see Omar, have them break in and kill Omar and his gang. Hold Marino in the warehouse temporarily. Let me know when you have him and I'll tell you what to do."

"Suppose Omar's not there and doesn't come?"

"Kill his gang and take Marino into custody. Then call me. I'll tell you what to do with him."

*       *       *

When Craig regained consciousness, he was naked, sitting in a wooden chair, his arms and legs tied tightly. His vision was foggy as he looked around, but he could tell he was in the center of a storage area of a warehouse. He saw oil barrels scattered on the floor and dirty paint cans on shelves. Craig's clothes were scattered on the floor near the chair.

Craig saw Mikhail and two other men, neither of whom was Omar. Seeing that he had regained consciousness, one of the men approached, aiming a gun straight at Craig's head.

"Why do you want to see Omar?" he asked.

"I want to hire Omar to do a job," Craig replied calmly. "If he's not in Grozny, tell me how I can contact him." The man with the gun looked dubious. He glanced at Mikhail questioningly.

Mikhail shook his head, his face hard. "He's lying," he said. "He's an agent of Kuznov. He wants to find Omar so Kuznov can kill him."

"That's ridiculous," Craig said. "I hate Kuznov. I wouldn't have anything to do with him."

The man with the gun studied Craig. Finally he said, "We'll find out if you're telling the truth."

He pointed to the third man who reached into a box on the ground. He pulled out a rope. At one end it had five steel balls. Craig could guess what was coming next. In case he had any doubt, the man wrapped the end of the rope around his hand and gave a practice swing. The steel balls struck a paint can so hard that it fell off the shelf.

"His balls will hit your balls," the man with the gun said, laughing sadistically. "Now, do you have anything else to tell me?"

Craig was out of ideas, but he tried to hang tough. "I've told you the truth. I want to hire Omar for a job. If you don't help me, you will be costing Omar a lot of money."

"I don't believe you," said the man.

"Then fuck you," Craig retorted. All he could think about was that Elizabeth had been right. He had been a fool to come to Grozny.

He watched the man wind up with the rope with a sick feeling in his stomach. But before he had a chance to swing it, Craig heard the firing of automatic weapons. The man with the steel balls hit the ground, and Craig saw his chest had been riddled with bullets. Six men in military uniforms burst into the warehouse firing at Mikhail and the man with the gun. They cut them down before either could get off a shot.

One of the soldiers untied Craig.

"Thank you," Craig said as he picked his clothes off the floor and hurriedly dressed.

"We take you back to the hotel," another soldier said.

Craig asked, "Who sent you?" but neither soldier responded.

They dropped Craig in front of the hotel. As soon as he entered, he glanced at the concierge desk, but it was deserted. He got into an elevator and hit the thirtieth floor. Gradually, his fright was passing. He didn't even want to imagine what would have happened to him if those soldiers hadn't come.

Craig got into the shower and let the water flow over his head, cleansing him from his ordeal. After his shower he checked airplane schedules on his iPad. The first plane with an available seat didn't leave Grozny for Moscow until 2:00 p.m. the next day. He made a reservation on that flight, grabbing one of the few remaining seats, and then on a connecting flight to Paris.

At this point, he just hoped he could get out of Grozny alive.

\*          \*          \*

Craig spent the morning in his hotel room, hoping Omar's gang wouldn't try to attack him there. He killed time until his flight by reading about Chechnya and its president, Daud Mollah. One thing was clear: Daud was a puppet of Russia.

At noon Craig got into a cab and asked the driver to take him to the airport. The man was silent the entire ride, and Craig breathed a sigh of relief when they arrived without incident.

Check-in also went smoothly, but Craig had no intention of relaxing until the plane took off. Waiting in the boarding area, he sipped lukewarm coffee and glanced around anxiously. The first ominous sign came when the monitor showed that their departure would be delayed one hour; no explanation was given. The other passengers groaned.

Twenty minutes later, two armed soldiers appeared in the boarding area and went up to the gate agent. After they spoke with her, the agent picked up the microphone and announced, "Will Enrico Marino please come to the desk."

Craig tried not to look worried as he approached. At the desk the agent asked to see his passport, then nodded to the two soldiers.

"Mr. Marino," one soldier said, "please come with us."

"For what reason?"

"On orders of our president."

Resisting was futile, Craig realized, so he followed the soldiers quietly.

Upon leaving the terminal, they put him into a military van waiting at the curb. Half an hour later, he was being escorted into the presidential palace and led to a suite of offices with a sign on a wooden door that read: Office of the President.

One of the soldiers knocked twice, and the door opened from inside. Craig immediately recognized President Daud Mollah from his research earlier that morning. The man was short, only five foot six, but squat and muscular, built like a tank with a short, pointed, reddish beard. He had a kindly smile, but Craig, who had read about Daud's cruelty, wasn't deceived.

"Come in Enrico," he said.

The door closed after Craig, and he found himself alone with Daud.

"I appreciate your coming," Daud said.

"It's an honor to meet the president of Chechnya," Craig replied in kind.

"I was surprised that you didn't come to thank me this morning for saving your manhood," Daud added.

Craig swallowed uncomfortably. "I really appreciate your help, and I mean that," he said, resisting the urge to add, "You cut it awfully close."

"Now I want to know why you came to Grozny," said Daud, his smile taking on a dangerous edge.

"I'm seeking possible investments," Craig replied smoothly. "I've heard that your economy is on the verge of taking off, and I want to get on the ground floor."

Daud looked angry. "I don't like it when people lie to me, Enrico Marino."

"I thought you'd like an investment in Chechnya by a famous race car driver."

"That story might have had a chance if you hadn't asked to see Omar Basayev yesterday. As you're no doubt aware, Omar is a terrorist, an enemy of Chechnya and Russia." He paused before adding, "Here's what we're going to do. In the next room I have certain implements that might prevail on you to talk. We can spend as long as you like there, but you will tell me why you came to Grozny, sooner or later."

Craig realized he didn't have much of a choice. His mind raced as he thought about what he could tell Daud, knowing the Chechen president would be sure to repeat it to Kuznov. The best approach, he thought, was to stick with the Amos Neir story and omit Peter Toth. He knew that Kuznov hated Omar, so if Kuznov believed Craig was hunting Omar for revenge, he might very well instruct Daud to let Craig go in the hope that he would succeed.

"I had a good friend," Craig began slowly, "Amos Neir, an Israeli Mossad agent who was killed in Paris on August second." As Craig spoke, he knew he had to give enough detail for his story to sound authentic. "Amos was living undercover as Ahmed Hussein in Clichy," he continued, "a Muslim suburb of Paris, trying to stop terrorist attacks. After Amos identified Omar in Clichy, he tried to find out what Omar was up to, but Omar realized Amos was tracking him. Amos's body was found in the river—he had been murdered. I'll do anything I can to locate Omar and kill him. I promised Amos's wife I would avenge his death, and I intend to do that."

Daud looked skeptically at Craig.

"You've heard the whole story," Craig added. "Now am I free to leave Grozny?"

"Tomorrow morning at eight, if your story checks out."

"How about this afternoon?"

"I need time to confirm what you told me."

Craig understood what that meant: Daud would tell Kuznov, and he had to give Kuznov enough time to check the facts and decide Craig's fate.

"My men will drive you to your hotel," said Daud. "It would be best if you stayed in this evening."

"You don't have to worry. I did enough sightseeing last evening."

Daud didn't even crack a smile. *Okay, the Chechen doesn't have a sense of humor*, thought Craig.

*       *       *

After Kuznov had heard Craig's story from Daud, he summoned Dimitri and asked him to see if it checked out.

An hour later, Kuznov received the answer: an Israeli undercover agent, Amos Neir, posing as Ahmed Hussein, had been murdered in Paris on August 2. His body had been pulled from the Seine, and the suspected murderer was Omar Basayev.

If in fact that was why Craig had gone to Grozny and he was trying to kill Omar, Kuznov would gladly let him leave. It would be wonderful if somebody other than Kuznov killed Omar. That way Kuznov wouldn't face another insurrection from the Chechens.

Kuznov still had some nagging doubts as to whether Craig was somehow involved in the plot Toth had set in motion, and he had one other way to get some information. He decided to delay calling Daud until he saw how that turned out.

*       *       *

That evening, Craig had another disappointing dinner alone in the hotel dining room, this time accompanied by a dismal bottle of Romanian wine.

After dinner, he returned to his suite. His plan was to shower, go to bed, and hopefully get on an 8:00 a.m. plane to Moscow, where he would connect to Paris.

While he was drying himself after his shower, he heard the doorbell ring. *What now*, Craig wondered as he slipped on a terrycloth robe and walked into the living room. He looked through the peephole and saw a gorgeous blonde woman in a room service uniform—a white skirt and tight fitting white blouse that accentuated her ample bosom. She was standing in the corridor with a cart holding a bottle of Taittinger Comtes de Vogue in an ice bucket and a platter of caviar and blinis.

Craig opened the door, and she wheeled in the cart.

"Hi, Mr. Marino," she said. "My name is Olga."

"I didn't order anything from room service."

"This is compliments of the hotel management. They understand that you had some trouble during your stay, and they don't want you to have an unfavorable view about Grozny."

"Well, that's very nice."

"Why don't you sit down? I'll pour you a glass of champagne and fix some caviar."

"That sounds wonderful," said Craig, sitting on a sofa.

She opened the bottle, poured a glass, and handed it to him. It was excellent and perfectly chilled. As he sipped, she spread caviar on a blini and held it in front of his mouth. He ate it.

"Would you like another?"

"Sure."

She returned to the cart, but instead of working with the caviar, she unbuttoned her blouse, exposing her full breasts. Then she unzipped her skirt, letting that fall to the floor. She wasn't wearing any underwear.

*Who sent her and what the hell is going on?* Craig wondered. He was determined to find out.

"Why don't you pull up a chair and join me for a glass," he suggested. "It's a shame for me to drink alone."

"Excellent idea," she agreed, pouring herself a glass before sitting down close to Craig.

She raised her glass. "To your good health, Mr. Marino."

"And yours, too," said Craig.

They both took a sip.

"Now for some more caviar," she said.

She returned to the cart, but this time instead of spreading it on a blini, she placed some caviar on each of her breasts, around the nipples. Then she walked over and stood in front of Craig.

"I thought you'd like to eat it this way."

"What a good idea."

As he licked off the caviar, she reached down and placed her hand between his legs. She played with his penis until it stiffened.

"Well, well, what do we have here?" she said. "You've obviously recovered from your ordeal."

"For sure. But I think we'd be more comfortable in the bedroom."

Once in the bedroom, she stretched out on the bed and raised her legs, opening herself up to him.

Craig turned on the radio next to the bed to a station playing classical music. Then he climbed on top of her, but didn't enter her. Instead, he swiftly grabbed a pillow and placed it over her face, pressing down firmly. He had no intention of harming her, but he needed answers and frightening her was the only way he could get them.

She tried to scream, but the pillow muffled the sound. She twisted, thrashed, and kicked to no avail. Craig was too strong. After a couple of minutes, he pulled the pillow away. She was gasping for breath.

"Listen Olga, you're going to answer some questions or I'll suffocate you. It's your choice."

Though he was bluffing, from the look of terror on her face, he was sure she believed him.

"What questions?" she asked, panting.

"I want to know who sent you and what you were told to do."

She gnashed her teeth, struggling to get away from him. "I'll tell you nothing, you bastard," she hissed.

"What a shame," he said, "for a beautiful woman to die so young."

Then he plastered the pillow over her face again, keeping it there for a full minute.

When he pulled it away this time, the color was gone from her face.

"Last chance, Olga. Tell me now or you'll die."

"I'll tell you," she stammered.

"I'm listening."

"President Kuznov sent me. He told me to find out why you came to Grozny. That's the truth. I swear."

"Where are you from?"

"Moscow."

"When did you fly to Grozny?"

"This afternoon. I flew from Moscow in President Kuznov's private plane."

Craig believed her. It made sense that once Kuznov knew Craig was coming to Grozny he would try anything to find out what Craig wanted.

He got up from the bed and said, "Get dressed. We have to talk. Let's go into the living room."

Once Craig had his robe on and Olga had dressed, he turned on the television in the living room. Then he dumped the two glasses of champagne into the ice bucket and poured two fresh ones.

"One thing I don't like is warm champagne," he said.

He handed her a glass. She looked worried now, and he understood why.

"You have a problem," he told her. "If you tell Kuznov what happened, he might kill you for failing him. I'm right, aren't I?"

"Yes," she stammered.

"So I have to give you a story that Kuznov will believe."

She nodded.

"Here's what you should tell him. You came into my suite with champagne. We had wonderful sex twice and we drank lots of champagne. After the second time while we were drinking champagne and talking, I told you that I came to Grozny to find Omar the Chechen and to kill him because he murdered a good friend of mine, Amos Neir."

He paused. "Do you understand what I said?"

"Yes," she said weakly.

"Good. I promise you," he added, "that if I am arrested by Kuznov's men after you leave here, I will tell them the exact same story. Our lives are both on the line. We're in this together, joined at the hip, whether we like it or not. We can save each other, but only if we stick to this story."

"I understand," she said, now with conviction.

"Good."

He walked over to the desk, where he had a pile of euros. He counted out five thousand and gave them to her.

"This is for your service tonight," he said. "And if Kuznov asks, you can tell him that you were so good in bed I wanted to reward you."

She smiled as she stuffed the money in her pocket.

"Can I go now?"

"No. I want you to go into the bedroom and moan for a couple of minutes as if we're having really good sex. Then come out here and watch television for an hour. After that, go back into the bedroom and make the moaning noises again. Can you do that?"

"Of course."

"Good. After that you can go."

The first time she went into the bedroom her cries sounded so real that Craig wondered what she was doing. From the door of the bedroom, he watched. She was naked lying on her back. With one hand she was playing with her breasts and with the other, she was stroking her vagina. Her eyes were closed; her body was writhing in ecstasy while she moaned. She clearly wasn't pretending. She obviously took her assignment seriously.

After she returned from her second trip to the bedroom, an hour later, Craig said, "Okay, Olga. I've had a very long couple of days and I'm tired. You should leave and let me get to sleep."

When she was gone, he wondered whether Kuznov would now send some thugs to test the veracity of the story Olga told by torturing him. Though the story she would tell was credible, it was about fifty-fifty, whether they would attack him, he decided. Nothing he could do about it now. Security men would almost undoubtedly stop him if he tried to leave the hotel.

*No sense worrying about what I can't control,* Craig thought, and he really was tired. He went into the bedroom and climbed into bed with the scent of Olga still in the air and on the sheets, where he fell into a sound sleep.

*          *          *

Kuznov had told Olga to call him as soon as she left Craig's hotel room, regardless of the hour. He was sleeping when the phone rang at 3:35 a.m.

"What took you so long?" he asked, rubbing the sleep out of his eyes.

"He's a virile man. He wanted to keep going. I couldn't tell him no."

"Sounds like you enjoyed yourself. What did you learn?"

"Enrico came to Grozny to find and kill Omar the Chechen because he murdered a friend of Enrico's in Paris last week, a man named Amos Neir."

"You think he was telling you the truth?"

"Yes, I made sure he drank a lot—it was clear his defenses were lowered."

"Did he pay you for your services?"

"Five thousand euros."

Kuznov laughed. "With the ten I paid you, not a bad day's work. Unfortunately, I needed my plane so it's back in Moscow. My secretary reserved a seat for you on the 8:00 a.m. Aeroflot to Moscow. So get a couple hours sleep and head to the airport."

Kuznov paced, thinking about what he had learned. It was possible that Craig had been telling the truth—that his mission to Grozny was unrelated to Peter Toth. Certainly in his CIA days he might have developed a relationship with a Mossad agent. He could be pursuing this separate from his help to Elizabeth with Nicholas Toth. In that case, torturing Craig to get him to talk would be a waste of time. It would make far more sense to let him fly back to Paris, have people follow him there, and hope that he found and killed Omar. Even if he was working to stop the ceremony in Budapest from taking place, Kuznov would find out about it beforehand and stop him.

Kuznov picked up the phone and called Daud. "Let Enrico Marino take the first plane out to Moscow."

Then he went back to bed, but he couldn't sleep. He had been reluctant to kill Omar himself for fear of risking another uprising in Chechnya, which he didn't want right now. But if Craig killed him, that would be perfect.

Kuznov could still remember Omar's attack on the concert hall in Moscow twenty-two years ago. Omar and his accomplices had taken more than fifty hostages. When Russian troops burst in, they killed thirty-four of the fifty, and all but one of the Chechens. But somehow Omar slipped way.

Craig Page killing Omar would be a stroke of good fortune. With that thought in mind, Kuznov fell back to sleep.

# Budapest

At six in the morning, Omar walked out of the front door of the castle into the cool morning air with a cup of tea in hand and a Glock holstered at his waist. The castle was perched on a crest in the rolling Buda hills west of the city center in Pest.

Omar looked eastward toward the Danube, with its beautiful bridges crossing into Pest, the commercial and business center of the city, and to the Great Hungarian Plains and farmland beyond where the sun was rising.

He was grateful to EU's free movement rule under the Schengen Agreement, which permitted him, along with the four men in his entourage, to cross freely without any border checks from France to Germany, Austria, and finally to Hungary, in their van loaded with weapons. He knew those were the rules, but he still breathed a sigh of relief when he crossed the border into Hungary.

Once they approached Budapest, it was easy to reach the deserted castle Peter Toth had told him to use during their planning session. Peter had given him keys both to the castle and to his office abutting Parliament Square. From his vantage point in the early morning light, Omar had a perfect view of the stately neo-Gothic parliament building, one of the largest in the world, its spires shooting up into the sky.

Today was only Friday morning. According to Peter, the ceremony was set for Wednesday at noon. Omar hated waiting.

The castle, complete with turrets, had been built in the nineteenth century by a nobleman whose descendants had been murdered by the Nazis—supposedly an ally of Hungary. Omar, once a professor of European history, knew that Hungary had the distinction of being on the losing side of almost every war in the nineteenth and twentieth centuries.

A few years ago, the castle had been refurbished inside and it was comfortable. Shamil brought in food and other supplies, but Omar refused to let the other three leave the building.

Though the nearest neighbor was a hundred yards away, he didn't want to risk raising suspicions that might bring a visit from the authorities.

As Omar looked out over the city, he heard the sound of footsteps from behind. Hand on his gun, Omar wheeled around. It was only Shamil.

"I have news," Shamil said.

"What's that?"

"I just learned that Peter Toth died in a fire in Washington."

Omar pulled back with a start. "How did you find out?"

"On the internet. I was trying to get information about the parliament building when I stumbled across a speech given by Janos Rajk, the Hungarian justice minister, at a memorial service for Peter Toth in Maryland."

Omar wasn't surprised they hadn't been aware of Peter's death. Neither Omar nor Shamil regularly read newspapers, looked at television, or checked news online.

While processing the information, Omar reached a conclusion: Peter's death could hardly be a coincidence. Kuznov must have found out what Peter was planning and arranged the fire. The Russian president had used arson to dispose of his political opponents in the past.

"You never received the second ten million euros that Peter Toth promised," Shamil pointed out. "You could simply take the ten million he already paid you and abandon the operation. Nobody is alive to care now, and that way we can avoid the serious risks in proceeding."

Omar rubbed his beard thinking about what Shamil had said. The castle was dark. He imagined the three men he had recruited were still sleeping. It was tempting to follow Shamil's suggestion. He could go back to Grozny and use the ten million euros to finance terrorist operations against Russia.

Omar would have done that if Hungarian Prime Minister Szabo were the only target. But Peter Toth had hired Omar to kill Kuznov as well as Szabo. The plans Omar had developed were airtight. He might never get a chance to kill Kuznov again and repay the Russian for what he had done to Omar's wife and children. And as long as he was killing Kuznov, he might as well take out Szabo as well. Of course, he'd never get the second ten million, but he didn't care.

"No, we keep going," Omar said with an air of finality.

He waited to hear whether Shamil would push back and argue with him, but instead he heard another man's voice coming from behind the castle. Did they have an intruder? Omar pulled out his gun, motioning to Shamil with a finger over his lips. With Shamil trailing behind, he walked softly toward the back of the castle and the sound of the voice.

A thick wooded area was in the back, and as he looked around the corner, Omar couldn't believe what he saw. One of the three Frenchmen—Rachid—was squatting down in a clump of trees, talking on a cell phone.

Omar was livid. He had told them they couldn't have cell phones. That fucking Rachid. He knew he would be trouble, even in Clichy. He should have never brought him along.

Omar heard Rachid say, "Don't worry," as he approached, white with rage.

"I told you not to bring cell phones," he hissed, aiming his gun at Rachid.

"Please don't kill me," Rachid cried out, holding his hands up.

"Who were you talking to?" Omar demanded.

"Only my sister, Ayanna. No one else, I swear," Rachid said in a terrified voice. "I won't make any more calls. I promise." Rachid raised his arm and threw the cell phone into the woods. "See? It's gone."

Omar ignored his plea, firing three shots, even though he knew Rachid was dead after the first.

Rachid collapsed to the ground in a pool of his own blood.

"Wake the other two," Omar told Shamil in an irate voice. "Order them to dig a hole and bury their buddy, that liar and sneak. Then have our friends in Clichy kill Ayanna as well. We don't know what he told her. We can't take any chances."

## Grozny and Paris

At six thirty in the morning, Craig walked through the revolving door of his hotel in Grozny and looked for a cab to take him to the airport. Horrified, he saw a military transport parked at the curb. Standing next to it were two soldiers.

One of the soldiers told Craig, "Our president is personally providing you with transport to the airport. Our taxis are not always dependable, and he doesn't want anything to happen to you."

Craig climbed into the vehicle. Kuznov must have not only accepted his story, Craig thought, but decided Craig could be valuable in finding and even killing Omar. That was fine with Craig.

The soldiers accompanied him to the boarding area where he was permitted to board first and given a seat in first class. At the end of the boarding process, he saw Olga get on the plane. She paused next to him, leaned over, and kissed him on the lips. "Great evening," she said. Reaching into her bag, she pulled out a card and handed it to him. "It has all of my contact info. Call me when you're in Moscow. I travel, too."

Then she made her way to the back of the plane. He wondered whether she meant it or if she was still playing the role he had given her.

Once they were in the air, Craig breathed a sigh of relief. But he didn't have a damn thing to show for all the pain and trauma he had suffered in Grozny.

When the plane landed in Moscow, Craig got off quickly and followed the signs for "connecting flights." He had no desire to talk with Olga. His connection to Paris was on time, and he landed at Charles de Gaulle at five in the afternoon.

Craig fully anticipated that Kuznov would have men following him from the time he arrived in Paris, but that didn't deter Craig. He rented a premium BMW from Avis, and as he left the lot, a dark blue Mercedes fell in behind him. The Mercedes followed him from the lot to the crowded highway, hanging back behind another car. Craig knew the roads around the airport by memory. He left the highway at the next exit. Then it only took him twenty minutes of fast driving, lane changes, and quick sharp turns, to lose the Mercedes.

Before proceeding to the Bristol, he found another Avis location, told them the engine was knocking, and traded the BMW for an Audi. He drove for ten more minutes, making sure he wasn't being followed. Then he pulled off the road at a service station, parked, and took out his phone. He dialed Elizabeth, who answered on the first ring.

"Craig."

"Hi Elizabeth."

"Where are you?"

"Paris."

"Oh my God. I'm so glad." She was crying. "I was so worried. Are you okay?"

"I'm completely fine. I'll give you the details later. Where are you?" Craig asked.

"Right where you left me."

"I'm on my way. Love you."

As soon as Craig entered the Bristol suite, he dropped his duffel bag and threw his arms around Elizabeth. They held each other tightly and kissed.

Pulling away, she said, "I was so worried. You have no idea."

"I'm really sorry I caused you so much pain."

"Was it worth going to Grozny?"

Craig shook his head. "I didn't learn a damn thing. It's frustrating."

"Listen, Giuseppe called. He wants to come over at ten this evening if you're back. He might have something for you."

"We need a break. How's Nick doing?" he asked.

"I was up there this afternoon. He's in good spirits. He just wants this to be over."

"Don't we all."

"Nobody suspicious has shown up at the clinic or here."

"That's good news."

"Why don't you shower and clean up," Elizabeth suggested. "I'll call Giuseppe and tell him to come at ten. Then I'll order some dinner from room service. We have something to discuss."

"That sounds ominous," he said, ducking into the bathroom.

After his shower, Craig and Elizabeth sat down to dinner in their suite. Craig was midway through a bite of steak when Elizabeth put her fork down decisively. Craig looked at her attentively.

"We've never spoken about children," she said, "so I haven't told you that when I was twenty-two I was diagnosed with endometriosis, which required surgery and left me with scarring. As a result, I can't have children."

His forehead wrinkled. "I'm sorry. I had no idea."

She hesitated, trying to frame her next words carefully. Before she had a chance to speak, Craig said, "You think we should adopt Nick? The two of us? Is that what you wanted to tell me?"

"How'd you know?"

"I can see how you feel about him."

"What do you think?" she asked, holding her breath.

"I think it's a great idea. He's a terrific kid, and I would love raising him with you."

"That's fantastic. I'm so glad," said Elizabeth excitedly. "I'll get started on the paperwork right away."

Craig raised his hand. "We better hold up until this is all over. People are trying to kill Nick. If we begin this proceeding now, we could be endangering him."

"Can I at least tell Nick?"

Craig thought about it for a moment, then replied, "You don't want to do that until we've seen Peter's will and we have a legal path forward. You don't want to raise Nick's hopes unless we're confident we can pull it off."

She nodded. "Yeah, you're right. Think it could ever happen?"

"Why not?"

"Peter's wife Reka had family in Cleveland. Chances are one of those relatives will want to raise Nick. And I'm not a lawyer, but my guess is they would have priority over us."

"What if Nick preferred us?"

"I don't know," Elizabeth said. "A friend of mine from Harvard, Daniel Metz, who I've stayed in touch with, went to Columbia Law and he's a partner in a big New York law firm. Can I ask him to recommend a lawyer in the field?"

Craig could tell how much this meant to Elizabeth. He reached his hand across the table and placed it on hers.

"If we do anything now, Elizabeth, I'm afraid it could endanger Nick. But I promise you as soon as this is all over, you can call Daniel for his recommendation."

She squeezed his hand. "Thank you, Craig."

                    *         *         *

Giuseppe came to the hotel at ten.

"Learn anything useful in Grozny?" he asked while Craig poured the three of them Armagnac.

"Not a damn thing."

"Well, at least you made it back, and you don't look any worse for it."

Craig had no intention of telling them what had happened. "Yeah, a pretty uneventful trip. I doubt that Omar is in Grozny. That's my one takeaway."

"Well that's something," Giuseppe said. "I wanted to talk to you about Sardinia."

"What'd you learn?"

"I had police in Sardinia show Peter's picture to cab drivers who work at Olbia Airport. One of them remembered taking him on July 26 to the compound on the Costa Smeralda of Yuri Brodervich, a Russian oligarch. After he fell out with Kuznov, the Russian president tried to have him killed, which is why he's living in Sardinia in a protected compound. The cab driver said he waited for three hours at the compound before taking Peter back to the airport."

Craig's mind was operating slowly after all he'd been through in the last couple of days—and thanks to Olga he had hardly slept the previous night—but the name Yuri Brodervich was familiar.

After a few seconds it clicked into place. "I know Yuri Brodervich."

"From where?" Giuseppe asked.

"I competed in rally races twice in Sardinia. The first time I crashed and was knocked out. The second time I won. After that second race when I was getting my trophy, Yuri came up to congratulate me. I remember he was accompanied by three thuggish-looking bodyguards. He introduced himself and he invited me to dinner that evening. I told him I had to get back to Milan, but promised to call him the next time I was in Sardinia. He gave me his card, so I could call him."

"Why don't you offer to have lunch with him tomorrow?"

"That place is a bitch to get to from Paris."

"I'll get you a private plane."

"Now you're talking."

He looked at Elizabeth. "What do you think? Should I go?"

She frowned. "I didn't think my opinion mattered about where you travel. Of course you should go and try to find out what Peter talked to Yuri about. It would be useful. And more important, I don't think there's much chance of you getting killed in Sardinia." She paused then added, "Although with you, Craig, danger is always a possibility."

"I'm going somewhere myself tomorrow," Giuseppe said, trying to change the subject.

"Where?" Craig asked.

"Brussels. I've convened a meeting of all the top security people in Belgium and France to go over our plans for apprehending Omar and stopping his attack on September 1."

# Costa Smeralda, Sardinia

The next morning Craig called Yuri from Paris. "It's Enrico Marino, Mr. Brodervich. I don't know if you remember me."

"Of course I do, the amazing race car driver. And please call me Yuri. I hope you're in Sardinia and we can get together."

"How about lunch today?"

"It'll be my pleasure. Come to my place at one." Yuri provided an address and directions.

Pleased at how smoothly it had gone, Craig called Giuseppe.

"The plane's waiting at Orly," Giuseppe said. "I'll have them fuel it."

At five minutes to one, Craig approached a walled compound next to the water in his rental car half a mile from Porto Cervo. An iron gate blocked access to the driveway, and two armed guards were standing in front.

As soon as Craig showed his Enrico Marino passport, they waved him through. Driving along a circular road, he approached the Moorish two-story house, which was concealed from the road by a high wall. Inside the front door, two more bodyguards lounged on chairs. An attractive, dark-haired woman came forward and said, "Mr. Marino, welcome. Please follow me."

Craig followed her through two rooms with elegant damask engravings, horseshoe arches, and turquoise ceilings. The furnishings were Italian with classic wooden pieces. Craig could smell the sea because the second room opened onto a patio facing the water.

Yuri, holding a glass in his left hand, dressed in white slacks and a navy polo, came forward to greet Craig. Behind Yuri, Craig saw an elegantly set table.

"So glad you could come," Yuri said, holding out his hand.

Craig shook it and winced. Yuri's grip was so strong it sent shock waves up Craig's arm.

"What would you like to drink?" Yuri asked. "I'm having vodka, but we have a white Arneis being chilled if you would prefer that."

"That sounds great."

Yuri pointed to the young woman who had led Craig out to the deck. "Vanessa, white wine for our guest."

Once Craig had a glass, Yuri raised his and said, "Salute. Now if you don't mind, let's sit at the table. I'm having back problems, and the straight chair helps."

"I'm sorry to hear that," said Craig, taking a seat across from Yuri.

The table was set with English bone china and Christofle silver. Between the house and the water, perfectly manicured grass with a lap pool in the center gave way to sand. Tied up at the dock was a large yacht sporting antennas and a helipad. Further out in the water a woman was water-skiing.

"Will you be driving in the October race this year?" Yuri asked.

"I'm planning to. I'd like to make it two in a row."

"I'll be betting on you," Yuri laughed. "I'm just afraid I may have to give long odds."

It struck Craig that Yuri seemed likable—surprising in view of his background as a hard-nosed businessman who some called a thief. Years earlier he had been caught stealing Middle Eastern assets from a large, Russian state-owned ore company. Craig's information, gleaned from the CIA at the time, was that Yuri avoided charges by paying off Kuznov and some of his friends. When their demands became too great for him to meet, Yuri got word that Kuznov was sending FSB agents to arrest him. His future was already stashed in foreign banks beyond Kuznov's reach. Leaving behind his wife and children, he escaped into Turkey, pretending to be a truck driver.

"I'll do my best to have you win your bet," Craig said.

"Speaking of racing, I read that your benefactor Federico Castiglione was murdered. I'd like to pick up Federico's share, whatever that was, and sponsor you."

Craig was flattered by the offer, but also appalled. The idea of being a partner with and in debt to the sinister Yuri Brodervich was a nonstarter. Still, he had to reject Yuri's offer gracefully. He needed the Russian's cooperation.

"That's a wonderful offer, Yuri, but fortunately Federico provided for me in his will, so I'm okay for now."

"Well, it's an expensive sport. If that money ever runs out, you know where to find me."

"Thank you."

Yuri signaled to Vanessa to refill their glasses. Seconds later, two waiters emerged from the house, one carrying a serving bowl covered by a dome, the other plates and a basket of rolls. Under the dome was an exquisite cold seafood salad loaded with calamari, octopus, mussels, and scallops. The waiters served the two men and withdrew.

"Tell me how it is," Yuri said.

Craig took a taste. "Outstanding."

"Good, because I just fired my chef. This one is new."

"He's a keeper."

"All right, Enrico, nobody comes to see me for a social visit. I thought you wanted me to invest in your racing. Now that we've established that's not the case, tell me why you're here."

Craig leaned forward in his chair. "I don't like it when somebody murders one of my friends. I think you can understand that." Yuri sat up with a start, back pain or not. If Craig were threatening him, he was prepared to call his bodyguards. He reached his hand under the table. Craig guessed he had a call button there.

"I'm not suggesting you had anything to do with it," he added swiftly.

Yuri relaxed. "Were you referring to Federico Castiglione?"

"No. Peter Toth."

"How did you know Peter?" Yuri asked, looking surprised.

"When he was still doing business in Hungary, we entered into a joint venture to bring rally racing to Hungary, and we became friends in the process." Craig sounded convincing as he spun out his yarn. "Then that prick Szabo shut down Peter's business. Now Peter's dead, and I'm sure as hell going to find out who's responsible and make them pay."

"What makes you think I know anything?"

"Peter told me that he was planning to visit you here in Sardinia a few days before the fire, but he didn't tell me why. I figured this was a good place to start in my effort to find out who killed Peter."

Yuri tapped his fingers on the table for a few seconds, then said, "When I was still in Moscow, Peter showed up at my energy company one day. He wanted to do a deal with me to buy oil for Hungary. We got to know each other. I liked Peter. We were close to finalizing an arrangement that made sense for both of us when I decided my health required resettlement to a warmer climate. That was the end of my Russian energy company."

"So why did Peter visit you here?"

Yuri drained his glass, picked up the vodka bottle on the table, and refilled it.

*That isn't water*, Craig thought with astonishment.

Yuri took a gulp and said, "Peter wanted me to recommend an assassin, somebody who hated Russia."

"Holy shit. Who did Peter want to have killed?"

"Peter told me he wanted to have Szabo killed because he was planning to enter into an agreement with Kuznov that would permit Russian troops into Hungary. By killing Szabo, he would block this agreement from going into effect—a huge blow for Kuznov."

"Did you give him a recommendation?" Craig asked.

Yuri nodded. "Omar the Chechen. I even told him where he could find Omar outside of Grozny, and I gave him a letter of recommendation."

"You've done business with Omar before?"

"Let's just say we know each other."

"So Peter flew off to Grozny to meet with Omar."

Yuri nodded again. "You should know one other fact."

"What's that?"

"Like Omar, I have reasons to hate Kuznov. So I told Peter that if he arranged for Omar to take out Kuznov as well as Szabo, I'd pay half his fee to Omar."

"What'd he say?"

"He was noncommittal. He told me he was willing to pay Omar ten million euros up front and another ten when the job was done. I told him if Omar got Kuznov as well as Szabo, I'd cover the second ten, but I never heard any more from him or Omar. Then I found out Peter was dead. Of course I'm convinced Kuznov arranged the fire outside of Washington. It was a good preemptive move—vintage Kuznov. He found out about Peter's plans and had him murdered."

"How do you know Szabo wasn't responsible for the fire and Peter's death?" Craig asked.

Yuri laughed. "The Hungarians, like the Poles, the Romanians, all of those Central Europeans, are too inept to light a fire in their fireplace at home."

Yuri may not be in Russia, Craig thought, but he certainly hadn't lost his Russian arrogance and contempt for Central Europeans that characterized the Soviet Union in the period from 1945 to 1991.

Craig asked Yuri, "Suppose Peter made the deal with Omar, as you described it, and Peter paid Omar ten million up front. Then suppose Omar found out that Peter died before Omar had a chance to do the job. What do you think he would do? Pocket the money and go back to Grozny? Or carry out the assignment?"

Yuri thought about it for a moment. "It depends."

"On what?"

"If Omar's only target was Szabo, he'd quit," Yuri explained. "On the other hand, I'm sure you know about Omar's hatred for Kuznov."

Craig recalled what Gideon had told him in Israel. "The man brutally killed his wife and children."

"Correct, so in view of Omar's hatred for Kuznov, if both men were his targets, or if Omar saw a way to kill Kuznov as well as Szabo, Omar would keep going."

After they had finished their lunch, Yuri walked Craig to the door. "You're always welcome here," he said. "Stay longer next time. We could have some fun. Women in Sardinia are incredible."

"For sure," Craig agreed as he made his way out.

Driving back to the airport, Craig tried to evaluate what he had learned. It seemed unlikely that Omar would miss a shot at taking out Kuznov, who had destroyed his life so utterly. So he had to assume that Omar was continuing his operation even after Peter's death—and that he had Kuznov as well as Szabo in his crosshairs.

But Kuznov wouldn't be coming to Brussels for the EU conference. So if Yuri were correct, Kuznov and Szabo must have plans to meet somewhere else, and that's where Omar planned to kill them.

The possibilities were endless. Moscow or Budapest? After that, anywhere else in Europe. He planned to brief Betty and Giuseppe when he returned to Paris. He would need their help.

The search for Omar had just gotten more difficult.

# Budapest

Omar left Shamil at the castle to watch the remaining two Frenchmen. Then he climbed into the white van, and for ten minutes he drove around the sparsely inhabited hills of Buda, taking random turns to make certain he wasn't being followed. He had a pistol in his jacket pocket and an automatic weapon on the floor in the front of the van.

If someone tried to tail him, he had a simple solution. He'd pull over the van to the side of the road and wait for his pursuer to do the same, then he would open fire on them with his automatic weapon.

After ten minutes of driving, once Omar was convinced he wasn't being followed, he started heading in a northeasterly direction. He wanted to make his way down from the hills of Buda to Pest on the east side of the river, but by a less trafficked route to minimize the chances of being stopped by a policeman. After fifteen minutes, he reached Margit Street, then crossed the Danube on Margit Bridge. Two blocks into Pest he turned right on Honved Street, where he parked his van. Omar concealed the assault weapon under the seat. Then, with the pistol in his pocket and a guidebook in his hand, he set off on foot parallel to the river for the parliament.

As Omar walked, he admired the majestic parliament building, which was modeled on the British Houses of Parliament. Hungary had managed to copy England's legislative palace, but was never able to duplicate Britain's governmental institutions.

It was a gorgeous summer day, and as Omar entered the large square in front of the parliament, he encountered thousands of tourists from around the world. While he heard a myriad of languages, a significant number were speaking Russian. That didn't surprise Omar. The former history professor was familiar with the Russian occupation of Hungary in the twentieth century and the 1956 revolution.

But most young Russians had no sense of history or familiarity with those events. For them, Budapest was a fun city, a great place to visit and party, a magnet that attracted young people from around the world.

Standing in the center of the square and looking around, Omar saw the drab office building that Peter Toth's company had occupied. On the west was the parliament building. From viewing photographs and videos of other ceremonies that had taken place in Budapest, Omar was sure that on Wednesday they would set up a platform on the side of the square in front of the parliament building. That's where the speakers would be, including Kuznov and Szabo. Hundreds of chairs would be arranged in rows for the audience on the concrete square in front of the speaker's platform. But at this point, none of these preparations had been made.

Omar closed his eyes and envisioned what would happen as he had planned it. Shamil and the two Frenchmen would be positioned near the square. When Omar gave the three of them the signal via an electronic communication device, they would each set off bombs they had planted very early that morning by remote control. They would then make their way back to the castle. This would produce chaos and pandemonium among the crowd. Omar, who would be waiting on the perimeter of the square, would shoot Kuznov and Szabo, and escape himself. Once they were all back at the castle, Omar and Shamil would direct the two Frenchmen to climb into the back of the van, telling them they were headed to France. In a deserted area of Western Hungary, Omar would direct Shamil to turn off onto a back road. After parking in a cluster of trees, Omar and Shamil would execute the two Frenchmen and hide their bodies in the woods. From there, Omar and Shamil would drive back to Grozny. It was a good plan, and Omar was confident it would work.

As he stood taking in the scene around him, his cell phone rang. Omar pulled the phone from his pocket and checked the caller ID. The number was blocked.

"Yes," Omar answered the phone as he moved away from the tourists to an isolated area.

"This is Peter Toth," Omar heard on the other end. He was so startled that he almost dropped the phone. *What the hell?* he thought. "But . . . I heard you died in a fire."

"Well, I'm still alive," said the man on the other end.

Omar was good at voice recognition, and he was convinced Peter Toth was on the phone, not an imposter. But how had Peter escaped what must have been a catastrophic fire?

"What happened?" Omar asked.

"That's not relevant. I'm calling to tell you to cancel the operation. You can keep the money I gave you, but I want you to abort. Do you understand?"

"Why?"

"That's also not relevant. It's my decision."

It only took Omar a few seconds to decide he would not obey Peter. He had worked too hard on his plan. Blood had been spilled to pay for his success. He was so close to his dream of killing Kuznov and avenging the murder of his wife and children. He would never quit now.

"No," he said in a firm voice. "I won't stop."

"It's my decision," said Peter, sounding incredulous.

But Omar had no intention of yielding. "It was your decision when you hired me. Now I'm in control."

"I won't pay your second installment."

"Keep your money. I don't care."

"You can't do this," Peter snarled.

"Watch the news. I will do it. And let me tell you something else. You are in this with me, whether you want to be or not. So if you go to the authorities to turn me in, you're going down as well."

The line was silent. Peter was too stunned to respond.

Omar continued, "When you came to talk with me in Grozny, I recorded our conversation. If I am arrested or anything happens to me, that recording, which fully identifies you, will be made public in addition to the details of my payment. So I would advise you against taking action against me."

"You dirty bastard," Peter rasped.

Omar laughed. He hadn't made a recording of their conversation, but he was confident Peter would never call his bluff.

"Goodbye, Peter," Omar said before hanging up on him.


# Paris

Peter Toth was sitting on a bench in the Place des Vosges in Paris staring at the phone in his hand. Omar had hung up. Though the humidity was low, perspiration was dotting his forehead, running down the sides of his face, and soaking his white shirt under a dark blue, pin-striped Lanvin suit jacket.

*What have I done? What in the world have I done?*

He realized now, albeit too late, that his desire for revenge against the Russians had clouded his judgment, causing him to set in motion a horrible set of events, resulting in the death of Emma, the woman he had loved, and undoubtedly causing tremendous pain and suffering for Nick, the only son he had left.

He now regretted everything he had done. If he had it to do all over again he never would have taken that fateful trip to Grozny to hire Omar. He felt as if he had released the brake on a freight train at the top of a steep grade, and he was now powerless to stop it. But perhaps he still had one chance. Perhaps Emma could still help him undo some of the damage.

Before exploring that, he had one other thing he had to do: walk by 98 Place des Vosges, the house he had bought for Emma, the house they had shared when he was in Paris, one final time and pay his respects to that remarkable woman. Peter wasn't worried about being recognized—he was sufficiently disguised and carrying a US passport in the name of Thomas Leahy.

Peter rose from the bench and exited the center grassy square. On the sidewalk he passed number 6 Place des Vosges, once the house of Victor Hugo. Now a museum, there was a line of tourists in front.

Approaching number ninety-eight, he saw the yellow police tape stretched across the front steps, forbidding access to the murder scene. Tears welled up in his eyes. Over the course of his long life, he had been intimate with three women: Tracy, Reka, and Emma. But Emma was the only one he had loved.

He stopped in front of the house and looked up at the second floor window of the bedroom they had shared. Emma had been beautiful, brilliant, intellectually challenging, witty, fun to be with, amazing in bed, and the mother of his child. And despite all of that, he had dragged her into a vendetta that wasn't hers, brushing aside her wise objections, and causing her death.

He closed his eyes and imagined being in the house with Emma—in the kitchen, in the living room, in the bedroom. After five minutes, he couldn't take it any longer. He forced himself to walk away.

Walking through the Marais, he worked his way to the Hôtel de Ville, the city hall. Across the street was a branch of the Bank of Paris. It had been Emma's idea to investigate Szabo's finances and Emma's idea that they open up a vault box in the bank with access by Emma and Thomas Leahy, the alias he had been using in Europe for the last month. When he had questioned the need for the vault box, Emma had told him that if anything happened to her, everything she had discovered would be waiting for him in the vault.

Peter climbed the cement steps of the majestic gray stone Bank of Paris with trepidation. He took an elevator to the lower level where he presented his Thomas Leahy passport and the vault key to a somber looking man in a dull gray suit and incongruous bright red tie.

The man removed the vault box and led Peter to a small windowless room. He pointed to a white button and said, "Please ring for me when you are finished." Then he closed the door, leaving Peter alone.

Peter's hands were shaking as he opened the gray metal box. He saw two sealed envelopes and opened the one on top. Inside he found a letter in Emma's handwriting. He began reading:

My dearest Peter,

If you are reading this, then I am no longer alive. I wanted you to know that I have no regret for anything I did and only great love for you.

I have used my contacts and relationships from many years in the banking community to obtain the following information.

Approximately two years ago, Prime Minister Szabo opened a numbered account at the Republic Bank in Lucerne. The other envelope contains all of the information about that account, including the name of a good friend, an officer of the bank, who promised to help you.

I hope you will take good care of Nick. I regret not seeing the fine young man he will turn out to be.

My eternal love,
Emma

Peter dropped the letter on the table and wept. When he had gotten himself under control, he dried his eyes and opened the second envelope.

Inside he found a piece of paper also in Emma's handwriting. Peter read: "Numbered account 26-512-640 at Republic Bank of Lucerne, opened by Franz Szabo two years ago with an initial deposit of five million euros from an account belonging to Szabo at the Hungarian National Bank. As of July 31 of this year, the account had five million euros. The bank's vice president, Hans Gerber, promised to be of assistance to you."

Peter read the note a second time with enormous disappointment. He had been hoping that Szabo's account would show the deposit of funds from a Russian bank that could be linked to Kuznov, implying that Szabo had accepted a bribe in return for entering into the Friendship Pact. But alas, Emma hadn't uncovered that. The five million euros deposited two years ago must have been a bribe for something else Szabo had done, but that didn't help Peter now.

Normally an optimistic person despite everything that had happened in his life, Peter had trouble finding a ray of hope in this dismal situation. Perhaps, he told himself, the payoff from Kuznov to Szabo hadn't come until after Emma's death.

He would fly to Lucerne that night. Hopefully he would be able to meet with Hans Gerber the next morning and convince him to disclose any recent activity in Szabo's account.

*     *     *

While he was driving from Orly Airport, stuck in Paris traffic, Craig's phone rang. It was a French number he didn't recognize.

He answered it, and a man's voice asked, "Is this Enrico Marino?"

The voice sounded familiar, but Craig couldn't identify it.

"Who's calling?" he asked.

"Habib from the Brasserie Rabat in Clichy."

Craig perked up. "Yes, Habib."

"Something has happened." Habib sounded anxious. "I would like to talk to you, but not in Clichy. Tell me where and when we can meet discreetly."

Craig gave him the location of his office at the race track, and they agreed to meet there in an hour. Craig was hoping this would be the break he needed.

Forty-five minutes later, Craig arrived at the track. It was deserted, which suited him perfectly.

When Habib arrived, he looked nervous. They sat down in Craig's office.

"Something to drink?" Craig asked.

Habib shook his head. "Your friend from the garage told me to call you."

"Abdullah?"

"Yeah. He said I could trust you."

"And you can."

"I hope so. When we spoke the last time, I knew some things that I couldn't tell you. Let me explain."

"I appreciate your coming to see me," said Craig.

"You showed me a picture of Omar Basayev and asked if I had seen him. I told you no because I wanted to protect someone. . . ." Habib hesitated. "In truth, Omar came into my brassiere several times in the last couple of weeks."

"Who was he with?"

"The most recent time he came in by himself. A little while later he was joined by three young men. Not Chechens. Men from North Africa who live in the area. He was recruiting them for a job. Eventually the three left with Omar and his assistant, Shamil, in a white van. It was around noon that Friday, the day of the police raid in Clichy."

"Where were they going?"

"I don't know. I tried to hear as much as I could without Omar noticing. I was afraid of him."

"Because he killed Ahmed Hussein?"

"I heard that from people . . . but I don't know for sure."

"Why didn't you tell me when we spoke the first time?"

Habib looked down at his hands. "One of the three men who went with Omar is Rachid. His sister, Ayanna, is an employee of mine—I care about her well-being. That's why I was trying to hear what they said. I was worried about her brother. But I didn't tell you when you came to the brasserie because I didn't want to do anything to endanger them."

"So what's changed?"

"Ayanna came to see me this morning in tears. She was on the phone with Rachid when she heard something happen—she believes that Omar may have hurt or even killed him. She asked me who she could reach out to."

"Did she tell you why she thought Omar might have killed her brother?"

Habib shook his head.

"Do you know where they were?"

Habib shook his head again.

"Where can I find Ayanna?" Craig asked.

"She stayed at my apartment after she came to see me this morning. She was terrified. She was convinced two Chechen men were following her and that they wanted to kill her."

"Why did she think that?"

"She heard Omar screaming at Rachid for having a cell phone, and she thinks he's probably afraid that he told her something."

"Is she sure that Rachid is dead?"

"She heard Omar and Rachid screaming. Then there were a lot of muffled noises and something that sounded like a shot, but she wasn't sure. After that, the phone went dead."

"What did Rachid tell her?"

"She wouldn't say, she just begged me to help her. She was sure the men following her hadn't seen her come to my place, so I told her she could hide out there. I didn't know what I could do to help her."

Craig thought about it for a minute, then said, "I think I can help her."

"How?" Habib asked.

"I have some connections in the French government. But I'll have to talk to her before I can try to use those. Where is she now?"

"In my apartment. I live alone."

"I could come there and talk to her."

"It's too risky," said Habib, shaking his head.

"Then suppose you hide her on the floor in the back of your car and bring her to me?"

"I have a van for my business."

"Good. Use that."

"Where should I bring her?"

"There's a wine bar called Vino Italiano about a block up from the Bristol Hotel on Rue du Faubourg Saint-Honoré. They have a private room in the back where we can talk. How about ten o'clock this evening?" When Habib hesitated, Craig added, "It's important that I talk to her. I won't harm her. Believe me."

Habib took a pack of Turkish cigarettes from his pocket and offered one to Craig, who declined. Habib lit one and closed his eyes meditatively.

"The girl has had a tough life," he finally said. "She works as a dishwasher at Rabat. She's only twenty-five." Habib took a puff of his cigarette before continuing, "Her parents came from Algeria, but she was born here. She still has dreams of getting out of Clichy, but she'll learn. What chance does a poor Muslim girl have?"

"You like Ayanna," Craig commented.

"After my wife died last year, she was kind to me. Her parents died a couple of years ago. It's just Ayanna and her brother now, and he hasn't been able to find work so she supports him." Habib narrowed his eyes at Craig. "You better not do anything to harm this girl."

"I promise you that I won't."

"Okay. I'll bring her to the wine bar this evening at ten."

*     *     *

A little before ten o'clock, Craig was sitting in the front area of the wine bar nursing a glass of Barbera when Habib walked in followed by an attractive woman wearing a black hijab. She was carrying a duffel bag, and she looked scared.

Craig motioned to Habib to follow him to a private room in the back with a table surrounded by four chairs. When they were seated, Habib said, "Ayanna, this is Enrico Marino. He's a friend of Abdullah who runs the garage. I think he can help you."

"Would you like something to drink?" Craig asked.

She nodded. "Just Perrier. I don't drink alcohol."

Craig went to the bar and returned with the Perrier and a glass of wine for Habib.

"I'm working with French intelligence," Craig said. "The man who may have killed your brother is Omar, a terrorist from Chechnya. If you tell me what you know, I may be able to protect you and find out what happened to your brother."

She had tears in her eyes. "If I talk to you, the Chechens will kill me," she said, barely above a whisper.

Craig leaned forward. "Nobody will find out," he reassured her.

"People in Clichy always find out who talked to the police. . . ." she replied, looking uncertain. Turning to Habib she asked, "What do you think?"

"I won't be able to protect you for very long," he said. "At least with this man you have a chance. And Abdullah said you can trust him."

Ayanna closed her eyes for a minute. When she opened them, she looked straight at Craig. "I'll talk to you, but on certain conditions." She sounded like a player who was holding the winning cards.

"What conditions?" Craig asked.

"You or the French government have to agree to get me out of Clichy, give me a new identity, and ten thousand euros for resettlement."

He thought about what Habib had said. Ayanna had a desire to get out of Clichy, and now she saw a chance to achieve that. He had to respect her for trying to convert her misfortune into an opportunity.

"I can't authorize what you want on my own," he replied. "But I should be able to tell you tomorrow if the French government will approve it. Meantime, it would help me if I knew what information you have about Omar."

She thought about it for a minute, then said, "I can tell you where Omar was early yesterday morning when he was with my brother."

"How do you know that?"

"Rachid told me where they were."

Craig tried to keep his excitement in check. "And where was that?" he asked.

Habib placed his hand on Ayanna's shoulder. "She'll tell you once you let her know that the French government will meet her conditions."

Craig nodded. "That's reasonable." The savvy Habib was right. Jean-Claude would be less likely to give Ayanna what she wanted if they already had this piece of critical information.

She turned to Habib, "Can I stay with you tonight?"

Habib looked uncomfortable, and Craig didn't like the idea. The Chechens might find her tonight and kill her.

Craig spoke up before Habib had a chance to respond, "My girl-friend, Elizabeth, could arrange a hotel room for you for tonight. Will that be okay?"

"Can Habib come with me until I'm settled in the room?"

"Sure."

"Okay then. I brought some clothes and other things in my bag. I didn't think I'd be going back home."

Craig called Elizabeth and told her what he wanted.

"I'll meet you in the hotel lobby in ten minutes," she said. "I'll make the arrangements with the Bristol before that."

Craig, Ayanna, and Habib walked down the Rue Saint-Honoré to the hotel. She looked scared, Craig thought. She seemed even more frightened when they walked in to the opulent Bristol lobby. In view of the hour, the lobby was deserted.

Elizabeth was standing next to the reception desk holding a room key. She immediately came forward. "You must be Ayanna," Elizabeth said warmly with a smile. "I'm very happy to meet you."

"Thank you," Ayanna said, some of her apprehension fading.

"I thought you and I would share a room tonight. That way, I'll be able to get you anything you need."

Ayanna smiled.

Craig was pleased that Elizabeth had thought of sharing a room with Ayanna. It was a great idea. It would make Ayanna more secure and minimize the chances of her changing her mind and leaving the hotel.

"Let's go up to your room," Elizabeth said.

Ayanna said goodbye to Habib. Then she and Elizabeth headed toward the glass door elevator. After Habib had gone, Craig called Giuseppe.

"I need your help," Craig said. "Where are you?"

"In Paris getting ready to go to sleep like a normal person."

Craig knew that Giuseppe lived off Avenue Victor Hugo, a short cab ride at this hour.

"Well, I hope you still have that 1962 Armagnac we had the last time."

"I only drink it with you."

"Good. I'm on my way."

\*       \*       \*

Half an hour later, as they were sipping the Armagnac, Craig gave Giuseppe a report on what had happened in Sardinia. Then he explained about his meetings with Habib and Ayanna. "This could be what we need," Craig said, sounding excited. "We have to sell the deal to Jean-Claude."

"I noticed you said *could*," Giuseppe remarked. "The problem is, we don't know what the girl can tell us. For all we know, she'll say they were on a highway in France or Belgium. That won't help us. We'll be shooting blind. That'll make it a tough sell with Jean-Claude. You know how he is."

Craig had a sick feeling in his stomach. What in the world could he do with Ayanna if Jean-Claude wouldn't make the deal?

"My gut tells me she can help us," Craig replied boldly.

Giuseppe laughed. "I don't want to hear about your gut. From my recollection it's wrong as often as it's right."

"Ouch, that stung."

Giuseppe laughed and reached for his phone. Craig heard him say, "Hi . . . Jean-Claude. Yes, Craig Page and I want to talk to you tomorrow morning about Omar the Chechen. The earliest you're available. Good, we'll be at your office at nine. I'll tell him that."

When Giuseppe put down the phone, he said, "We're all set for his office at nine tomorrow. And he wants to talk to you about a shootout at Häagen-Dazs last Sunday. You don't know anything about that, do you?"

*Uh-oh*, Craig thought. *I'm in trouble.*

*       *       *

The next morning at nine Craig and Giuseppe filed into Jean-Claude's office. The Frenchman was glaring at Craig.

"How was Elizabeth's baseball game last Sunday in the Bois de Boulogne?" he asked.

"Very good," Craig replied. "She pitched and hit the game-winning homer."

"It's too bad you didn't have a chance to finish your ice cream after the game," Jean Claud remarked caustically.

"Oh, that," said Craig, trying to sound casual. "We had a little excitement. How'd you find out?"

"People in the shop described the shooter and the woman with him. She was wearing a Paris Yanks baseball shirt. I'm not a moron, although you apparently think so."

Craig was glad Jean-Claude hadn't zeroed in on Nick. In the confusion, the shop employees might not have noticed the boy or thought he wasn't important. Craig had no reason to tell Jean-Claude that the Russians had come for Nick. Instead, he saw a way to deflect Jean-Claude's inquiry. "I guess I ruffled some feathers in Clichy," he said.

Jean-Claude wrinkled his forehead. "Possibly, but these thugs were members of a gang from Moscow. What happened doesn't make sense."

"Right now, none of this makes sense."

"Lucky for you the witnesses said it was self-defense."

"It was."

"And no bystanders were hit."

"I do good work."

Jean-Claude was shaking his head. "Well, Lone Ranger, you managed to turn the streets of Paris into the American Wild West."

"I'm sorry for that, really I am." *At least that's a truthful statement,* Craig thought.

"Dammit, Craig," said Jean-Claude raising his voice. "You should have called and let me know what happened right after this incident."

"You're right. I should have," Craig replied, doing his best to look penitent.

"Humph. I feel as if you're hiding something from me. What's your game here?"

"To find Omar and kill him," Craig admitted.

"Because he killed your friend, Amos Neir?"

"That's right."

"Is that why you went to Grozny?" Jean-Claude asked.

Craig wondered how he knew about that—Giuseppe never would have told him.

As if reading his mind, Jean-Claude said, "After the ice cream shoot out, I had the airport customs people let me know about any Enrico Marino trips."

"Yes, that's why I went to Grozny, but I didn't find Omar. I think he's still here in Europe."

"We have half the police in Brussels and northern France looking for him—so far not even a trace."

*What a perfect opening,* Craig thought. "That's why Giuseppe and I are here," he said. "We have a way of finding out where Omar is." Craig then explained about his conversations with Habib and

Ayanna. "The bottom line is that Omar took Ayanna's brother, Rachid, and two other young men from Clichy with him to a location outside of Paris. He called her yesterday morning from that location."

"What's the location?"

"She'll only tell us if the French government agrees to move her out of Clichy, give her a new identity, and ten thousand euros for resettlement."

Jean-Claude looked dubious. "And you think I should agree to this?"

"Definitely. Omar's attack could take place at any time. Ayanna is our only hope of finding out where he is and stopping him."

Giuseppe interjected, "For her information, she's not asking much in return."

Jean-Claude tapped his fingers on the table. "I could have my men bring her in and toss her into jail. She'll talk eventually."

Craig couldn't let that happen. "Based on talking with her," Craig said, "I don't think she will talk. Still, even if you're right, we'll lose precious time that we don't have. The clock is ticking."

Creases marked Jean-Claude forehead. Craig could tell that he'd finally gotten through to the Frenchman.

"I can't authorize this myself," he said. "I'll need the minister's approval."

"How soon can you get it?"

"It's August. He's at his house in Saint-Tropez." Jean-Claude turned to his computer. "Let me check his schedule."

After a couple of minutes, Jean-Claude said, "He's out on his boat this morning. He'll be back in his house for lunch. The earliest I can talk to him is one o'clock this afternoon. You two come back a little before one. I want you to be here for the call in case he has questions."

"By the way," Craig said, "we haven't confirmed that the attack will take place in Brussels. Why don't you tell the minister it could occur in the south of France, perhaps even Saint-Tropez—the perfect place for a terrorist attack in August?"

Before the scowling Jean-Claude could reply to that, Giuseppe said, "We'll be back a little before one."

Jean-Claude turned to Craig. "That gives you a few hours. You can take your girlfriend, Elizabeth, for an ice cream," he said sarcastically.

Craig fired back, "What a good idea. I heard they have a Häagen-Dazs near the Bois de Boulogne."

*       *       *

Jean-Claude didn't put the phone on speaker, but listening, Craig had to admit that he made the case clearly and forcefully for giving Ayanna what she wanted, even tossing in the possibility that Omar's attack could take place in Saint-Tropez.

When Jean-Claude put down the phone, Giuseppe asked, "What's the verdict?"

"He approved the deal Ayanna wants. He's afraid of another terrorist attack happening somewhere in France on his watch. I just hope what she tells us is helpful. I went out on a long limb for her, and a relocation like this costs money."

"Right now she's our best chance," Giuseppe pointed out.

"That's what I said. How soon can you get her in here so we can talk to her?"

Craig took out his phone and called Elizabeth. "You can tell Ayanna we have good news—the answer is yes. Have her meet me in the Bristol lobby in half an hour, and tell her to bring her clothes and other things with her."

Craig turned back to Jean-Claude and Giuseppe. "I'll have her here in an hour."

# Lucerne

Peter had spent the night at the stately and grand Palace Hotel along the lake in Lucerne. Though his room with a view of the lake was comfortable and modern, having been recently renovated, the stone exterior harkened back to an era of a hundred years ago when European aristocracy customarily stayed in Lucerne. Now it was tourists from around the world shopping for watches and eating the most incredible chocolate.

After breakfast, Peter walked along Lake Lucerne into the heart of the city. He crossed a wooden covered bridge into the business center. Three blocks from the railroad station on Pilatusstrasse, he saw the Republic Bank. Afraid that Hans Gerber might not want to talk to him now that Emma was dead, Peter had decided not to call in advance. He would do best just showing up and taking Gerber by surprise.

The Republic Bank occupied a four-story, gray stone structure that reminded Peter of a fortress. It had small windows and an armed guard posted on each side of the large metal front door. They didn't stop Peter as he entered the building. Inside, he saw a young blonde woman with a tight, drawn face sitting behind a large wooden desk. Facing out was a nameplate that identified her as Hilda Werner.

"I'd like to see Hans Gerber," Peter said in English.

"Do you have an appointment?" she asked.

"No, but please tell Mr. Gerber that my name is Thomas Leahy and Emma Miller suggested I talk with him."

Peter took the Thomas Leahy passport from his pocket and showed it to her. After studying it, she directed Peter to a sitting area across the room.

Several minutes later she returned, saying, "Please wait here, Mr. Leahy. Someone will come down and take you to Mr. Gerber."

After another several minutes, a tall, comely, gray-haired woman fashionably dressed in a burgundy suit got off the elevator and walked over to Peter.

"Mr. Leahy?" she said.

"Yes," said Peter, standing up.

"Please come with me."

They rode in the elevator to the top floor. Then, with Peter following her clicking heels across the marble floor, she led the way to a corner office where Hans Gerber was sitting behind a red leather-topped desk. Gerber, wearing a three-piece charcoal suit and wire-framed glasses, had a large, round face and shaved head.

Gerber stood up and introduced himself.

*I'm one-third of the way home*, Peter thought. *Now comes the hard part: getting the information.*

"I was very sorry to hear about the death of Emma Miller," Gerber said as they both took a seat. "We knew each other for many years. I was fond of her."

Peter decided he had the best chance of getting Gerber's cooperation by leveling with the banker.

"Emma was murdered," Peter said, "because she was helping me investigate corruption in Hungary."

When Gerber didn't respond, Peter continued, "I'm sure you'll want to help me, as she told me you promised to do. In that way, you'll be doing something to avenge her death."

"Help you how?" Gerber asked skeptically.

"Provide me with information on recent transactions in your numbered account 26-512-640."

The banker leaned back in his chair and linked the fingers of his two hands together. "I'm afraid that's quite impossible," he said. "We have strict banking regulations in Switzerland that prohibit divulging such information. I would be dismissed if our president learned I had ignored these legal requirements."

Peter had been anticipating this response. "My dear Mr. Gerber," Peter said calmly, "you have already broken these regulations by telling Emma that on July 31 of this year that account had five million euros, funds which were deposited approximately two years ago in a transfer from a Hungarian National Bank account in the name of Franz Szabo. If I were to disclose to your president that you had given this information to Emma Miller, you undoubtedly would be dismissed."

Gerber's face turned bright red. "I gave her that information because we were friends."

Peter ignored him and kept talking. "If your president asked me why you provided the information to Emma Miller, I would simply show him a picture of Emma in a bathing suit, which I took last year at the Eden Roc in Ascona. She's such a beautiful woman that I'm sure he would understand that you hoped for some sexual favors in return for this information. Or perhaps you received them."

Gerber pounded his fist on the desk. "You're totally reprehensible. You defile Emma's memory."

"No, Mr. Gerber. You defile her memory by refusing to give me information that will enable me to bring to justice those who killed her."

When Gerber didn't respond, Peter realized he was wavering. "I can assure you," he said pressing ahead, "I will never disclose how I obtained this information. If asked, I will say that I had the assistance of IT experts who hacked into the bank's computer."

Gerber shook his head with an angry expression on his face. He was an intelligent man, Peter thought. He had to realize that he had no choice.

Without saying another word, Gerber swiveled in his chair to the computer on one side of his desk. He punched in some numbers, then said to Peter, "On August 7, fifty million euros were transferred from the Moscow Federal Bank to this account."

"I need a printout of this information," said Peter, keeping his excitement in check.

"You ask for too much."

"I promise I won't give you away."

Gerber unwillingly hit a couple more buttons. Then he stood up and reached over to the printer behind this desk, which was spitting out a document.

Gerber studied it, and then handed it to Peter, who glanced at it briefly. This was exactly what he needed, including the names on the two accounts, France Szabo on the Republic Bank account, and the Russian Treasury on the Moscow Federal Bank account.

"Thank you," Peter said.

"Take it and go," Gerber said angrily.

Peter was thrilled. He now had a way to destroy Szabo and block the Friendship Pact from going into effect without killing Szabo or Kuznov.

At last the killing would stop.


# Paris

Craig rode with Ayanna in the back of an unmarked Ministry of Defense car. She had her duffel bag at her feet.

"Where are we going?" she asked.

"Ministry of Defense," Craig replied.

She looked frightened.

"You can trust me, Ayanna."

"I don't know if I can or not, but I'm prepared to take a chance."

She looked worried as they walked into the ministry building on Boulevard Saint-Germain. A security guard led them to Jean-Claude's office where he and Giuseppe were waiting.

When she sat down at the conference table, her hands were shaking. Craig hoped that Jean-Claude would show her compassion.

"You're asking a lot from the French government, mademoiselle," Jean-Claude said.

Craig was preparing to jump in when Ayanna steadied her hands, leaned forward, and boldly replied, "I have valuable information to give you in return, monsieur."

Craig felt admiration for this tenacious Muslim woman willing to stand her ground with one of the powers in French intelligence.

"I'll listen," Jean-Claude said. "And if it's valuable, I promise we will provide you what you're asking."

"Thank you," she acknowledged.

Jean-Claude pointed to Craig. It was his show.

Craig took a photograph of Omar from his pocket and showed it to her. "Have you ever seen this man?" he asked.

She studied it for a moment. "I saw him once on the street in Clichy when I was walking with my brother, Rachid. My brother told me that his name was Omar. He was a Chechen who came into Clichy about ten days ago. The Chechens seemed to revere him. My brother said it was because he killed many Russian soldiers. Omar had made it known that he was recruiting three men for a job. He promised good payments, and Rachid was interested. But Omar refused to tell the men he was recruiting where they would be going. He said they would find out when they left Paris."

"How do you know so much about this?" Jean-Claude asked skeptically.

"Rachid told me everything. I tried to convince him not to go. I told him he would be a fool to do it. But Rachid, like so many young men in Clichy, couldn't find work. He didn't like relying on me to support him. He thought he could gain self-respect if he went with Omar."

"So did Rachid agree to go with Omar?" Craig asked.

She nodded. "Before they left, Rachid gave me five thousand euros and said I should hide it, that it would cover his share of the rent for many months. I pleaded with him not to go, but it was futile. Our parents are both dead, so there are only the two of us. I didn't have anyone to appeal to for help."

"Did you hear from Rachid after he left?"

A veil of sadness descended over her face. "Rashid called me yesterday morning around six o'clock. He told me that he was fine, and that I shouldn't worry. They had finished traveling and were in Budapest."

"Are you certain he said Budapest?" Craig asked.

"Yes. That is what he said."

She paused for a second. Craig couldn't believe it. He now knew where Omar was, where the hit would take place. Not Brussels, but Budapest.

Ayanna continued. "During the phone call yesterday, as soon as Rachid told me not to worry, I heard a man shouting in the background about how he had forbidden them to bring cell phones. I heard my brother cry out for him not to kill him, and then the connection became muffled. I thought I heard what sounded like a shot, but then the phone went dead. I called back several times, but I could not get through," Tears were streaming down her face. "I am so afraid that my brother is hurt or dead. It's all my fault. He told me he wouldn't be able to call after he left, but I pleaded with him to at least let me know he was okay."

"You can't blame yourself," Craig said.

Wiping the tears from her eyes, Ayanna continued, "A couple hours later I had gone out to the market, and I noticed two Chechen men following me. I was sure they wanted to kill me because of what I had heard on the phone. I ran away from them, and I went to my friend Habib, who owns the Brasserie Rabat. He told me to talk to you." Here she pointed to Craig.

"Have you spoken about this to anybody other than Habib and me?" Craig asked.

"Nobody. I was too frightened."

Craig had Ayanna write down Rachid's phone number and asked if he had more questions.

The Frenchman shook his head. Then he turned to Ayanna. "This is valuable information. I don't think you should go back to your place in Clichy. It would be too dangerous."

"I thought that might be the situation," she said. "So I brought some things with me." She motioned to the duffel.

Jean-Claude reached for the phone and called Corrine, one of his assistants. When she entered the office, Jean-Claude told her, "This is Ayanna. We're giving her a new identity and relocating her to Marseille in the morning. I don't want her going back to Clichy where she lives, so I want you to arrange for a new identity and put her up in a hotel for tonight. Also, please make the arrangements for her resettlement. Then in the morning give her a card linked to an account with 15,000 euros in her new name, and put her on a plane to Marseille."

Craig raised his eyebrows at Jean-Claude upping the payment to Ayanna of his own accord. The Frenchman wasn't a total hard-ass.

After the two women left, Giuseppe said, "Now that we know Omar is in Budapest, we have a problem. Szabo hates all of us in law enforcement in Western Europe including Jean-Claude and me. He won't even return our calls."

Jean-Claude nodded.

"Craig, you should talk to your friend Betty at the CIA," Giuseppe continued. "Perhaps Szabo is still talking to the Americans. But even if Betty is on board, you know how reluctant the American government can be to intervene in foreign issues these days. I suspect, Craig, that if you want to avenge Amos's death, you will have to go to Budapest and find Omar yourself."

*       *       *

"Omar's in Budapest," Craig said to Elizabeth as soon as he entered the Bristol suite. "We have to brief President Worth and Betty."

Elizabeth called Betty on the encrypted phone and told her what they wanted. "Let me check with the White House." The CIA director put her on hold for a minute.

When Betty returned, she said, "Can you and Craig get to the embassy communications room in one hour? We'll call you there on the red phone."

An hour later, the call came through on the red phone at the embassy, and President Worth said, "I gather you had some developments."

"Bottom line, Mr. President," Craig said, "Omar is in Budapest. I believe he's planning to assassinate Szabo and possibly Kuznov."

"Well that's a mouthful," Worth whistled. "You better explain."

Craig took him through his discussion with Yuri in Sardinia and what Ayanna had said. When he finished, there was a silence on the other end.

Finally, Worth said, "I agree with you that Szabo is undoubtedly Omar's target, but your evidence that Omar is going after Kuznov as well is extremely weak. We don't even know that Kuznov will be in Budapest."

"Even if I'm wrong on that, Mr. President, somebody still has to locate Omar in Budapest and stop him."

"Yes, but that should be Szabo's responsibility. I intend to call and alert him."

Craig got a sinking feeling in his stomach. He saw where this was headed. Szabo would take over the hunt for Omar, which he would probably fuck up, and Craig would lose his chance to avenge Amos's death.

Worth continued, "You two stay on the line. If I can get hold of Szabo, I'll conference him in without telling him you're listening. You'll be on mute. That way you'll be able to hear what he says."

"Thank you, Mr. President." Craig said.

A few moments later, Craig heard a woman's voice, "Prime Minister Szabo, please hold for President Worth."

"Hello Prime Minister Szabo," Worth said.

"What do you have to tell me that's so urgent?" came Szabo's voice.

"My CIA director has received information that Omar Basayev, a notorious Chechen terrorist, is in Budapest and that he is planning to assassinate you and perhaps Russian President Kuznov as well."

"Thank you for the information," Szabo replied smoothly, "but I'm afraid your CIA director must be mistaken. President Kuznov has no plans to be in Budapest."

"I'm just trying to warn you."

"I appreciate the effort on your part, President Worth, however, I have an outstanding security detail. Do you have anything else to tell me?"

"Nothing."

There was a click. Szabo had ended the call.

Betty said, "Hang up, Craig. We'll call you right back."

Seconds later Worth called back with Betty on the line. "That ungrateful, arrogant, SOB," the president said.

"Perhaps you should call Kuznov and warn him," Craig said.

"Our evidence that he's a target isn't strong enough," Worth replied dismissively. "And Szabo told us that Kuznov has no plans to be in Budapest. When we have stronger evidence that Kuznov's a target, we'll revisit the issue." Worth continued. "After my conversation with Szabo, what I'd like us to do is stay on the sidelines and let Omar kill Szabo if he can."

"But when we were in Washington, Mr. President," Craig said, "you concluded that we couldn't stand by and let Omar assassinate Szabo."

"I did say that, didn't I? Well, we gave Szabo ample warning. We did our part. If you feel the need to go to Budapest yourself, that's your decision."

Craig was disappointed, but he wasn't going to let that stop him. He would go to Budapest, with or without Worth's backing.

# Budapest

Prime Minister Szabo was sitting at his desk, staring at the phone and replaying in his mind the call with President Worth. He doubted that the Americans knew that his Friendship Pact with Kuznov would be signed on Wednesday. If they had, Worth would have threatened him or tried to offer incentives to persuade Szabo not to go through with it.

As far as the possibility of Omar assassinating him and Kuznov, he would alert his personal security detail that he had received word of an unsubstantiated threat against his life and ask them to tighten security. That should be sufficient.

He would also inform his chief of Military Intelligence that a Chechen terrorist, Omar Basayev, might be in Budapest planning some type of attack. They would obtain a photo of Omar from Interpol and begin a search for him in Budapest.

Szabo had no intention of calling Kuznov and warning him—he didn't want to take the chance of Kuznov calling off the agreement and refusing to pay Szabo the rest of his money. Fifty million euros was too much to risk losing.

Szabo picked up an economic report on his desk. But as he began reading the dismal forecasts for the next year, he couldn't concentrate. He kept thinking about the events that had occurred in the last couple of weeks. Kuznov, having learned from Szabo that Peter knew about their plan, must have arranged the deaths of Peter and Emma. But now Omar Basayev, a Chechen, planning to assassinate him. . . . The Hungarian prime minister had never even heard of Omar. That meant someone had hired the Chechen. But who?

Szabo's immediate thought was Peter Toth, the most likely candidate, but Peter was dead. All of these facts somehow had to be interrelated. Suppose Peter had hired Omar before he died in the fire? That would make sense. If he had hired Omar to kill both Szabo and Kuznov and the Russian had found out, he would undoubtedly have Peter killed. The fire might have been murder, not an accident.

Szabo had a burning desire to get to the bottom of this, but he didn't dare approach Kuznov. That might put his fifty million euros in jeopardy.

He racked his brain trying to think about how he could gain some additional information. Then it struck him—Gyorgy, Toth's business partner and confidante, might know what Peter had planned.

Szabo summoned the head of military intelligence and told him, "I want you to arrest Gyorgy Kovacs. Interrogate him to find out whether he knows anything about a plan by Peter Toth to hire a Chechen by the name of Omar Basayev to conduct a terrorist attack in Budapest."

"Are there any limitations on what I can do to Gyorgy Kovacs?" the head of intelligence asked.

Szabo thought about it for a minute. Gyorgy's father was still revered by some for what he had done in the 1956 revolution. Those people would be upset at Szabo's plan to give Russia a role in Hungary. He couldn't do anything to further incite them.

"Yes, you can only keep him twelve hours, and you cannot do anything that will leave marks on his body. We have to be able to deny any charges he makes after he is released."

## Paris

After they had ended the call with President Worth and Betty, Craig had reserved a seat on the first plane to Budapest the following morning at eight, and Elizabeth hadn't tried to stop him.

Then they went to Market on Avenue Matignon for a casual dinner. As soon as they ordered—sole meunière with salad for both of them, and a Latour Meursault Blagny—Elizabeth said, "I should be going with you to Budapest. Having just been there, I could be of help."

"I know you could," Craig replied, "and I'd love to have you, but what about Nick? Do you really want to leave him by himself in Paris?"

Elizabeth looked glum. "I guess you're right," she said.

An hour and a half later, they were walking back to the Bristol when Elizabeth's encrypted phone rang.

"Where are you?" Betty asked.

"Craig and I are on the street fifteen minutes away from our hotel."

"Call me as soon as you get into your suite."

Elizabeth put away the phone, saying, "It sounds important."

"I wonder what could have happened in the last two hours," Craig mused.

They hurried back to the hotel and immediately called Betty, putting the call on speaker.

"You will not believe this," Betty said.

"Go ahead," Elizabeth told her.

"I just received a call from the FBI director. He had no idea why it took so long, but the analysis of dental records of the two dead bodies in the fire in Peter's house just came back. *They are not Peter and Reka.*"

"What?" Craig blurted out. "Then who the hell are they?"

"The FBI has no idea. Their dental expert thinks that based on the dental work they had done, both bodies were Russian males."

"Of course," Craig said. "I get it."

"You get what?" Betty asked.

"Nick heard two Russian intruders in the house, but he didn't stick around long enough to find out what happened next. After he had left, Peter must have killed the intruders and burnt down the house himself. Then he and Reka escaped and hid away somewhere, pretending they had died in the fire."

"But why do that?" Elizabeth asked Craig.

"Peter realized Kuznov had a hit out on him. He wanted to make sure Omar killed Kuznov before they could get to him."

"If you're right," Elizabeth said, "Peter will be in Budapest. He'll want to make sure that Omar completes the job. He'll also want to celebrate Szabo's death and help shape the new Hungarian government."

"Correct," Craig said. "So if I can talk to Peter before Omar strikes, I might be able to convince him to call off the attack. He may know where Omar is hiding—he may have even arranged that hiding place."

"Terrific," Elizabeth said. "You'll be able to tell Peter that we know he planned Omar's attack. Unless he calls it off, he'll spend the rest of his life in jail. After everything he's put at risk, I doubt if that will influence him, though."

"Why don't we find Peter first," Craig said. "Then we'll decide how to play it."

"I hate to prick your balloon, you two," Betty said, "but how do you think you'll be able to locate Peter in Budapest? He'll no doubt be in hiding himself."

"What about your friend, Gyorgy Kovacs?" Craig said to Elizabeth. "Maybe Gyorgy can lead us to Peter."

Elizabeth shook her head. "I doubt that he'd let Gyorgy know he was alive, and even if he did, Gyorgy would never tell us."

"I can't argue with that. You know Gyorgy better than I do. But there has to be a way we can get to Peter." Then it struck Craig. "Nick. Of course. That's the answer."

"What do you mean?" Elizabeth asked.

"If Nick called Peter—he must have Peter's cell phone number—and asked Peter to come and see him in Budapest, Peter would never turn Nick down. Then you and I would take Nick with us to Budapest."

"I don't like it," Elizabeth said.

"Why not? From everything we know about Nick's relationship with Peter, Peter would come."

"That's not what's bothering me."

"What then?"

"With all Nick's been through, you think we should raise the kid's hopes that his grandfather is still alive and in Budapest when we have no evidence of either of those facts? I'm afraid if his hopes were dashed, he'd never recover emotionally."

"What do you think Betty?" Craig asked.

"It seems to me that you're making a wild guess based on no facts that Peter will be in Budapest, even if he is alive. For all we know Kuznov may have learned that Peter escaped the fire and found another way to kill him."

"Thanks, Betty," Craig said glumly.

"Don't get me wrong," Betty clarified. "I hope you're right. And as for Elizabeth's concern about Nick and the impact of all this on him, I think you need the advice of a professional on that."

"Great idea," Craig said. "Elizabeth, why don't you call your friend who runs the clinic and ask him?"

"I guess I can do that," she conceded reluctantly.

"Can you trust him?" Betty asked.

"Absolutely," Elizabeth replied.

"Good. Talk to him and let me know how it turns out," Betty said. Then she added, "So I guess you're going to Budapest either way, Craig."

"That's right."

"I'll alert Douglas Caldwell, our station chief whose office is in the embassy in Budapest. As a favor, I'll tell him to give you anything you need."

\*        \*        \*

Elizabeth wanted to wait and talk to Dr. Cardin in person the following morning at the clinic, but Craig convinced her time was too critical, so she called him at home.

"I'm involved with US intelligence people in a complicated national security issue," she said. "We believe Jonathan's grandfather may be in Budapest, and it's important we talk to him. Jonathan believes that his grandfather is dead."

Dr. Cardin interrupted her to say, "You want to know whether you can ask the boy to help you get in touch with his grandfather?"

She was impressed at how well Dr. Cardin had sized up the situation. "That's exactly right."

After a short pause, Cardin said, "I think you can do it. Jonathan has an amazing ability to cope and a maturity beyond his years. And in any event, I would recommend that you give him as much information as you can."

"But what if his grandfather isn't in Budapest or we later find out he's not alive? I don't want to raise his hopes only to crush them."

"If you explain the uncertainty to Jonathan from the beginning, I think he should be okay."

She thanked Dr. Cardin, put down the phone, and then explained to Craig what he had said.

"I'll reserve seats for you and Nick on my flight to Budapest in the morning," he said, pleased with the result.

She raised her hand. "Not so fast. What about the risk to Nick? If the Russians find out he's there, they may attack him."

"Good point. We'll take Pierre with us. You and I may be busy. He'll be able to guard Nick."

\*       \*       \*

Early Monday morning as Craig and Elizabeth drove to the clinic with Pierre following them, they decided on a plan. Elizabeth would go in and talk to Nick while Craig remained outside and briefed Pierre on what they wanted him to do in Budapest.

Walking up the stairs into the clinic, Elizabeth realized how delicate this conversation would be. It was wonderful news that Nick's grandparents hadn't died in the fire, but she couldn't prove that they were still alive, and even if they were, Peter being in Budapest was still a guess on their part. The last thing she wanted to do was raise Nick's hopes only to disappoint him. She had to be careful.

When Elizabeth went into Nick's room, the boy was still sleeping. She turned on the light next to the bed and tapped him on the shoulder gently. "Hey Nick, it's Elizabeth."

The boy sprang up to a sitting position, then relaxed on seeing her. He leaned back against the headboard. "Did you play baseball yesterday?" he asked, yawning.

She smiled. "The Paris Yanks had the week off. But I have something I need to talk to you about."

"What happened?" he asked anxiously.

Elizabeth sat down on the bed next to Nick.

"The FBI analyzed dental records from the two bodies found in your house after the fire. They weren't from your grandfather and grandmother."

"Then they're still alive?" Nick asked doubtfully, almost unable to believe it could be true.

Recalling what Dr. Cardin had said, she continued, "I don't want to mislead you. We don't know where they are, or even that they're still alive," she cautioned. "We only know that they didn't die in the fire."

"Then who died?" Nick asked.

"The FBI thinks it was two Russian men."

"I bet my grandpa killed the two who broke into the house. I bet he's still alive—he's too smart to have let them kill him." For the first time Nick let a look of wild hope steal across his face.

"I hope you're right. Craig and I want you to help us find him, if he's still alive."

"How can I do that?"

"We think there's a chance that your grandpa may be in Budapest. You know his phone number, don't you?"

"Sure. I used to call him all the time."

Elizabeth told Nick what to say, and he placed the call.

As he dialed, his hand shook. Elizabeth tried to imagine what he was feeling emotionally.

In a quavering voice, Nick said, "Grandpa? It's Nick. . . ." Then he started to cry. "I'm so glad that you and Grandma didn't die in the fire. . . . I'm safe now. Some wonderful people are taking care of me. They told me that dental records show you didn't die in the fire, so I tried your cell phone. . . . Where are you? They're taking me to Budapest. We'll be at the Four Seasons Hotel this evening in a room registered to Elizabeth Crowder. . . Okay. I'll see you then." Nick put down the phone, wiping his face with his sleeve.

"What did he say?" Elizabeth asked, anxiously.

"He was very surprised. He told me he was sorry he caused me so much pain. When he sees me, he'll explain what happened and why he had no choice. He hopes that I will forgive him. He said he will come to our hotel suite this evening at eleven in disguise, so I may not recognize him. And he said that he loves me."

Elizabeth was thrilled that Nick had handled the call so well. She had gotten exactly what she had hoped for. Now it would be up to Craig to convince Peter to cooperate in finding and stopping Omar.

"This is very helpful," Elizabeth told Nick. "I'm glad you'll see your grandpa this evening. Now let's go to Budapest!"

Nick started peeling off his pajamas. "I'm getting dressed. I'll be ready to go in two minutes."

Nick was true to his word. Two minutes later they were on their way to the airport.

## Budapest

Prime Minister Szabo was disappointed as he listened to the report from the director of Military Intelligence. An enhanced interrogation of Gyorgy Kovacs, including waterboarding, hadn't produced any information about Peter Toth's plans to hire Chechen terrorists.

"I'm convinced Gyorgy doesn't know anything," the director concluded.

"Okay, release him," Szabo fumed, "and warn him that if he tells anyone what happened to him he'll be charged with undermining state security and given a ten-year jail sentence."

\*       \*       \*

At Ferenc Liszt airport in Budapest Pierre rented a gray Audi and drove the other three the twenty minutes to the Four Seasons Hotel along the Danube River, a short distance south of the parliament.

The art nouveau building, once the Gresham Palace, had been totally renovated after being damaged in World War II and was now Budapest's most luxurious hotel. With Craig leading the way, they walked across the marble lobby lit by ornate glass chandeliers and up to the front desk.

Elizabeth registered for a two-bedroom suite to keep Nick close by in the second bedroom, and a room adjacent to the suite for Pierre.

Once they were in the suite and the bellman had gone, Craig made sure there were no bugs.

Elizabeth told Nick, "I'm glad you'll see your grandpa this evening." She turned to Craig. "I think it would be best if Nick and I stayed in the suite. You probably have some things you want to do."

"Correct. I want to try and hook up with Lieutenant General Nemeth. When I was the head of EU Counterterrorism, Nemeth commanded Hungarian Special Forces. He's a good guy, and I think I can trust him. I'm hoping he'll help us in locating Omar."

As Craig headed toward the door, Elizabeth's encrypted phone rang. She handed it to Craig.

"Yes, Betty," he said.

"Are you in Budapest?"

"Yeah. In the Four Seasons Hotel with Elizabeth and Nick."

"Can you get to the embassy? Doug Caldwell's expecting you."

"Sure. I'm on my way."

"Use your Enrico Marino passport to get through security. Doug knows who you really are."

Betty clicked off.

"Keep the phone," Elizabeth told Craig. "You may have to call Betty when you're not in the embassy. Also, do you know Caldwell?"

Craig shook his head.

"I checked his bio this morning," Elizabeth continued. "He's a kid. Been with the agency five years, an Iowa farm boy and a graduate of Wisconsin with an econ major. His first assignment was in London. Now this."

"So that's who the heirs are to the swashbuckling, charismatic Yalies of the CIA's glamour days."

"Don't be such a snob. As I recall, you went to Carnegie Mellon."

As Craig walked the seven blocks to the embassy, the blazing sun beat down on him. It was a hot summer day, and as he passed by St. Stephen's Basilica he was struck by the beauty of the cathedral. In front of the US Embassy was a small grassy area with an unsightly stone statute on a pedestal at the center. It was the Soviet Army memorial, which inexplicably had not been torn down after the Russians left in 1991.

The embassy, a five-story, pale yellow stone structure with a lovely art nouveau façade, would have looked like any other office building in the area but for the extreme security. A six-foot-high, heavy, metal black fence surrounded the building. Access was possible only through one entry gate, which was guarded by several Marines clutching assault rifles. After the 9/11 bombings, security at US embassies around the world had been enhanced. However, Craig wondered what justified so much security in Budapest. To his knowledge, the embassy had never been attacked, and Hungary was on friendly terms with the US, although Szabo seemed determined to change that.

Doug Caldwell, tall and broad shouldered with a blonde crew cut, was waiting for Craig in his cubby hole of an office on the third floor. Craig regarded these surroundings with amusement. They exemplified what many in the State Department thought of their CIA colleagues. In fairness to the CIA leadership, it was hard to run a spy agency when Congress kept brutally cutting funds and committee chairmen wanted to be involved in planning every mission. Then there was the press, constantly making the CIA a whipping boy. The Company had fallen on hard times in its recruitment as well.

"It's a great honor to meet you, Mr. Page."

"You can call me Craig."

"And I'm Doug. I heard all about you in my training at the agency's farm. You're almost a mythical figure within the CIA."

"Yeah. I'm mythical okay. Did they also tell you that I set the record for shortest time as CIA director? Three weeks, as I recall. Not even long enough for them to take my picture to hang on the seventh floor at Langley."

"There were extenuating circumstances, I heard."

"Yeah. Like a weak livered spineless president following the advice of an asshole Washington lawyer."

Caldwell smiled. "I was pleased to hear from Director Richards this morning that we'd be working together."

"Don't worry, Doug, you'll get over it."

Doug's enthusiasm wasn't dampened. "Would you like some coffee?" he asked.

"That'd be great. Black and strong."

Doug left the office and returned a couple of minutes later holding two Styrofoam cups. *What happened to English bone china?* Craig thought.

Craig moved files from a chair in front of Doug's overcrowded desk and sat down facing the station chief.

"Now tell me," Craig said to Doug, "what happened that Betty asked me to drop everything and get over here?"

Caldwell took a deep breath and said, "About an hour ago, I received a call from my primary contact in Hungarian military intelligence. He told me that Russian President Kuznov will be coming to Budapest Wednesday morning. Then at noon on Wednesday, in front of the parliament building, Kuznov and Szabo will announce an agreement between Hungary and Russia. My contact, General Horvath, doesn't know what it provides."

Craig felt triumphant. All the pieces had fallen into place now, confirming what Craig and Elizabeth had guessed. Peter must have found out about this agreement between Hungary and Russia. With his enormous hatred of the Russians and Szabo, he then traveled to Chechnya where he hired Omar to assassinate both Kuznov and Szabo during the ceremony. Omar was thrilled to do it because of his own hatred for Kuznov, and Peter funneled the payment through Emma Miller. This also confirmed why Omar didn't abort, even when he thought Peter was dead. With Omar's hatred of Kuznov, he'd never pass up a chance to kill the Russian president.

"And you told Betty what you learned from General Horvath?" Craig asked Doug.

"Yes, sir, as soon as I heard it from General Horvath."

"What did she tell you to do?"

"That I was to brief you and remain on standby until she called back."

The phone on Caldwell's desk rang. "Yes ma'am. He's here. . . . I'll do that right away."

He put down the phone. "Director Richards wants us to go to the communications room in the basement to take her call."

The communications room was a twelve-foot square with depressingly drab gray walls, badly in need of fresh paint. It held a battered metal table with a red phone and three rickety wooden chairs.

Doug hit several buttons, and Craig heard Betty say, "Craig, are you with Doug?"

"Yeah. We're both here."

"Did Doug tell you what he learned from General Horvath?"

"He did. It confirms everything Elizabeth and I deduced. Omar's planning to kill both Szabo and Kuznov at the ceremony on Wednesday."

"I agree."

"I hope President Worth will call Kuznov now and warn him."

"He just made the call, urging him not to go to Budapest until Omar is apprehended. Kuznov rejected the warning. He thinks this is all a ploy by the US to block Russia and Hungary from executing their Friendship agreement."

"What's the president want me to do?"

"He has decided to back your attempt. Peter Toth was a US citizen, and he is responsible for developing this plot. If Omar succeeds or even if he attempts to carry out the attack, the US could be blamed. Worth doesn't want to risk it. He thinks it's better to try and stop Omar, even if that means the Russian–Hungarian treaty goes forward. The president is hoping you'll work with the Hungarians to apprehend Omar and his men before Kuznov arrives Wednesday morning."

"I assume apprehend means capture or kill."

"I didn't say that. But if Omar is shot while trying to escape, I'm sure you couldn't help that."

"Suppose the Hungarians won't work with me?" Craig asked.

"You're charming, Craig. You'll persuade them."

"Thanks."

"You have only one limitation—no US troops can be involved. Do you understand?"

"I do."

"Okay. Good luck."

*This is great*, Craig thought sarcastically. *There are 1.8 million people in Budapest, and somewhere among them Omar and his men are holed up. I have less than forty-eight hours to find and stop him, and I don't even have the vaguest idea where he is.*

Craig needed help, but he declined Doug's offer for assistance. The CIA station chief had nothing that would be useful to him. Once Craig was outside of the embassy, he called Lieutenant General Nemeth.

"Good to hear from you Craig," Nemeth said in a booming voice. "Where are you?"

"Budapest, and I'd like to talk to you."

"How about coming to my office in the Defense Ministry?"

"Off-site will be better. I'm close to the parliament."

After a short silence, Nemeth said, "Special Forces has a small office at number 12 Bathory Street. I can meet you there in an hour."

"I'll see you then."

Craig thought about the last time he'd seen Nemeth, who headed up a unit that was a combination of military intelligence and special ops.

It was about three years ago, he thought. Craig had been the head of EU Counterterrorism, and he had received information that two ISIS terrorists had infiltrated a group of Syrian refugees who had arrived in Hungary before Szabo shut down access routes from Southern Europe. Working closely together, Nemeth and Craig had located the two, trapped them in Castle Hill in Buda where they were trying to set off bombs, and killed both of them. Craig and Nemeth solidified their bond that evening, celebrating by getting so drunk in a café with wine and Slivovitz that Craig could barely make it back to his hotel.

With an hour to kill until his meeting with Nemeth, Craig passed the Soviet Army memorial and headed toward the parliament, its neo-Renaissance dome shooting up into the air providing a marker for the entire city.

Arriving in the square, he saw workmen erecting a platform with an overhanging roof in front of the parliament. That must be where the event would take place Wednesday. As Craig walked the periphery of the parliament square he passed Peter's old office building with the defaced name plate that Elizabeth had told him about. Unfortunately, Peter and Szabo's vendetta was no longer personal. Nations were involved, with potential consequences for millions of people.

When Craig arrived at number 12 Bathory, Nemeth was waiting inside the front door. He took a look at Craig and a puzzled expression crossed his face. Reading his mind, Craig explained, "I had some work done to stay alive."

"Same voice. Same walk. It's hard to change those."

Nemeth led Craig up a flight of stairs and into a drab corner office with a view of the parliament. Other than the two of them the building seemed deserted.

The forty-five-year-old Nemeth had aged since Craig had last seen him. The brown crew cut was now gray, and his face showed wrinkles. His was a tough job with the constant threat of Islamic terrorists; and working for Szabo couldn't be a picnic. It had all taken a toll over the last three years.

Nemeth settled behind a desk while Craig sat in front of him.

"I was sorry that you left the EU Counterterrorism job," Nemeth said. "Giuseppe's a good man."

"For sure. But he's no Craig Page."

"Yeah, well, I've made some career choices that didn't work out too well. How are Katalin and your daughters?"

"All good, thanks. I can guess why you're here."

"Go ahead."

Nemeth reached into his pocket and pulled out a picture of Omar the Chechen. He put it down on the desk.

"How'd you guess?" Craig asked.

"Szabo called me this morning and said he was reported to be in Budapest and might be planning to carry out some type of terrorist attack. Szabo said we should try to find and kill him. Is that right?"

"Part way."

"It figures with Szabo. You and I had a rule we could tell each other anything without fearing it would be repeated. Can we impose that again?"

"For sure."

"Then I'll tell you I disliked Szabo when we last worked together. The man's gotten much worse. He's a horror—a megalomaniac, consumed with the power he has and always wanting more."

"That fits with what I've heard."

"Why are you here?" Nemeth asked. "To locate Omar? And who sent you? Giuseppe?"

"It's complicated."

Nemeth laughed. "With you, Craig, it's always complicated. Tell me about it."

Knowing he could trust Nemeth and that he desperately needed the Hungarian's help, Craig told him about Amos's and Emma's murders. He omitted Nick, and after talking for ten minutes, he came to the bottom line. "Szabo omitted some information when he told you about Omar. Omar's plan is to kill Szabo and Kuznov, probably at Wednesday's ceremony."

"You sure Szabo knows he's a target?"

"President Worth personally called Szabo and gave him the warning."

"Tell me again how you know that Omar is in Budapest," Nemeth requested. "It may help us figure out where he is."

Craig told him about Ayanna and Rachid.

When he was finished, Nemeth said, "Do you have her brother's cell number?"

"I do."

"Perhaps the phone was overlooked. It could have been left where it fell."

"But how likely is that?" Craig asked skeptically.

Nemeth shrugged. "Only a slight chance, but sometimes even seasoned terrorists make mistakes. At any rate, I can't think of a better way of locating Omar. Perhaps you can."

Craig shook his head. "You could give the cell number to your tech people and see if they could locate it."

"Our tech people are back in the Stone Age. It could take them six weeks. But your embassy must have some good IT people. Perhaps they could provide guidance."

Craig wasn't optimistic this would succeed, but he was willing to give it a try.

They split, promising to remain in contact, and Craig raced back to the embassy where he told Doug that he wanted the techies at the embassy to work with their Hungarian counterparts to locate the phone.

"I'll do that, but their IT is rudimentary."

"I know that. It's why I'm asking you to have our people involved."

"Do I need approval for that?"

Craig wanted to scream but he kept himself under control. "Of course not," he said calmly and with confidence. "We're on an assignment authorized by POTUS. I've been authorized to use all the resources that our country has except for American troops. Now get moving."

*         *         *

Omar hated being cooped up in the castle. During the day, he had to get outside to clear his mind and to walk around. It didn't seem to bother the other men. They were always playing cards and video games; they could play all day.

Omar wanted to run through the plans for Wednesday's attack, so he and Shamil went out to the back of the house and sat down on the ground. Using a stick, Omar scratched a square in the dirt representing the area in front of the parliament where the ceremony would take place.

As he scratched, he heard a sound in the bushes near where Rachid had been hiding when he made that call on his cell phone. He got up and walked over with Shamil following. A small wild boar raced away.

"Maybe he was looking for Rachid's cell phone," said Shamil.

"What'd you say?" Omar asked.

"Maybe that boar was looking for Rachid's cell phone."

Omar had heard Shamil perfectly well the first time. His words hit Omar like a ton of bricks. Omar realized he had made a serious error by not finding the cell phone that Rachid had tossed into the woods and destroying it so it couldn't be used to locate them. Maybe it wasn't too late. Omar had the number of Rachid's cell because he had used it in Clichy.

Now he took out his own phone and walked into the woods in the area where Rachid had thrown it. As he walked, Omar repeatedly dialed Rachid's number. After a few minutes he heard a faint, "Beep . . . beep . . . beep." He followed the noise into the trees, disregarding the branches that were scratching his arms, until finally he found the phone, still intact. It hadn't rained since Rachid had used it.

Omar examined the phone and saw there was a voicemail from the previous day. He listened to it. "Rachid, this is Ayanna. Are you okay? Please call me."

In a rage as he thought about what Rachid had done, Omar handed the phone to Shamil. "I want you to destroy the SIM card and the phone with a hammer. Then I want you to drive it down to the river and throw it into the Danube."

*       *       *

Doug was right, Craig realized. The Hungarian IT was rudimentary. Even working with Americans at the embassy it took them until six o'clock that evening to conclude that Rachid's cell phone could not be located.

Trying not to feel discouraged, Craig told himself that it had been a long shot anyway. His only hope now was that Peter might have some information that would help them locate Omar. Craig called Nemeth to tell him that they had struck out on the phone.

"I have one other possibility," he said. "I'll let you know in the morning if that works."

When Craig returned to the hotel, he said hello to Pierre, who was seated in the corridor outside of their suite. He found Elizabeth hunched over her laptop in the living room of the suite. She came over and kissed him.

"Where's Nick?" he asked.

"In his bedroom playing a video game on my iPad."

"Good. I want to tell you what happened."

When he was finished she said, "So you're no closer to finding Omar."

He smiled. "You have a very concise way of summing it up. And how was your day?"

"Not nearly as exciting. I've been editing pieces for the *Herald*. But I have a plan for us before Peter gets here at eleven."

"I'm listening."

"I'm going down to the gym to work out for about an hour."

"Accompanied by Pierre."

"Of course. Then there's an excellent restaurant, Baraka, about two or three blocks from the hotel. You, Nick, and I should go for dinner."

"We can't risk Nick being seen in a restaurant," Craig interrupted.

"Agreed. So I called and found out they have a private dining room. We'll take Pierre with us. The kid needs a night out. What do you think?"

"We all need a night out," Craig agreed with a sigh. "Let's do it."

"You're really willing?" She sounded surprised.

"Yeah. I think that either I shook the Russian tail or Kuznov called off the dogs. At this point, Szabo probably doesn't know we're in Budapest, and Omar's hiding from us. It's good to be the hunter instead of the hunted for once."

*     *     *

They returned to the hotel suite at ten fifteen. Nick had enjoyed being able to get out of the hotel for a few hours, and thanked them for taking him to dinner. Then he went into his bedroom to await his grandfather's arrival. He seemed anxious, and Craig couldn't blame him. His grandfather, who he had loved dearly, was returning from the dead.

Precisely at eleven o'clock, Craig heard a knock on the door. He had seen pictures of Peter, with his thinning gray hair, and he knew Peter would be in disguise. But he was still surprised to see the man who walked into the suite with a thick head of brown hair—a very professional toupee—and a matching mustache. He was wearing wire-framed glasses, which Peter didn't need, and he had a sandpaper beard, unlike the clean-shaven Peter that Craig had seen in photos.

"Hello. I'm Peter Toth."

While Craig stared at the visitor, Elizabeth came forward. "Elizabeth Crowder," she said.

"The reporter?"

"Correct. And this is my friend Craig."

"Where's Nick?"

She went into the bedroom and brought Nick out. He stopped dead in his tracks and did a double take looking at Peter.

"It's me," Peter said. The voice must have satisfied the boy because he ran to Peter and gave him a big hug.

"I'm so glad you're okay, Nick. I'm sorry that I caused you so much pain," Peter said, his voice cracking.

"I did everything you said, Grandpa." Nick said, overcome with emotion. "I ran away from the house, and I called Emma. Then I flew to Paris just as you told me."

"I'm so proud of you."

"But I was scared after the fire and finding out Emma was dead as soon as I got to Paris."

"I had no idea that would happen. I was terrified for you when I heard about Emma's death."

"I don't know what I would have done if Elizabeth didn't take me home with her," Nick continued. "And she's taken good care of me ever since. Craig, too. He's a superspy. You should have seen him kill those two Russians in the Häagen-Dazs!"

"I'm very grateful to both of you," Peter said. "I don't know how I could possibly repay you for taking care of Nick."

Peter turned to Nick. "I want you to know how hard I tried to find you that night. I hadn't been able to sleep, although I pretended to when you looked into our bedroom before you snuck down to watch the game."

"You knew?"

"Of course. Then I heard the Russian intruders. I grabbed the gun in the table next to the bed, figuring they would come upstairs to kill me and your grandmother. I was hiding behind a door on the landing, and as soon as they were in sight, I surprised them. Only one fired a shot, and it missed me. I killed both of them. Then I went downstairs to find you. I saw the open window in the basement and realized you had followed the escape plan I gave you. On the way down, I saw the gasoline and other stuff the Russians had brought to set the house on fire after they killed me and your grandmother, so I decided to use it. I wanted everyone to think I was dead. That way the Russians would stop hunting me."

"You did a good job," Craig said.

"How did you realize I was alive?" Peter asked.

"FBI analysis of dental records of the bodies found in the house."

Peter turned to Nick. "After I set the fire, your grandma and I got into the car. We drove around the area for a long time, trying to find you, but we couldn't. I even thought of driving to Dulles Airport, because you would be there for a flight to Paris as I had arranged with Emma, but I thought that would be too dangerous because the Russians might know I had escaped and they would be looking for me there. I didn't think they'd be looking for you. I wanted you to be safe. I thought you would be okay because you would fly to Paris and Emma would take care of you. I never thought the Russians would kill Emma as well."

"Where's Grandma?" Nick asked.

"I drove her to Cleveland and hid her there with your cousins Margaret and Hal."

"Then where did you go?" Nick asked, his eyes wide.

"I had a fake passport. I flew to Budapest."

"Did you want to be here when Omar killed Kuznov and Szabo?" Craig asked. "To gloat?"

"So you know about that. . . ." Peter looked vaguely confused by Craig's unexpected knowledge.

"Also that you agreed to pay Omar twenty million euros to kill Szabo and perhaps Kuznov, and that you already paid the first ten million, funneling the money through Emma."

Peter pulled back in surprise. "I'm not sure Nick should hear this," he said finally.

Elizabeth intervened. "The boy's been through a lot. He's entitled to know what happened."

"I even met with President Worth," Nick chimed in.

Craig smiled. The kid was sharp. Craig was hoping that with Nick listening they could convince Peter to call off Omar. "Why don't you tell us what you had in mind Peter?" Craig said.

"It's true that I did hire Omar to kill Szabo and Kuznov, but you have to understand why. The Russians caused so much pain and suffering to millions of Hungarians, not just to me and my family. Now Szabo would be letting Russian troops back into the country again. I couldn't let it happen."

"And you think that justified the assassination of two national leaders?" Elizabeth asked.

"Initially I did." He sounded defensive. "But after Emma's murder, I realized I was wrong. Assassination isn't the solution. I had to find another way to block the agreement from being finalized."

"Omar's still in Budapest," Craig said.

"You never called him off," Elizabeth added.

"I tried," Peter said with a sigh. "I pleaded with him to keep my first payment and to go back to Grozny. He refused. I threatened to withhold the second payment, but it didn't matter to him. Omar hates Kuznov. He's now operating on his own agenda."

Craig was flabbergasted. He had not expected to hear this from Peter.

"You set him in motion," Craig said.

"True, but I'm not responsible for what he does now."

Craig opened his mouth to argue with Peter, reconsidered, and moved on. "Have you found another way to block the agreement from being finalized?"

"I'm working on it, but I don't want to tell you about it yet because I'm not sure it will succeed."

"And meantime Omar is on the loose somewhere in this city of almost two million people, and we have no idea where," Craig retorted.

"Listen, Craig. I told you that I tried to stop Omar. I don't want him to kill Szabo or Kuznov either."

"Then tell us where to find him."

When Peter didn't reply, Craig was convinced that he knew where Omar was and was considering whether or not to tell them. Did he want to hedge his bets? If his other way of blocking the agreement didn't pan out, would he still prefer that Omar kill Kuznov and Szabo? The moment of truth had come.

"If you don't tell us and Omar succeeds, you'll be treated as an accomplice to murder. The police will arrest you," Elizabeth pointed out, adding pressure for Peter.

Nick burst into tears. "I don't want you to be arrested, Grandpa."

"So which is more important to you," Elizabeth continued, on a roll, "revenge for what was done to you and your mother by Colonel Suslov or your future with Nick?"

"How do you know about Colonel Suslov?" Peter asked startled.

"Tracy Thomas and I spent time together after the moving memorial service for you at the Church of the Little Flower."

He looked chagrined at the mention of Tracy. *And he should*, Elizabeth thought. After all she had done for him, Peter had treated Tracy like a used tissue.

"Tell them," Nick said. "Please tell them. I don't want to lose you again."

Peter took a deep breath and said, "I rented a deserted castle for Omar in the hills outside of Buda. He and his men are probably there now or they will be by tomorrow."

"Where's the castle?" Craig asked.

Peter walked over to the desk, pulled a piece of stationery out of the drawer and a pen from his pocket. With Craig looking over his shoulder, he drew a map, placing an x at the location of the castle. He handed it to Craig, looking him in the eye. "I hope you find Omar and stop him."

Then Peter walked around to Nick. "This will all be over in two days," Peter told his grandson, "and when it is, I promise to make everything up to you. We will always be together."

Nick still looked worried as Peter hugged him goodbye.

"I have to leave now," Peter said. "I have work to do to destroy Szabo and to block the treaty from going into effect. But nothing involving violence. I promise you."

Once Peter was gone, Craig turned to Nick. "Do you have any idea what your grandfather meant when he said he was working on a way to block the agreement from being finalized?"

Nick shook his head.

"Think back to his phone call with Emma," Elizabeth said, "when you were eavesdropping during the baseball game. Can you recall anything else they talked about?"

Nick thought about it for a few minutes. Then he said, "There is something else I remember. Grandpa said he still had his key to their vault box in Paris."

"Anything else?" Elizabeth asked.

Nick shook his head.

Craig interjected, "Maybe Emma left something for Peter in the vault box? Since she was working with him to dismantle the agreement, it could have been something to do with that."

Nick yawned. "I'm tired," he said. "I'm going to sleep."

While Elizabeth walked Nick into the bedroom, Craig called Betty on the encrypted phone and reported what they had learned.

"Excellent," she said. "Email me the map. I'll get satellite and drone surveillance on it at daybreak. Can you get to the embassy at five tomorrow morning? I'll arrange for you to get real-time video feed."

*　　　*　　　*

At five in the morning, as darkness was giving way to light in Budapest, Craig, Doug Caldwell, and a thermos of hot, strong black coffee were in the communications room in the embassy. The red phone was on the table, and a video screen on one wall.

Moments later, images appeared on the screen, and Betty was on the phone.

"Morning, Craig and Doug," she said.

"And good evening to you," Craig replied.

"Look at the screen. The castle Peter identified is in the center."

Craig saw a gray stone building with turrets shooting up into the air. It had an almost medieval look. The only other structure on the screen was another similar looking castle that Craig guessed was about a hundred yards away.

"We're zooming in on the castle Peter identified," Betty said.

The castle came into clear focus.

"That's it," Betty said.

"We should destroy the castle with a missile or a drone," Craig said.

"I knew you'd want to do that, so I already ran it by the president."

"And?"

"He said positively not. First, we don't know for a fact that Omar is inside. Second, even if he is, the two young Frenchmen may be with him."

"But they're part of an assassination team. They hardly qualify as collateral damage," Craig argued.

"There may be other civilians inside as well," Betty countered.

"I doubt if they're innocent."

"Sorry, but the president was clear."

"Suppose Omar goes outside, and we get a line on Omar alone. Can we at least hit him?" he asked.

"Worth said I should let him know. He wasn't ready to make that decision yet."

For the next forty-five minutes they watched the screen, but nothing happened. Finally at two minutes to six, a man walked through the front door of the castle alone. He was smoking a cigarette.

"That's Omar," Craig said.

"You sure?" Betty asked.

"Positive. I've been studying Omar's photo for days. Let's take him out."

"I'll call the president."

"He'll be gone by then."

"I can't authorize this without approval. Stand by. I'll call you back."

Craig was salivating at the thought of killing Omar. They had a perfect shot. No collateral damage. Surely Worth would approve it.

*     *     *

With increasing apprehension, Omar stood in front of the castle and looked up into the cloudless morning sky. He saw an object overhead. That must be a drone. Omar was convinced it was focused on the castle and, at this instant, on him.

Omar didn't think the Hungarians had sophisticated drone technology, so he guessed it was Russian.

*Kuznov has found me.*

Omar considered his options. He could race into the castle, grab the keys to the van, and drive away. No point doing that. They would see him and fire a rocket at his van. Hiding in the castle was also futile— they would blast it to smithereens, and him as well.

Besides, those were a coward's choices for death. Not Omar's. He was a courageous warrior. He would die a heroic martyr's death.

He remained calm, bracing himself, expecting the missile to come from the drone any second and kill him. At long last he would be joining his wife and daughters in paradise.

$$* \qquad * \qquad *$$

Betty was back on the line with Craig and Doug. "The answer is no."

Craig was dumbfounded. "No, what?"

"No, we won't take Omar out with a missile."

"I don't fucking believe it. Why not?"

"President Worth says Hungary is a sovereign country. It isn't Pakistan, where we had far better reasons for taking out Osama bin Laden. If we do this without Szabo's approval, he'll go berserk. It'll drive him into the arms of the Russians."

"He's already there."

"Worth wants you to talk to Szabo. You can tell Szabo that we now have direct evidence that Omar is in Budapest. If you get Szabo's approval, we'll hit Omar."

"Omar will be gone by then."

Ignoring Craig's words, Betty said, "If you need an intro to get access to Szabo, Worth will call him."

Craig knew that Nemeth had access to the Hungarian prime minister. He decided that was the better way.

"I don't need it," Craig said glumly. "I have a high-ranking Hungarian military officer who can get me in."

"Keep me posted."

Damn politicians, Craig thought as he put down the phone.

"What can I do to help?" Doug asked.

The station chief had been so quiet that Craig had forgotten he was there. "Not a damn thing unfortunately," Craig said angrily.

Craig took out his phone and called Nemeth. "We have to talk."

"Same location as yesterday," Nemeth said. "In thirty minutes."

"I'll be there."

*　　*　　*

*The missile never came.* Incredulous, Omar opened his eyes. Kuznov and Szabo didn't want to kill him. Why not?

Omar could think of only one explanation. They wanted him alive in order to interrogate him, to learn who had sent him on this mission. Omar was familiar with the Russian torture techniques, and knew the Hungarians would permit Russia to control his fate. He had no intention of letting them capture him. He would fortify the castle so well that any attack they launched would produce heavy casualties on their side. And if he couldn't prevail or escape, he intended to die in the castle. But they would never take him alive, he vowed.

Omar went into the castle to prepare for the attack that would come—and soon.

*　　*　　*

Craig couldn't let Szabo know that Peter Toth was the source of his information about Omar's location. So he developed a cover, which he told to Nemeth, about how he learned the information from an anonymous source in Paris. Craig then described the location of the castle for Nemeth by drawing a map of his own, a copy of Peter's map from memory.

Craig added, "I passed the info along to my friends in the CIA who put a satellite and drone in the air for surveillance. Before I called you I was looking at video feed in our embassy. I made visual confirmation of Omar. I wanted to take him out with a missile."

"In which case, I'd still be sleeping."

"That's right. The powers in Washington decided they wouldn't do it unless Szabo gave the US prior approval. President Worth intends to respect Hungarian sovereignty."

"Very polite of him," Nemeth commented. "The US doesn't always operate that way."

"Personally, I disagreed," Craig said.

Nemeth laughed. "I'm not surprised. But since you were overruled, you called me to gain access to Szabo."

"That's right."

Without hesitating, Nemeth took out his phone. For the next couple of minutes, he was engaged in a spirited conversation in Hungarian. Craig had no idea what he was saying or who he was talking to. Nemeth was frowning. When he put down the phone he told Craig, "I spoke to Szabo. He won't see us until eleven."

"*Eleven*? Omar could have left the country by then."

"That's what I said, but Szabo told me that if Omar leaves the castle, your people will track him from the sky. The fact is, Szabo doesn't want to look like he's doing the bidding of President Worth."

"Who, by the way, is trying to save his life."

"Look Craig, you know Szabo's not one of my favorite people. Now let's go have some breakfast. After that we can come back here and plot an operation to capture the castle with ground troops, just in case Szabo doesn't approve a drone attack."

Nemeth obviously felt Szabo would nix the drone attack. Craig got a sick feeling in the pit of his stomach. This would not go well.

*       *       *

Craig always formed snap impressions of people. After only two minutes with Szabo and Nemeth in the prime minister's large and stately office, he viewed Szabo as a "disgusting little man." Szabo, five foot two with thick gray hair and a high forehead, leaned back in his black plush chair, feet up on a green leather topped desk, puffing on a cigar while Craig repeated for Szabo the story he had told Nemeth earlier about the anonymous tip from Paris.

At the end, Craig said, "I'm here, Mr. Prime Minister, at the request of President Worth to obtain your approval to kill the notorious Chechen terrorist, Omar Basayev, with a missile from a drone. We now have direct evidence Omar is in Budapest, and we know his location. We will, of course, do our best to ensure that no one else is injured."

Before the words were even out of Craig's mouth, Szabo said, "No."

"No what, Mr. Prime Minister?"

"No, you can't do it."

"Can I ask why?"

Szabo puffed on the cigar and put it down. "First, only the Hungarian government carries out operations on Hungarian soil and in Hungarian airspace. Second, I want this terrorist captured alive. We will interrogate him to find out who sent him. We have people who are expert at this type of interrogation, and we don't have some of the restraints that the US has."

Craig thought about his visit when he had been the director of EU Counterterrorism to a museum on Andrassy Boulevard in Budapest known as the House of Terror. It portrayed not only torture in Hungary conducted by the Gestapo and the Russians, but also by AVH, the Hungarian secret police, who Stalin's puppet government unleashed and whose brutality was a factor in leading to the 1956 revolt. So repugnant were AVH's actions that during the early days of the revolt before the Russians had taken control, numerous AVH agents were lynched in the streets and hung up by their feet from trees and lampposts.

Craig wondered whether Szabo suspected that Peter had hired Omar and wanted to prove it. *And there may be something else motivating Szabo*, Craig thought. After his people were finished with Omar, he could turn over to Kuznov what was left of the terrorist for his own interrogation, thereby currying favor with the Russian leader.

Szabo turned to Nemeth. "Since I've ruled out an attack from the air, I want you to develop a plan for capturing Omar in a ground operation."

"I've already thought of that, Mr. Prime Minister," Nemeth said, his tone respectful.

"Describe it for me in detail."

*Wonderful*, Craig thought. *Another civilian head of state who wants to micromanage a military operation.*

Nemeth then presented the plan he and Craig had developed. It meant taking over an abandoned castle a hundred yards away to use as a staging area. "We expect to be able to launch our attack by two o'clock this afternoon," Nemeth said.

While Nemeth was talking, Szabo frowned. When he had finished, Szabo said, "I don't like it."

"Why not, Mr. Prime Minister?"

"We have to assume that Omar and his people will be heavily armed. Am I correct?"

"You are," Nemeth replied.

"During daylight our casualties will be too great. I want you to get your forces in place in the nearby castle but wait for nighttime. Launch your attack at midnight."

Craig refused to remain silent any longer. "With all due respect, Mr. Prime Minister, Omar will undoubtedly realize we are setting up for an attack. Waiting until midnight will give him plenty of time to fortify his castle and to strengthen his defenses. As a result, our casualties will be increased. Also, there will be a greater chance of Omar escaping."

Szabo was red in the face. The man wasn't used to being challenged and certainly not by a foreigner. "How dare you question me?" he spat.

"With all due respect, sir, I've had considerable experience in matters like this."

"I don't care what you've had. This attack will take place at midnight."

Szabo was so adamant that Craig tried to think of his motive, apart from wanting to be in charge. It struck Craig that Szabo might not want to disclose an attack on his life in the media and believed that if the fighting took place at night, he'd have a better chance of keeping the incident quiet.

"And one other thing," Szabo said, pausing to light another cigar, "you can help General Nemeth in planning, but I don't want any US troops or other personnel involved in the actual attack in any way. And that includes you. Is that understood?"

"Understood."

"Finally, let me emphasize that I want Omar captured not killed. Is that understood by both of you?"

"Understood," they replied.

Leaving Szabo's office with Nemeth, Craig considered appealing Szabo's decision on the drone and midnight attack to Washington, but he assumed the prime minister would dig in and Craig would be blocked from participating. The home team makes the rules, after all. But Craig wouldn't be sidelined. He didn't care that Szabo told him he shouldn't participate in the attack or that Omar should be taken alive.

Craig had no intention of following those orders. He was working on his own agenda. He would storm the castle with the Hungarian troops, and the instant he saw Omar, even if the Chechen was in custody, Craig intended to kill him. It was payback for Amos Neir. Also, Craig couldn't risk Omar telling Szabo that Peter had hired him, for Nick's sake.

\*        \*        \*

As soon as Omar got back into the castle following the drone attack that never came, he assembled Shamil and the two Frenchmen, Muhammad and Yassir, in the living room.

"An attack may be coming," Omar said, "but we have an advantage."

"What's that?" Yassir asked, sounding frightened.

"We have to fortify and booby-trap this castle. It won't matter how many men they send. We'll drive them off."

"And after that?" Muhammad asked.

"I have a second hiding spot. Once we've driven off the attackers and it's dark, we go there."

Omar could tell that the two Frenchmen were nervous, but they knew he had killed Rachid. They were too frightened to defy him. They didn't want Omar to kill them, too. That suited Omar. Obedience was what he needed from them.

\*        \*        \*

Craig was fuming as he worked with Nemeth and ten Hungarian soldiers, including two medics, to develop a plan for the midnight attack on Omar's castle. If they moved now, Omar wouldn't have had much time to prepare. Thanks to Szabo, that advantage would be lost.

As Craig and Nemeth spoke about operational details, the Hungarian general told his troops that they would have to follow Szabo's orders, emphasizing the need to capture Omar alive. Craig's instinct was that Omar would be likely to expect a frontal assault, would station more of his men behind the front door to the castle, and would strongly fortify that entrance. As a result, he told Nemeth they should break in from the back or side door, which they had seen from air recognizance, or through windows, but avoid the front door. Craig's assumption was that Omar wouldn't want to booby trap all the doors in case he had to escape.

The directive to capture Omar precluded the use of grenades, but Craig had persuaded Nemeth to use tear gas and to outfit his soldiers with gas masks.

Their plans were set by three in the afternoon, and the next nine hours of waiting were interminable. The soldiers ate and some slept while others smoked and played cards.

Craig paced in the castle. He called Elizabeth to tell her he wouldn't be back until quite late. "Please don't wait up and don't worry." Even with an encrypted phone, he didn't want to tell her any more than that.

Finally, at fifteen minutes before midnight, the Hungarian soldiers gathered their equipment and picked up their guns. Craig's plan was to be in front of the onrushing troops, then cut to the left, to the side door. He wanted to be one of the first in the castle in order to kill Omar before he was captured.

At midnight as they waited outside the castle, Nemeth gave the signal. Craig was out in front running toward Omar's castle, which appeared to be completely dark inside. The ground was rocky and uneven. With only a sliver of a moon and clouds in the sky, Craig had to use the flashlight he had in one hand to avoid losing his footing. He had a gun in his other hand, and Nemeth was running beside him carrying a tear gas gun.

While the two of them ran toward the side door, Craig noticed one of the Hungarian soldiers heading straight for the front door of the castle. Damn fool didn't believe in following orders. One of Omar's men opened fire from an upstairs window, mowing him down.

As Craig reached the side door, he heard an explosion from the front door of the castle. He had been correct. It was booby trapped.

Craig smashed in the side door, and Nemeth immediately fired tear gas into the darkened castle. While Craig paused at the door and looked around, three Hungarian soldiers entered the castle through the back door. They took heavy gunfire from Omar and his men.

In seconds, it was chaos in the castle with guns firing in every direction.

Craig saw a bearded man rushing toward the back door carrying a duffel bag. Certain it was Omar, Craig raised his gun and screamed, "That's Omar. Stop him!"

Before Craig had a clear shot, Omar wheeled around and fired in Craig's direction. Craig ducked. The bullet hit Nemeth in the chest, and he went down.

To reach Omar before he escaped through the back door, Craig would have had to make it through the crossfire. He would have tried, but he couldn't leave Nemeth. The general was bleeding profusely. Craig dragged him into a side bedroom, tore a sheet off the bed and bandaged him. The shooting was dying down.

Craig went out to the main room and cried, "Medic!" One of the Hungarians rushed over. The firing had stopped. Craig surveyed the scene. All three of Omar's men were dead, as well as five of the ten Hungarians.

Craig returned to Nemeth.

"I called for an ambulance," the medic said.

"What do you think?" Craig asked.

"A serious wound."

Craig gave the medic his phone number. "Please call and let me know how he is."

Realizing there was nothing else he could do for Nemeth, Craig had to try and find Omar.

A Hungarian soldier tapped Craig on the shoulder and said, "Omar?"

Craig pointed to the back door.

The soldier nodded and said, "Dogs." Then he took out his digital radio, calling for reinforcements and dogs to help in the search.

Craig wasn't about to wait for the dogs. With a flashlight in one hand and a gun in the other, he raced out the back door.

Shining the light into the thickly wooded area, he couldn't see a damn thing. He listened carefully. Up ahead he heard twigs snap. He gave chase in that direction, firing at the source of the noise as he ran. Then he stopped and listened. He didn't hear anything. He shined his flashlight on the ground, looking for footprints. Nothing. Trying to figure out which way Omar had gone was hopeless. The Chechen had too much of a head start.

Despondent, Craig returned to the castle and waited for the dogs. Thirty minutes later, Craig and two Hungarian soldiers followed the dogs into the woods.

*      *      *

Elizabeth lay in bed at the Gresham Palace suite trying to sleep, but she was too worried about Craig. She was tossing in bed when she heard a tapping on the door. She sat up with start and turned on the lamp.

"Who is it?" she called out.

"Nick. Can I come in, Elizabeth?"

"Sure."

Nick came in and sat in a chair next to the bed. "I'm frightened for Grandpa," he whispered. "What if he doesn't come back?"

"Your grandpa is tough, and he knows what he's doing," she reassured him, trying to display a confidence she didn't feel.

"But the Russians tried to kill him in Potomac. They'll try to kill him here, too."

"He's escaped from them before, and they won't find him this time. He has a good disguise."

For the next several minutes, she tried to reassure Nick, but he wasn't buying it. The kid was too smart. Finally, she convinced him to try and sleep. She walked with him back to his bedroom, tucked him in, and kissed him on the cheek.

*      *      *

Omar continued running through the woods, carrying the duffel. A few minutes earlier he had heard gun shots. Now from behind in the distance he heard dogs barking. His arms were bruised and bloodied from tree branches he had crashed into, and he had lost his balance once, falling and wrenching his knee. Ignoring the pain, he kept running.

What drove Omar and gave him strength was visualizing the scene in his house in Grozny that had happened so many years ago but still felt like yesterday. Kuznov directing four foul, smiling Russian soldiers, and the horrific things they had done.

Though the sky was filled with clouds, at long last Omar saw an opening in the trees ahead, an end to the forest. Ignoring the dogs, which were getting closer, he willed his legs to go faster. Bursting through the trees onto a road, he spotted a nearby villa with a black SUV parked in front.

Omar ran to the car and used a gun from his duffel to break the driver side window. Once he had the door open, he tossed his duffel inside the car and in minutes was racing down the hill toward the Danube.

When he reached the castle district, a medieval walled area on a limestone plateau towering above the river, he slowed down to avoid being stopped by the police. He took the winding Attila út down the hill to the river, then turned left, following the river north until he reached the bottom of the Sikló, the funicular railway that climbed the hill. There, he left the car, crossing the bridge on foot and passing the Gresham Palace Hotel. Then he turned left, heading toward the parliament. He checked his watch. It was almost 4:00 a.m.

Fifteen minutes later, Omar reached the square in front of parliament. It was set up for the ceremony happening later that day, the chairs all neatly arranged facing the raised platform in front of the building. Fortunately, it was deserted. Straight ahead, he focused on the two six-story office buildings abutting the square on the north side. Either would be perfect for his purpose.

Approaching the one on the left, he saw a plaque on the wall in front that said Peter Toth Industries, splattered with black paint. The building looked badly in need of repair. Plastered on the front door was a sign in Hungarian and English. He could read the English. It said: "This building will be closed on Wednesday by order of the government." Undoubtedly because of the ceremony, Omar thought. It would be perfect for his purpose. Using the key Peter had given him, he unlocked the front door. He also removed a gun with a silencer, then tossed the bag inside, leaving the door unlocked.

Omar walked to the other building. On the front, it had the same sign stating that the building would be closed that day. Using his pistol, he smashed the lock, forcing the door open. He went inside and rubbed his bloody arm against the wall. Then he exited the building through the front door.

Omar returned to the Peter Toth Industries building. When he was inside, he locked the door and grabbed his duffel. Using a flashlight, he climbed six flights of stairs to the top floor.

The offices had an abandoned look. Computers and files were piled on most of the desks. He kept walking until he reached an office with large floor-to-ceiling windows that faced Parliament Square. It gave him an excellent view of the platform that would be used for the ceremony.

Omar checked the window in the center. It opened. He moved over a small table and chair and placed them in front of the window. Hungry, he removed cheese, sausage laced with garlic, and bread from the duffel and placed it on the table.

He had no intention of sleeping. After he had eaten, he planned to sit at the table and wait until noon for the ceremony. Twenty minutes before that, he would set up his sniper's rifle on the table and keep the handgun close at hand. If anyone came for him, he would be ready for them.

*      *      *

After two hours of following the dogs, who barked occasionally raising his hopes, Craig realized it was futile. When they reached the road at the end of the woods, the dogs lost the scent.

He tried to place himself in Omar's head. What would he do now?

All of his men were dead. Whatever plan he had developed to kill Kuznov and Szabo with their help was no longer viable. On the other hand, Omar would never admit defeat and return to Grozny—not this close to murdering Kuznov and avenging the brutal deaths of his wife and children.

But what could he do on his own? After a moment of thought, the answer came to Craig. Regardless of what Omar's original plan had been, on his own, Omar's best alternative would be to take out Kuznov and Szabo with a sniper's rifle. That meant Omar had probably gone to Parliament Square after he left the forest. It would be easier to break into a building there and to set up under the cover of darkness.

Armed with a Glock and a flashlight in his pocket, Craig asked one of the soldiers to drive him to Parliament Square and leave him there.

Once he climbed out of the military transport, Craig looked around. He concluded that Omar had two likely buildings to set up for his sniper attack—the decrepit Peter Toth Industries building or the one next to it.

As he walked across the square, heading toward the Peter Toth building, Craig noticed the sun was beginning to rise behind the eastern plateau adjoining the city.

\*      \*      \*

Omar watched anxiously from his sixth-floor window as a solitary figure walked across Parliament Square toward the Peter Toth building. Omar picked up his binoculars and studied the man. He had been one of the attackers at the castle—and he had recognized Omar and known his name.

Omar had no idea who the man was but it was obvious he had come to Parliament Square to find Omar and stop him.

If he entered the building, Omar decided he would find a good hiding place and then ambush the man. Killing him would be easy in the dimly lit building.

\*      \*      \*

Craig stopped in front of the Peter Toth building and read the sign. Closing the building today for security was a good move on Szabo's part. Craig tried the door. It was locked. He walked over to the other building and looked at the lock. It had been damaged. Craig twisted it, and the door opened.

Omar must have wrecked the lock to force his way in. This had to be the building Omar had selected. Craig went inside and shined his flashlight around. He noticed stains on the wall. It had to be blood. Omar was definitively inside.

Craig took the elevator to the top, sixth floor. Systematically, gun in one hand and flashlight in the other, he searched each floor, room by room. Finding nothing, he went down to the basement. He even looked in the furnace room.

No trace of Omar.

No indication Omar was in the building.

Weary and despondent, Craig climbed back up to the building lobby, contemplating his next move, when his phone rang. It was Elizabeth.

"Are you okay?" she asked.

"I'm fine but still searching for the man from Grozny."

"I was afraid that might be the case. I have an idea for you to accomplish what you want to do today."

Craig perked up. He needed help. "What's your idea?"

"It would be better if I told you in person. Can you come back to the hotel?"

"I'm on my way."

Fifteen minutes later, Craig entered the suite.

"You look like hell," she said.

"Thanks. I had a tough night."

After he gave her a summary of what had happened she said, "Why don't you take a shower? I'll fix you coffee and order up some breakfast."

"Sounds good. Where's Nick?"

"Still sleeping. Poor kid. He was up much of the night worrying about his grandpa. I think it's all too much for him."

A few minutes later, Craig emerged from the bathroom wearing a white terrycloth robe.

"The reason I lost Omar," he said glumly, "is because Prime Minister Szabo decided to play military commander."

"All right," said Elizabeth patiently. "But it's over. We have to move on."

"Hey, that's my line," said Craig with a wry smile.

"We've been together such a long time, we're starting to sound alike," she said, tousling his damp hair as she went to answer the door for room service.

Breakfast was wheeled in on a table, and once they had sat down, Craig said, "Okay. Tell me your idea."

"I'll start with the fact that you know Kuznov, right?"

"Know is a bit of an exaggeration. I met with him in Moscow at the time I was dealing with Zhou."

"And you saved his ass when he was in a tight spot with the Chinese."

"Yeah, but people like Kuznov don't repay favors," said Craig with a shrug. "They demand more concessions."

"Suppose you were to talk to Kuznov when he arrives in Budapest this morning before the noon ceremony. And you tell him about the threat from Omar."

"President Worth already did that. Kuznov brushed it aside."

"But you can tell Kuznov what happened last night at the castle and your efforts to find Omar, all of which show how committed Omar is to killing him and Szabo. That might convince him to skip the ceremony and fly home. At least that way you'd be saving Kuznov's life, which is all the US cares about. After that Prime Minister Szabo is on his own with Omar. Szabo has been warned."

Elizabeth paused, swirling a spoon in her coffee thoughtfully before continuing, "It will be up to Szabo's troops to defend him. But it's also likely that Omar might abort if Kuznov goes home. Omar doesn't care about Szabo, Kuznov is the one he hates, and he's already pocketed his upfront money. Well, what do you think, Craig?"

Craig shook his head. "Your idea's creative, but it won't work."

"Why not?" she asked.

"Kuznov will never want to seem as if he's frightened of Omar. He'll stay and hope that the Hungarians and his own security forces can thwart Omar's attack."

"I don't think you're right," she said stubbornly. "Kuznov's no fool. He has to know how vulnerable he'll be in a public ceremony in Parliament Square in Budapest. They'll never be able to protect him from someone as clever and brutal as Omar."

"It won't work," Craig repeated.

"At least try it. What do you have to lose?" Then she answered her own question. "You don't want to do it because you want Omar to come out of hiding to try and assassinate Kuznov and Szabo. You'll be in Parliament Square. Once he exposes himself by firing shots at them, you'll move in to kill Omar and avenge Amos Neir's death."

Of course she was right, but Craig didn't want to admit it. Instead he told her, "Your great plan has another flaw."

"What's that?"

"How will I get in to see Kuznov?"

"I've already thought of that."

"And?"

"Kuznov travels with his press aide, Eugeny, who I've gotten to know. He gave me material for a couple of stories, and I've always treated Kuznov fairly well in my articles. It's likely that Kuznov and Eugeny will be at the Russian Embassy until the ceremony. If I told Eugeny that you want an urgent meeting with Kuznov in advance of the ceremony, I'll bet that Kuznov will see you."

"Have I ever told you that you're persistent?"

"All the time," Elizabeth said with a smile, taking a sip of her coffee.

"Okay, I surrender. Let's try it."

"Listen, Craig. I know you didn't agree to talk to Kuznov and urge him to abort merely because of my pestering. If it were only that, you'd let him go through with the ceremony to give you a better chance of killing Omar."

He wanted to make her spell it out to make sure she really understood. "So why am I doing it?"

"Because deep down, you're an American patriot. You realize that if we let the Russian president be assassinated without doing everything we can to stop it, it would be wrong."

"You're right, of course. I know it's the correct thing to do. On the other hand, Szabo is such a scoundrel, and Peter Toth's reasons for wanting to thwart the Russian–Hungarian pact were sound. If I manage to stop Omar, that means the Russian–Hungarian pact will be finalized and Nick's life was torn apart for no reason."

Elizabeth reached across the table and clasped Craig's hand. "You're a good person, Craig. That's why I love you."

He laughed. "Even though I do stupid things like going to Grozny."

She wasn't smiling. "Even though you do stupid things."

*       *       *

Craig and Elizabeth decided that she would initially go alone to the Russian Embassy to meet with Eugeny, that way Craig could stay with Nick and support Pierre in guarding the boy.

She took the gray Audi Pierre had rented to the Russian Embassy on Bajza Street—a ten minute ride. On the way, she kept thinking about Peter's life in Russia-controlled Budapest. The city must have been a frightening place then. Now, notwithstanding Szabo's politics, Budapest, like Prague, was a magnet for young people around the world who came to party and luxuriate in the city's rich culture and history. The bizarre fact was that the Hungarian people had thirty years of freedom from Russian dominance, but Szabo wanted to let the bear into the tent again.

Elizabeth had decided not to call ahead. She preferred the element of surprise in dealing with Eugeny. Inside the front door she encountered a receptionist, a tough looking young woman with short blonde hair seated behind a plate glass window. Two armed Russian soldiers were on each side of the window.

Elizabeth showed her press ID from the *Herald* and asked to see Eugeny.

"Do you have an appointment?" the woman asked.

"No, but if you tell him it's Elizabeth Crowder, I'm sure he'll see me."

Five minutes later, the door leading inside opened. Elizabeth was directed to a library room off to one side. It had a piano, a couple of sofas, chairs, and an end table. The walls were lined with books.

Eugeny was waiting for her. "I'm surprised to see you," he said. "We haven't publicized this visit to Budapest by President Kuznov."

Elizabeth wanted to add, "Or the secret treaty he's about to announce," but she didn't. Instead she replied, "Good journalists always find a story. I'm sure you remember that from your days as a reporter with *Pravda*."

He laughed and said, "Touché. Would you like me to give you some comments about the purpose of President Kuznov's visit, which is to strengthen and solidify the relations between Russia and Hungary?"

"Actually, I have another purpose in coming."

"What's that?" he asked, suddenly guarded.

"I want you to tell President Kuznov that Craig Page is here with me in Budapest. Craig knows President Kuznov and would like to see him for a few minutes as soon as possible and before Kuznov leaves the embassy this morning."

Eugeny frowned. "I'm afraid that's quite impossible. President Kuznov's schedule is very tight."

Elizabeth narrowed her eyes. In a stern tone she said, "Eugeny, we've always been very honest with each other so I'll be very blunt and lay my cards on the table. Craig isn't looking for a social visit to renew old acquaintances. He has information about a threat to President Kuznov's life that is real and immediate."

"Then he should send an email to Dimitri, Kuznov's aide. Dimitri will evaluate it and if—"

"Let me be clear," she replied in a sharp voice, "if you do not pass my request on to Kuznov right now and something happens to your president, I will write an article for the *Herald* explaining that you refused to move your ass to save your president's life. Now do you understand?"

Eugeny looked shaken. "Wait here," he said. "I'll be right back." Looking grim, he left the room.

Ten minutes later, Eugeny returned. "President Kuznov will see Craig Page in one hour. When he comes here, tell him to ask for Dimitri."

"Thank you. He will do that. And tell President Kuznov that Craig looks a little different. He had some work done on his face."

As soon as she left the embassy, she called Craig and told him, "Success. He'll see you in an hour. I'm on my way back to the hotel."

"Great work."

"I'll leave the car for you in front of the hotel."

\*        \*        \*

When Craig entered the embassy reception area an hour later, Dimitri was waiting for him.

"Craig Page?" Dimitri asked.

Craig nodded.

"Good. Come with me."

They climbed a flight of stairs to a large office overlooking the street in front of the building. Craig guessed that Kuznov had commandeered the ambassador's office.

Kuznov was sitting behind a desk reading some papers when Craig followed Dimitri into the office.

The Russian president stood up, came forward, and shook Craig's hand.

"You certainly did change your appearance," Kuznov said. "Personally, I think it's an improvement. You look much younger. I was considering a little cosmetic touch-up myself. Perhaps you can tell me where you had it done."

"In Switzerland, but it wasn't cosmetic. I was trying to avoid being killed by our good friends the Zhou brothers. I'm sure you remember them."

Kuznov turned to Dimitri. "Will you excuse us?"

Dimitri quickly retreated and closed the door behind him. Kuznov signaled Craig to a sofa and they both sat down. Smiling, Kuznov said, "Olga sends her regards."

Craig smiled as well. "I didn't realize I had you to thank for that little treat."

"Friends do favors for friends. Grozny can be a little drab and dull at night. I thought you might enjoy some company and what Olga had to offer."

"And to be sure, I did."

"Well, now we have something in common. We both appreciate her many attributes and talents. Anyhow, it's unfortunate our last meeting didn't produce the result you and I intended." He paused and added, "Or at least that I intended. You may have had your own agenda."

"I was surprised as well. It just proves that no matter how much one plans, there is a human factor. Let's just say it was a bittersweet ending for both of us. Although not for your man Orlov."

"Orlov was a fool. He deserved what happened to him. But I gather you're not here to rehash old stories."

"That's right. I'm here to save your life."

"I already heard about that so-called threat from President Worth. I firmly believe that the US wants to stop me from solidifying my relationship with the Hungarian people, and that's what I told him. Personally, I doubt that Omar is within a thousand miles of Budapest."

"I personally saw Omar with my own eyes just last night." Craig then described for Kuznov what had happened the previous night at the castle.

"You're sure it was Omar?"

"Beyond any doubt. I've studied that bastard's photograph until my eyes hurt. I have a score to settle with him for killing a friend of mine."

"Then why didn't you pursue him last night."

"I was delayed taking care of a wounded Hungarian colleague. By the time I gave chase, it was too late. Omar had too much of a head start. Even with dogs we couldn't catch him."

The smile was gone. Kuznov sat up with a start. "How do you know Omar's objective is to assassinate me and Prime Minister Szabo?"

"Financing came from Peter Toth, who, as you know, hated both Russia and Szabo. We traced the money trail from Peter to Omar. And of course, you no doubt know that Peter wanted to prevent your agreement with Szabo." He continued, "I assume that's why you had Peter killed. And for the same reason, you arranged Emma Miller's murder."

"I won't respond to those baseless accusations," said Kuznov, his face unreadable.

"I didn't expect you to."

"Is Prime Minister Szabo aware of your claim that Omar is here and intends to kill us?"

"He authorized last night's attack. He even micromanaged it, which was why it failed. I gather he didn't tell you."

When Kuznov didn't reply, Craig added, "I guess he didn't want to risk your turning around and going back to Moscow. He must want this agreement as much as you do." Craig decided to twist the knife, so he added, "It can't give you a good feeling forming an alliance with a partner who withholds key information."

After a moment's silence, Kuznov said, "Listen, Craig, your concern for my welfare is genuinely appreciated. However, I'm no coward. I don't run and hide. I brought soldiers with me, and I'm confident they'll be able to protect me."

Kuznov paused. He was hesitating, as if he had something else to say and he wasn't sure whether he should. Finally, he continued, "And besides. Omar has been a nemesis of mine for a long time. He has managed to elude me from the time that I was in Grozny."

*When you killed his wife and children*, Craig was thinking.

"If Omar is in Budapest," Kuznov continued, "and he rears his head, that is good news. It means that I will at last get a chance to cut it off. Now you'll have to excuse me. I have somewhere to be."

Craig guessed Kuznov was going to meet Szabo before they went to the ceremony.

Having failed again, Craig left the Russian Embassy, thinking about his next move. He checked his watch. The ceremony would be starting in another thirty minutes. He could always do what Elizabeth had said: be present in Parliament Square and try to kill Omar once he attacked Kuznov and Szabo, but the two leaders might be dead by then.

There had to be a better way. He racked his brain. Then it struck him. Earlier that morning, he had made a serious error by not searching the other building, the Peter Toth building in Parliament Square. Omar must have given him a false trail with the broken lock and blood on the wall so he'd think Omar had holed up in the other building. And Craig had fallen for it, hook, line, and sinker. Omar must have picked the lock on the door of the Peter Toth building, gone in, and then locked it from the inside.

At breakneck speed, Craig drove to Parliament Square. From the car, he called Elizabeth. "I struck out with our friend, but I'm on to plan B. I want you to get a cab and come with Nick and Pierre to Parliament Square in time for the ceremony. Stay in the car until you hear from me. I'll let you know when it's all clear."

He was ready to put down the phone when he realized he needed Elizabeth's help for something else. He couldn't just break into the Peter Toth building. Soldiers would be all over the square. He'd never be able to explain it to them, and they'd arrest him. Nor did he have time to get Szabo's authorization to break in.

He told Elizabeth, "Call your friend Gyorgy. Have him get to his office building on Parliament Square with the key to the front door to let me in. I'll meet him in front."

*    *    *

When Craig arrived in Parliament Square it was fifteen minutes to the start of the ceremony. The crowd was large, and the chairs were filling up. Hungarian music was playing. Craig counted twenty-five soldiers and scores of policeman in the area.

His phone rang. It was the medic from the castle. Craig held his breath. "General Nemeth just got out of surgery," the medic said. "He's going to be okay."

Craig sighed with relief. "Thank you for calling."

Calmly and nonchalantly, Craig walked over to the Peter Toth building. Nobody was standing near the door. He just hoped to hell Elizabeth had reached Gyorgy. He thought of calling her, but concluded that she would have called if she'd hit a snag.

Impatiently, he paced near the door. *C'mon Gyorgy*, he thought. *You have to get here.*

Two minutes later, a gray-haired man got out of a car on the edge of the square and limped toward the Peter Toth building. The man looked pale and frightened.

"Gyorgy," Craig said.

"Yes, Elizabeth called."

"Step behind me," Craig said. "I'll cover you. The building is off-limits today. We don't want soldiers to ask any questions."

Gyorgy nodded and did what Craig told him. Once Craig heard the click of the door opening, he said, "Switch positions."

Craig moved around Gyorgy and slipped into the building. Gun in one hand and flashlight in another, he decided to climb the stairs, not wanting to alert Omar to his presence and figuring he would be on the top floor for the best vantage point. If he didn't find Omar on six, he'd work his way down, one floor at a time.

As he climbed, he checked his watch. He still had seven minutes until the start of the ceremony. Not much, but it had to be enough. Omar had better be in this building.

Treading softly, Craig opened the door leading from the inside staircase to the sixth floor corridor. He had four minutes. As he stepped onto the floor with its fading and frayed carpet, he smelled something. It was garlic. Omar must be on this floor.

Walking softly, gun in hand, Craig followed the scent. It led him toward the side of the building facing Parliament Square. A door opening on to the corridor was ajar. Craig nudged it open all the way with his foot. From one of the outside offices, he heard a sound: a rifle being loaded.

As quietly as possible, Craig went through one interior door, then another. On the toes of his feet, he passed three deserted desks with disconnected phones and old computers. When he passed through the second door, he saw the back of a man crouched down on a low table in front of the window aiming a sniper's rifle.

Omar had no idea Craig was there. Craig raised his gun. He could have just pulled the trigger and blown Omar's head away, but he wanted the Chechen to die knowing what had happened to him.

Though it was risky, Craig cried out, "Omar!"

The Chechen dropped his rifle. He grabbed a pistol resting on the table and wheeled around.

Craig locked eyes with Omar. In a penetrating voice he shouted, "This is for Amos Neir, my friend whose body you dumped in the Seine."

Before Omar had a chance to respond, Craig pulled the trigger. The bullet ripped into Omar's head. Blood and tissue splattered against the window, and his lifeless body dropped to the floor.

Craig let out a deep breath and called Elizabeth. "Omar's dead," he said.

"Are you okay?"

"Perfect. Head over to the ceremony, I'll meet you there."

*       *       *

The ceremony was just beginning. Practically every seat was taken. Nick was sitting between Craig and Elizabeth, and a band was playing the Hungarian national anthem. Craig watched Szabo and Kuznov climb the stairs onto the platform.

Craig felt a strange ambivalence. While he had avenged the death of Amos Neir and rid the world of a terrorist, now the Russian–Hungarian agreement would go into effect. It might not only destabilize Europe, but lead to another war.

When the music stopped, a beaming Szabo moved up to the lectern. The television cameras were rolling. He was opening his mouth to speak when suddenly two men in suits and ties, followed by a contingent of twenty armed soldiers, climbed onto the podium.

Nick said, "Hey, there's Grandpa on the stage. And he's not in disguise."

*What the hell's going on?* Craig wondered.

Elizabeth leaned behind Nick and poked Craig in the ribs. "The man with Peter is Janos Rajk, the justice minister," she whispered.

Janos roughly shoved Szabo aside. He leaned over the microphone. Looking into the television cameras, he announced, "I am Janos Rajk, the Hungarian justice minister. With me is Peter Toth, known to many of you as one of our most successful business people and a true patriot. Thanks to Peter, we have regrettably found evidence that Prime Minister Szabo has taken a bribe of fifty million euros from the Russian government to enter into the Friendship Pact he planned to announce today. This agreement would have permitted Russia to station their troops in our country once again." Janos took a piece of paper from his pocket and waved it around. "I am here with an order from the Curia, the Supreme Court, to arrest Prime Minister Szabo for this crime, making his agreement with Russia null and void."

A gasp went up from the crowd.

The justice minister continued, "I assure all of you that there will be a free election within sixty days and a new prime minister will be selected."

An outraged Szabo reached for the microphone, but before he could get his hands on it, the justice minister gave the soldiers the order to arrest him. While Szabo thrashed his arms, two soldiers grabbed him and slapped on handcuffs. Then they led him away.

Craig, who had been watching and listening to the justice minister, now turned his head toward the chair Kuznov had occupied. It was empty. The Russian president was walking down the side stairs and away from the platform looking furious. Kuznov may have escaped with his life, but his plans for the reconquest of Central Europe had just suffered a huge setback. This had been a major defeat for Kuznov.

Janos announced, "This ceremony is now concluded," and the crowd began drifting away.

Another man in a suit and tie approached Craig, Elizabeth, and Nick. He told them, "I'm an aide to the justice minister. He would like to talk to the three of you in the parliament building. Will you please come with me?"

"Sure, and my security man comes with us," Craig said, pointing to Pierre.

The aide led them up a wide, ornate staircase. At the top in the center of the domed hall, the crown of St. Stephen, the country's most important national icon, was on display in a thick glass case. They followed him to a caucus room off the legislative chamber. Peter and Janos were already in the room. Then the aide departed, closing the door behind him.

As soon as Nick saw his grandfather, he ran up and hugged him.

"Hello Elizabeth," Janos said. "Good to see you again."

"And you. This is Craig Page," she added, introducing him.

"I know all about you, Craig," Janos responded. "What happened to Omar?"

Craig guessed that Peter had briefed Janos. "You'll find his dead body on the sixth floor of Peter's office building."

"I'm very happy to hear that," Janos said. "I want to thank you and Elizabeth on behalf of the Hungarian people for everything you did." Janos turned to Peter. "I'm extremely grateful to you for uncovering the bribe that Szabo took from the Russians. I'm hoping to be appointed the next prime minister, and if I do, I'd like you to come back to Hungary and take a position in my government as finance minister."

Craig watched Nick's face fall. He was no doubt afraid his grandfather would abandon him again in Washington. But to Craig's pleasant surprise, Peter told Janos, "Thank you for offering me such an honor. However, I must decline. I want to spend my time with my grandson, Nick, in Washington." Peter turned to Nick. "I plan to build a new house in Potomac and live there full-time with you and your grandmother."

Before the gathering broke up, Elizabeth took Peter off to one side while Pierre and Janos took Nick to look at St. Stephen's crown. Craig stuck around, eavesdropping. He heard Peter thanking Elizabeth for taking such good care of Nick.

She replied softly, "Your son is a wonderful boy."

"You mean my grandson," Peter corrected her.

"I know about you and Emma."

Peter was taken aback. "Does Nick know?"

"I didn't tell him. That's up to you."

With a trembling hand, Peter reached out and grasped Elizabeth's arm. "Thank you."

The three of them left the room and went to the hall outside where Janos was explaining to Nick about the crown and how the US had kept it for thirty-two years after the Second World War.

Then it was time for Craig and Elizabeth to say goodbye to Nick. With tears in her eyes, Elizabeth promised to see him when she came to Washington.

Once they were alone, walking back to the hotel, Elizabeth said to Craig, "Will Peter be safe? Do you think Kuznov will try to have him killed again?"

Craig shook his head. "It's unlikely. Kuznov has more important things to focus on now that we quashed his alliance with Hungary. He'll have to find another way to achieve his ambitious goals for Russia."

She thought about it for a minute and said, "You're right. I have to say, though, Peter is a very complex man."

"That's true. What really matters is that you did a great thing. You saved Nick's life. You can be proud of yourself."

"And I could never have succeeded without you."

"We're a good combination."

He stopped walking, took her into his arms, and kissed her.

# About the Author

Allan Topol is the author of fourteen novels of international intrigue. Two of them, *Spy Dance* and *Enemy of My Enemy*, were national best sellers. His novels have been translated into Chinese, Japanese, Portuguese, and Hebrew. One was optioned, and three are in development for movies.

In addition to his fiction writing, Allan Topol coauthored a two-volume legal treatise entitled *Superfund Law and Procedure*. He wrote a weekly column for Military.com, and has published articles in numerous newspapers and periodicals, including the *New York Times*, *Washington Post*, and *Yale Law Journal*.

He is a graduate of Carnegie Institute of Technology who majored in chemistry, abandoned science, and obtained a law degree from Yale University. He later became a partner in a major Washington law firm. An avid wine collector and connoisseur, he has traveled extensively researching dramatic locations for his novels.

For more information, visit www.allantopol.com.